IL
LA

ILL MET IN LANKHMAR

Fritz Leiber

This edition copyright © Fritz Leiber/1995
All rights reserved

The right of Fritz Leiber to be identified as the author
of this work has been asserted by him in accordance with
the Copyright, Designs and Patents Act 1988.

First published in Great Britain in 1999 by
Millennium
An imprint of Orion Books Ltd
Orion House, 5 Upper St Martin's Lane, London WC2H 9EA

To receive information on the Millennium list, e-mail us at:
smy@orionbooks.co.uk

A CIP catalogue record for this book is available
from the British Library

ISBN 185798 810 8

Typset by Deltatype Ltd, Birkenhead, Merseyside
Printed in Great Britain by
Clays Ltd, St Ives plc

CONTENTS

INTRODUCTION

Michael Moorcock

Cele Goldsmith (later Lalli) is one of the great editors of science fantasy and, with Judith Merril, godmother to the American sf New Wave of the 1960s. She published all the Young Turks, most of them for the first time, in the magazines she edited – the venerable *Fantastic Stories* and *Amazing Stories*, two of the oldest specialised pulps in print.

Lalli had a liking for what one of her contributors had christened 'Sword and Sorcery' and she commissioned a young John Jakes to write her a series of Conan-like adventures, Brak the Barabarian. She published an early fantasy of mine called 'Earl Aubec and the Golem', which she retitled 'Master of Chaos'. She published the first Roger Zelazny story – and published many more. She published Thomas M. Disch and J. G. Ballard and Samuel R. Delany and all the exciting talents which helped create that wonderful sea-change of the 1960s. She also liked Philip K. Dick and Keith Laumer, but I think her favourite writer, whose talent stood so far above the majority of his more financially successful peers, was Fritz Leiber.

Like so many of us, Cele Goldsmith treasured the handful of stories which Leiber (pronounced, if someone hasn't already mentioned this, in the original German fashion – as Lie~ber – Fritz could be sensitive about that) had published in John W. Campbell's much-loved fantasy classic *Unknown*. These included 'Adept's Gambit' and the others which appeared in a small-press edition in 1947 called *Two Sought Adventure*. Those of us lucky to have a copy treasured it in common with our rare editions of Dunsany and Morris. Leiber was perceived as a writer of literary adventure fantasy, a stylist with the same sense of touch that marked Stevenson or Chesterton, a modern (and, some thought, superior) James Branch Cabell.

In those days the kind of supernatural romance which dominates today's best-seller lists had virtually no commercial market. Leiber had done no better with his first Gray Mouser book than I had done with my first Elric book. Not only publishers scoffed at the notion of mass-market editions of these books, we authors scoffed equally. We knew there were only about twenty of us – readers and writers – spread thin across Britain and America … So Cele Goldsmith, when she commissioned Fritz Leiber to write a new series of Fafhrd and Gray Mouser stories for *Fantastic*, was taking a big gamble with her circulation figures.

As Merill did with her opinion-moulding *Year's Best SF Stories*, Goldsmith had to create a climate for the kind of fiction she enjoyed. J. R. R. Tolkien was still an obscure academic who had published a peculiar trilogy with a William Morris/Anglo-Saxon ring to it and had yet to become the core of a somewhat unhealthy cult. Few recognised the tradition in which we wrote and the public for our work numbered a few thousand throughout the world. The works of most of our predecessors – whether commerical writers like Howard, Burroughs and Merritt or literary writers like Dunsany and Cabell – were largely out of print and hard to find. If Goldsmith had been a modern editor, she would have known that statistically she could not publish such fiction and would have followed commercial wisdom by buying stories which were exactly like all the other stories she was publishing.

But, happily, Goldsmith was an old-fashioned editor willing to back her tastes and instincts with her own job and the circulations of the magazines she produced for Ziff Davis. Like Merill, she preferred to publish what was good and frequently off-beat rather than what was safe. And, not surprisingly, her circulation figures improved ...

If Goldsmith had been a 1990s corporate editor, the majority of Fritz Leiber's outstanding Mouser/Fafhrd stories would never have appeared. Modern American heroic fantasy could be said to owe its existence chiefly to her efforts and the enthusiasms of Donald A. Wollheim who discovered a loophole in the copyright law and brought out an unauthorised mass-market edition of *The Lord of The Rings*, and also discovered that by an oversight Edgar Rice Burroughs's *A Princess Of Mars* was out of copyright and published that. Together – and a little later with Lin Carter's programme of classic reprints for Ballantine – they launched what has now become the dominant genre in modern fantastic fiction.

Meanwhile the Young Turks given a public by Lalli and Merril, rejecting their immediate predecessors as Young Turks will, were all agreed that there were two writers of the earlier generation whose literary standards and skills, whose talent and sensibility they still admired. One was Philip K. Dick. The other was Fritz Leiber, whose masterly prose and urbane wit continued to outshine our callow talents. We revered him. We still do.

Fritz Leiber Jr, son of the (at one time) more famous Fritz Leiber Sr, had the benefit of a good, old-fashioned education, a thorough reading in the classics, a casual knowledge of Shakespeare and a relish for oratory inherited from his father. Fritz Leiber Sr was a very famous Shakespearean stage actor who occasionally appeared in films, much as Alec Guinness pops up in *Star*

Wars, to give them a bit of class. The Leiber profile was familiar to pre-war audiences both in silent epics and in talkies. Anyone who has seen *Captain Blood* will remember Fritz Sr as Judge Jeffreys in the tremendous court-room scene designed by Anton Grot, and anyone who has seen *Camille* will remember Fritz Jr as Robert Taylor's handsome friend.

In short, while he loved the stories he read in *Weird Tales*, supernatural fiction was not his only reading and his experience and expectations of the world were greater, far more sophisticated and more varied than those, say, of Lovecraft or Clark Ashton Smith, whom he enjoyed. His own literary skills were generally far better than the majority of writers he admired and, because he had read so widely and with such relish, his ambitions, his standards were considerably higher than most of the excellent writers who appeared beside him in *Unknown*, *Galaxy*, or *Fantastic Stories of the Imagination*. I once asked him why he wrote for commercial magazines whose audiences sometimes actively disliked his best work. He said that in the late '30s and '40s writers like himself – and he named Robert Bloch and Henry Kuttner amongst them – had no market at all, if they didn't have the pulp sf market. The literary market simply wasn't interested in their 'surrealist' fantasies. So they adapted them to the pulp market and earned a little money while they learned.

Ultimately, Fritz admitted, one found oneself getting increasingly interested in the genre for its own sake. Fritz, together with a handful of other fine writers of his generation, was one of those who helped create the literary conventions which exist in all popular science fiction today, from *Star Trek* to *Blade Runner*.

It became a familiar refrain, amongst Leiber enthusiasts, that he was too good for his markets, and that he was ahead of his time. Both these things were to some extent true: The markets of those days were far less sophisticated than those of today and a lot of sf readers – who made up the majority in an extremely small market – were deeply conservative, actively disliking anything which was not the 'hard' sf of the kind appearing in *Astounding* (later *Analog*) and believing Sword and Sorcery to be an illogical and unwholesome abomination. Amongst the horror fans, any form of humour was regarded almost as blasphemy.

Unknown, which specialised in fine humorous fantasy, including the Harold Shea stories of L. Sprague de Camp and the Compleat Werewolf stories of Anthony Boucher, had never been a great commercial success. Its taste was regarded as being tat of a relatively small elite. Leiber's science fiction, such as his classic *Gather, Darkness!*, in which he cleverly rationalised the same images he was using in his fantasy, was far more successful. For a long time he wrote mostly sf, much of it highly original and seminal in its influence, some of it baffling to audiences of the day. He could not help himself. He was innovative, he was a writer with a lot of ideas he wanted to explore, in as many ways as he could, and a glance through his collected short stories will tell you how well he could write in many different forms.

Judith Merril, a great supporter of Leiber's work, used to reckon that it took the public twenty years to catch up with Fritz. But being pretty much always twenty years ahead of his time and, it should be admitted, inclined to drink his profits rather than put them in a savings account, Fritz managed to die with too much of his best work unavailable to the general reader.

I've never forgotten a particular trip to New York in the mid-1960s. Four of us had driven in from the country. Merril, a native New Yorker, refused to drive in the city. I had no licence and Jim Sallis (author of *Moth* and other fine thrillers) who had never driven in New York before was the only one of us capable of driving. Three of us sat in the front and the back seat was given over to Fritz who lay sprawled and fairly stoned reciting *Lepanto* by G. K. Chesterton in all its many verses in his deep, massive, stage-trained voice.

Suddenly Jim, who was horribly underslept, stopped the car in the middle of the street and announced that he refused to drive any further. We were in the middle of Sixth Avenue traffic at four o'clock in the afternoon on an August week-day and the traffic around us was not at one with itself. We rapidly (and fairly) became the chief focus of its disapproval. At Judy's insistence, Fritz was brought down to about five feet above ground level and told to drive. Without missing a verse, Fritz climbed behind the wheel and flew us with graceful panache to our destination (don't try this at home, children). Until it deteriorated beyond recovery, I had a tape of *Lepanto* which Fritz had made for me to remind me of that occasion. He could be a generous, extravagant soul and his relish for life comes out in particular in those wonderful stories.

Fritz, amongst others, has told the story of how the little Mouser and the burly Fafhrd were created – almost as people these days create role-playing worlds for their own pleasure – by himself and his friend Harry Otto Fischer. These stories were never written to make money. Indeed, just as with my Elric stories of the early '60s, Fritz considered them chiefly a labour of love, written for the pleasure of the telling, the delight in his characters and their wonderfully imaginative world of Nehwon.

Cele Goldsmith's enthusiasm had encouraged Fritz to write the stories for her magazine, but Fritz did not really expect them to appear in book form. And then Donald A. Wollheim, that extraordinary and indefatigable catalyst, commissioned him to turn them into the series of novels being so deservedly republished. The fantasy genre owes those two editors an enormous debt. Perhaps because they worked mostly as pulp fiction editors, they have never been given the considerable credit they deserve, just as

Fritz himself – who wrote so much that was illuminating on the subject of literary fantasy and who wrote some of the best examples there will ever be – still does not receive sufficient credit for his enormous contribution to the genre. The publication of these volumes by Millennium should do much to help remind readers of fantasy of their debt to a writer who is, in my opinion, still the greatest of us all.

Michael Moorcock
Lost Pines, Texas, May 1995.

SWORDS
AND DEVILTRY

Book 1 in the Swords Series

CONTENTS

I: INDUCTION

Sundered from us by gulfs of time and stranger dimensions dreams the ancient world of Nehwon with its towers and skulls and jewels, its swords and sorceries. Nehwon's known realms crowd about the Inner Sea: northward the green-forested fierce Land of the Eight Cities, eastward the steppe-dwelling Mingol horsemen and the desert where caravans creep from the rich Eastern Lands and the River Tilth. But southward, linked to the desert only by the Sinking Land and further warded by the Great Dike and the Mountain of Hunger, are the rich grainfields and walled cities of Lankhmar, eldest and chiefest of Nehwon's lands. Dominating the Land of Lankhmar and crouching at the silty mouth of the River Hlal in a secure corner between the grainfields, the Great Salt Marsh, and the Inner Sea is the massive-walled and mazy-alleyed metropolis of Lankhmar, thick with thieves and shaven priests, lean-framed magicians and fat-bellied merchants – Lankhmar the Imperishable, the City of the Black Toga.

In Lankhmar on one murky night, if we can believe the runic books of Sheelba of the Eyeless Face, there met for the first time those two dubious heroes and whimsical scoundrels, Fafhrd and the Gray Mouser. Fafhrd's origins were easy to perceive in his near seven-foot height and limber-looking ranginess, his hammered ornaments and huge longsword: he was clearly a barbarian from the Cold Waste north even of the Eight Cities and the Trollstep

5

Mountains. The Mouser's antecedents were more cryptic and hardly to be deduced from his childlike stature, gray garb, mouse-skin hood shadowing flat swart face, and deceptively dainty rapier; but somewhere about him was the suggestion of cities and the south, the dark streets and also the sun-drenched spaces. As the twain eyed each other challengingly through the murky fog lit indirectly by distant torches, they were already dimly aware that they were two long-sundered, matching fragments of a greater hero and that each had found a comrade who would outlast a thousand quests and a lifetime – or a hundred lifetimes – of adventuring.

No one at that moment could have guessed that the Gray Mouser was once named Mouse, or that Fafhrd had recently been a youth whose voice was by training high-pitched, who wore white furs only, and who still slept in his mother's tent although he was eighteen.

II: THE SNOW WOMEN

At Cold Corner in midwinter, the women of the Snow Clan were waging a cold war against the men. They trudged about like ghosts in their whitest furs almost invisible against the new-fallen snow, always together in female groups, silent or at most hissing like angry shades. They avoided Godshall with its trees for pillars and walls of laced leather and towering pine-needle roof.

They gathered in the big, oval Tent of the Women, which stood guard in front of the smaller home tents, for sessions of chanting and ominous moaning and various silent practises designed to create powerful enchantments that would tether their husbands' ankles to Cold Corner, tie up their loins, and give them sniveling, nose-dripping colds, with the threat of the Great Cough and Winter Fever held in reserve. Any man so unwise as to walk alone by day was apt to be set upon and snowballed and, if caught, thrashed – be he even skald or mighty hunter.

And a snowballing by Snow Clan women was nothing to laugh at. They threw overarm, it is true, but their muscles for that had been greatly strengthened by much splitting of firewood, lopping of high branches, and pounding of hides, including the iron-hard one of the snowy behemoth. And they sometimes froze their snowballs.

The sinewy, winter-hardened men took all of this with

immense dignity, striding about like kings in their conspic-
uous black, russet, and rainbow-dyed ceremonial furs,
drinking hugely but with discretion, and trading as
shrewdly as Ilth-marts their bits of amber and ambergris,
their snow-diamonds visible only by night, their glossy
animal pelts, and their ice-herbs, in exchange for woven
fabrics, hot spices, blued and browned iron, honey, waxen
candles, fire-powders that flared with a colored roar, and
other products of the civilized south. Nevertheless, they
made a point of keeping generally in groups, and there was
many a nose a-drip among them.

It was not the trading the women objected to. Their
men were good at that and they – the women – were the
chief beneficiaries. They greatly preferred it to their
husbands' occasional piratings, which took those lusty men
far down the eastern coasts of the Outer Sea, out of reach
of immediate matriarchal supervision and even, the
women sometimes feared, of their potent female magic.
Cold Corner was the farthest south ever got by the entire
Snow Clan, whose members spent most of their lives on
the Cold Waste and among the foothills of the untopped
Mountains of the Giants and the even more northerly
Bones of the Old Ones, and so this midwinter camp was
their one yearly chance to trade peaceably with venturesome Mingols, Sarheenmarts, Lankhmarts, and even an
occasional Eastern desert-man, heavily beturbaned,
bundled up to the eyes, and elephantinely gloved and
booted.

Nor was it the guzzling which the women opposed.
Their husbands were great quaffers of mead and ale at all
times and even of the native white snow-potato brandy, a
headier drink than most of the wines and boozes the
traders hopefully dispensed.

No, what the Snow Women hated so venomously and
which each year caused them to wage cold war with hardly
any material or magical holds barred, was the theatrical

8

show which inevitably came shivering north with the traders, its daring troupers with faces chapped and legs chilblained, but hearts a-beat for soft northern gold and easy if rampageous audiences – a show so blasphemous and obscene that the men preempted Godshall for its performance (God being unshockable) and refused to let the women and youths view it; a show whose actors were, according to the women, solely dirty old men and even dirtier scrawny southern girls, as loose in their morals as in the lacing of their skimpy garments, when they went clothed at all. It did not occur to the Snow Women that a scrawny wench, her dirty nakedness all blue goosebumps in the chill of drafty Godshall, would hardly be an object of erotic appeal besides her risking permanent all-over frostbite.

So the Snow Women each midwinter hissed and magicked and sneaked and sniped with their crusty snowballs at huge men retreating with pomp, and frequently caught an old or crippled or foolish, young, drunken husband and beat him soundly.

This outwardly comic combat had sinister undertones. Particularly when working all together, the Snow Women were reputed to wield mighty magics, particularly through the element of cold and its consequences: slipperiness, the sudden freezing of flesh, the gluing of skin to metal, the frangibility of objects, the menacing mass of snow-laden trees and branches, and the vastly greater mass of avalanches. And there was no man wholly unafraid of the hypnotic power in their ice-blue eyes.

Each Snow Woman, usually with the aid of the rest, worked to maintain absolute control of her man, though leaving him seemingly free, and it was whispered that recalcitrant husbands had been injured and even slain, generally by some frigid instrumentality. While at the same time witchy cliques and individual sorceresses played against each other a power game in which the brawniest and boldest of men, even chiefs and priests, were but counters.

During the fortnight of trading and the two days of the Show, hags and great strapping girls guarded the Tent of the Women at all quarters, while from within came strong perfumes, stenches, flashes and intermittent glows by night, clashings and tinklings, cracklings and quenchings, and incantational chantings and whisperings that never quite stopped.

This morning one could imagine that the Snow Women's sorcery was working everywhere, for the weather was windless and overcast, and there were wisps of fog in the moist freezing air, so that crystals of ice were rapidly forming on every bush and branch, every twig and tip of any sort, including the ends of the men's moustaches and the eartips of the tamed lynxes. The crystals were as blue and flashing as the Snow Women's eyes and even mimicked in their forms, to an imaginative mind, the Snow Women's hooded, tall, and white-robed figures, for many of the crystals grew upright, like diamond flames.

And this morning the Snow Women had caught, or rather got a near certain chance of trapping, an almost unimaginably choice victim. For one of the Show girls, whether by ignorance or foolhardy daring, and perhaps tempted by the relatively mild, gem-begetting air, had strolled on the crusty snow away from the safety of the actors' tents, past Godshall on the precipice side, and from thence between two sky-thrusting copses of snow-laden evergreens, out onto the snow-carpeted natural rock bridge that had been the start of the Old Road south to Gnampf Nar until some five man-lengths of its central section had fallen three score years ago.

A short step from the up-curving, perilous brink she had paused and looked for a long while south through the wisps of mist that, in the distance, grew thin as pluckings of long-haired wool. Below her in the canyon's overhung slot, the snow-capped pines flooring Trollstep Canyon looked tiny as the white tents of an army of Ice Gnomes. Her gaze slowly traced Trollstep Canyon from its far eastern beginnings to where, narrowing, it passed directly beneath her and then, slowly widening, curved south, until the buttress opposite her with its matching, jutting section of the one-time rock bridge, cut off the view south. Then her gaze went back to trace the New Road from where it began its descent beyond the actors' tents and clung to the far wall of the canyon until, after many a switchback and many a swing into great gully and out again – unlike the far swifter, straighter descent of the Old Road – it plunged into the midst of the flooring pines and went with them south.

From her constant yearning look, one might have thought the actress a silly homesick soubrette, already regretting this freezing northern tour and pining for some hot, flea-bitten actors' alley beyond the Land of the Eight Cities and the Inner Sea – except for the quiet confidence of her movements, the proud set of her shoulders, and the perilous spot she had chosen for her peering. For this spot was not only physically dangerous, but also as near the Tent of the Snow Women as it was to Godshall, and in addition the spot was taboo because a chief and his children had plunged to their deaths when the central rock-span had cracked away three score years ago, and because the wooden replacement had fallen under the weight of a brandy-merchant's cart some two score years later. Brandy of the fieriest, a loss fearsome enough to justify the sternest of taboos, including one against ever rebuilding the bridge.

And as if even those tragedies were not sufficient to glut the jealous gods and make taboo absolute, only two years past the most skillful skier the Snow Clan had produced in decades, one Skif, drunk with snow brandy and an icy pride, had sought to jump the gap from the Cold Corner side. Towed to a fast start and thrusting furiously with his sticks, he had taken off like a gliding hawk, yet missed the opposite snowy verge by an arm's length; the prows of his skis had crashed into rock, and he himself smashed in the rocky depths of the canyon.

The bemused actress wore a long coat of auburn fox fur belted with a light, gold-washed brass chain. Icy crystals had formed in her high-piled, fine, dark brown hair.

From the narrowness of her coat, her figure promised to be scrawny or at least thinly muscular enough to satisfy the Snow Women's notion of female players, but she was almost six feet tall – which was not at all as actresses should be and definitely an added affront to the tall Snow Women now approaching her from behind in a silent white rank.

An over-hasty white fur boot sang against the glazed snow.

The actress spun around and without hesitation raced back the way she had come. Her first three steps broke the snowcrust, losing her time, but then she learned the trick of running in a glide, feet grazing the crust.

She hitched her russet coat high. She was wearing black fur boots and bright scarlet stockings.

The Snow Women glided swiftly after her, pitching their hard-packed snowballs.

One struck her hard on the shoulder. She made the mistake of looking back.

By ill chance two snowballs took her in jaw and forehead, just beneath painted lip and on an arched black eyebrow.

She reeled then, turning fully back, and a snowball thrown almost with the force of a slinger's stone struck her in the midriff, doubling her up and driving the breath from her lungs in an open-mouthed *whoosh*.

She collapsed. The white women rushed forward, blue eyes a-glare.

A big, thinnish, black-moustached man in a drab quilted jacket and a low black turban stopped watching from beside a becrystalled, rough-barked living pillar of God-shall, and ran toward the fallen woman. His footsteps broke the crust, but his strong legs drove him powerfully on.

Then he slowed in amaze as he was passed almost as if he were at a standstill by a tall, white, slender figure glide-running so swiftly that it seemed for a moment it went on skis. Then for another instant, the turbaned man thought it was another Snow Woman, but then he noted that it wore a short fur jerkin rather than a long fur robe – and so was presumably a Snow Man or Snow Youth, though the black-turbaned man had never seen a Snow Clan male dressed in white.

The strange, swift figure glide-ran, with chin tucked down and eyes bent away from the Snow Women, as if fearing to meet their wrathful blue gaze. Then, as he swiftly knelt by the felled actress, long reddish-blond hair spilled from his hood. From that and the figure's slender-ness, the black-turbaned man knew an instant of fear that the intercomer was a very tall Snow Girl, eager to strike the first blow at close quarters.

But then he saw a jut of downy male chin in the reddish-blond hair and also a pair of massive silver bracelets of the sort one gained only by pirating. Next the youth picked up the actress and glide-ran away from the Snow Women, who now could see only their victim's scarlet-stockinged legs. A volley of snowballs struck the rescuer's back. He staggered a little, then sped deter-minedly on, still ducking his head.

The biggest of the Snow Women, one with the bearing of a queen and a haggard face still handsome, though the hair falling to either side of it was white, stopped running and shouted in a deep voice, 'Come back, my son! You hear me, Fafhrd, come back now!'

The youth nodded his ducked head slightly, though he did not pause in his flight. Without turning his head, he called in a rather high voice, 'I will come back, revered Mor my mother ... later on.'

The other women took up the cry of 'Come back now!' Some of them added such epithets as 'Dissolute youth!' 'Curse of your good mother Mor!' and 'Chaser after whores!'

Mor silenced them with a curt, sidewise sweep of her hands, palms down. 'We will wait here,' she announced with authority.

The black-turbaned man paused a bit, then strolled after the vanished pair, keeping a wary eye on the Snow Women. They were supposed not to attack traders, but with barbarian females, as with males, one could never tell.

Fafhrd reached the actors' tents, which were pitched in a circle around a trampled stretch of snow at the altar end of Godshall. Farthest from the precipice was the tall, conical tent of the Master of the Show. Midway stretched the common actors' tent, somewhat fish-shaped, one-third for the girls, two-thirds for the men. Nearest Trollstep Canyon was a medium-size, hemicylindrical tent supported on half hoops. Across its middle, an evergreen sycamore thrust a great heavy branch balanced by two lesser branches on the opposite side, all spangled with crystals. In this tent's semicircular front was a laced entry-flap, which Fafhrd found difficult to open, since the long form in his arms was still limp.

A swag-bellied little old man came strutting toward him with something of the bounce of youth. This one wore ragged finery touched up with gilt. Even his long gray moustache and goatee glittered with specks of gold above and below his dirty-toothed mouth. His heavily pouched eyes were rheumy and red all around, but dark and darting at center. Above them was a purple turban supporting in turn a gilt crown set with battered gems of rock crystal, poorly aping diamonds.

Behind him came a skinny, one-armed Mingol, a fat Easterner with a vast black beard that stank of burning, and two scrawny girls who, despite their yawning and the heavy blankets huddled around them, looked watchful and evasive as alley cats.

'What's this now?' the leader demanded, his alert eyes taking in every detail of Fafhrd and his burden. 'Vlana slain? Raped and slain, eh? Know, murderous youth, that you'll pay high for your fun. You may not know who I am, but you'll learn. I'll have reparations from your chiefs, I will! Vast reparations! I have influence, I have. You'll lose those pirate's bracelets of yours and that silver chain peeping from under your collar. Your family'll be beggared, and all your relatives, too. As for what *they'll* do to *you*—'

'You are Essedinex, Master of the Show,' Fafhrd broke in dogmatically, his high tenor voice cutting like a trumpet through the other's hoarse, ranting baritone. 'I am Fafhrd, son of Mor and of Nalgron the Legend-Breaker. Vlana the culture dancer is not raped or dead, but stunned with snowballs. This is her tent. Open it.'

'We'll take care of her, barbarian,' Essedinex asserted, though more quietly, appearing both surprised and somewhat intimidated by the youth's almost pedantic precision as to who was who, and what was what. 'Hand her over. Then depart.'

'I will lay her down,' Fafhrd persisted. 'Open the tent!'

Essedinex shrugged and motioned to the Mingol, who with a sardonic grin used his one hand and elbow to unlace and draw aside the entry-flap. An odor of sandalwood and closetberry came out. Stooping, Fafhrd entered. Midway down the length of the tent he noted a pallet of furs and a low table with a silver mirror propped

15

against some jars and squat bottles. At the far end was a rack of costumes.

Stepping around a brazier from which a thread of pale smoke wreathed, Fafhrd carefully knelt and most gently deposited his burden on the pallet. Next he felt Vlana's pulse at jaw-hinge and wrist, rolled back a dark lid and peered into each eye, delicately explored with his fingertips the sizable bumps that were forming on jaw and forehead. Then he tweaked the lobe of her left ear and, when she did not react, shook his head and, drawing open her russet robe, began to unbutton the red dress under it.

Essedinex, who with the others had been watching the proceedings in a puzzled fashion cried out, 'Well, of all – Cease, lascivious youth!'

'Silence,' Fafhrd commanded and continued unbuttoning.

The two blanketed girls giggled, then clapped hands to mouths, darting amused gazes at Essedinex and the rest.

Drawing aside his long hair from his right ear, Fafhrd laid that side of his face on Vlana's chest between her breasts, small as half pomegranates, their nipples rosy bronze in hue. He maintained a solemn expression. The girls smothered giggles again. Essedinex strangledly cleared his throat, preparing for large speech.

Fafhrd sat up and said, 'Her spirit will shortly return. Her bruises should be dressed with snow-bandages, renewed when they begin to melt. Now I require a cup of your best brandy.'

'My best brandy—!' Essedinex cried outragedly. 'This goes too far. First you must have a help-yourself peep show, then strong drink! Presumptuous youth, depart at once!'

'I am merely seeking—' Fafhrd began in clear and at last slightly dangerous tones.

His patient interrupted the dispute by opening her eyes, shaking her head, wincing, then determinedly sitting up –

whereupon she grew pale and her gaze wavered. Fafhrd helped her lie down again and put pillows under her feet. Then he looked at her face. Her eyes were still open and she was looking back at him curiously.

He saw a face small and sunken-cheeked, no longer girlish-young, but with a compact catlike beauty despite its lumps. Her eyes, being large, brown-irised and long-lashed, should have been melting, but were not. There was the look of the loner in them, and purpose, and a thoughtful weighing of what she saw.

She saw a handsome, fair-complexioned youth of about eighteen winters, wide-headed and long-jawed, as if he had not done growing. Fine red-gold hair cascaded down his cheeks. His eyes were green, cryptic, and as staring as a cat's. His lips were wide, but slightly compressed, as if they were a door that locked words in and opened only on the cryptic eyes' command.

One of the girls had poured a half cup of brandy from a bottle on the low table. Fafhrd took it and lifted Vlana's head for her to drink it in sips. The other girl came with powder snow folded in woolen cloths. Kneeling on the far side of the pallet, she bound them against the bruises.

After inquiring Fafhrd's name and confirming that he had rescued her from the Snow Women, Vlana asked, 'Why do you speak in such a high voice?'

'I study with a singing skald,' he answered. 'They use that voice and are the true skalds, not the roaring ones who use deep tones.'

'What reward do you expect for rescuing me?' she asked boldly.

'None,' Fafhrd replied.

From the two girls came further giggles, quickly cut off at Vlana's glance.

Fafhrd added, 'It was my personal obligation to rescue you, since the leader of the Snow Women was my mother.

I must respect my mother's wishes, but I must also prevent her from performing wrong actions.'

'Oh. Why do you act like a priest or healer?' Vlana continued. 'Is that one of your mother's wishes?' She had not bothered to cover her breasts, but Fafhrd was not looking at them now, only at the actress's lips and eyes.

'Healing is part of the singing skald's art,' he answered. 'As for my mother, I do my duty toward her, nor less, nor more.'

'Vlana, it is not politic that you talk thus with this youth,' Essedinex interposed, now in a nervous voice. 'He must—'

'Shut up!' Vlana snapped. Then, back to Fafhrd, 'Why do you wear white?'

'It is proper garb for all Snow Folk. I do not follow the new custom of dark and dyed furs for males. My father always wore white.'

'He is dead?'

'Yes. While climbing a tabooed mountain called White Fang.'

'And your mother wishes you to wear white, as if you were your father returned?'

Fafhrd neither answered nor frowned at that shrewd question. Instead he asked, 'How many languages can you speak – besides this pidgin-Lankhmarese?'

She smiled at last. 'What a question! Why, I speak – though not too well – Mingol, Kvarchish, High and Low Lankhmarese, Quarmallian, Old Ghoulish, Desert-talk, and three Eastern tongues.'

Fafhrd nodded. 'That's good.'

'Forever why?'

'Because it means you are very civilized,' he answered.

'What's so great about that?' she demanded with a sour laugh.

'You should know, you're a culture dancer. In any case, I am interested in civilization.'

'One comes,' Essedinex hissed from the entry. 'Vlana, the youth must—'

'He must not!'

'As it happens, I must indeed leave now,' Fafhrd said, rising. 'Keep up the snow-bandages,' he instructed Vlana. 'Rest until sundown. Then more brandy, with hot soup.'

'Why must you leave?' Vlana demanded, rising on an elbow.

'I made a promise to my mother,' Fafhrd said without looking back.

'Your mother!'

Stooping at the entry, Fafhrd finally did stop to look back. 'I owe my mother many duties,' he said. 'I owe you none, as yet.'

'Vlana, he *must* leave. It's *the* one,' Essedinex stage-whispered hoarsely. Meanwhile he was shoving at Fafhrd, but for all the youth's slenderness, he might as well have been trying to push a tree off of its roots.

'Are you afraid of him who comes?' Vlana was buttoning up her dress now.

Fafhrd looked at her thoughtfully. Then, without replying in any way whatever to her question, he ducked through the entry and stood up, waiting the approach through the persistent mist of a man in whose face anger was gathering.

This man was as tall as Fafhrd, half again as thick and wide, and about twice as old. He was dressed in brown sealskin and amethyst-studded silver except for the two massive gold bracelets on his wrists and the gold chain about his neck, marks of a pirate chief.

Fafhrd felt a touch of fear, not at the approaching man, but at the crystals which were now thicker on the tents than he recalled them being when he had carried Vlana in. The element over which Mor and her sister witches had most power was cold – whether in a man's soup or loins, or in his sword or climbing rope, making them shatter. He often wondered whether it was Mor's magic that had made his own heart so cold. Now the cold would close in on the dancer. He should warn her, except she was civilized and would laugh at him.

The big man came up.

'Honorable Hringorl,' Fafhrd greeted softly.

For reply, the big man aimed a backhanded uppercut at Fafhrd with his near arm.

Fafhrd leaned sharply away, slithering under the blow, and then simply walked off the way he had first come.

Hringorl, breathing heavily, glared after him for a couple of heartbeats, then plunged into the hemi-cylindrical tent.

Hringorl was certainly the most powerful man in the Snow Clan, Fafhrd reflected, though not one of its chiefs because of his bullying ways and defiances of custom. The Snow Women hated, but found it hard to get a hold of him, since his mother was dead and he had never taken a wife, satisfying himself with concubines he brought back from his piratings.

From wherever he'd been inconspicuously standing, the black-turbaned and black-moustached man came up quietly to Fafhrd. 'That was well done, my friend. And when you brought in the dancer.'

Fafhrd said impassively, 'You are Vellix the Venturer.'

The other nodded. 'Bringing brandy from Klelg Nar to this mart. Will you sample the best with me?'

Fafhrd said, 'I am sorry, but I have an engagement with my mother.'

'Another time then,' Vellix said easily.

'Fafhrd!'

It was Hringorl who called. His voice was no longer angry. Fafhrd turned. The big man stood by the tent, then came striding up when Fafhrd did not move. Meanwhile, Vellix faded back and away in a fashion as easy as his speech.

'I'm sorry, Fafhrd,' Hringorl said gruffly. 'I did not know you had saved the dancer's life. You have done me a great service. Here.' He unclasped from his wrist one of the heavy gold bracelets and held it out.

Fafhrd kept his hands at his sides. 'No service whatever,' he said. 'I was only saving my mother from committing a wrong action.'

'You've sailed under me,' Hringorl suddenly roared, his face reddening though he still grinned somewhat, or tried to. 'So you'll take my gifts as well as my orders.' He caught hold of Fafhrd's hand, pressed the weighty torus into it, closed Fafhrd's lax fingers on it, and stepped back.

Instantly Fafhrd knelt, saying swiftly, 'I am sorry, but I may not take what I have not rightly won. And now I must keep an engagement with my mother.' Then he swiftly rose, turned, and walked away. Behind him, on an unbroken crust of snow, the golden bracelet gleamed.

He heard Hringorl's snarl and choked-back curse, but did not look around to see whether or not Hringorl picked up his spurned gratuity, though he did find it a bit difficult not to weave in his stride or duck his head a trifle, in case Hringorl decided to throw the massive wristlet at his skull.

Shortly he came to the place where his mother was sitting amongst seven Snow Women, making eight in all. They stood up. He stopped a yard short. Ducking his head and looking to the side, he said, 'Here I am, Mor.'

'You took a long while,' she said. 'You took too long.' Six heads around her nodded solemnly. Only Fafhrd noted, in the blurred edge of his vision, that the seventh and slenderest Snow Woman was moving silently backward.

'But here I am,' Fafhrd said.

'You disobeyed my command,' Mor pronounced coldly. Her haggard and once beautiful face would have looked very unhappy, had it not been so proud and masterful.

'But now I am obeying it,' Fafhrd countered. He noted

that the seventh Snow Woman was now silently running, her great white cloak a-stream, between the home tents toward the high white forest that was Cold Corner's boundary everywhere that Trollstep Canyon wasn't.

'Very well,' Mor said. 'And now you will obey me by following me to the dream tent for ritual purification.'

'I am not defiled,' Fafhrd announced. 'Moreover, I purify myself after my own fashion, one also agreeable to the gods.'

There were clucks of shocked disapproval from all Mor's coven. Fafhrd had spoken boldly, but his head was still bent, so that he did not see their faces, and their entrapping eyes, but only their long-robed white forms, like a clump of great birches.

Mor said, 'Look me in the eyes.'

Fafhrd said, 'I fulfill all the customary duties of a grown son, from food-winning to sword-guarding. But as far as I can ascertain, looking my mother in the eyes is not one of those duties.'

'Your father always obeyed me,' Mor said ominously.

'Whenever he saw a tall mountain, he climbed her, obeying no one but himself,' Fafhrd contradicted.

'Yes, and died doing so!' Mor cried, her masterfulness controlling grief and anger without hiding them.

Fafhrd said hardly, 'Whence came the great cold that shattered his rope and pick on White Fang?'

Amidst the gasps of her coven, Mor pronounced in her deepest voice, 'A mother's curse, Fafhrd, on your disobedience and evil thinking!'

Fafhrd said with strange eagerness, 'I dutifully accept your curse, Mother.'

Mor said, 'My curse is not on you, but on your evil imaginings.'

'Nevertheless, I will forever treasure it,' Fafhrd cut in. 'And now, obeying myself, I must take leave of you, until the wrath-devil has let you go.'

And with that, head still bent down and away, he walked rapidly toward a point in the forest east of the home tents, but west of the great tongue of forest that stretched south almost to Godshall. The angry hissings of Mor's coven followed him, but his mother did not cry out his name, nor any word at all. Fafhrd would almost rather that she had.

Youth heals swiftly, on the skin-side. By the time Fafhrd plunged into his beloved wood without jarring a single becrystalled twig, his senses were alert, his neck-joint supple, and the outward surface of his inner being as cleared for new experience as the unbroken snow ahead. He took the easiest path, avoiding bediamonded thorn bushes to left and huge pinescreened juttings of pale granite to right.

He saw bird tracks, squirrel tracks, day-old bear tracks; snow birds snapped their black beaks at red snowberries; a furred snow-snake hissed at him, and he would not have been startled by the emergence of a dragon with ice-crusted spines.

So he was in no wise amazed when a great high-branched pine opened its snow-plastered bark and showed him its dryad – a merry, blue-eyed, blonde-haired girl's face, a dryad no more than seventeen years old. In fact, he had been expecting such an apparition ever since he had noted the seventh Snow Woman in flight.

Yet he pretended to be amazed for almost two heartbeats. Then he sprang forward crying, 'Mara, my witch,' and with his two arms separated her white-cloaked self from her camouflaging background, and kept them wrapped around her while they stood like one white column, hood to hood and lips to lips for at least twenty heartbeats of the most thuddingly delightful sort.

Then she found his right hand and drew it into her cloak and, through a placket, under her long coat, and pressed it against her crisply-ringleted lower belly.

23

'Guess,' she whispered, licking his ear.

'It's part of a girl. I do believe it's a—' he began most gayly, though his thoughts were already plunging wildly in a direly different direction.

'No, idiot, it's something that belongs to you,' the wet whisper coached.

The dire direction became an iced chute leading toward certainty. Nevertheless he said bravely, 'Well, I'd hoped you hadn't been trying out others, though that's your right. I must say I am vastly honored—'

'Silly beast! I meant it's something that belongs to *us*.'

The dire direction was now a black icy tunnel, becoming a pit. Automatically and with an appropriately great heart-thump, Fafhrd said, 'Not—?'

'Yes! I'm certain, you monster. I've missed twice.'

Better than ever in his life before, Fafhrd's lips performed their office of locking in words. When they opened at last, they and the tongue behind them were utterly under control of the great green eyes. There came forth in a joyous rush: 'O gods! How wonderful! I am a father! How clever of you, Mara!'

'Very clever indeed,' the girl admitted, 'to have fashioned anything so delicate after your rude handling. But now I must pay you off for that ungracious remark about "trying out others."' Hitching up her skirt behind, she guided both his hands under her cloak to a knot of thongs at the base of her spine. (Snow women wore fur hoods, fur boots, a high fur stocking on each leg gartered to a waist thong, and one or more fur coats and cloaks – it was a practical garb, not unlike the men's except for the longer coats.)

As he fingered the knot, from which three thongs led lightly off, Fafhrd said, 'Truly, Mara dearest, I do not favor these chastity girdles. They are not a civilized device. Besides, they must interfere with the circulation of your blood.'

24

'You and your fad for civilization! I'll love and belabor you out of it. Go on, untie the knot, making sure you and no other tied it.'

Fafhrd complied and had to agree that it was his knot and no other man's. The task took some time and was a delightful one to Mara, judging from her soft squeals and moans, her gentle nips and bites. Fafhrd himself began to get interested. When the task was done, Fafhrd got the reward of all courteous liars: Mara loved him dearly because he had told her all the right lies and she showed it in her beguiling behavior, and his interest in her and his excitement became vast.

After certain handlings and other tokens of affection, they fell to the snow side by side, both mattressed and covered entirely by their white fur cloaks and hoods.

A passerby would have thought that a snow mound had come alive convulsively and was perhaps about to give birth to a snowman, elf, or demon.

After a while the snow-mound grew utterly quiescent and the hypothetical passerby would have had to lean very close to catch the voices coming from inside it.

MARA: Guess what I'm thinking.

FAFHRD: That you're the Queen of Bliss. Aaah!

MARA: Aaaah back at you, and ooooh! And that you're the King of Beasts. No, silly, I'll tell you. I was thinking of how glad I am that you've had your southward adventurings before marriage. I'm sure you've raped or even made indecent love to dozens of southern women, which perhaps accounts for your wrongheadedness about civilization. But I don't mind a bit. I'll love you out of it.

FAFHRD: Mara, you have a brilliant mind, but just the same you greatly exaggerate that one pirate cruise I made under Hringorl, and especially the opportunities it afforded for amorous adventures. In the first place, all the inhabitants, and especially all the young women of any shore town we sacked, ran away to the hills before we'd

25

even landed. And if there were any women raped, I being youngest would have been at the bottom of the list of rapists and so hardly tempted. Truth to tell, the only interesting folk I met on that dreary voyage were two old men held for ransom, from whom I learned a smattering of Quarmallian and High Lankhmarese, and a scrawny youth apprenticed to a hedge-wizard. He was deft with the dagger, that one, and had a legend-breaking mind, like mine and my father's.

MARA: Do not grieve. Life will become more exciting for you after we're married.

FAFHRD: That's where you're wrong, dearest Mara. Hold, let me explain! I know my mother. Once we're married, Mor will expect you to do all the cooking and tent-work. She'll treat you as seven-eighths slave and – perhaps – one-eighth my concubine.

MARA: Ha! You really will have to learn to rule your mother, Fafhrd. Yet do not fret, dearest, even about that. It's clear you know nothing of the weapons a strong and untiring young wife has against an old mother-in-law. I'll put her in her place, even if I have to poison her – oh, not to kill, only to weaken sufficiently. Before three moons have waxed, she'll be trembling at my gaze and you'll feel yourself much more a man. I know that you being an only child and your wild father perishing young, she got an unnatural influence over you, but—

FAFHRD: I feel myself very much the man at this instant, you immoral and poisoning witchlet, you ice-tigress; and I intend to prove it on you without delay. Defend yourself! Ha, would you—!

Once more the snow-mound convulsed, like a giant ice-bear dying of fits. The bear died to a music of sistrums and triangles, as there clashed together and shattered the flashing ice crystals which had grown in unnatural numbers and size on Mara's and Fafhrd's cloaks during their dialogue.

The short day raced toward night, as if even the gods who govern the sun and stars were impatient to see the Show.

Hringorl conferred with his three chief henchmen, Hor, Harrax, and Hrey. There was scowling and nodding, and Fafhrd's name was mentioned.

The youngest husband of the Snow Clan, a vain and thoughtless cockerel, was ambushed and snowballed unconscious by a patrol of young Snow Wives who had seen him in brazen converse with a Mingol stage girl. Thereafter, a sure casualty for the two-day run of the Show, he was tenderly but slowly nursed back toward life by his wife, who had been the most enthusiastic of the snowballers.

Mara, happy as a snow dove, dropped in on this household and helped. But as she watched the husband so helpless and the wife so tender, her smiles and dreamy grace vanished. She grew tense and, for an athletic girl, fidgety. Thrice she opened her lips to speak, then pursed them, and finally left without saying a word.

In the Women's Tent, Mor and her coven put a spell on Fafhrd to bring him home and another to chill his loins, then went on to discuss weightier measures against the whole universe of sons, husbands, and actresses.

The second enchantment had no effect on Fafhrd, probably because he was taking a snow-bath at the time – it being a well-known fact that magic has little effect on those who are already inflicting upon themselves the same results which the spell is trying to cause. After parting with Mara, he had stripped, plunged into a snowbank, then rubbed every surface, crack and cranny of his body with the numbing powdery stuff. Thereafter he used thickly-needled pine branches to dust himself off and beat his blood back into motion. Dressed, he felt the pull of the first enchantment, but opposed it and secretly made his way into the tent of two old Mingol traders, Zax and Effendrit, who had been his father's friends, and he snoozed amidst a

27

pile of pelts until evening. Neither of his mother's spells were able to follow him into what was, by trading custom, a tiny area of Mingol territory though the Mingols' tent did begin to sag with an unnaturally large number of ice crystals, which the Mingol oldsters, wizened and nimble as monkeys, beat off janglingly with poles. The sound penetrated pleasantly into Fafhrd's dream without arousing him, which would have irked his mother had she known – she believed that both pleasure and rest were bad for men. His dream became one of Vlana dancing sinuously in a dress made of a net of fine silver wires from the intersections of which hung myriads of tiny silver bells, a vision which would have irked Mor beyond endurance; fortunate indeed that she was not at that moment using her power of reading minds at a distance.

Vlana herself slumbered while one of the Mingol girls, paid a half smerduk in advance by the injured actress, renewed the snow-bandages as necessary and, when they looked dry, wet Vlana's lips with sweet wine, of which a few drops trickled between. Vlana's mind was a-storm with anticipations and plots, but whenever she waked, she stilled it with an Eastern circle-charm that went something like, 'Creep, sleep; rouse, drowse; browse, soughs; slumber, umber; raw, claw; burnt, earn'd; cumber, number; left, death; cunt, won't; count, fount; mount, down't; leap, deep; creep, sleep,' and so on back around the incestuous loop. She knew that a woman can get wrinkles in her mind as well as her skin. She also knew that only a spinster looks after a spinster. And finally she knew that a trouper, like a soldier, does well to sleep whenever possible.

Vellix the Venturer, idly slipping about, overheard some of Hringorl's plottings, saw Fafhrd enter his tent of retreat, noted that Essedinex was drinking beyond his wont, and eavesdropped for a while on the Master of the Show.

In the girls' third of the actors' fish-shaped tent, Essedinex was arguing with the two Mingol girls, who were twins, and a barely nubile Ilthmarix, about the amount of grease they proposed to smear on their shaven bodies for tonight's performance.

'By the black bones, you'll beggar me,' he wailingly expostulated. 'And you'll look no more lascivious than lumps of lard.'

'From what I know of Northerners, they like their women well larded, and why not outside as well as in?' the one Mingol girl demanded.

'What's more,' her twin added sharply, 'if you expect us to freeze off our toes and tits, to please an audience of smelly old bearskins, you've got your head on upside-down.'

'Don't worry, Seddy,' the Ilthmarix said, patting his flushed cheek and its sparse white hairs, 'I always give my best performance when I'm all gooey. We'll have them chasing us up the walls, where we'll pop from their grabs like so many slippery melon seeds.'

'Chasing—?' Essedinex gripped the Ilthmarix by her slim shoulder. 'You'll provoke no orgies tonight, do you hear me? Teasing pays. Orgies don't. The point is to—'

'We know just how far to tease, daddy-pooh,' one of the Mingol girls put in.

'We know how to control them,' her sister continued.

'And if we don't, Vlana always does,' the Ilthmarix finished.

As the almost imperceptible shadows lengthened and the mist-wreathed air grew dark, the omnipresent crystals seemed to be growing even a little more swiftly. The palaver at the trading tents, which the thick snowy tongue of the forest shut off from the home tents, grew softer-voiced then ceased. The unending low chant from the Women's Tent became more noticeable and also higher pitched. An evening breeze came from the north making all the crystals tinkle. The chanting grew gruffer and the breeze and the tinkling ceased as if on command. The mist came wreathing back from east and west, and the crystals were growing again. The women's chanting faded to a murmur. All the Cold Corner grew tautly and expectantly silent with the approach of night.

Day ran away over the ice-fanged western horizon as if she were afraid of the dark.

In the narrow space between the actors' tents and Godshall there was movement, a glimmer, a bright spark that sputtered for nine, ten, eleven heartbeats, then a flash, a flaring, and there rose up – slowly at first, then swifter and swifter – a comet with a brushy tail of orange fire that dribbled sparks. High above the pines, almost on the edge of heaven – twenty-one, twenty-two, twenty-three – the comet's tail faded and it burst with a thunderclap into nine white stars.

It was the rocket signaling the first performance of the Show.

Godshall on the inside was a tall crazy longship of chill blackness inadequately lit and warmed by an arc of candles in the prow, which all the rest of the year was an altar, but now a stage. Its masts were eleven vast living pines thrusting up from the ship's bow, stern, and sides. Its sails – in sober fact, its walls – were stitched hides laced tautly to the masts. Instead of sky overhead there were thickly interthrusting pine branches, white with drifting snow, beginning a good five man's-heights above the deck.

The stern and waist of this weird ship, which moved only on the winds of imagination, were crowded with Snow Men in their darkly colorful furs and seated on stumps and thick blanket rolls. They were laughing with drink and growling out short talk and jokes at each other, but not very loudly. Religious awe and fear touched them on entering Godshall, or more properly, God's Ship, despite or more likely because of the profane use to which it was being put tonight.

There came a rhythmic drumming, sinister as the

padding of a snow leopard and at first so soft that no man might say exactly when it began, except that one moment there was talk and movement in the audience and the next none at all, only so many pairs of hands gripping or lightly resting on knees, and so many pairs of eyes scanning the candlelit stage between two screens painted with black and gray whorls.

The drumming grew louder, quickened, complicated itself into weaving arabesques of tapped sound, and returned to the leopard's padding.

There loped onto the stage, precisely in time with the drum beats, a silver-furred, short-bodied, slender feline with long legs, long ears a-prick, long whiskers, and long, white fangs. It stood about a yard high at the shoulder and rump. The only human feature was a glossy mop of long, straight black hair falling down the back of its neck and thence forward over its right shoulder.

It circled the stage thrice, ducking its head and sniffing as if on a scent and growling deep in its throat.

Then it noticed the audience and with a scream crouched back from them rampant, menacing them with the long, glittering claws which terminated its forelegs.

Two members of the audience were so taken in by the illusion that they had to be restrained by neighbors from pitching a knife or hurling a short-handled axe at what they were certain was a genuine and dangerous beast.

The beast scanned them, writhing its black lips back from its fangs and lesser teeth. As it swiftly swung its muzzle from side to side, inspecting them with its great brown eyes, its short-furred tail lashed back and forth in time.

Then it danced a leopardly dance of life, love, and death, sometimes on hind legs, but mostly on all fours. It scampered and investigated, it menaced and shrank, it attacked and fled, it caterwauled and writhed cat-lasciviously.

31

Despite the long black hair, it became no easier for the audience to think of it as a human female in a close-fitting suit of fur. For one thing, its forelegs were as long as its hindlegs and appeared to have an extra joint in them.

Something white squawked and came fluttering upward from behind one of the screens. With a swift leap and slash of foreleg, the great silvery cat struck.

Everyone in Godshall heard the scream of the snow pigeon and the crack of its neck.

Holding the dead bird to its fangs, the great cat, standing womanly now, gave the audience a long look, then walked without haste behind the nearest screen. There came from the audience a sigh compounded of loathing and longing, of a wonder as to what would happen next and of a wish to see what was going on now.

Fafhrd, however, did not sigh. For one thing, the slightest movement might have revealed his hiding place. For another, he could clearly see all that was going on behind both whorl-marked screens.

Being barred from the Show by his youth, let alone by Mor's wishes and witcheries, half an hour before showtime he had mounted one of the trunk-pillars of Godshall on the precipice side when no one was looking. The strong lacings of the hide walls made it the easiest of climbs. Then he had cautiously crawled out onto two of several stout pine branches growing inward close together over the hall, being very careful to disturb neither browning needles nor drifted snow, until he had found a good viewing hole, one opening toward the stage, but mostly hidden from the audience. Thereafter, it had been simply a matter of holding still enough so that no betraying needles or snow dropped down. Anyone looking up through the gloom and chancing to see parts of his white garb would take it for snow, he hoped.

Now he watched the two Mingol girls rapidly pull off from Vlana's arms the tight fur sleeves together with the fur-covered, claw-tipped, rigid extra lengths in which they ended and which her hands had been gripping. Next they dragged from Vlana's legs *their* fur coverings, while she sat on a stool and, after drawing her fangs off her teeth, speedily unhooked her leopard mask and shoulder piece.

A moment later she slouched back on stage – a cave woman in a brief sarong of silvery fur and lazily gnawing at the end of a long, thick bone. She mimed a cave woman's day: fire-and-baby-tending, brat-slapping, hide-chewing, and laborious sewing. Things got a bit more exciting with the return of her husband, an unseen presence made visible by her miming.

Her audience followed the story easily, grinning when she demanded what meat her husband had brought, showed dissatisfaction with his meager kill, and refused him an embrace. They guffawed when she tried to clobber him with her chewing bone and got knocked sprawling in return, her children cowering around her.

From that position she scuttled off stage behind the other screen, which hid the actors' doorway (normally the Snow Priest's) and also concealed the one-armed Mingol, whose flickering five fingers did all the drum music on the instrument clutched between his feet. Vlana whipped off the rest of her fur, changed the slant of her eyes and eyebrows by four deft strokes of makeup, seemingly in one movement shouldered into a long gray gown with hood, and was back on stage in the persona of a Mingol woman of the Steppes.

After another brief session of miming, she squatted gracefully down at a low, jar-stocked table stage front, and began carefully to make up her face and do her hair, the audience serving as her mirror. She dropped back hood and gown, revealing the briefer red silk garment her fur one had hidden. It was most fascinating to watch her apply the variously colored salves and powders and glittering dusts to her lips, cheeks, and eyes, and see her comb up

33

her dark hair into a high structure kept in place by long, gem-headed pins.

Just then Fafhrd's composure was tested to the uttermost, when a large handful of snow was clapped to his eyes and held there.

He stayed perfectly still for three heartbeats. Then he captured a rather slender wrist and dragged it down a short distance, meantime gently shaking his head and blinking his eyes.

The trapped wrist twisted free and the clot of snow fell down the neck of the wolfskin coat of Hringorl's man Hor seated immediately below. Hor gave a strange low cry and started to glare upward, but fortunately at that moment Vlana pulled down her red silk sarong and began to anoint her nipples with a coral salve.

Fafhrd looked around and saw Mara grinning fiercely at him from where she lay outstretched on the two branches next his, her head level with his shoulder.

'If I'd been an ice gnome, you'd be dead!' she hissed at him. 'Or if I'd set my four brothers to trap you, as I should have. Your ears *were* dead, your mind all in your eyes straining toward that skinny harlot. I've heard how you challenged Hringorl for her! And refused his gift of a gold bracelet!'

'I admit, dear, that you slithered up behind me most skillfully and silently,' Fafhrd breathed at her softly, 'while you seem to have eyes and ears for all things that transpire and some that don't – at Cold Corner. But I must say, Mara—'

'Hah! Now you'll tell me I shouldn't be here, being a woman. Male prerogatives, intersexual sacrilege, and so forth. Well, neither should you be here.'

Fafhrd gravely considered part of that. 'No, I think all the women should be here. What they would learn would be much to their interest and advantage.'

'To caper like a cat in heat? To slouch about like a silly

34

slave? Yes, I saw those acts too – while you were drooling dumb and deaf! You men will laugh at anything, especially when your stupid, gasping, red-faced lust's been aroused by a shameless bitch making a show of her scrawny nakedness!'

Mara's heated hissings were getting dangerously loud and might well have attracted the attention of Hor and others, but once again good fortune intervened, in that there was a ripple of drumming as Vlana streaked off the stage, and then there began a wild, somewhat thin, but galloping music, the one-armed Mingol being joined by the little Ilthmarix playing a nose flute.

'I did not laugh, my dear,' Fafhrd breathed somewhat loftily, 'nor did I drool or flush or speed my breath, as I am sure you noted. No, Mara, my sole purpose in being here is to learn more about civilization.'

She glared at him, grinned, then of a sudden smiled tenderly. 'You know, I honestly think you believe that, you incredible infant,' she breathed back wonderingly. 'Granting that the decadence called civilization could possibly be of interest to anyone, and a capering whore able to carry its message, or rather absence of message.'

'I neither think nor believe, I *know* it,' Fafhrd replied, ignoring Mara's other remarks. 'A whole world calls and have we eyes only for Cold Corner? Watch with me, Mara, and gain wisdom. The actress dances the cultures of all lands and ages. Now she is a woman of the Eight Cities.'

Perhaps Mara was in some small part persuaded. Or perhaps it was that Vlana's new costume covered her thoroughly – sleeved, green bodice, full, blue skirt, red stockings, and yellow shoes – and that the culture dancer was panting a trifle and showing the cords in her neck from the stamping and whirling dance she was doing. At any rate, the Snow Girl shrugged and smiled indulgently and whispered, 'Well, I must admit it all has a certain disgusting interest.'

'I knew you'd understand, dearest. You have twice the mind of any woman of our tribe, aye, or of any man,' Fafhrd cooed, caressing her tenderly but somewhat absently as he peered at the stage.

In succession, always making lightning costume changes, Vlana became a houri of the Eastern Lands, a custom-hobbled Quarmallian queen, a languorous concubine of the King of Kings, and a haughty Lankhmar lady wearing a black toga. This last was theatrical license: only the men of Lankhmar wear the toga, but the garment was Lankhmar's chiefest symbol across the world of Nehwon.

Meanwhile Mara did her best to share the eccentric whim of her husband-to-be. At first she was genuinely intrigued and made mental notes on details of Vlana's dress styles and tricks of behavior which she might herself adopt to advantage. But then she was gradually overwhelmed by a realization of the older woman's superiority in training, knowledge and experience. Vlana's dancing and miming clearly couldn't be learned except with much coaching and drill. And how, and especially where, could a Snow Girl ever wear such clothes? Feelings of inferiority gave way to jealousy and that to hatred.

Civilization was nasty, Vlana ought to be whipped out of Cold Corner, and Fafhrd needed a woman to run his life and keep his mad imagination in check. Not his mother, of course – that awful and incestuous eater of her own son – but a glamorous and shrewd young wife. Herself.

She began to watch Fafhrd intently. He didn't look like an infatuated male, he looked cold as ice, but he was certainly utterly intent on the scene below. She reminded herself that a few men were adept at hiding their true feelings.

Vlana shed her toga and stood in a wide-meshed tunic

of fine silver wires. At each crossing of the wires a tiny silver bell stood out. She shimmied and the bells tinkled, like a tree of tiny birds all chirruping together a hymn to her body. Now her slenderness seemed that of adolescence, while from between the strands of her sleekly cascading hair, her large eyes gleamed with mysterious hints and invitations.

Fafhrd's controlled breathing quickened. So his dream in the Mingols' tent had been true! His attention, which had half been off to the lands and ages Vlana had danced, centered wholly on her and became desire.

This time his composure was put to an even sorer test for, without warning, Mara's hand clutched his crotch.

But he had little time in which to demonstrate his composure. She let go and crying, 'Filthy beast! You are lusting!' struck him in the side, below the ribs.

He tried to catch her wrists, while staying on his branches. She kept trying to hit him. The pine boughs creaked and shed snow and needles.

In landing a clout on Fafhrd's ear, Mara's upper body overbalanced, though her feet kept hooked to branchlets.

Growling, 'God freeze you, you bitch!' Fafhrd gripped his stoutest bough with one hand and lunged down with the other to catch Mara's arm just beneath the shoulder.

Those looking up from below – and by now there were some, despite the strong counter-attraction of the stage – saw two struggling, white-clad torsos and fair-haired heads dipping out of the branchy roof, as if about to descend in swan dives. Then, still struggling, the figures withdrew upward.

An older Snow Man cried out, 'Sacrilege!' A younger, 'Peepers! Let's thrash 'em!' He might have been obeyed, for a quarter of the Snow Men were on their feet by now, if it hadn't been that Essedinex was keeping a close eye on things through a peephole in one of the screens and that he was wise in the ways of handling unruly audiences. He shot a finger at the Mingol behind him, then sharply raised that hand, palm upward.

The music surged. Cymbals clashed. The two Mingol girls and the Ilthmarix bounded on stage stark naked and began to caper around Vlana. The fat Easterner clumped past them and set fire to his great black beard. Blue flames crawled up and flickered before his face and around his ears. He didn't put the fire out – with a wet towel he carried – until Essedinex hoarsely stage-whispered from his peephole, 'That's enough. We've got 'em again.' The length of the black beard had been halved. Actors make great sacrifices, which the yokels and even their co-mates rarely appreciate.

Fafhrd, dropping the last dozen feet, lighted in the high drift outside Godshall at the same instant Mara finished her downward climb. They faced each other calf-deep in crusted snow, across which the rising, slightly gibbous moon threw streaks of white glimmer and made shadow between them.

Fafhrd asked, 'Mara, where did you hear that lie about me challenging Hringorl for the actress?'

'Faithless lecher!' she cried, punched him in the eye, and ran off toward the tent of the women, sobbing and crying, 'I *will* tell my brothers! You'll see!'

Fafhrd jumped up and down, smothering a howl of pain, sprinted after her three steps, stopped, clapped snow to his pain-stabbed eye and, as soon as it was only throbbing, began to think.

He looked around with the other eye, saw no one, made his way to a clump of snow-laden evergreens on the edge of the precipice, concealed himself among them, and continued to think.

His ears told him that the Show was still going at a hot pace inside Godshall. There were laughs and cheers, sometimes drowning the wild drumming and fluting. His eyes – the hit one was working again – told him there was no one near him. They swiveled to the actors' tents at that end of Godshall which lay nearest the new road south, and at the stables beyond them, and at the traders' tents beyond the stables. Then they came back to the nearest tent: Vlana's hemicylindrical one. Crystals clothed it, twinkling in the moonlight, and a giant crystal flatworm seemed to be crawling across its middle just below the evergreen sycamore bough.

He slitheringly walked toward it across the bediamonded snow crust. The knot joining the lacings of its doorway was hidden in shadow and felt complex and foreign. He went to the back of the tent, loosened two pegs, went on belly through the crack like a snake, found himself amongst the hems of the skirts of Vlana's racked garments, loosely replaced the pegs, stood up, shook himself, took four steps and lay down on the pallet. A little heat radiated from a banked brazier. After a while he reached to the table and poured himself a cup of brandy.

At last he heard voices. They grew louder. As the lacings of the door were being unknotted and loosened, he felt for his knife and also prepared to draw a large fur rug over him.

Saying with laughter but also decision, 'No, no, *no*,' Vlana swiftly stepped in backward over the slack lashings, held the door closed with one hand while she gave the lashings a tightening pull with the other, and glanced over her shoulder.

Her look of stark surprise was gone almost before Fafhrd marked it, to be replaced by a quick welcoming grin that wrinkled her nose comically. She turned away from him, carefully drew the lashings tight, and spent some time tying a knot on the inside. Then she came over and knelt beside him where he lay, her body erect from her knees. There was no grin now as she looked down at him, only a composed, enigmatic thoughtfulness, which he sought to match. She was wearing the hooded robe of her Mingol costume.

'So you changed your mind about a reward,' she said quietly but matter-of-factly. 'How do you know that I too may not have changed mine since?'

Fafhrd shook his head, replying to her first statement. Then, after a pause, he said, 'Nevertheless, I have discovered that I desire you.'

Vlana said, 'I saw you watching the show from ... from the gallery. You almost stole it, you know – I mean the show. Who was the girl with you? Or was it a youth? I couldn't be quite sure.'

Fafhrd did not answer her inquiries. Instead he said, 'I also wish to ask you questions about your supremely skillful dancing and ... and acting in loneliness.'

'Miming.' She supplied the word.

'Miming, yes. *And* I want to talk to you about civilization.'

'That's right, this morning you asked me how many languages I knew,' she said, looking straight across him at the wall of the tent. It was clear that she too was a thinker. She took the cup of brandy out of his hand, swallowed half of what was left, and returned it to him.

'Very well,' she said, at last looking down at him, but with unchanged expression. 'I will give you your desire, my dear boy. But now is not the time. First, I must rest and gather strength. Go away and return when the star Shadah sets. Wake me if I slumber.'

'That's an hour before dawn,' he said, looking up at her. 'It will be a chilly wait for me in the snow.'

'Don't do that,' she said quickly. 'I don't want you three-quarters frozen. Go where it's warm. To stay awake, think of me. Don't drink too much wine. Now go.'

He got up and made to embrace her. She drew back a step, saying, 'Later. Later – everything.' He started toward

40

the door. She shook her head, saying, 'You might be seen. As you came.'

Passing her again, his head brushed something hard. Between the hoops supporting the tent's middle, the supple hide of the tent bulged down, while the hoops themselves were bowed out and somewhat flattened bearing the weight. He cringed down for an instant, ready to grab Vlana and jump any way, then began methodically to punch and sweep at the bulges, always striking outward. There was a crashing and a loud tinkling as the massed crystals, which outside had reminded him of a giant flatworm – must be a giant snow serpent by now! – broke up and showered off.

Meanwhile he said, 'The Snow Women do not love you. Nor is Mor my mother your friend.'

'Do they think to frighten me with ice crystals?' Vlana demanded contemptuously. 'Why, I know of Eastern fire sorceries compared to which their feeble magickings—'

'But you are in *their* territory now, at the mercy of *their* element, which is crueler and subtler than fire,' Fafhrd interposed, brushing away the last of the bulgings, so that the hoops stood up again and the leather stretched almost flat between them. 'Do not underrate their powers.'

'Thank you for saving my tent from being crumbled. But now – and swiftly – go.'

She spoke as if of trivial matters, but her large eyes were thoughtful.

Just before snaking under the back wall, Fafhrd looked over his shoulder. Vlana was gazing at the side wall again, holding the empty cup he had given her, but she caught his movement and, now smiling tenderly, put a kiss on her palm and blew it toward him.

Outside the cold had grown bitter. Nevertheless, Fafhrd went to his clump of evergreens, drew his cloak closely around him, dropped its hood over his forehead, tightened the hood's drawstring, and sat himself facing Vlana's tent.

When the cold began to penetrate his furs, he thought of Vlana.

Suddenly he was crouching and had loosened his knife in its sheath.

A figure was approaching Vlana's tent, keeping to the shadows when it could. It appeared to be clad in black.

Fafhrd silently advanced.

Through the still air came the faint sound of fingernails scratching leather.

There was a flash of dim light as the doorway was opened.

It was bright enough to show the face of Vellix the Venturer. He stepped inside and there was the sound of lacings being drawn tight.

Fafhrd stopped ten paces from the tent and stood there for perhaps two dozen breaths. Then he softly walked past the tent, keeping the same distance.

There was a glow in the doorway of the high, conical tent of Essedinex. From the stables beyond, a horse whickered twice.

Fafhrd crouched and peered through the low, glowing doorway a knife-cast away. He moved from side to side. He saw a table crowded with jugs and cups set against the sloping wall of the tent opposite the doorway.

To one side of the table sat Essedinex. To the other, Hringorl.

On the watch for Hor, Harrax, or Hrey, Fafhrd circled the tent. He approached it where the table and the two men were faintly silhouetted. Drawing aside his hood and hair, he set his ear against the leather.

'Three gold bars – that's my top,' Hringorl was saying surlily. The leather made his voice hollow.

'Five,' Essedinex answered, and there was the *slup* of wine mouthed and swallowed.

'Look here, old man,' Hringorl countered, his voice at

its most gruffly menacing, 'I don't need you. I can snatch the girl and pay you nothing.'

'Oh no, that won't do, Master Hringorl.' Essedinex sounded merry. 'For then the Show would never return again to Cold Corner, and how would your tribesmen like that? Nor would there be any more girls brought you by me.'

'What matter?' the other answered carelessly. The words were muffled by a gulp of wine, yet Fafhrd could hear the bluff in them. 'I have my ship. I can cut your throat this instant and snatch the girl tonight.'

'Then do so,' Essedinex said brightly. 'Only give me a moment for one more quaff.'

'Very well, you old miser. Four gold bars.'

'Five.'

Hringorl cursed sulfurously. 'Some night, you ancient pimp, you will provoke me too far. Besides, the girl is old.'

'Aye, in the ways of pleasure. Did I tell you that she once became an acolyte of the Wizards of Azorkah? – so that she might be trained by them to become a concubine of the King of Kings and their spy in the court at Horborixen. Aye, and eluded those dread necromancers most cleverly when she had gained the erotic knowledge she desired.'

Hringorl laughed with a forced lightness. 'Why should I pay even one silver bar for a girl who has been possessed by dozens? Every man's plaything.'

'By hundreds,' Essedinex corrected. 'Skill is gained only by experience, as you know well. And the greater the experience, the greater the skill. Yet this girl is never a plaything. She is the instructress, the revelator; she plays with a man for his pleasure, she can make a man feel king of the universe and perchance – who knows? – even *be* that. What is impossible to a girl who knows the pleasure-ways of the gods themselves – aye, and of the arch-demons? And yet – you won't believe this, but it's true –

43

she remains in her fashion forever virginal. For no man has ever mastered her.'

'That will be seen to!' Hringorl's words were almost a laughing shout. There was the sound of wine gulped. Then his voice dropped. 'Very well, five gold bars it is, you usurer. Delivery after tomorrow night's Show. The gold paid against the girl.'

'Three hours after the Show, when the girl's drugged and all's quiet. No need to rouse the jealousy of your fellow tribesmen so soon.'

'Make it two hours. Agreed? And now let's talk of next year. I'll want a black girl, a full-blooded Kleshite. And no five-gold-bar deal ever again. I'll not want a witchy wonder, only youth and great beauty.'

Essedinex answered, 'Believe me, you won't ever again desire another woman, once you've known and – I wish you luck – mastered Vlana. Oh, of course, I suppose—'

Fafhrd reeled back from the tent a half dozen paces and there planted his feet firm and wide, feeling strangely dizzy, or was it drunk? He had early guessed they were almost certainly talking of Vlana, but hearing her name spoken made a much greater difference than he'd expected.

The two revelations, coming so close, filled him with a mixed feeling he'd never known before; an overmastering rage and also a desire to laugh hugely. He wanted a sword long enough to slash open the sky and tumble the dwellers in paradise from their beds. He wanted to find and fire off all the Show's sky-rockets into the tent of Essedinex. He wanted to topple Godshall with its pines and drag it across all the actors' tents. He wanted—

He turned around and swiftly made for the stable tent. The one groom was snoring on the straw beside an empty jug and near the light sleigh of Essedinex. Fafhrd noted with a fiendish grin that the horse he knew best happened to be one of Hringorl's. He found a horse collar and a long

44

coil of light, strong rope. Then, making reassuring mumbles behind half-closed lips, he led out the chosen horse – a white mare – from the rest. The groom only snored louder.

He again noted the light sleigh. A risk-devil seized him and he unlaced the stiff, pitchy tarpaulin covering the storage space behind the two seats. Beneath it among other things was the Show's supply of rockets. He selected three of the biggest – with their stout ash tails they were long as ski sticks – and then took time to replace the tarpaulin. He still felt the mad desire for destruction, but now it was under a measure of control.

Outside he put the collar on the mare and firmly knotted to it one end of the rope. The other end he fashioned into a roomy noose. Then, coiling the rest of the rope and gripping the rockets under his left elbow, he nimbly mounted the mare and walked it near the tent of Essedinex. The two dim silhouettes still confronted each other across the table.

He whirled the noose above his head and cast. It settled around the apex of the tent with hardly a sound, for he was quick to draw in the slack before it rattled against the tent's wall.

The noose tightened around the top of the tent's central mast. Containing his excitement, he walked the mare towards the forest across the moon-bright snow, paying out the rope. When there were only four coils of it left, he urged the mare into a lope. He crouched over the collar, holding it firm, his heels clamped to the mare's sides. The rope tightened. The mare strained. There was a satisfying, muffled *crack* behind him. He shouted a triumphant laugh. The mare plunged on against the rope's irregular restraint. Looking back, he saw the tent dragging after them. He saw fire and heard yells of surprise and anger. Again he shouted his laughter.

At the edge of the forest he drew his knife and slashed

the rope. Vaulting down, he buzzed approvingly in the mare's ear and gave her a slap on the flank that set her cantering toward the stable. He considered firing off the rockets toward the fallen tent, but decided it would be anticlimactic. With them still clamped under his elbow, he walked into the edge of the woods. So hidden, he started home. He walked lightly to minimize footprints, found a branch of fringe pine and dragged it behind him and, when he could, he walked on rock.

His mountainous humor was gone and his rage too, replaced by black depression. He no longer hated Vellix or even Vlana, but civilization seemed a tawdry thing, unworthy of his interest. He was glad he had spilled Hringorl and Essedinex, but they were woodlice. He himself was a lonely ghost, doomed to roam the Cold Waste.

He thought of walking north through the woods until he found a new life or froze, of fetching and strapping on his skis and attempting to leap the tabooed gap that had been the death of Skif, of getting sword and challenging Hringorl's henchmen all at once, and of a hundred other doom-treadings.

The tents of the Snow Clan looked like pale mushrooms in the light of the crazily glaring moon. Some were cones topping a squat cylinder; others, bloated hemispheres, turnip shapes. Like mushrooms, they did not quite touch the ground at the edges. Their floors of packed branches, carpeted with hides and supported by heavier boughs, stood on and overhung chunky posts, so that a tent's heat would not turn the frozen ground below it to a mush.

The huge, silvery trunk of a dead snow oak, ending in what looked like a giant's split fingernails, where an old lightning bolt had shattered it midway up, marked the site of Mor's and Fafhrd's tent – and also of his father's grave, which the tent overlay. Each year it was pitched just so.

There were lights in a few of the tents and in the great

Tent of the Women lying beyond in the direction of Godshall, but Fafhrd could see no one abroad. With a dispirited grunt he headed for his home door then, remembering the rockets, he veered toward the dead oak. It was smooth surfaced, the bark long gone. The few remaining branches were likewise bare and broken off short, the lowest of them appearing well out of reach.

A few paces away he paused for another look around. Assured of secrecy, he raced toward the oak and making a vertical leap more like a leopard's than a man's, he caught hold of the lowest branch with his free hand and whipped himself up onto it before his upward impetus was altogether spent.

Standing lightly on the dead branch with a finger touching the trunk, he made a final scan for peepers and late walkers, then with pressure of fingers and tease of fingernails, opened in the seemingly seamless gray wood a doorway tall as himself but scarcely half as wide. Feeling past skis and ski sticks, he found a long thin shape wrapped thrice around with lightly oiled sealskin. Undoing it, he uncovered a powerful looking bow and a quiver of long arrows. He added the rockets to it, replaced the wrappings, then shut the queer door of his tree-safe and dropped to the snow below, which he brushed smooth.

Entering his home tent, he felt again like a ghost and made as little noise as one. The odors of home comforted him uncomfortably and against his will; smells of meat, cooking, old smoke, hides, sweat, the chamber pot, Mor's faint, sour-sweet stench. He crossed the springy floor and, fully clad, he stretched himself in his sleeping furs. He felt tired as death. The silence was profound. He couldn't hear Mor's breathing. He thought of his last sight of his father, blue and shut-eyed, his broken limbs straightened, his best sword naked at his side with his slate-colored fingers fitted around the hilt. He thought of Nalgron now in the earth under the tent, worm-gnawed to a skeleton, the sword

47

black rust, the eyes open now – sockets staring upward through solid dirt. He remembered his last sight of his father alive: a tall wolfskin cloak striding away with Mor's warnings and threats spattering against it. Then the skeleton came back into his mind. It was a night for ghosts.

'Fafhrd?' Mor called softly from across the tent.

Fafhrd stiffened and held his breath. When he could no longer, he began to let it out and draw it in, open-mouthed, in noiseless draughts.

'Fafhrd?' The voice was a little louder, though still like a ghost cry. 'I heard you come in. You're not asleep.'

No use keeping silent. 'You haven't slept either, Mother?'

'The old sleep little.'

That wasn't true, he thought. Mor wasn't old, even by the Cold Waste's merciless measure. At the same time, it *was* the truth. Mor was as old as the tribe, the Waste itself, as old as death.

Mor said composedly – Fafhrd knew she had to be lying on her back, staring straight upward – 'I am willing that you should take Mara to wife. Not pleased, but willing. There is need for a strong back here, so long as you daydream, shooting your thoughts like arrows loosed high and at random, and prank about and gad after actresses and such gilded dirt. Besides, you have got Mara with child and her family does not altogether lack status.'

'Mara spoke to you tonight?' Fafhrd asked. He tried to keep his voice dispassionate, but the words came out strangledly.

'As any Snow Girl should. Except she ought to have told me earlier. And you earlier still. But you have inherited threefold your father's secretiveness along with his urge to neglect his family and indulge himself in useless adventurings. Except that in you the sickness takes a more repulsive form. Cold mountain-tops were his mistresses, while you are drawn to civilization, that putrid festering of the hot

48

south, where there is no natural stern cold to punish the foolish and luxurious and to see that the decencies are kept. But you will discover that there is a witchy cold that can follow you anywhere in Nehwon. Ice once went down and covered all the hot lands, in punishment for an earlier cycle of lecherous evil. And wherever ice once went, witchery can send it again. You will come to believe that, and shed your sickness, or else you will learn as your father learned.'

Fafhrd tried to make the accusation of husband-murder that he had hinted at so easily this morning, but the words stuck, not in his throat, but in his very mind, which felt invaded. Mor had long ago made his heart cold. Now, up in his brain, she was creating among his most private thoughts crystals which distorted everything and prevented him from using against her the weapons of duty coldly performed and joined by a cold reason which let him keep his integrity. He felt as if there were closing in on him forever the whole world of cold, in which the rigidity of ice and the rigidity of morals and the rigidity of thought were all one.

As if sensing her victory and permitting herself to joy in it a little, Mor said in the same dead, reflective tones, 'Aye, your father now bitterly regrets Gran Hanack, White Fang, the Ice Queen, and all his other mountain paramours. They cannot help him now. They have forgotten him. He stares up endlessly from lidless sockets at the home he despised and now yearns for, so near, yet so impossibly far. His fingerbones scrabble feebly against the frozen earth, he tries futilely to twist under its weight ...'

Fafhrd heard a faint scratching, perhaps of icy twigs against tent leather, but his hair rose. Yet he could move no other part of him, he discovered as he tried to lift himself. The blackness all around him was a vast weight. He wondered if Mor had magicked him down under the ground beside his father. Yet it was a greater weight than

49

that of eight feet of frozen earth that pressed on him. It was the weight of the entire Cold Waste and its killingness, of the taboos and contempts and shutmindedness of the Snow Clan, of the pirate greed and loutish lust of Hringorl, of even Mara's merry self-absorption and bright, half-blind mind, and atop them all Mor with ice crystals forming on her fingertips as she wove them in a binding spell.

And then he thought of Vlana.

It may not have been the thought of Vlana that did it. A star may have chanced to crawl across the tent's tiny smoke-hole and shoot its tiny silver arrow into the pupil of one of his eyes. It may have been that his held breath suddenly puffed out and his lungs automatically sucked another breath in, showing him that his muscles *could* move.

At any rate he shot up and dashed for the doorway. He dared not stop for the lashings, because Mor's ice-jagged fingers were clutching at him. Instead he ripped the brittle, old leather with one downward sweep of his clawed right hand and then *leaped* from the door, because Nalgron's skeletal arms were straining toward him from the narrow black space between the frozen ground and the tent's elevated floor.

And then he ran as he had never run before. He ran as if all the ghosts of the Cold Waste were at his heels – and in some fashion they were. He passed the last of the Snow Clan's tents, all dark, and the faintly tinkling Tent of the Women, and sprinted out onto the gentle slope, all silvered by the moon, leading down to the upcurving lip of Trollstep Canyon. He felt the urge to dash off that verge, challenging the air to uphold him and bear him south or else hurl him to instant oblivion – and for a moment there seemed nothing to choose between those two fates.

Then he was running not so much away from the cold

and its crippling, supernatural horrors, as toward civilization, which was once again a bright emblem in his brain, an answer to all small-mindedness.

He slowed down a little and some sense came back into his head, so that he peered for living late-walkers as well as for demons and fetches.

He noted Shadah twinkling blue in the western treetops.

He was walking by the time he reached Godshall. He went between it and the canyon's rim, which no longer tugged him.

He noted that Essedinex's tent had been set up again and was once more lit. No new snow worm crawled across Vlana's tent. The snow sycamore bough above it glittered with crystals in the moonlight.

He entered without warning by the back door, silently drawing out the loosened pegs and then thrusting together under the wall and the hems of the racked costumes his head and right fist, the latter gripping his drawn knife.

Vlana lay asleep alone on her back on the pallet, a light red woolen blanket drawn up to her naked armpits. The lamp burned yellow and small, yet brightly enough to show all the interior and no one but her. The unbanked and newly stoked brazier radiated heat.

Fafhrd came all the way in, sheathed his knife, and stood looking down at the actress. Her arms seemed very slender, her hands long-fingered and a shade large. With her big eyes shut, her face seemed rather small at the center of its glory of outspread, dark brown hair. Yet it looked both noble and knowing and its moist, long, generous lips, newly and carefully carmined, roused and tempted him. Her skin had a faint sheen of oil. He could smell its perfume.

For a moment Vlana's supine posture reminded him of both Mor and Nalgron, but this thought was instantly swept away by the brazier's fierce heat, like that of a small wrought-iron sun, by the rich textures and graceful

51

instruments of civilization all around him, and by Vlana's beauty and couth grace, which seemed self-aware even in sleep. She was civilization's sigil.

He moved back toward the rack and began to strip off his clothes and neatly fold and pile them. Vlana did not wake, or at least her eyes did not open.

Getting back under the red blanket again some time later, after crawling out to relieve himself, Fafhrd said, 'Now tell me about civilization and your part in it.'

Vlana drank half of the wine Fafhrd had fetched her on his way back, then stretched luxuriously, her head resting on her interwined hands.

'Well, to begin with, I'm not a princess, though I liked being called one,' she said lightly. 'I must inform you that you have not got yourself even a lady, darlingest boy. As for civilization, it stinks.'

'No,' Fafhrd agreed, 'I have got myself the skillfullest and most glamorous actress in all Nehwon. But why has civilization an ill odor for you?'

'I think I must disillusion you still further, beloved,' Vlana said, somewhat absently rubbing her side against his. 'Otherwise you might get silly notions about me and even devise silly plans.'

'If you're talking about pretending to be a whore in order to gain erotic knowledge and other wisdoms—' Fafhrd began.

She glanced at him in considerable surprise and interrupted rather sharply: 'I'm worse than a whore, by some standards. I'm a thief. Yes, Red Ringlets, a cutpurse and filchpocket, a roller of drunks, a burglar and alleybasher. I was born a farm girl, which I suppose makes me lower still to a hunter, who lives by the death of animals and keeps his hands out of the dirt and reaps no harvest except with the sword. When my parents' plot of land was confiscated by the law's trickery to make a tiny corner of one of the new, vast, slave-worked, Lankhmar-owned grain farms, and they in consequence starved to death, I determined to get my own back from the grain merchants. Lankhmar City would feed me, aye, feed me well! – and be paid only with lumps and perhaps a deep scratch or two. So to Lankhmar I went. Falling in there with a clever girl of the same turn of mind and some experience, I did well for two full rounds of moons and a few more. We worked only in black garb, and called ourselves to ourselves the Dark Duo.

'For a cover, we danced, chiefly in the twilight hours, to fill in the time before the big-name entertainers. A little later we began to mime too, taught by one Hinerio, a famous actor fallen by wine on evil days, the darlingest and courtliest old trembler who ever begged for a drink at dawn or contrived to fondle a girl one quarter his age at dusk. And so, as I say, I did quite well ... until I fell afoul, as my parents had, of the law. No, not the Overlord's courts, dear boy, and his prisons and racks and head-and-hand-chopping blocks, though they are a shame crying to the stars. No, I ran afoul of a law older even than Lankhmar's and a court less merciful. In short, my friend's and my own cover was finally blown by the Thieves' Guild, a most ancient organization with locals in every city of the civilized world with a hidebound law against female membership and with a deep detestation of all freelance pilferers. Back on the farm I had heard of the Guild and hoped in my innocence to become worthy to join it, but soon learned their byword, "Sooner give a cobra a kiss, than a secret to a woman." Incidentally, sweet scholar of civilization's arts, such women as the Guild must use as lures and attention-shifters and such, they hire by the half hour from the Whores' Guild.

'I was lucky. At the moment when I was supposed to be slowly strangling somewhere else, I was stumbling over my friend's body, having looped swiftly home to get a key I'd

53

forgot. I lit a lamp in our close-shuttered abode and saw the long agony in Vilis' face and the red silken cord buried deep in her neck. But what filled me with the hottest rage and coldest hate – besides a second measure of knee-melting fear – was that they had strangled old Hinerio too. Vilis and I were at least competitors and so perhaps fair game by civilization's malodorous standards, but he had never even suspected us of thievery. He had assumed merely that we had other lovers or else – and also – erotic clients.

'So I scuttled out of Lankhmar as swiftly as a spied crab, eyes behind me for pursuit, and in Ilthmar encountered Essedinex' troupe, headed north for the off-season. By good fortune they needed a leading mime and my skill was sufficient to satisfy old Seddy.

'But at the same time, I swore an oath by the morning star to avenge the deaths of Vilis and Hinerio. And some day I shall! With proper plans and help and a new cover. More than one high potentate of the Thieves' Guild will learn how it feels to have his weasand narrowed a fingerclip's breadth at a time, aye, and worse things!

'But this is a hellish topic for a comfy morning, lover, and I raise it only to show you why you must not get deeply involved with a dirty and vicious one such as me.'

Vlana turned her body then so that it leaned against Fafhrd's and she kissed him from the corner of the lip to the lobe of the ear, but when he would have returned these courtesies in full measure and more, she carried away his groping hands and, bracing herself on his arms, thereby confining them, pushed herself up and gazed at him with her enigmatic look, saying, 'Dearest boy, it is the gray of dawn and soon comes the pink and you must leave me at once, or at most after a last engagement. Go home, marry that lovely and nimble tree-girl – I'm sure now it was not a male youth – and live your proper, arrow-straight life far from the stinks and snares of civilization. The Show packs up and leaves early, day after tomorrow, and I have my crooked destiny to tread. When your blood has cooled, you will feel only contempt for me. Nay, deny it not – I know men! Though there is a tiny chance that you, being you, will recall me with a little pleasure. In which case I advise one thing only: never hint of it to your wife!'

Fafhrd matched her enigmatic look and answered, 'Princess, I've been a pirate, which is nothing but a water thief, who often raids folk poor as your parents. Barbarism can match civilization's every stench. Not one move in our frostbit lives but is strictured by a mad god's laws, which we call customs, and by black-handed irrationalities from which there is no escape. My own father was condemned to death by bone-breaking by a court I dare not name. His offense: climbing a mountain. And there are murders and thievings and pimpings and – Oh, there are tales I could tell you if—'

He broke off to lift his hands so that he was holding her half above him, grasping her gently below the armpits, rather than she propped on her arms. 'Let me come south with you, Vlana,' he said eagerly, 'whether as member of your troupe or moving alone – though I *am* a singing skald, I can also sword dance, juggle four whirling daggers, and hit with one at ten paces a mark the size of my thumbnail. And when we get to Lankhmar City, perhaps disguised as two Northerners, for you are tall, I'll be your good right arm of vengeance. I can thieve by land, too, believe me, and stalk a victim through alleys, I should think, as sightlessly and silently as through forests. I can—'

Vlana, supported by his hands, laid a palm across his lips while her other hand wandered idly under the long hair at the back of his neck. 'Darling,' she said, 'I doubt not that you are brave and loyal and skillful for a lad of eighteen. And you make love well enough for a youth – quite well enough to hold your white-furred girl and mayhap a few more wenches, if you choose. But, despite your ferocious words – forgive my frankness – I sense in you honesty, nobility even, a love of fair play, and a hatred of torture. The lieutenant I seek for my revenge must be cruel and treacherous and fell as a serpent, while knowing at least as much as I of the fantastically twisty ways of the great cities and the ancient guilds. And, to be blunt, he must be old as I, which you miss by almost the fingers of two hands. So come kiss me, dear boy, and pleasure me once more and—'

Fafhrd suddenly sat up, and lifted her a little and sat her down, so that she sat sideways on his thighs, he shifting his grasp to her shoulders.

'No,' he said firmly. 'I see nothing to be gained by subjecting you once more to my inexpert caresses. But—'

'I was afraid you would take it that way,' she interrupted unhappily. 'I did not mean—'

'But,' he continued with cool authority, 'I want to ask you one question. Have you already chosen your lieutenant?'

'I will not answer that,' she replied, eyeing him as coolly and confidently.

'Is he—?' he began and then pressed his lips together, catching the name 'Vellix' before it was uttered.

She looked at him with undisguised curiosity as to what his next move would be. 'Very well,' he said at last, dropping his hands from her shoulders and propping himself with them. 'You have tried, I think, to act in what you believe to be my best interests, so I will return like with like. What I have to reveal indites barbarism and civilization equally.' And he told her of Essedinex' and Hringorl's plan for her.

She laughed heartily when he was done, though he fancied she had turned a shade pale.

'I must be slipping,' she commented. 'So that was why my somewhat subtle mimings so easily pleased Seddy's rough and ready tastes, and why there was a place open

for me in the troupe, and why he did not insist I whore for
him after the Show, as the other girls must.' She looked at
Fafhrd sharply. 'Some pranksters overset Seddy's tent this
midnight. Was it—?'

He nodded. 'I was in a strange humor, last night, merry
yet furious.'

Honest, delighted laughter from her then, followed by
another of the sharp looks. 'So you did not go home when
I sent you away after the Show?'.

'Not until afterward,' he said. 'No, I stayed and
watched.'

She looked at him in a tender, mocking, wondering way
which asked quite plainly, 'And what did you see?' But this
time he found it very easy not to name Vellix.

'So you're a gentleman, too,' she joked. 'But why didn't
you tell me about Hringorl's base scheme earlier? Did you
think I'd become too frightened to be amorous?'

'A little of that,' he admitted, 'but it was chiefly that I
did not decide until this moment to warn you. Truth to
tell, I only came back to you tonight because I was
frightened by ghosts, though later I found other good
reasons. Indeed, just before I came to your tent, fear and
loneliness – yes, and a certain jealousy too – had me
minded to hurl myself into Trollstep Canyon, or else don
skis and attempt the next-to-impossible leap which has
teased my courage for years ...'

She clutched his upper arm, digging in fingers. 'Never
do that,' she said very seriously. 'Hold onto life. Think
only of yourself. The worst always changes for the better –
or oblivion.'

'Yes, so I was thinking when I would have let the air
over the canyon decide my destiny. Would it cradle me or
dash me down? But selfishness, of which I've a plenty
whatever you think – that and a certain leeriness of all
miracles – quashed that whim. Also, I was earlier half
minded to trample your tent before pulling down the

Show Master's. So there *is* some evil in me, you see. Aye, and a shut-mouthed deceitfulness.'

She did not laugh, but studied his face most thoughtfully. Then for a time the enigma-look came back into her eyes. For a moment Fafhrd thought he could peer past it, and he was troubled, for what he thought he glimpsed behind those large, brown-irised pupils was not a sibyl surveying the universe from a mountaintop, but a merchant with scales in which he weighed objects most carefully, at whiles noting down in a little book old debts and new bribes and alternate plans for gain.

But it was only one troubling glimpse, so his heart joyed when Vlana, whom his big hands still held tilted above him, smiled down into his eyes and said, 'I will now answer your question, which I would and could not earlier. For I have only this instant decided that my lieutenant will be ... *you.* Hug me on it!'

Fafhrd grappled her with eager warmth and a strength that made her squeal, but then just before his body had fired unendurably, she pushed up from him, saying breathlessly, 'Wait, wait! We must first lay our plans.'

'Afterward, my love. Afterward,' he pleaded, straining her down.

'No!' she protested sharply. 'Afterward loses too many battles to Too Late. If you are lieutenant, I am captain and give directions.'

'Harkening in obedience,' he said, giving way. 'Only be swift.'

'We must be well away from Cold Corner before kidnap time,' she said. 'Today I must gather my things together and provide us with sleigh, swift horses, and a store of food. Leave all that to me. You behave today exactly as is your wont, keeping well away from me, in case our enemies set spies on you, as both Seddy and Hringorl are most like to do—'

58

'Very well, very well,' Fafhrd agreed hurriedly. 'And now, my sweetest—'

'Hush and have patience! To cap your deception, climb into the roof of Godshall well before the Show, just as you did last night. There just might be an attempt to kidnap me during the Show – Hringorl or his men becoming overeager, or Hringorl seeking to cheat Seddy of his gold – and I'll feel safest with you on watch. Then when I exit after wearing the toga and the silver bells, come you down swiftly and meet me at the stable. We'll escape during the break between the first and second halves of the Show, when one way or another all are too intent on what more's coming, to take note of us. You've got that? Stay far away today? Hide in the roof? Join me at the halves break? Very well! And now, darlingest lieutenant, banish all discipline. Forget every atom of respect you owe your captain and—'

But now it was Fafhrd's turn to delay. Vlana's talk had allowed time for his own worries to rouse and he held her away from him although she had knit her hands behind his neck and was straining to draw their two bodies together.

He said, 'I will obey you in every particular. Only one warning more, which it's vital you heed. Think as little as you can today about our plans, even while performing actions vital to them. Keep them hid behind the scenery of your other thoughts. As I shall mine, you may be sure. For Mor my mother is a great reader of minds.'

'Your mother! Truly she has overawed you inordinately, darling, in a fashion which makes me itch to set you wholly free – oh, do not hold me off! Why, you speak of her as if she were the Queen of Witches.'

'And so she is, make no mistake,' Fafhrd assured her dourly. 'She is the great white spider, while the whole Cold Waste, both above and below, is her web, on which we flies must go tippy-toe, o'erstepping sticky stretches. You *will* heed me?'

'Yes, yes, yes! And now—'

He brought her slowly down toward him, as a man might put a wineskin to his mouth, tantalizing himself. Their skins met. Their lips poised.

Fafhrd became aware of a profound silence above, around, below as if the very earth were holding her breath. It frightened him.

They kissed, drinking deeply of each other, and his fear was drowned.

They parted for breath. Fafhrd reached out and pinched the lamp's wick so that the flame fled and the tent was dark except for the cold silver of dawn seeping in by cranny and crack. His fingers stung. He wondered why he'd done it – they'd loved by lamplight before. Again fear came.

He clasped Vlana tightly in the hug that banishes all fears.

And then of a sudden – he could not possibly have told why – he was rolling over and over with her toward the back of the tent. His hands gripping her shoulders, his legs clamping hers together, he was hurling her sideways over him and then himself over her in swiftest alteration.

There was a *crack* like thunder and the jolt of a giant's fist hammered against the granite-frozen ground behind them, where the middle of the tent became nothing high, while the hoops above them leaned sharply that way, drawing the tent's leather skin after.

They rolled into the racked garments spilling down. There was a second monster *crack* followed by a crashing and a crunching like some super-giant beast snapping up a behemoth and crunching it between its jaws. Earth quivered for a space.

Then all was silent after that great noise and ground-shaking, except for the astonishment and fear buzzing in their ears. They clutched each other like terrified children.

Fafhrd recovered himself first. 'Dress!' he told Vlana

and squirmed under the back of the tent and stood up naked in the biting cold under the pinkening sky.

The great bough of the snow sycamore, its crystals dashed off in a vast heap, lay athwart the middle of the tent, pressing it and the pallet beneath into the frozen earth.

The rest of the sycamore, robbed of its great balancing bough, had fallen entire in the opposite direction and lay mounded around with shaken-off crystals. Its black, hairy, broken-off roots were nakedly exposed.

All the crystals shone with a pale flesh-pink from the sun.

Nothing moved anywhere, not even a wisp of breakfast smoke. Sorcery had struck a great hammerstroke and none had noted it except the intended victims.

Fafhrd, beginning to shake, slithered under again. Vlana had obeyed his word and was dressing with an actress's swiftness. Fafhrd hurried into his own garments, piled so providentially at this end of the tent. He wondered if he had been under a god's directions in doing that and in snuffing out the lamp, which else by now would have had the crushed tent flaming.

His clothes felt colder than the icy air, but he knew that would change.

He crawled with Vlana outside once more. As they stood up, he faced her toward the fallen bough with the great crystal heap around it and said, 'Now laugh at the witchy powers of my mother and her coven and all the Snow Women.'

Vlana said doubtfully, 'I see only a bough that was overweighted with ice.'

Fafhrd said, 'Compare the mass of crystals and snow that was shaken off that bough with those elsewhere. Remember: hide your thoughts!'

Vlana was silent.

A black figure was racing toward them from the traders' tents. It grew in size as it grotesquely bounded.

Vellix the Venturer was gasping as he stamped to a stop and seized Vlana's arms. Controlling his breathing, he said, 'I dreamed a dream of you struck down and pashed. Then a thunderclap waked me.'

Vlana answered, 'You dreamed the beginning of the truth, but in a matter like this, almost is as good as not at all.'

Vellix at last saw Fafhrd. Lines of jealous anger engraved his face and his hand went to the dagger at his belt.

'Hold!' Vlana commanded sharply. 'I had indeed been mashed to a mummy, except that this youth's senses, which ought to have been utterly engrossed in something else, caught the first cues of the bough's fall, and he whipped me out of death's way in the very nick. Fafhrd's his name.'

Vellix changed his hand's movement into part of a low bow, sweeping his other arm out wide.

'I am much indebted to you, young man,' he said warmly and then after a pause, 'for saving the life of a notable *artiste*.'

By now other figures were in view, some hurrying toward them from the nearby actors' tents, others at the doors of the far-off Snow Tribe's tents and not moving at all.

Pressing her cheek to Fafhrd's, as if in formal gratitude, Vlana whispered rapidly, 'Remember my plan for tonight and for all our future rapture. Do not depart a jot from it. Efface yourself.'

Fafhrd managed, 'Beware ice and snow. Act without thought.'

To Vellix, Vlana said more distantly, though with courtesy and kindness, 'Thank you, sir, for your concern for me, both in your dreams and your wakings.'

From out a fur robe, whose collar topped his ears, Essedinex greeted with gruff humor, 'It's been a hard night on tents.' Vlana shrugged.

The women of the troupe gathered around her with anxious questions and she talked with them privately as they walked to the actors' tent and went in through the girls' door-flap.

Vellix frowned after her and pulled at his black moustache.

The male actors stared and shook their heads at the beating the hemicylindrical tent had taken.

Vellix said to Fafhrd with warm friendliness, 'I offered you brandy before and now I'd guess you need it. Also, since yestermorning I've had a great desire to talk with you.'

'Your pardon, but once I sit I will not be able to stay awake for a word, were they wise as owls', nor for even a brandy swig,' Fafhrd answered politely, hiding a great yawn which was only half feigned. 'But I thank you.'

'It appears I am fated always to ask at the wrong time,' Vellix commented with a shrug. 'Perhaps at noon? Or mid-afternoon?' he added swiftly.

'The latter, if it please you,' Fafhrd replied and rapidly walked off, taking great strides toward the trading tents. Vellix did not seek to keep up with him.

Fafhrd felt more satisfied than he ever had in his life. The thought that tonight he would forever escape this stupid snow world and its man-chaining women almost made him nostalgic about Cold Corner. Thought-guard! he told himself. Feelings of eerie menace or else his hunger for sleep turned his surroundings spectral, like a childhood scene revisited.

He drained a white porcelain tankard of wine given him by his Mingol friends Zax and Effendrit, let them conduct him to a glossy pallet hidden by piles of other furs, and fell at once into a deep sleep.

After eons of absolute, pillowy darkness, lights came softly on. Fafhrd sat beside Nalgron his father at a stout banquet table crowded with all savory foods smoking hot and all fortified wines in jugs of earthenware, stone, silver, crystal and gold. There were other feasters lining the table, but Fafhrd could make nothing of them except their dark silhouettes and the sleepy sound of their unceasing talk too soft to be understood, like many streams of murmuring water, though with occasional bursts of low laughter, like small waves running up and returning down a gravelly beach. While the dull clash of knife and spoon against plate and each other was like the clank of the pebbles in that surf.

Nalgron was clad and cloaked in ice-bear furs of the whitest with pins and chains and wristlets and rings of purest silver, and there was silver also in his hair, which troubled Fafhrd. In his left hand he held a silver goblet, which at intervals he touched to his lips, but he kept his eating hand under his cloak.

Nalgron was discoursing wisely, tolerantly, almost tenderly of many matters. He directed his gaze here and there around the table, yet spoke so quietly that Fafhrd knew his conversation was directed at his son alone.

Fafhrd also knew he should be listening intently to every word and carefully stowing away each aphorism, for Nalgron was speaking of courage, of honor, of prudence, of thoughtfulness in giving and punctilio in keeping your word, of following your heart, of setting and unswervingly striving toward a high, romantic goal, of self-honesty in all these things but especially in recognizing your aversions and desires, of the need to close your ears to the fears and naggings of women, yet freely forgive them all their jealousies, attempted trammelings, and even extremest wickednesses, since those all sprang from their ungovernable love, for you or another, and of many a different

64

matter most useful to know for a youth on manhood's verge.

But although he knew this much, Fafhrd heard his father only in snatches, for he was so troubled by the gauntness of Nalgron's cheek and by the leanness of the strong fingers lightly holding the silver goblet and by the silver in his hair, and a faint overlay of blue on his ruddy lips, although Nalgron was most sure and even sprightly in every movement, gesture, and word, that he was compelled to be forever searching the steaming platters and bowls around him for especially succulent portions to spoon or fork onto Nalgron's wide, silver plate to tempt his appetite.

Whenever he did this, Nalgron would look toward him with a smile and a courteous nod, and with love in his eyes, and then touch his goblet to his lips and return to his discoursings, but never would he uncover his eating hand.

As the banquet progressed, Nalgron began to speak of matters yet more important, but now Fafhrd heard hardly one of the precious words, so greatly agitated was he by his concern for his father's health. Now the thin skin seemed stretched to bursting on the jutting cheekbone, the bright eyes ever more sunken and dark-ringed, the blue veins more bulgingly a-crawl across the stout tendons of the hand lightly holding the silver goblet – and Fafhrd had begun to suspect that although Nalgron often let the wine touch his lips he drank never a drop.

'Eat, father,' Fafhrd pleaded in a low voice taut with concern. 'At least drink.'

Again the look, the smile, the agreeable nod, the bright eyes warmer still with love, the brief tipping of goblet against unparted lips, the looking away, the tranquil, unattendable discourse resumed.

And now Fafhrd knew fear, for the lights were growing blue and he realized that none of the black, unfeatured fellow-feasters were or had all the while been lifting so much as hand, let alone cup-rim, to mouth, though making an unceasing dull clatter with their cutlery. His concern for his father became an agony and before he rightly knew what he was doing, he had brushed back his father's cloak and gripped his father's right forearm and wrist and so shoved his eating hand toward his high-piled plate.

Then Nalgron was not nodding, but thrusting his head at Fafhrd, and not smiling, but grinning in such fashion as to show all his teeth of old ivory hue, whilst his eyes were cold, cold, cold.

The hand and arm that Fafhrd gripped felt like, looked like, *were* bare brown bone.

Of a sudden shaking violently in all his parts, but chiefly in his arms, Fafhrd recoiled swift as a serpent down the bench.

Then Fafhrd was not shaking, but being shaken by strong hands of flesh on his shoulders, and instead of the dark there was the faintly translucent hide of the Mingols' tent-roof, and in place of his father's face the sallow-cheeked, black-moustached one, somber yet concerned, of Vellix the Venturer.

Fafhrd stared dazedly, then shook his shoulders and head to bring a quicker-tempoed life back into his body and throw off the gripping hands.

But Vellix had already let go and seated himself on the next pile of furs.

'Your pardon, young warrior,' he said gravely. 'You appeared to be having a dream no man would care to continue.'

His manner and the tone of his voice were like the nightmare-Nalgron's. Fafhrd pushed up on an elbow, yawned, and with a shuddery grimace shook himself again.

'You're chilled in body, mind, or both,' Vellix said. 'So we've good excuse for the brandy I promised.'

He brought up from beside him two small silver mugs in

one hand and in the other a brown jug of brandy which he now uncorked with that forefinger and thumb.

Fafhrd frowned inwardly at the dark tarnish on the mugs and at the thought of what might be crusted or dusted in their bottoms, or perhaps that of one only. With a troubled twinge, he reminded himself that this man was his rival for Vlana's affections.

'Hold,' he said as Vellix prepared to pour. 'A silver cup played a nasty role in my dream. Zax!' he called to the Mingol looking out the tent door. 'A porcelain mug, if you please!'

'You take the dream as a warning against drinking from silver?' Vellix inquired softly with an ambiguous smile.

'No,' Fafhrd answered, 'but it instilled an antipathy into my flesh, which still crawls.' He wondered a little that the Mingols had so casually let in Vellix to sit beside him. Perhaps the three were old acquaintances from the trading camps. Or perhaps there'd been bribery.

Vellix chuckled and became freer of manner. 'Also, I've fallen into filthy ways, living without a woman or servant. Effendrit! Make that two porcelain mugs, clean as newly-debarked birch!'

It was indeed the other Mingol who had been standing by the door — Vellix knew them better than Fafhrd did. The Venturer immediately handed over one of the gleaming white mugs. He poured a little of the nose-tickling drink into his own porcelain mug, then a generous gush for Fafhrd, then more for himself — as if to demonstrate that Fafhrd's drink could not possibly be poisoned or drugged. And Fafhrd, who had been watching closely, could find no fault in the demonstration. They lightly clinked mugs and when Vellix drank deeply, Fafhrd took a large though carefully slow sip. The stuff burned gently.

'It's my last jug,' Vellix said cheerfully. 'I've traded my whole stock for amber, snow-gems, and other smalls — aye, and my tent and cart too, everything but my two horses and our gear and winter rations.'

'I've heard your horses are the swiftest and hardiest on the Steppes,' Fafhrd remarked.

'That's too large a claim. Here they rank well, no doubt.'

'Here!' Fafhrd said contemptuously.

Vellix eyed him as Nalgron had in all but the last part of the dream. Then he said, 'Fafhrd – I may call you that? Call me Vellix. May I make a suggestion? May I give you advice such as I might give a son of mine?'

'Surely,' Fafhrd answered, feeling not only uncomfortable now but wary.

'You're clearly restless and dissatisfied here. So is any sound young man, anywhere, at your age. The wide world calls you. You've an itching foot. Yet let me say this: it takes more than wit and prudence – aye, and wisdom, too – to cope with civilization and find any comfort. That requires low cunning, a smirching of yourself as civilization is smirched. You cannot climb to success there as you climb a mountain, no matter how icy and treacherous. The latter demands all your best. The former, much of your worst: a calculated self-evil you have yet to experience, and need not. I was born a renegade. My father was a man of the Eight Cities who rode with the Mingols. I wish now I had stuck to the Steppes myself, cruel as they are, nor harkened to the corrupting call of Lankhmar and the Eastern Lands.

'I know, I know, the folk here are narrow-visioned, custom-bound. But matched with the twisted minds of civilization, they're straight as pines. With your natural gifts you'll easily be a chief here – more, in sooth, a chief paramount, weld a dozen clans together, make the Northerners a power for nations to reckon with. Then, if you wish, you can challenge civilization. On your terms, not hers.'

68

Fafhrd's thoughts and feelings were like choppy water, though he had outwardly become almost preternaturally calm. There was even a current of glee in him, that Vellix rated a youth's chances with Vlana so high that he would ply him with flattery as well as brandy.

But across all other currents, making the chop sharp and high, was the impression, hard to shake, that the Venturer was not altogether dissimulating, that he did feel like a father toward Fafhrd, that he was truly seeking to save him hurt, that what he said of civilization had an honest core. Of course that might be because Vellix felt so sure of Vlana that he could afford to be kind to a rival. Nevertheless ...

Nevertheless, Fafhrd now once again felt more uncomfortable than anything else.

He drained his mug. 'Your advice is worth thought, sir – Vellix, I mean. I'll ponder it.'

Refusing another drink with a headshake and smile, he stood up and straightened his clothes.

'I had hoped for a longer chat,' Vellix said, not rising.

'I've business to attend,' Fafhrd answered. 'My hearty thanks.'

Vellix smiled thoughtfully as he departed.

The concourse of trodden snow winding amongst the traders' tents was racketty with noise and crowdedly a-bustle. While Fafhrd slept, the men of the Ice Tribe and fully half of the Frost Companions had come in and now many of these were gathered around two sunfires – so called for their bigness, heat, and the height of their leaping flames – quaffing steaming mead and laughing and scuffling together. To either side were oases of buying and bargaining, encroached on by the merry-makers or given careful berth according to the rank of those involved in the business doings. Old comrades spotted one another and shouted and sometimes drove through the press to embrace. Food and drink were spilled, challenges made and accepted, or more often laughed down. Skalds sang and roared.

The tumult irked Fafhrd, who wanted quiet in which to disentangle Vellix from Nalgron in his feelings, and banish his vague doubts of Vlana, and unsmirch civilization. He walked as a troubled dreamer, frowning yet unmindful of elbowings and other shoves.

Then all at once he was tinglingly alert, for he glimpsed angling toward him through the crowd Hor and Harrax, and he read the purpose in their eyes. Letting an eddy in the crush spin him around, he noted Hrey, one other of Hringorl's creatures, close behind him.

The purpose of the three was clear. Under guise of comradely scuffling, they would give him a vicious beating or worse.

In his moody concern with Vellix, he had forgotten his more certain enemy and rival, the brutally direct yet cunning Hringorl.

Then the three were upon him. In a frozen instant he noted that Hor bore a small bludgeon and that Harrax' fists were overly large, as if they gripped stone or metal to heavy their blows.

He lunged backward, as if he meant to dodge between that couple and Hrey; then as suddenly reversed course and with a shocking bellow raced toward the sunfire ahead. Heads turned at his yell and a startled few dodged from his way. But the Ice Tribesmen and Frost Companions had time to take in what was happening: a tall youth pursued by three huskies. This promised sport. They sprang to either side of the sunfire to block his passage past it. Fafhrd veered first to left, then to right. Jeering, they bunched more closely.

Holding his breath and throwing up an arm to guard his eyes, Fafhrd leaped straight through the flames. They lifted his fur cloak from his back and blew it high. He felt the stab of heat on hand and neck.

He came out with his furs a-smolder, blue flames running up his hair. There was more crowd ahead except for a swept, carpeted, and canopied space between two tents, where chiefs and priests sat intently around a low table where a merchant weighed gold dust in a pair of scales.

He heard bump and yell behind, someone cried, 'Run, coward,' another, 'A fight, a fight'; he saw Mara's face ahead, red and excited.

Then the future chief paramount of Northland – for so he happened at that instant to think of himself – half sprang, half dived a-flame across the canopied table, unavoidably tumbling the merchant and two chiefs, banging aside the scales, and knocking the gold dust to the winds before he landed with a steaming zizzle in the great, soft snowbank beyond.

He swiftly rolled over twice to make sure all his fires were quenched, then scrambled to his feet and ran like a deer into the woods, followed by gusts of curses and gales of laughter.

Fifty big trees later he stopped abruptly in the snowy gloom and held his breath while he listened. Through the soft pounding of his blood, there came not the faintest sound of pursuit. Ruefully he combed with his fingers his stinking, diminished hair and sketchily brushed his now patchy, equally fire-stinking furs.

Then he waited for his breath to quiet and his awareness to expand. It was during this pause that he made a disconcerting discovery. For the first time in his life the forest, which had always been his retreat, his continent-spanning tent, his great private needle-roofed room, seemed hostile to him, as if the very trees and the cold-fleshed, warm-boweled mother-earth in which they were rooted knew of his apostasy, his spurning, jilting and intended divorce of his native land.

It was not the unusual silence, nor the sinister and

71

suspicious quality of the faint sounds he at last began to hear: scratch on bark of small claw, pitter of tiny paw-steps, hoot of a distant owl anticipating night. Those were effects, or at most concomitants. It was something unnameable, intangible, yet profound, like the frown of a god. Or goddess.

He was greatly depressed. At the same time he had never known his heart feel as hard.

When at last he set out again, it was as silently as might be, and not with his unusual relaxed and wide-open awareness, but rather the naked-nerved sensitivity and bent-bow readiness of a scout in enemy territory.

And it was well for him that he did so, since otherwise he might not have dodged the nearly soundless fall of an icicle, sharp, heavy, and long as a siege-catapult's missile, nor the down-clubbing of a huge snow-weighted dead branch that broke with a single thunderous crack, nor the venomous dart of a snow-adder's head from its unaccustomed white coil in the open, nor the sidewise slash of the narrow, cruel claws of a snow-leopard that seemed almost to materialize a-spring in the frigid air and that vanished as strangely when Fafhrd slipped aside from its first attack and faced it with dirk drawn. Nor might he have spotted in time the up-whipping, slip-knotted snare, set against all custom in this home-area of the forest and big enough to strangle not a hare but a bear.

He wondered where Mor was and what she might be muttering or chanting. Had his mistake been simply to dream of Nalgron? Despite yesterday's curse – and others before it – and last night's naked threats, he had never truly and wholly imagined his mother seeking to kill him. But now the hair on his neck was lifted in apprehension and horror, the watchful glare in his eyes was febrile and wild, while a little blood dripped unheeded from the cut in his cheek where the great icicle down-dropping had grazed it.

So intent had he become on spying dangers that it was with a little surprise that he found himself standing in the glade where he and Mara had embraced only yesterday, his feet on the short trail leading to the home tents. He relaxed a little then, sheathing his dirk and pressing a handful of snow to his bleeding cheek – but he relaxed only a little, with the result that he was aware of one coming to meet him before he consciously heard footsteps.

So silently and completely did he then melt into the snowy background that Mara was three paces away before she saw him.

'They hurt you,' she exclaimed.

'No,' he answered curtly, still intent on dangers in the forest.

'But the red snow on your cheek. There was a fight?'

'Only a nick got in the woods. I outran 'em.'

Her look of concern faded. 'First time I saw you run from a quarrel.'

'I had no mind to take on three or more,' he said flatly.

'Why do you look behind? They're trailing you?'

'No.'

Her expression hardened. 'The elders are outraged. The younger men call you scareling. My brothers among them. I didn't know what to say.'

'Your brothers!' Fafhrd exclaimed. 'Let the stinking Snow Clan call me what they will. I care not.'

Mara planted her fists on her hips. 'You've grown very free with your insults of late. I'll not have my family berated, do you hear? Nor myself insulted, now that I think of it.' She was breathing hard. 'Last night you went back to that shriveled old whore of a dancer. You were in her tent for hours.'

'I was not!' Fafhrd denied, thinking *An hour and a half at most.* The bickering was warming his blood and quelling his supernatural dread.

73

'You lie! The story's all around the camp. Any other girl would have set her brothers on you ere this.'

Fafhrd came back to his schemy self almost with a jerk. On this eve of all eves he must not risk needless trouble – the chance of being crippled, it might even be, or dead.

Tactics, man, tactics, he told himself as he moved eagerly toward Mara, exclaiming in hurt, honeyed tones, 'Mara, my queen, how can you believe such of me, who love you more than—'

'Keep off me, liar and cheat!'

'And you carrying my son,' he persisted, still trying to embrace her. 'How does the bonny babe?'

'Spits at his father. Keep off me, I say.'

'But I yearn to touch your ticklesome skin, than which there is no other balm for me this side of Hell, oh most beauteous made more beautiful by motherhood.'

'Go to Hell, then. And stop these sickening pretenses. Your acting wouldn't deceive a drunken she-scullion. Hamfatter!'

Stung to his blood, which instantly grew hot, Fafhrd retorted, 'And what of your own lies? Yesterday you boasted of how you'd cow and control my mother. Instanter you went sniveling to tell her you were with child by me.'

'Only after I knew you lusted after the actress. And was it anything but the complete truth? Oh, you twister!'

Fafhrd stood back and folded his arms. He pronounced, 'Wife of mine must be true to me, must trust me, must ask me first before she acts, must comport herself like the mate of a chief paramount to-be. It appears to me that in all of these you fall short.'

'True to you? You're one to talk!' Her fair face grew unpleasantly red and strained with rage. 'Chief paramount! Set your sights merely on being called a man by the Snow Clan, which they've not done yet. Hear me now, sneak and dissembler. You will instantly plead for my

74

pardon on your knees and then come with me to ask my mother and aunts for my hand, or else—'

'I'd sooner kneel to a snake! Or wed a she-bear!' Fafhrd cried out, all thoughts of tactics vanished.

'I'll set my brothers on you,' she screamed back. 'Cowardly boor!'

Fafhrd lifted his fist, dropped it, set his hands to his head and rocked it in a gesture of maniacal desperation, then suddenly ran past her toward the camp.

'I'll set the whole tribe on you! I'll tell it in the Tent of the Women. I'll tell your mother ...' Mara shrieked after him, her voice fading fast with the intervening boughs, snow, and distance.

Barely pausing to note that none were abroad amongst the Snow Clan's tents, either because they were still at the trading fair or inside preparing supper, Fafhrd bounded up his treasure tree and flipped open the door of his hidey hole. Cursing the fingernail he broke doing so, he got out the sealskin-wrapped bow and arrows and rockets and added thereto his best pair of skis and ski sticks, a somewhat shorter package holding his father's second-best sword well-oiled, and a pouch of smaller gear. Dropping to the snow, he swiftly bound the longer items into a single pack, which he slung over shoulder.

After a moment of indecision, he hurtled inside Mor's tent, snatching from his pouch a small firepot of bubble-stone, and filled it with glowing embers from the hearth, sprinkled ashes over them, laced the pot tight shut, and returned it to his pouch.

Then turning in frantic haste toward the doorway, he stopped dead. Mor stood in it, a tall silhouette white-edged and shadow-faced.

'So you're deserting me and the Waste. Not to return. You think.'

Fafhrd was speechless.

'Yet you will return. If you wish it to be a-crawl on four

feet, or blessedly on two, and not stretched lifeless on a litter of spears, weigh soon your duties and your birth.'

Fafhrd framed a bitter answer, but the very words were a gag in his gullet. He stalked toward Mor.

'Make way, Mother,' he managed in a whisper.

She did not move.

His jaws clamped in a horrid grimace of tension, he shot forth his hands, gripped her under the armpits – his flesh crawling – and set her to one side. She seemed as stiff and cold as ice. She made no protest. He could not look her in the face.

Outside, he started at a brisk pace for Godshall, but there were men in his way – four hulking young blond ones flanked by a dozen others.

Mara had brought not only her brothers from the fair, but all her available kinsmen.

Yet now she appeared to have repented of her act, for she was dragging at her eldest brother's arm and talking earnestly to him, to judge by her expression and the movements of her lips.

Her eldest brother marched on as if she weren't there. And now as his gaze hit Fafhrd he gave a joyous shout, jerked from her grasp, and came on a-rush followed by the rest. All waved clubs or their scabbarded swords.

Mara's agonized, 'Fly, my love!' was anticipated by Fafhrd by at least two heartbeats. He turned and raced for the woods, his long, stiff pack banging his back. When the path of his flight joined the trail of footprints he'd made running out of the woods, he took care to set a foot in each without slackening speed.

Behind him they cried, 'Coward!' He ran faster.

When he reached the juttings of granite a short way inside the forest, he turned sharply to the right and leaping from bare rock to rock, making not one additional print, he reached a low cliff of granite and mounted it with only two hand-grabs, then darted on until the cliff's edge hid him from anyone below.

He heard the pursuit enter the woods, angry cries as in veering around trees they bumped each other, then a masterful voice crying for silence.

He carefully lobbed three stones so that they fell along his false trail well ahead of Mara's human hounds. The thud of the stones and the rustle of branches they made falling drew cries of 'There he goes!' and another demand for silence.

Lifting a larger rock, he hurled it two-handed so that it struck solidly the trunk of a stout tree on the nearer side of the trail, jarring down great branchfuls of snow and ice. There were muffled cries of startlement, confusion, and rage from the showered and likely three-quarters buried men. Fafhrd grinned, then his face sobered and his eyes grew dartingly watchful as he set off at a lope through the darkening woods.

But this time he felt no inimical presences and the living and the lifeless, whether rock or ghost, held off their assaults. Perhaps Mor, deeming him sufficiently harried by Mara's kinsmen, had ceased to energize her charms. Or perhaps – Fafhrd left off thinking and devoted all of himself to silent speeding. Vlana and civilization lay ahead. His mother and barbarism behind – but he endeavored not to think of her.

Night was near when Fafhrd left the woods. He had made the fullest possible circuit through them, coming out next to the drop into Trollstep Canyon. The strap of his long pack chafed his shoulder.

There were the lights and sounds of feasting amongst the traders' tents. Godshall and the actors' tents were dark. Still nearer loomed the dark bulk of the stable tent.

He silently crossed the frosty, rutted gravel of the New Road leading south into the canyon.

Then he saw that the stable tent was not altogether dark. A ghostly glow moved inside it. He approached its door cautiously and saw the silhouette of Hor peering in. Still the soul of silence, he came up behind Hor and peered over his shoulder.

Vlana and Vellix were harnessing the latter's two horses to Essedinex' sleigh, from which Fafhrd had stolen the three rockets.

Hor tipped up his head and lifted a hand to his lips to make some sort of owl or wolf cry.

Fafhrd whipped out his knife and, as he was about to slash Hor's throat, reversed his intent and his knife too, and struck him senseless with a blow of the pommel against the side of his head. As Hor collapsed, Fafhrd hauled him to one side of the doorway.

Vlana and Vellix sprang into the sleigh, the latter touched his horses with the reins, and they came thud-slithering out. Fafhrd gripped his knife fiercely ... then sheathed it and shrank back into the shadows.

The sleigh went gliding off down the New Road. Fafhrd stared after it, standing tall, his arms as straight down his sides as those of a corpse laid out, but with his fingers and thumbs gripped into tightest fists.

He suddenly turned and fled toward Godshall.

There came an owl-hooting from behind the stable tent. Fafhrd skidded to a stop in the snow and turned around, his hands still fists.

Out of the dark, two forms, one trailing fire, raced toward Trollstep Canyon. The tall form was unmistakably Hringorl's. They stopped at the brink. Hringorl swung his torch in a great circle of flame. The light showed the face of Harrax beside him. Once, twice, thrice, as if in signal to someone far south down the canyon. Then they raced for the stable.

Fafhrd ran for Godshall. There was a harsh cry behind him. He stopped and turned again. Out of the stable galloped a big horse. Hringorl rode it. He dragged by rope a man on skis: Harrax. The pair careened down the New Road in a flaring upswirl of snow.

Fafhrd raced on until he was past Godshall and a quarter way up the slope leading to the Tent of the Women. He cast off his pack, opened it, drew his skis from it and strapped them to his feet. Next he unwrapped his father's sword and belted it to his left side, balancing his pouch on right.

Then he faced Trollstep Canyon where the Old Road had gone. He took up two of his ski sticks, crouched, and dug them in. His face was a skull, the visage of one who casts dice with Death.

At that instant, beyond Godshall, the way he had come, there was a tiny yellow sputtering. He paused for it, counting heartbeats, he knew not why.

Nine, ten, eleven – there was a great flare of flame. The rocket rose, signaling tonight's Show. Twenty-one, twenty-two, twenty-three – and the tail-flame faded and the nine white stars burst out.

Fafhrd dropped his ski sticks, picked up one of the three rockets he'd stolen, and drew its fuse from its end, pulling just hard enough to break the cementing tar without breaking the fuse.

Holding the slender, finger-long, tarry cylinder delicately between his teeth, he took his fire-pot out of his pouch. The bubblestone was barely warm. He unlaced the top and brushed away the ashes below until he saw – and was stung by – a red glow.

He took the fuse from between his teeth and placed it so that one end leaned on the edge of the fire-pot while the other end touched the red glow. There was a sputtering. Seven, eight, nine, ten, eleven, twelve – and the sputtering became a flaring jet, then was done.

Setting his fire-pot on the snow, he took up the two remaining rockets, and hugged their thick bodies under his

79

arms and dug their tails into the snow, testing them against the ground. The tails were truly as stiff and strong as ski sticks.

He held the rockets propped parallel in one hand and blew hard on the glowing fire-patch in his firepot and brought it up toward the two fuses.

Mara ran out of the dark and said, 'Darling, I'm so glad my kin didn't catch you!'

The glow of the fire-pot showed the beauty of her face.

Staring at her across it, Fafhrd said, 'I'm leaving Cold Corner. I'm leaving the Snow Tribe. I'm leaving you.'

Mara said, 'You can't.'

Fafhrd set down the fire-pot and the rockets.

Mara stretched out her hands.

Fafhrd took the silver bracelets off his wrists and put them in Mara's palms.

Mara clenched them and cried, 'I don't ask for these. I don't ask for anything. You're the father of my child. You're mine!'

Fafhrd whipped the heavy silver chain off his neck, laid it across her wrists, and said, 'Yes! You're mine forever, and I'm yours. Your son is mine. I'll never have another Snow-Clan wife. We're married.'

Meanwhile he had taken up the two rockets again and held their fuses to the fire-pot. They sputtered simultaneously. He set them down, thonged shut the fire-pot and thrust it in his pouch. Three, four …

Mor looked over Mara's shoulder and said, 'I witness your words, my son. Stop!'

Fafhrd grabbed up the rockets, each by its sputtering body, dug in the stick ends and took off down the slope with a great shove. Six, seven …

Mara screamed, 'Fafhrd! Husband!' As Mor shouted, 'No son of mine!'

Fafhrd shoved again with the sputtering rockets. Cold air whipped his face. He barely felt it. The moonlit lip of

80

the jump was close ahead. He felt its up-curve. Beyond it, darkness. Eight, nine …

He hugged the rockets fiercely to his sides, under his elbows, and was flying through darkness. Eleven, twelve …

The rockets did not fire. The moonlight showed the opposite wall of the canyon rushing toward him. His skis were directed at a point just beneath its top and that point was steadily falling. He tilted the rockets down and hugged them more fiercely still.

They fired. It was as if he were clinging to two great wrists that were dragging him up. His elbows and sides were warm. In the sudden glare the rock wall showed close, but now below. Sixteen, seventeen …

He touched down smoothly on the fair crust of snow covering the Old Road and hurled the rockets to either side. There was a double thunderclap and white stars were shooting around him. One smote and stung, then tortured his cheek as it died. There was time for the one great laughing thought, *I depart in a burst of glory.*

Then no time for large thoughts at all, as he gave all his attention to skiing down the steep slope of the Old Road, now bright in the moonlight, now pitchblack as it curved, crags to his right, a precipice to his left. Crouching and keeping his skis locked side to side, he steered by swaying his hips. His face and his hands grew numb. Reality was the Old Road hurled at him. Tiny bumps became great jolts. White rims came close. Black shoulders threatened.

Deep, deep down there were thoughts nevertheless. Even as he strained to keep all his attention on his skiing, they were there. *Idiot, you should have grabbed a pair of sticks with the rockets. But how would you have held them when casting aside the rockets? In your pack? – then they'd be doing you no good now. Will the fire-pot in your pouch prove more worthwhile than sticks? You should have stayed with Mara. Such loveliness you'll never see again. But it's Vlana you want. Or is it? How, with Vellix? If you weren't so cold-hearted and good, you'd have killed Vellix in the stable, instead of speeding to — Did you truly intend killing yourself? What do you intend now? Can Mor's charms out-speed your skiing? Were the rocket wrists really Nalgron's, reaching from Hell? What's that ahead?*

That was a hulking shoulder skidded around. He lay over on his right side as the white edge to his left narrowed. The edge held. Beyond it, on the opposite wall of the widening canyon, he saw a tiny streak of flame. Hringorl still had his torch, as he galloped down the New Road dragging Harrax? Fafhrd lay over again to his right as the Old Road curved farther that way in a tightening turn. The sky reeled. Life demanded that he lay still farther over, braking to a stop. But Death was still an equal player in this game. Ahead was the intersection where Old and New Road met. He must reach it as soon as Vellix and Vlana in their sleigh. Speed was the essence. Why? He was uncertain. New curves ahead.

By infinitesimal stages the slope grew less. Snow-freighted treetops thrust from the sinister depths — to the left — then shot up to either side. He was in a flat black tunnel. His progress became soundless as a ghost's. He coasted to a stop just at the tunnel's end. His numb fingers went up and feather-touched the bulge of the star-born blister on his cheek. Ice needles crackled very faintly inside the blister.

No other sound but the faint tinkle of the crystals growing all around in the still, damp air.

Five paces ahead of him, down a sudden slope, was a bulbous roll bush weighted with snow. Behind it crouched Hringorl's chief lieutenant Hrey — no mistaking that pointed beard, though its red was gray in the moonlight. He held a strung bow in his left hand.

Beyond him, two dozen paces down slope, was the fork where New and Old Road met. The tunnel going south through the trees was blocked by a pair of roll bushes higher than a man's head. Vellix' and Vlana's sleigh was stopped short of the pile, its two horses great loomings. Moonlight struck silvery manes and silver bushes. Vlana sat hunched in the sleigh, her head fur-hooded. Vellix had got down and was casting the roll bushes out of the way.

Torchlight came streaking down the New Road from Cold Corner. Vellix gave up his work and drew his sword. Vlana looked over her shoulder.

Hringorl galloped into the clearing with a laughing cry of triumph, and threw his torch high in the air, reined his horse to a stop behind the sleigh. The skier he towed – Harrax – shot past him and halfway up the slope. There Harrax braked to a stop and stooped to unlace his skis. The torch came down and went out sizzling.

Hringorl dropped from his horse, a fighting axe ready in his hand.

Vellix ran toward Hringorl. Clearly he understood that he must dispose of the giant pirate before Harrax got off his skis or he would be fighting two at once. Vlana's face was a small white mask in the moonlight and she half lifted from her seat to stare after him. The hood fell back from her head.

Fafhrd could have helped Vellix, but he still hadn't made a move to unlash his skis. With a pang – or was it relief? – he remembered he'd left his bow and arrows behind. He told himself that he should help Vellix. Hadn't he skied down here at incalculable risk to save the Venturer and Vlana, or at least warn them of the ambush he had suspected ever since he'd seen Hringorl whirl his torch on the precipice's edge? And didn't Vellix look like Nalgron, now more than ever in his moment of bravery? But the phantom Death still stood at Fafhrd's side, inhibiting all action.

Besides, Fafhrd felt there was a spell on the clearing, making all action inside it futile. As if a giant spider, white-furred, had already spun a web around it, shutting it off from the rest of the universe, making it a volume inscribed,

83

'This space belongs to the White Spider of Death.' No matter that this giant spider spun not silk, but crystals – the result was the same.

Hringorl aimed a great axe swipe at Vellix. The Venturer evaded it and thrust his sword into Hringorl's forearm. With a howl of rage, Hringorl shifted his axe to his left hand, lunged forward and struck again.

Taken by surprise, Vellix barely dodged back out of the way of the hissing curve of steel, bright in the moonlight. Yet he was nimbly on guard again, while Hringorl advanced more warily, axe-head high and a little ahead of him, ready to make short chops.

Vlana stood up in the sleigh, steel flashing in her hand. She made as if to hurl it, then paused uncertainly.

Hrey rose from his bush, an arrow nocked to his bow.

Fafhrd could have killed him, by hurling his sword spearwise if in no other way. But the sense of Death beside him was still paralyzingly strong, and the sense of being in the White Ice Spider's great womblike trap. Besides, what did he really feel toward Vellix, or even Nalgron?

The bowstring twanged. Vellix paused in his fencing, transfixed. The arrow had struck him in the back, to one side of his spine, and protruded from his chest, just below the breastbone.

With a chop of the axe, Hringorl knocked the sword from the dying man's grip as he started to fall. He gave another of his great, harsh laughs. He turned toward the sleigh.

Vlana screamed.

Before he quite realized it, Fafhrd had silently drawn his sword from its well-oiled sheath and, using it as a stick, pushed off down the white slope. His skis sang very faintly, though very high-pitched, against the snow crust.

Death no longer stood at his side. Death had stepped inside him. It was Death's feet that were lashed to the skis. It was Death who felt the White Spider's trap to be home.

Hrey turned, just in convenient time for Fafhrd's blade to open the side of his neck in a deep, slicing thrust that slit gullet as well as jugular. His sword came away almost before the gushing blood, black in the moonlight, had wet it, and certainly before Hrey had lifted his great hands in a futile effort to stop the great choking flow. It all happened very easily. His skis had thrust, Fafhrd told himself, not he. His skis, that had their own life, Death's life, and were carrying him on a most doomful journey.

Harrax, too, as if a very puppet of the gods, finished unlacing his skis and rose and turned just in time for Fafhrd's thrust, made upward from a crouch, to take him high in the guts, just as his arrow had taken Vellix, but in reverse direction.

The sword grated against Harrax's spine, but came out easily. Fafhrd sped downhill with hardly a check. Harrax stared wide-eyed after him. The great brute's mouth was wide open, too, but no sound came from it. Likely the thrust had sliced a lung and his heart as well, or else some of the great vessels springing from it.

And now Fafhrd's sword was pointed straight at the back of Hringorl, who was preparing to mount into the sleigh, and the skis were speeding the bloody blade faster and faster.

Vlana stared at Fafhrd over Hringorl's shoulder, as if she were looking at the approach of Death himself, and she screamed.

Hringorl swung around and instantly raised his axe to strike Fafhrd's sword aside. His wide face had the alert, yet sleepy look of one who has stared at Death many times and is never surprised by the sudden appearance of the Killer of All.

Fafhrd braked and turned so that, his rush slowing, he went past the back end of the sleigh. His sword strained all the while toward Hringorl without quite reaching him. It evaded the chop Hringorl made at it.

Then Fafhrd saw, just ahead, the sprawled body of Vellix. He made a right-angle turn, braking instantly, even thrusting his sword into the snow so that it struck sparks from the rock below, to keep from tumbling over the corpse.

He wrenched his body around then, as far as he could when his feet were still lashed to the skis, just in time to see Hringorl rushing down on him, out of the snow thrown up by the skis, and aiming his axe in a great blow at Fafhrd's neck.

Fafhrd parried the blow with his sword. Held at right angle to the sweep of the axe, the blade would have been shattered, but Fafhrd held his sword at just the proper angle for the axe to be deflected with a screech of steel and go whistling over his head.

Hringorl louted past him, unable to stop his rush.

Fafhrd again wrenched around his body, cursing the skis that now nailed his feet to the earth. His thrust was too late to reach Hringorl.

The thicker man turned and came rushing back, aiming another axe-swipe. This time the only way Fafhrd could dodge it was by falling flat on the ground.

He gimpsed two streakings of moonlit steel. Then he used his sword to thrust himself to his feet, ready for another blow at Hringorl, or another dodge, if there was time.

The big man had dropped his axe and was clawing at his own face.

Lunging by making a clumsy sidewise step with his ski – no place this for style! – Fafhrd ran him through the heart.

Hringorl dropped his hands as his body pitched over backward. From his right eye socket protruded the silver pommel and black grip of a dagger. Fafhrd wrenched out his sword. Hringorl hit with a great soft thud and an out-blow of snow around him, writhed violently twice, and was still.

Fafhrd poised his sword and his gaze darted around. He was ready for any other attack, by anyone at all

But not one of the five bodies moved – the two at his feet, the two sprawled on the slope, nor Vlana's erect in the sleigh. With a little surprise he realized that the gasping he heard was his own breath. Otherwise the only sound was a faint, high tinkling, which for the present he ignored. Even Vellix' two horses hitched to the sleigh and Hringorl's big mount, standing a short way up the Old Road, were unaccountably silent.

He leaned back against the sleigh, resting his left arm on the icy tarpaulin covering the rockets and other gear. His right hand still held his sword poised, a little negligently now, but ready.

He inspected the bodies once more, ending at Vlana's. Still none of them had moved. Each of the first four was surrounded by its blotches of blood-blackened snow, huge for Hrey, Harrax, and Hringorl, tiny for the arrow-slain Vellix.

He fixed his gaze on Vlana's staring, whiterimmed eyes. Controlling his breath, he said, 'I owe you thanks for slaying Hringorl. Perhaps. I doubt I could have bested him, he on his feet, I on my back. But was your knife aimed at Hringorl, or at my back? And did I 'scape death simply by falling, while the knife passed over me to strike down another man?'

She answered not a word. Instead her hands flew up to press her cheeks and lips. She continued to stare, now over her fingers, at Fafhrd.

He continued, his voice growing still more casual, 'You chose Vellix over me, after making me a promise. Why not Hringorl then over Vellix – and over me – when Hringorl seemed the likelier man to win? Why didn't you help Velli with your knife, when he so bravely tackled Hringorl? Why did you scream when you saw me, spoiling my chance to kill Hringorl with one silent thrust?'

87

He emphasized each question by idly poking his sword in her direction. His breath was coming easily now, weariness departing from his body even as black depression filled his mind.

Vlana slowly took her hands from her lips and swallowed twice. Then she said, her voice harsh, but clear, and not very loud, 'A woman must always keep all ways open, can you understand that? Only by being ready to league with any man, and discard one for another as fortune shifts the plan, can she begin to counter men's great advantage. I chose Vellix over you because his experience was greater and because – believe this or not, as you will – I did not think a partner of mine would have much chance for long life and I wanted you to live. I did not help Vellix here at the roadblock because I thought then that he and I were doomed. The roadblock and from it the knowledge that there must be ambushers around it cowed me – though Vellix seemed not to think so, or to care. As for my screaming when I saw you, I did not recognize you. I thought you were Death himself.'

'Well, it appears I was,' Fafhrd commented softly, looking around for a third time at the scattered corpses. He unlashed his skis. Then, after stamping his feet, he kneeled by Hringorl and jerked the dagger from his eye and wiped in on the dead man's furs.

Vlana continued, 'And I fear death even more than I detested Hringorl. Yes, I would eagerly flee with Hringorl, if it were away from death.'

'This time Hringorl was headed in the wrong direction,' Fafhrd commented, hefting the dagger. It balanced well for thrusting or throwing.

Vlana said, 'Now of course I'm yours. Eagerly and happily – again believe it or not. If you'll have me. Perhaps you still think I tried to kill you.'

Fafhrd turned toward her and tossed the dagger. 'Catch,' he said. She caught.

He laughed and said, 'No, a showgirl who's also been a thief would be apt to be expert at knife-throwing. And I doubt that Hringorl was struck in his brains through his eye by accident. Are you still minded to have revenge on the Thieves' Guild?'

'I am,' she answered.

Fafhrd said, 'Women are horrible. I mean, quite as horrible as men. Oh, is there anyone in the wide world that has aught but ice water in his or her veins?'

And he laughed again, more loudly, as if knowing there could be no answer to that question. Then he wiped his sword on Hringorl's furs, thrust it in his scabbard, and without looking at Vlana strode past her and the silent horses to the pile of roll bushes and began to cast their remainder aside. They were frozen to each other and he had to tug and twist to get them loose, putting more effort into it, fighting the bushes more than he recalled Vellix having to do.

Vlana did not look at him, even as he passed. She was gazing straight up the slope with its sinuous ski track leading to the black tunnel-mouth of the Old Road. Her white gaze was not fixed on Harrax and Hrey, nor on the tunnel mouth. It went higher.

There was a faint tinkling that never stopped.

Then there was a crystal clatter and Fafhrd wrenched loose and hurled aside the last of the ice-weighted roll bushes.

He looked down the road leading south. To civilization, whatever that was worth now.

This road was a tunnel, too, between snow-shouldered pines.

And it was filled, the moonlight showed, with a web of crystals that seemed to go on forever, strands of ice stretching from twig to twig and bough to bough, depth beyond icy depth.

Fafhrd recalled his mother's words, *There is a witchy cold, that can follow you anywhere in Nehwon. Wherever ice once went witchery can send it again. Your father now bitterly regrets ...*

He thought of a great white spider, spinning its frigid way around this clearing.

He saw Mor's face, beside Mara's, atop the precipice, the other side of the great leap.

He wondered what was being chanted now in the Tent of the Women, and if Mara was chanting too. Somehow he thought not.

Vlana cried out softly, 'Women indeed are horrible. Look. Look. Look!'

At that instant, Hringorl's horse gave a great whinny. There was the pound of hooves as he fled up the Old Road.

An instant later, Vellix' horses reared and screamed.

Fafhrd smote the neck of the nearest horse with the outside of his arm. Then he looked toward the small, big-eyed, triangular white mask of Vlana's face and followed her gaze.

Growing up out of the slope that led to the Old Road were half dozen tenuous forms high as trees. They looked like hooded women. They got solider and solider as Fafhrd watched.

He crouched down in terror. This movement caught his pouch between his belly and his thigh. He felt a faint warmth.

He sprang up and dashed back the way he had come. He ripped the tarpaulin off the back of the sleigh. He grabbed the eight remaining rockets one by one and thrust the tail of each into the snow so that their heads pointed at the vast, thickening ice-figures.

Then he reached in his pouch, took out his fire-pot, unthonged its top, shook off its gray ashes, shook its red ashes to one side of the bowl, and rapidly touched them to the fuses of the rockets.

Their multiple spluttering in his ears, he sprang into the sleigh.

Vlana did not move as he brushed her. But she chinked. She seemed to have put on a translucent cloak of ice crystals that held her where she stood. Reflected moonlight shone stolidly from the crystals. He felt it would move only as the moon moved.

He grabbed the reins. They stung his fingers like frozen iron. He could not stir them. The ice web ahead had grown around the horses. They were part of it – great equine statues enclosed in a greater crystal. One stood on four legs, one reared on two. The walls of the ice womb were closing in. *There is a witchy cold that can follow you ...*

The first rocket roared, then the second. He felt their warmth. He heard the mighty tinkling as they struck their up-slope targets.

The reins moved, slapped the backs of the horses. There was a glassy smashing as they plunged forward. He ducked his head and, holding the reins in his left hand, swung up his right and dragged Vlana down into the seat. Her ice-cloak jingled madly and vanished. Four, five ...

There was a continuous jangling as horses and sleigh shot forward through the ice web. Crystals showered onto and glanced off his ducked head. The jangling grew fainter. Seven, eight ...

All icy constraints fell away. Hooves pounded. A great north wind sprang up, ending the calm of days. Ahead the sky was faintly pink with dawn. Behind, it was faintly red with fire of pine-needles ignited by the rockets. It seemed to Fafhrd that the north wind brought the roaring of flames.

He shouted, 'Gnamph Nar, Mlurg Nar, great Kvarch Nar – we'll see them all! All the cities of the Forest Land! All the Land of the Eight Cities.'

Beside him Vlana stirred warm under his embracing arm and took up his cry with, 'Sarheenmar, Ilthmar,

Lankhmar! All the cities of the south! Quarmall! Horborixen! Slimspired Tisilinilit! The Rising Land.'

It seemed to Fafhrd that mirages of all those unknown
cities and places filled the brightening horizon. 'Travel,
love, adventure, the world!' he shouted, hugging Vlana to
him with his right arm while his left slapped the horses
with the reins.

He wondered why, although his imagination was
roaringly aflame like the canyon behind him, his heart was
still so cold.

III: THE UNHOLY GRAIL

Three things warned the wizard's apprentice that something was wrong: first the deep-trodden prints of iron-shod hooves along the forest path – he sensed them through his boots before stooping to feel them out in the dark; next, the eerie drone of a bee unnaturally abroad by night; and finally, a faint aromatic odor of burning. Mouse raced ahead, dodging treetrunks and skipping over twisted roots by memory and by a bat's feeling for rebounding whispers of sound. Gray leggings, tunic, peaked hood and streaming cloak made the slight youth, skinny with asceticism, seem like a rushing shadow.

The exaltation Mouse had felt at the successful completion of his long quest and his triumphal return to this sorcerous master, Glavas Rho, now vanished from his mind and gave way to a fear he hardly dared put into thoughts. Harm to the great wizard, whose mere apprentice he was? – 'My Gray Mouse, still midway in his allegiance between white magic and black,' Glavas Rho had once put it – no, it was unthinkable that that great figure of wisdom and spiritual might should come to harm. The great magician ... (There was something hysterical about the way Mouse insisted on that 'great', for to the world Glavas Rho was but a hedge-wizard, no better than a Mingol necromancer with his second-sighted spotted dog or a conjurer beggar of Quarmall) ... the great magician

93

and his dwelling were alike protected by strong enchantments no impious outsider could breach – not even (the heart of Mouse skipped a beat) the lord paramount of these forests, Duke Janarrl, who hated all magic, but white worse than black.

And yet the smell of burning was stronger now and Glavas Rho's low cottage was built of resinous wood.

There also vanished from Mouse's mind the vision of a girl's face, perpetually frightened yet sweet – that of Duke Janarrl's daughter Ivrian, who came secretly to study under Glavas Rho, figuratively sipping the milk of his white wisdom side by side with Mouse. Indeed, they had privately come to call each other Mouse and Misling, while under his tunic Mouse carried a plain green glove he had teased from Ivrian when he set forth on his quest, as if he were her armored and beweaponed knight and not a swordless wizardling.

By the time Mouse reached the hilltop clearing he was breathing hard, not from exertion.

There the gathering light showed him at a glance the hoof-hacked garden of magic herbs, the over-turned straw beehive, the great flare of soot sweeping up the smooth surface of the vast granite boulder that sheltered the wizard's tiny house.

But even without the dawn light he would have seen the fire-shrunken beams and fire-gnawed posts a-creep with red ember-worms and the wraithlike green flame where some stubborn sorcerous ointment still burned. He would have smelled the confusion of precious odors of burned drugs and balms and the horribly appetizing kitchen-odor of burned flesh.

His whole lean body winced. Then, like a hound getting the scent, he darted forward.

The wizard lay just inside the buckled door. And he had fared as his house: the beams of his body bared and blackened; the priceless juices and subtle substances boiled, burned, destroyed forever or streamed upward to some cold hell beyond the moon.

From all around came very faintly a low sad hum, as the unhoused bees mourned.

Memories fled horror-stricken through Mouse's mind: these shriveled lips softly chanting incantations, those charred fingers pointing at the stars or stroking a small woodland animal.

Trembling, Mouse drew from the leather pouch at his belt a flat green stone, engraved on the one side with deep-cut alien hieroglyphs, on the other with an armored, many-jointed monster, like a giant ant, that trod among tiny fleeing human figures. That stone had been the object of the quest on which Glavas Rho had sent him. For sake of it, he had rafted across the Lakes of Pleea, tramped the foot-hills of the Mountains of Hunger, hidden from a raiding party of red-bearded pirates, tricked lumpish peasant-fishermen, flattered and flirted with an elderly odorous witch; robbed a tribal shrine, and eluded hounds set on his trail. His winning the green stone without shedding blood meant that he had advanced another grade in his apprenticeship. Now he gazed dully at its ancient surface and then, his trembling controlled, laid it carefully on his master's blackened palm. As he stooped he realized that the soles of his feet were painfully hot, his boots smoking a little at the edges, yet he did not hurry his steps as he moved away.

It was lighter now and he noticed little things, such as the anthill by the threshold. The master had studied the black-armored creatures as intently as he had their cousin bees. Now it was deeply dented by a great heelmark showing a semicircle of pits made by spikes – yet something was moving. Peering closely he saw a tiny heat-maimed warrior struggling over the sand-grains. He remembered the monster on the green stone and shrugged at a thought that led nowhere.

He crossed the clearing through the mourning bees to where pale light showed between the treetrunks and soon was standing, hand resting on a gnarly bole, at a point where the hillside sloped sharply away. In the wooded valley below was a serpent of milky mist, indicating the course of the stream that wound through it. The air was heavy with the dissipating smoke of darkness. The horizon was edged to the right with red from the coming sun. Beyond it, Mouse knew, lay more forest and then the interminable grain fields and marshes of Lankhmar and beyond even those the ancient world-center of Lankhmar city, which Mouse had never seen, yet whose overlord ruled in theory even this far.

But near at hand, outlined by the sunrise red, was a bundle of jagged-topped towers – the stronghold of Duke Janarrl. A wary animation came into Mouse's masklike face. He thought of the spiked heelmark, the hacked turf, the trail of hoofmarks leading down this slope. Everything pointed to the wizard-hating Janarrl as the author of the atrocity behind him, except that, still revering his master's skills as matchless, Mouse did not understand how the Duke had broken through the enchantments, strong enough to dizzy the keenest woodsman, which had protected Glavas Rho's abode for many a year.

He bowed his head … and saw, lying lightly on the springing grassblades, a plain green glove. He snatched it up and digging in his tunic drew forth another glove, darkly mottled and streakily bleached by sweat, and held them side by side. They were mates.

His lips writhed back from his teeth and his gaze went again to the distant stronghold. Then he unseated a thick round of scraggy bark from the tree-trunk he'd been touching and delved shoulder-deep in the black cavity revealed. As he did these things with a slow tense automatism, the words came back to him of a reading

Glavas Rho had smilingly given him over a meal of milkless gruel.

'Mouse,' the mage had said, firelight dancing on his short white beard, 'when you stare your eyes like that and flare your nostrils, you are too much like a cat for me to credit you will ever be a sheep-dog of the truth. You are a middling dutiful scholar, but secretly you favor swords over wands. You are more tempted by the hot lips of black magic than the chaste slim fingers of white, no matter to how pretty a misling the latter belong – no, do not deny it! You are more drawn to the beguiling sinuosities of the left-hand path than the straight steep road of the right. I fear me you will never be mouse in the end but mouser. And never white but gray – oh well, that's better than black. Now, wash up these bowls and go breathe an hour on the newborn ague-plant, for 'tis a chill night, and remember to talk kindly to the thorn bush.'

The remembered words grew faint, but did not fade, as Mouse drew from the hole a leather belt furred green with mold and dangling from it a moldy scabbard. From the latter he drew, seizing it by the thong-wrapped grip, a tapering bronze sword showing more verdigris than metal. His eyes grew wide, but pinpoint-pupiled, and his face yet more mask-like, as he held the pale-green, brown-edged blade against the red hump of the rising sun.

From across the valley came faintly the high, clear, ringing note of a hunting horn, calling men to the chase.

Abruptly Mouse strode off down the slope, cutting over to the trail of the hooves, moving with long hasty strides and a little stiff-leggedly, as if drunk, and buckling around his waist as he went the mold-furred sword-belt.

A dark four-footed shape rushed across the sun-specked forest glade, bearing down the underbrush with its broad low chest and trampling it with its narrow cloven hooves. From behind sounded the notes of a horn and the harsh shouts of men. At the far edge of the glade, the boar turned. Breath whistled through its nostrils and it swayed. Then its half-glazed little eyes fixed on the figure of a man on horseback. It turned toward him and some trick of the sunlight made its pelt grow blacker. Then it charged. But before the terrible up-turning tusks could find flesh to slash, a heavy-bladed spear bent like a bow against the knob of its shoulder and it went crashing over half backward, its blood spattering the greenery.

Huntsmen clad in brown and green appeared in the glade, some surrounding the fallen boar with a wall of spear points, others hurrying up to the man on the horse. He was clad in rich garments of yellow and brown. He laughed, tossed one of his huntsmen the bloodied spear and accepted a silver-worked leather wine flask from another.

A second rider appeared in the glade and the Duke's small yellow eyes clouded under the tangled brows. He drank deep and wiped his lips with the back of his sleeve. The huntsmen were warily closing their spear-wall on the boar, which lay rigid but with head lifted a finger's breadth off the turf, its only movements the darting of its gaze from side to side and the pulse of bright blood from its shoulder. The spearwall was about to close when Janarrl waved the huntsmen to a halt.

'Ivrian!' he called harshly to the newcomer. 'You had two chances at the beast, but you flinched. Your cursed dead mother would already have sliced thin and tasted the beast's raw heart.'

His daughter stared at him miserably. She was dressed as the huntsmen and rode astride with a sword at her side and a spear in her hand, but it only made her seem more the thin-faced, spindle-armed girl.

'You are a milksop, a wizard-loving coward,' Janarrl continued. 'Your abominable mother would have faced the boar a-foot and laughed when its blood gushed in her face. Look here, this boar is scotched. It cannot harm you. Drive your spear into it now! I command you!'

The huntsmen broke their spear-wall and drew back to either side, making a path between the boar and the girl. They sniggered openly at her and the Duke smiled at them approvingly. The girl hesitated, sucking at her underlip, staring with fear and fascination too at the beast which eyed her, head still just a-lift.

'Drive in your spear!' Janarrl repeated, sucking quickly at the flask. 'Do so, or I will whip you here and now.'

Then she touched her heels to the horse's flanks and cantered down the glade, her body bent low, the spear trained at its target. But at the last instant its point swerved aside and gouged the dirt. The boar had not moved. The huntsmen laughed raucously.

Janarrl's wide face reddened with anger as he whipped out suddenly and trapped her wrist, tightened on it. 'Your damned mother could cut men's throats and not change color. I'll see you flesh your spear in that carcass, or I'll make you dance, here and now, as I did last night, when you told me the wizard's spells and the place of his den.'

He leaned closer and his voice sank to a whisper. 'Know, chit, that I've long suspected that your mother, fierce as she could be, was – perhaps ensorceled against her will – a wizard-lover like yourself ... and you the whelp of that burned charmer.'

Her eyes widened and she started to pull away from him, but he drew her closer. 'Have no fear, chit, I'll work the taint out of your flesh one way or another. For a beginning, prick me that boar!'

She did not move. Her face was a cream-colored mask of fear. He raised his hand. But at that moment there was an interruption.

A figure appeared at the edge of the glade at the point where the boar had turned to make its last charge. It was that of a slim youth, dressed all in gray. Like one drugged or in a trance, he walked straight toward Janarrl. The three huntsmen who had been attending the Duke drew swords and moved leisurely toward him.

The youth's face was white and tensed, his forehead beaded with sweat under the gray hood half thrown back. Jaw muscles made ivory knobs. His eyes, fixed on the Duke, squinted as if they looked at the blinding sun.

His lips parted wide, showing his teeth. 'Slayer of Glavas Rho! Wizard-killer!'

Then his bronze sword was out of its moldy scabbard. Two of the huntsmen moved in his way, one of them crying, 'Beware poison!' at the green of the newcomer's blade. The youth aimed a terrific blow at him, handling his sword as if it were a sledge. The huntsman parried it with ease, so that it whistled over his head, and the youth almost fell with the force of his own blow. The huntsman stepped forward and with a snappy stroke rapped the youth's sword near the hilt to disarm him, and the fight was done before begun – almost. For the glazed look left the youth's eyes and his features twitched like those of a cat and, recovering his grip on his sword, he lunged forward with a twisting motion at the wrist that captured the huntsman's blade in his own green one and whipped it out of its startled owner's grasp. Then he continued his lunge straight toward the heart of the second huntsman, who escaped only by collapsing backward to the turf.

Janarrl leaned forward tensely in his saddle, muttering, 'The whelp has fangs,' but at that instant the third huntsman, who had circled past, struck the youth with sword-pommel on the back of his neck. The youth dropped his sword, swayed and started to fall, but the first huntsman grabbed him by the neck of his tunic and hurled him toward his companions. They received him in their own jocular fashion with cuffs and slaps, slashing his head and ribs with sheathed daggers, eventually letting him fall to the ground, kicking him, worrying him like a pack of hounds.

Janarrl sat motionless, watching his daughter. He had not missed her frightened start of recognition when the youth appeared. Now he saw her lean forward, lips twitching. Twice she started to speak. Her horse moved uneasily and whinnied. Finally she hung her head and cowered back while low retching sobs came from her throat. Then Janarrl gave a satisfied grunt and called out, 'Enough for the present! Bring him here!'

Two huntsmen dragged between them the half-fainting youth clad now in red-spattered gray.

'Coward,' said the Duke. 'This sport will not kill you. They were only gentling you in preparation for other sports. But I forget you are a pawky wizardling, an effeminate creature who babbles spells in the dark and curses behind the back, a craven who fondles animals and would make the forests mawkish places. Faught! My teeth are on edge. And yet you sought to corrupt my daughter and – Hearken to me, wizardling, I say!' And leaning low from his saddle he caught the youth's sagging head by the hair, tangling in his fingers. The youth's eyes rolled wildly and he gave a convulsive jerk that took the huntsmen by surprise and almost tumbled Janarrl out of the saddle.

Just then there was an ominous crackling of underbrush and the rapid thud of hooves. Someone cried, 'Have a care, master! Oh Gods, guard the Duke!'

The wounded boar had lurched to its feet and was charging the group by Janarrl's horse.

The huntsmen scattered back, snatching for their weapons.

Janarrl's horse shied, further overbalancing its rider. The boar thundered past, like red-smeared midnight. Janarrl almost fell atop it. The boar swung sharply around for a return charge, evading three thrown spears that thudded into the earth just beside it. Janarrl tried to stand, but one of his feet was snagged in a stirrup and his horse, jerking clear, tumbled him again.

The boar came on, but other hooves were thudding now. Another horse swept past Janarrl and a firmly-held spear entered near the boar's shoulder and buried itself deep. The black beast, jarred backward, slashed once at the spear with its tusk, fell heavily on its side and was still.

Then Ivrian let go the spear. The arm with which she had been holding it dangled unnaturally. She slumped in her saddle, catching its pommel with her other hand.

Janarrl scrambled to his feet, eyed his daughter and the boar. Then his gaze traveled slowly around the glade, full circle.

Glavas Rho's apprentice was gone.

'North be south, east be west. Copse be glade and gully crest. Dizziness all paths invest. Leaves and grasses, do the rest.'

Mouse mumbled the chant through swollen lips almost as though he were talking into the ground on which he lay. His fingers arranging themselves into cabalistic symbols, he thumbed a pinch of green powder from a tiny pouch and tossed it into the air with a wrist-flick that made him wince. 'Know it, hound, you are wolf-born, enemy to whip and horn. Horse, think of the unicorn, uncaught since the primal morn. Weave off from me, by the Norn!'

The charm completed, he lay still and the pains in his bruised flesh and bones became more bearable. He listened to the sounds of the hunt trail off in the distance.

His face was pushed close to a patch of grass. He saw an ant laboriously climb a blade, fall to the ground, and then continue on its way. For a moment he felt a bond of kinship between himself and the tiny insect. He remembered the black boar whose unexpected charge had given him a chance to escape and for a strange moment his mind linked it with the ant.

Vaguely he thought of the pirates who had threatened

his life in the west. But their gay ruthlessness had been a different thing from the premeditated and presavored brutality of Janarrl's huntsmen.

Gradually anger and hate began to swirl in him. He saw the gods of Glavas Rho, their formerly serene faces white and sneering. He heard the words of the old incantations, but they twanged with a new meaning. Then these visions receded, and he saw only a whirl of grinning faces and cruel hands. Somewhere in it the white, guilt-stricken face of a girl. Swords, sticks, whips. All spinning. And at the center, like the hub of a wheel on which men are broken, the thick form of the Duke.

What was the teaching of Glavas Rho to that wheel? It had rolled over him and crushed him. What was white magic to Janarrl and his henchmen? Only a priceless parchment to be besmirched. Magic gems to be trampled in filth. Thoughts of deep wisdom to be pulped with their encasing brain.

But there was the other magic. The magic Glavas Rho had forbidden, sometimes smilingly but always with an underlying seriousness. The magic Mouse had learned of only by hints and warnings. The magic which stemmed from death and hate and pain and decay, which dealt in poisons and night-shrieks, which trickled down from the black spaces between the stars, which, as Janarrl himself had said, cursed in the dark behind the back.

It was as if all Mouse's former knowledge – of small creatures and stars and beneficial sorceries and Nature's codes of courtesy – burned in one swift sudden holocaust. And the black ashes took life and began to stir, and from them crept a host of night shapes, resembling those which had been burned, but all distorted. Creeping, skulking, scurrying shapes. Heartless, all hate and terror, but as lovely to look on as black spiders swinging along their geometrical webs.

To sound a hunting horn for that pack! To set them on the track of Janarrl!

Deep in his brain an evil voice began to whisper, 'The Duke must die. The Duke must die.' And he knew that he would always hear that voice, until its purpose was fulfilled.

Laboriously he pushed himself up, feeling a stabbing pain that told of broken ribs; he wondered how he had managed to flee this far. Grinding his teeth, he stumbled across a clearing. By the time he had gotten into the shelter of the trees again, the pain had forced him to his hands and knees. He crawled on a little way, then collapsed.

Near evening of the third day after the hunt. Ivrian stole down from her tower room, ordered the smirking groom to fetch her horse, and rode through the valley and across the stream and up the opposite hill until she reached the rock-sheltered house of Glavas Rho. The destruction she saw brought new misery to her white taut face. She dismounted and went close to the fire-gutted ruin, trembling lest she come upon the body of Glavas Rho. But it was not there. She could see that the ashes had been disturbed as though someone had been searching through them and sifting them for any objects that might have escaped the flames. Everything was very quiet.

An inequality in the ground off toward the side of the clearing caught her eye and she walked in that direction. It was a new-made grave, and in place of a headstone was, set around with gray pebbles, a small flat greenish stone with strange carvings on its surface.

A sudden little sound from the forest set her trembling and made her realize that she was very much afraid, only that up to this point her misery had outweighed her terror. She looked up and gave a gasping cry, for a face was peering at her through a hole in the leaves. It was a wild face, smeared with dirt and grass stains, smirched here and there with old patches of dried blood, shadowed by a stubble of beard. Then she recognized it.

'Mouse,' she called haltingly.

She hardly knew the answering voice.

'So you have returned to gloat over the wreckage caused by your treachery.'

'No, Mouse, no!' she cried. 'I did not intend this. You must believe me.'

'Liar! It was your father's men who killed him and burned his house.'

'But I never thought they would!'

'Never thought they would! – as if that's any excuse. You are so afraid of your father that you would tell him anything. You live by fear.'

'Not always, Mouse. In the end I killed the boar.'

'So much the worse – killing the beast the gods had sent to kill your father.'

'But truly I never killed the boar. I was only boasting when I said so – I thought you liked me brave. I have no memory of that killing. My mind went black. I think my dead mother entered me and drove the spear.'

'Liar and changer of lies! But I'll amend my judgment: you live by fear except when your father whips you to courage. I should have realized that and warned Glavas Rho against you. But I had dreams about you.'

'You called me Misling,' she said faintly.

'Aye, we played at being mice, forgetting cats are real. And then while I was away, you were frightened by mere whippings into betraying Glavas Rho to your father!'

'Mouse, do not condemn me.' Ivrian was sobbing. 'I know that my life has been nothing but fear. Ever since I was a child my father has tried to force me to believe that cruelty and hate are the laws of the universe. He has tortured and tormented me. There was no one to whom I could turn, until I found Glavas Rho and learned that the universe has laws of sympathy and love that shape even death and the seeming hates. But now Glavas Rho is dead and I am more frightened and alone than ever. I need your help, Mouse. You studied under Glavas Rho. You know his teachings. Come and help me.'

His laughter mocked her. 'Come out and be betrayed? Be whipped again while you look on? Listen to your sweet lying voice, while your father's huntsmen creep closer? No, I have other plans.'

'Plans?' she questioned. Her voice was apprehensive. 'Mouse, your life is in danger so long as you lurk here. My father's men are sworn to slay you on sight. I would die, I tell you, if they caught you. Don't delay, get away. Only tell me first that you do not hate me.' And she moved toward him.

Again his laughter mocked her.

'You are beneath my hate,' came the stinging words. 'I feel only contempt for your cowardly weakness. Glavas Rho talked too much of love. There are laws of hate in the universe, shaping even its loves, and it is time I made them work for me. Come no closer! I do not intend to betray my plans to you, or my new hidey holes. But this much I will tell you, and listen well. In seven days your father's torment begins.'

'My father's torment—? Mouse, Mouse, listen to me. I want to question you about more than Glavas Rho's teachings. I want to question you about Glavas Rho. My father hinted to me that he knew my mother, that he was perchance my very father.'

This time there was a pause before the mocking laughter, but when it came, it was doubled. 'Good, good, good! It pleasures me to think that Old Whitebeard enjoyed life a little before he became so wise, wise, wise. I dearly hope he did tumble your mother. That would explain his nobility. Where so much love was – love for each creature ever born – there must have been lust and guilt before. Out of that encounter – and all your mother's evil – his white magic grew. It is true! Guilt and white magic side by side – and the gods never lied! Which leaves you the daughter of Glavas Rho, betraying your true father to his sooty death.'

And then his face was gone and the leaves framed only a dark hole. She blundered into the forest after him, calling out 'Mouse! Mouse!' and trying to follow the receding laughter. But it died away, and she found herself in a gloomy hollow, and she began to realize how evil the apprentice's laughter had sounded, as if he laughed at the death of all love, or even its unbirth. Then panic seized her, and she fled back through the undergrowth, brambles catching at her clothes and twigs stinging her cheeks, until she had regained the clearing and was galloping back through the dusk, a thousand fears besetting her and her heart sick with the thought there was now no one in the wide world who did not hate and despise her.

When she reached the stronghold, it seemed to crouch above her like an ugly jag-crested monster, and when she passed through the great gateway, it seemed to her that the monster had gobbled her up forever.

Come nightfall on the seventh day, when dinner was being served in the great banquet hall, with much loud talk and crunching of rushes and clashing of silver plates, Janarrl stifled a cry of pain and clapped his hand to his heart.

'It is nothing,' he said a moment later to the thin-faced henchman sitting at his side. 'Give me a cup of wine! That will stop it twinging.'

But he continued to look pale and ill at ease, and he ate little of the meat that was served up in great smoking slices. His eyes kept roving about the table, finally settling on his daughter.

'Stop staring at me in that gloomy way, girl!' he called. 'One would think that you had poisoned my wine and were watching to see green spots come out on me. Or red ones edged with black, belike.'

This brought a general guffaw of laughter which seemed to please the Duke, for he tore off the wing of a fowl and gnawed at it hungrily, but the next moment he gave another sudden cry of pain, louder than the first, staggered to his feet, clawed convulsively at his chest, and then pitched over on the table where he lay groaning and writhing in his pain.

'The Duke is stricken,' the thin-faced henchman announced quite unnecessarily and yet most portentously after bending over him. 'Carry him to bed. One of you loosen his shirt. He gasps for air.'

A flurry of whispering went up and down the table. As the great door to his private apartments was opened for the Duke, a heavy gust of chill air made the torches flicker and turn blue, so that shadows crowded into the hall. Then one torch flared white-bright as a star, showing the face of a girl. Ivrian felt the others draw away from her with suspicious glances and mutterings, as if they were certain there had been truth in the Duke's jest. She did not look up. After a while someone came and told her that the Duke commanded her presence. Without a word she rose and followed.

The Duke's face was gray and furrowed with pain, but he had control of himself, though with each breath his hand tightened convulsively on the edge of the bed until his knuckles were like knobs of rock. He was propped up with pillows and a furred robe had been tucked closely about his shoulders and long-legged braziers glowed around the bed. In spite of all he was shivering convulsively.

'Come here, girl,' he ordered in a low, labored voice that hissed against his drawn lips. 'You know what has happened. My heart pains as though there were a fire under it and yet my skin is cased in ice. There is a stabbing in my joints as if long needles pierced clear through the marrow. It is wizard's work.'

'Wizard's work, beyond doubt,' confirmed Giscorl, the thin-faced henchman, who stood at the head of the bed. 'And there is no need to guess who. That young serpent whom you did not kill quickly enough ten days ago! He's been reported skulking in the woods, aye, and talking to … certain ones,' he added, eyeing Ivrian narrowly, suspiciously.

A spasm of agony shook the Duke. 'I should have stamped out whelp with sire,' he groaned. Then his eyes shifted back, to Ivrian. 'Look, girl, you've been seen poking about in the forest where the old wizard was killed. It's believed you talked with his cub.'

Ivrian wet her lips, tried to speak, shook her head. She could feel her father's eyes probing into her. Then his fingers reached out and twisted themselves in her hair.

'I believe you're in league with him!' His whisper was like a rusty knife. 'You're helping him do this to me. Admit it! Admit!' And he thrust her cheek against the nearest brazier so that her hair smoked and her 'No!' became a shuddering scream. The brazier swayed and Giscorl steadied it. Through Ivrian's scream the Duke snarled, 'Your mother once held red coals to prove her honor.'

A ghostly blue flame ran up Ivrian's hair. The Duke jerked her from the brazier and fell back against the pillows …

'Send her away,' he finally whispered faintly, each word an effort. 'She's a coward and wouldn't dare to hurt even me. Meantime, Giscorl, send out more men to hunt through the woods. They must find his lair before dawn, or I'll rupture my heart withstanding the pain.'

Curtly Giscorl motioned Ivrian toward the door. She cringed, and slunk from the room, fighting down tears. Her cheek pulsed with pain. She was not aware of the strangely speculative smile with which the hawk-faced henchman watched her out.

Ivrian stood at the narrow window of her room watching the little bands of horsemen come and go, their torches glowing like will-o'-the-wisps in the woods. The stronghold was full of mysterious movement. The very stones seemed restlessly alive, as if they shared the torment of their master.

She felt herself drawn toward a certain point out there in the darkness. A memory kept recurring to her of how one day Glavas Rho had showed her a small cavern in the hillside and had warned her that it was an evil place, where much baneful sorcery had been done in the past. Her fingertips moved around the crescent-shaped blister on her cheek and over the rough streak in her hair.

Finally her uneasiness and the pull from the night became too strong for her. She dressed in the dark and edged open the door of her chamber. The corridor seemed for the moment deserted. She hurried along it, keeping close to the wall, and darted down the worn rounded hummocks of the stone stair. The tramp of footsteps sent her hurrying into a niche, where she cowered while two huntsmen strode glum-faced toward the Duke's chamber. They were dust-stained and stiff from riding.

'No one'll find him in all that dark,' one of them muttered. 'It's like hunting an ant in a cellar.'

The other nodded. 'And wizards can change landmarks and make forest paths turn on themselves, so that all searchers are befuddled.'

As soon as they were past Ivrian hastened into the banquet hall, now dark and empty, and through the kitchen with its high brick ovens and its huge copper kettles glinting in the shadows.

Outside in the courtyard torches were flaring and there was a bustle of activity as grooms brought fresh horses or led off spent ones, but she trusted to her huntsman's costume to let her pass unrecognized. Keeping to the shadows, she worked her way around to the stables. Her horse moved restlessly and neighed when she slipped into the stall, but quieted at her low whisper. A few moments and it was saddled, and she was leading it around to the open fields at the back. No searching parties seemed to be near, so she mounted and rode swiftly toward the wood.

Her mind was a storm of anxieties. She could not explain to herself how she had dared come this far, except that the attraction toward that point in the night – the cavern against which Glavas Rho had warned her – possessed a sorcerous insistence not to be denied.

Then, when the forest engulfed her, she suddenly felt that she was committing herself to the arms of darkness and putting behind forever the grim stronghold and its cruel occupants. The ceiling of leaves blotted out most of the stars. She trusted to a light rein on her horse to guide her straight. And in this she was successful, for within a half hour she reached a shallow ravine which led past the cavern she sought.

Now, for the first time, her horse became uneasy. It balked and uttered little whinnying cries of fear and tried repeatedly to turn off as she urged it along the ravine. Its pace slowed to a walk. Finally it refused to move further. Its ears were laid back and it was trembling all over.

Ivrian dismounted and moved on. The forest was portentously quiet, as if all animals and birds – even the insects – had gone. The darkness ahead was almost tangible, as if built of black bricks just beyond her hand.

Then Ivrian became aware of the green glow, vague and faint at first as the ghosts of an aurora. Gradually it grew brighter and acquired a flickering quality, as the leafy curtains between her and it became fewer. Suddenly she found herself staring directly at it – a thick, heavy, soot-edged flame that writhed instead of danced. If green slime could be transmuted to fire, it would have that look. It burned in the mouth of a shallow cavern.

Then, beside the flame, she saw the face of the apprentice of Glavas Rho, and in that instant an agony of horror and sympathy tore at her mind.

The face seemed inhuman – more a green mask of torment than anything alive. The cheeks were drawn in; the eyes were unnaturally wild; it was very pale, and dripping with cold sweat induced by intense inward effort. There was much suffering in it, but also much power – power to control the thick twisting shadows that seemed to crowd around the green flame, power to master the forces of hate that were being marshaled. At regular intervals the cracked lips moved and the arms and hands made set gestures.

It seemed to Ivrian that she heard the mellow voice of Glavas Rho repeating a statement he had once made to Mouse and to her. 'None can use black magic without straining the soul to the uttermost – and staining it into the bargain. None can inflict suffering without enduring the same. None can send death by spells and sorcery without walking on the brink of death's own abyss, aye, and dripping his own blood into it. The forces black magic evokes are like two-edged poisoned swords with grips studded with scorpion stings. Only a strong man, leather-handed, in whom hate and evil are very powerful, can wield them, and he only for a space.'

In Mouse's face Ivrian saw the living example of those words. Step by step she moved toward him, feeling no more power to control her movements than if she were in a nightmare. She became aware of shadowy presences, as if she were pushing her way through cobweb veils. She came so near that she could have reached out her hand and touched him, and still he did not notice her, as if his spirit were out beyond the stars, grappling the blackness there.

Then a twig snapped under her foot and Mouse sprang up with terrifying swiftness, the energy of every taut muscle released. He snatched up his sword and lunged at the intruder. But when the green blade was within a hand's breadth of Ivrian's throat, he checked it with an effort. He glared, lips drawn back from his teeth. Although he had checked his sword, he seemed only half to recognize her.

At that instant Ivrian was buffeted by a mighty gust of wind, which came from the mouth of the cavern, a strange wind, carrying shadows. The green fire burned low, running rapidly along the sticks that were its fuel, and almost snuffing out.

Then the wind ceased and the thick darkness lifted, to be replaced by a wan gray light heralding the dawn. The fire turned from green to yellow. The wizard's apprentice staggered, and the sword dropped from his fingers.

'Why did you come here?' he questioned thickly.

She saw how his face was wasted with hunger and hate, how his clothing bore the signs of many nights spent in the forest like an animal, under no roof. Then suddenly she realized that she knew the answer to his question.

'Oh, Mouse,' she whispered, 'let us go away from this place. Here is only horror.' He swayed, and she caught hold of him. 'Take me with you, Mouse,' she said.

He stared frowningly into her eyes. 'You do not hate me then, for what I have done to your father? Or what I have done to the teachings of Glavas Rho?' he questioned puzzledly. 'You are not afraid of me?'

'I am afraid of everything,' she whispered, clinging to him. 'I am afraid of you, yes, a great deal afraid. But that fear can be unlearned. Oh, Mouse, will you take me away? – to Lankhmar or to Earth's End?'

He took her by the shoulders. 'I have dreamed of that,' he said slowly. 'But you …?'

'Apprentice of Glavas Rho!' thundered a stern, triumphant voice. 'I apprehend you in the name of Duke Janarrl for sorceries practiced on the Duke's body!'

Four huntsmen were springing forward from the undergrowth with swords drawn and Giscorl three paces behind them. Mouse met them halfway. They soon found that this time they were not dealing with a youth blinded by anger, but with a cold and cunning swordsman. There was a kind of magic in his primitive blade. He ripped up the arm of his first assailant with a well-judged thrust, disarmed the second with an unexpected twist, then cooly warded off the blows of the other two, retreating slowly. But other huntsmen followed the first four and circled around. Still fighting with terrible intensity and giving blow for blow, Mouse went down under the sheer weight of their attack. They pinioned his arms and dragged him to his feet. He was bleeding from a cut in the cheek, but he carried his head high, though it was beast-shaggy. His bloodshot eyes sought out Ivrian.

'I should have known,' he said evenly, 'that having betrayed Glavas Rho you would not rest until you had betrayed me. You did your work well, girl. I trust you take much pleasure in my death.'

Giscorl laughed. Like a whip, the words of Mouse stung Ivrian. She could not meet his eyes. Then she became aware that there was a man on horseback behind Giscorl and, looking up, she saw that it was her father. His wide body was bent by pain. His face was a death's mask. It seemed a miracle that he managed to cling to the saddle.

'Quick, Giscorl!' he hissed.

But the thin-faced henchman was already sniffing around in the cavern's mouth like a well trained ferret. He gave a cry of satisfaction and lifted down a little figure from a ledge above the fire, which he next stamped out. He carried the figure as gingerly as if it were made of cobweb. As he passed by her, Ivrian saw that it was a clay doll wide as it was tall and dressed in brown and yellow leaves, and that its features were a grotesque copy of her father's. It was pierced in several places by long bone needles.

'This is the thing, oh Master,' said Giscorl, holding it up, but the Duke only repeated, 'Quick, Giscorl!' The henchman started to withdraw the largest needle which pierced the doll's middle, but the Duke gasped in agony and cried, 'Forget not the balm!' Whereupon Giscorl uncorked with his teeth and poured a large vial of sirupy liquid over the doll's body and the Duke sighed a little with relief. Then Giscorl very carefully withdrew the needles, one by one, and as each needle was withdrawn the Duke's breath whistled and he clapped his hand to his shoulder or thigh, as if it were from his own body that the needles were being drawn. After the last one was out, he sat slumped in his saddle for a long time. When he finally looked up the transformation that had taken place was astonishing. There was color in his face, and the lines of pain had vanished, and his voice was loud and ringing.

'Take the prisoner back to our stronghold to await our judgment,' he cried. 'Let this be a warning to all who would practice wizardry in our domain. Giscorl, you have proved yourself a faithful servant.' His eyes rested on Ivrian. 'You have played with witchcraft too often, girl, and need other instruction. As a beginning you will witness the punishment I shall visit on this foul wizardling.'

'A small boon, oh Duke!' Mouse cried. He had been hoisted onto a saddle and his legs tied under the horse's belly. 'Keep your foul, spying daughter out of my sight. And let her not look at me in my pain.'

'Strike him in the lips, one of you,' the Duke ordered. 'Ivrian, ride close behind him – I command it.'

Slowly the little cavalcade rode off toward the stronghold through the brightening dawn. Ivrian's horse had been brought to her and she took her place as bidden, sunk in a nightmare of misery and defeat. She seemed to see the pattern of her whole life laid out before her – past, present, and future – and it consisted of nothing but fear, loneliness, and pain. Even the memory of her mother, who had died when she was a little girl, was something that still brought a palpitation of panic to her heart: a bold, handsome woman, who always had a whip in her hand, and whom even her father had feared. Ivrian remembered how when the servants had brought word that her mother had broken her neck in a fall from a horse, her only emotion had been fear that they were lying to her, and that this was some new trick of her mother's to put her off guard, and that some new punishment would follow.

Then, from the day of her mother's death, her father had shown her nothing but a strangely perverse cruelty. Perhaps it was his disgust at not having a son that made him treat her like a cowardly boy instead of a girl and encourage his lowliest followers to maltreat her – from the maids who played at ghosts around her bed to the kitchen wenches who put frogs in her milk and nettles in her salad.

Sometimes it seemed to her that anger at not having a son was too weak an explanation for her father's cruelties, and that he was revenging himself through Ivrian on his dead wife, whom he had certainly feared and who still influenced his actions, since he had never married again or openly taken mistresses. Or perhaps there was truth in what he had said of her mother and Glavas Rho – no, surely that must be a wild imagining of his anger. Or perhaps, as he sometimes told her, he was trying to make her live up to her mother's vicious and blood-thirsty example, trying to recreate his hated and adored wife in the person of her daughter, and finding a queer pleasure in the refractoriness of the material on which he worked and the grotesquerie of the whole endeavor.

Then in Glavas Rho Ivrian had found a refuge. When she had first chanced upon the white-bearded old man in her lonely wanderings through the forest, he had been mending the broken leg of a fawn and he had spoken to her softly of the ways of kindness and of the brotherhood of all life, human and animal. And she had come back day after day to hear her own vague intuitions revealed to her as deep truths and to take refuge in his wide sympathy … and to explore her timid friendship with his clever little apprentice. But now Glavas Rho was dead and Mouse had taken the spider's way, or the snake's track, or the cat's path, as the old wizard had sometimes referred to bale magic.

She looked up and saw Mouse riding a little ahead and to one side of her, his hands bound behind him, his head and body bowed forward. Conscience smote her, for she knew she had been responsible for his capture. But worse than conscience was the pang of lost opportunity, for there ahead of her rode, doomed, the one man who might have saved her from her life.

A narrowing of the path brought her close beside him. She said hurriedly, ashamedly, 'If there is anything I can do so that you will forgive me a little …'

The glance he bent on her, looking sidewise up, was sharp, appraising, and surprisingly alive.

'Perhaps you can,' he murmured softly, so the huntsmen ahead might not hear. 'As you must know, your father will have me tortured to death. You will be asked to watch it. Do just that. Keep your eyes riveted on mine the whole time. Sit close beside your father. Keep your hand on his arm. Aye, kiss him too. Above all, show no sign of fright or revulsion. Be like a statue carved of marble. Watch to the end. One other thing – wear, if you can, a gown of your mother's, or if not a gown, then some article of her clothing.' He smiled at her thinly. 'Do this and I will at least have the consolation of watching you flinch – and flinch – and flinch!'

'No mumbling charms now!' cried the huntsman suddenly, jerking Mouse's horse ahead.

Ivrian reeled as if she had been struck in the face. She had thought her misery could go no deeper, but Mouse's words had beaten it down a final notch. At that instant the cavalcade came into the open, and the stronghold loomed up ahead – a great horned and jag-crested blot on the sunrise. Never before had it seemed so much like a hideous monster. Ivrian felt that its high gates were the iron jaws of death.

Janarrl, striding into the torture chamber deep below his stronghold, experienced a hot wave of exultation, as when he and his huntsmen closed in around an animal for the kill. But atop the wave was a very faint foam of fear. His feelings were a little like those of a ravenously hungry man invited to a sumptuous banquet, but who has been warned by a fortune-teller to fear death by poison. He was haunted by the feverish frightened face of the man arm-wounded by the wizardling's corroded bronze sword. His eyes met those of Glavas Rho's apprentice, whose half-naked body was stretched – though not yet painfully so – upon the rack, and the Duke's sense of fear sharpened. They were too searching, those eyes, too cold and menacing, too suggestive of magical powers.

He told himself angrily that a little pain would soon change their look to one of trapped panic. He told himself that it was natural that he should still be on edge from last night's horrors, when his life had almost been pried from him by dirty sorceries. But deep in his heart he knew that fear was always with him – fear of anything or anyone that some day might be stronger than he and hurt him as he had hurt others – fear of the dead he had harmed and could hurt no longer – fear of his dead wife, who had indeed been stronger and crueler than he and who had

118

humiliated him in a thousand ways that no one but he remembered.

But he also knew that his daughter would soon be here and that he could then shift off his fear on her; by forcing her to fear, he would be able to heal his own courage, as he had done innumerable times in the past.

So he confidently took his place and gave order that the torture begin.

As the great wheel creaked and the leathern wristlets and anklets began to tighten a little, Mouse felt a qualm of helpless panic run over his body. It centered in his joints – those little deep-set hinges of bone normally exempt from danger. There was yet no pain. His body was merely stretched a little, as if he were yawning.

The low ceiling was close to his face. The flickering light of the torches revealed the mortices in the stone and the dusty cobwebs. Toward his feet he could see the upper portion of the wheel, and the two large hands that gripped its spokes, dragging them down effortlessly, very slowly, stopping for twenty heartbeats at a time. By turning his head and eyes to the side he could see the big figure of the Duke – not wide as his doll of him, but wide – sitting in a carven wooden chair, two armed men standing behind him. The Duke's brown hands, their jeweled rings flashing fire, were closed over the knobs on the chair-arms. His feet were firmly planted. His jaw was set. Only his eyes showed any uneasiness or vulnerability. They kept shifting from side to side – rapidly, regularly, like the pivoted ones of a doll.

'My daughter should be here,' he heard the Duke say abruptly in a flat voice. 'Hasten her. She is not to be permitted to delay.'

One of the men hurried away.

Then the twinges of pain commenced, striking at random in the forearm, the back, the knee, the shoulder. With an effort Mouse composed his features. He fixed his attention on the faces around him, surveying them in detail as if they formed a picture, noting the highlights on the cheeks and eyes and beards and the shadows, wavering with the torchflames, that their figures cast upon the low walls.

Then those low walls melted and, as if distance were no longer real, he saw the whole wide world he'd never visited beyond them: great reaches of forest, bright amber desert, and turquoise sea; the Lake of Monsters, the City of Ghouls, magnificent Lankhmar, the Land of the Eight Cities, the Trollstep Mountains, the fabulous Cold Waste and by some chance striding there an open-faced, hulking red-haired youth he'd glimpsed among the pirates and later spoken with – all places and persons he'd never now encounter, but showing in wondrous fine detail, as if carved and tinted by a master miniaturist.

With startling suddenness the pain returned and increased. The twinges became needle stabs – a cunning prying at his insides – fingers of force crawling up his arms and legs toward his spine – an unsettling at the hips. He desperately tensed his muscles against them.

Then he heard the Duke's voice, 'Not so fast. Stop a while.' Mouse thought he recognized the overtones of panic in the voice. He twisted his head despite the pangs it cost him and watched the uneasy eyes. They swung to and fro, like little pendulums.

Suddenly then, as if time were no longer real, Mouse saw another scene in this chamber. The Duke was there and his eyes swinging from side to side, but he was younger and there was open panic and horror in his face. Close beside him was a boldly handsome woman in a dark red dress cut low in the bosom and with slashes inset with yellow silk. Stretched upon the rack itself in Mouse's place was a strappingly beautiful but now pitifully whimpering maid, whom the woman in red was questioning, with great coldness and insistence on detail, about her amorous encounters with the Duke and her attempt on the life of herself, the Duke's wife, by poison.

Footsteps broke that scene, as stones destroy a reflection in water, and brought the present back. Then a voice: 'Your daughter comes, oh Duke.'

Mouse steeled himself. He had not realized how much he dreaded this meeting, even in his pain. He felt bitterly certain that Ivrian would not have heeded his words. She was not evil, he knew, and she had not meant to betray him, but by the same token she was without courage. She would come whimpering, and her anguish would eat at what little self-control he could muster and doom his last wild wishful schemings.

Lighter footsteps were approaching now – hers. There was something curiously measured about them.

It meant added pain for him to turn his head so he could see the doorway; yet he did so, watching her figure define itself as it entered the region of ruddy light cast by the torches.

Then he saw the eyes. They were wide and staring. They were fixed straight on him. And they did not turn away. The face was pale, calm with a deadly serenity.

He saw she was dressed in a gown of dark red, cut low in the bosom and with slashes inset with yellow silk.

And then the soul of Mouse exulted, for he knew that she had done what he had bidden her. Glavas Rho had said, 'The sufferer can hurl his suffering back upon his oppressor, if only his oppressor can be tempted to open a channel for his hate.' Now there was a channel open for him, leading to Janarrl's inmost being.

Hungrily, Mouse fastened his gaze on Ivrian's unblinking eyes, as if they were pools of black magic in a cold moon. Those eyes, he knew, could receive what he could give.

He saw her seat herself by the Duke. He saw the Duke peer sidewise at his daughter and start up as if she were a ghost. But Ivrian did not look toward him, only her hand stole out and fastened on his wrist, and the Duke sank shuddering back into his chair.

'Proceed!' he heard the Duke call out to the torturers, and this time the panic in the Duke's voice was very close to the surface.

The wheel turned. Mouse heard himself groan piteously. But there was something in him now that could ride on top of the pain and that had no part in the groan. He felt that there was a path between his eyes and Ivrian's – a rock-walled channel through which the forces of human spirit and of more than human spirit could be sent roaring like a mountain torrent. And still she did not turn away. No expression crossed her face when he groaned, only her eyes seemed to darken as she grew still more pale. Mouse sensed a shifting of feelings in his body. Through the scalding waters of pain, his hate rose to the surface, rode atop too. He pushed his hate down the rock-walled channel, saw Ivrian's face grow more deathlike as it struck her, saw her tighten her grip on her father's wrist, sensed the trembling that her father no longer could master.

The wheel turned. From far off Mouse heard a steady, heart-tearing whimpering. But a part of him was outside the room now – high, he felt, in the frosty emptiness above the world. He saw spread out below him a nighted panorama of wooded hills and valleys. Near the summit of one hill was a tight clump of tiny stone towers. But as if he were endowed with a magical vulture's eye, he could see through the walls and roofs of those towers into the very foundations beneath, into a tiny murky room in which men tinier than insects clustered and cowered together. Some were working at a mechanism which inflicted pain on a creature that might have been a bleached and writhing ant. And the pain of that creature, whose tiny thin cries he could faintly hear, had a strange effect on him at this height, strengthening his inward powers and tearing away a veil from his eyes – a veil that had hitherto hidden a whole black universe.

For he began to hear about him a mighty murmuring. The frigid darkness was beaten by wings of stone. The steely light of the stars cut into his brain like painless knives. He felt a wild black whirlpool of evil, like a torrent of black tigers, blast down upon him from above, and he knew that it was his to control. He let it surge through his body and then hurled it down the unbroken path that led to two points of darkness in the tiny room below – the two staring eyes of Ivrian, daughter of Duke Janarrl. He saw the black of the whirlwind's heart spread on her face like an inkblot, seep down her white arms and dye her fingers. He saw her hand tighten convulsively on her father's arm. He saw her reach her other hand toward the Duke and lift her open lips to his cheek.

Then, for one moment while the torch flames whipped low and blue in a physical wind that seemed to blow through the morticed stones of the buried chamber ... for one moment while the torturers and guards dropped the tools of their trades ... for one indelible moment of hate fulfilled and revenge accomplished, Mouse saw the strong, square face of Duke Janarrl shake in the agitation of ultimate terror, the features twisted like heavy cloth wrung between invisible hands, then crumpled in defeat and death.

The strand supporting Mouse snapped. His spirit dropped like a plummet toward the buried room.

An agonizing pain filled him, but it promised life, not death. Above him was the low stone ceiling. The hands on the wheel were white and slender. Then he knew that the pain was that of release from the rack.

Slowly Ivrian loosened the rings of leather from his wrists and ankles. Slowly she helped him down, supporting him with all her strength as they dragged their way across the room, from which everyone else had fled in terror save for one crumpled jeweled figure in a carven chair. They paused by that and he surveyed the dead thing with the cool, satisfied, masklike gaze of a cat. Then on and up they went, Ivrian and the Gray Mouser, through corridors emptied by panic, and out into the night.

IV: ILL MET IN LANKHMAR

Silent as specters, the tall and the fat thief edged past the dead, noose-strangled watch-leopard, out the thick, lock-picked door of Jengao the Gem Merchant, and strolled east on Cash Street through the thin black night-smog of Lankhmar, City of Sevenscore Thousand Smokes.

East on Cash it had to be, for west at the intersection of Cash and Silver was a police post with unbribed guardsmen in browned-iron cuirasses and helms, restlessly grounding and rattling their pikes, while Jengao's place had no alley entrance or even window in its stone walls three spans thick and the roof and floor almost as strong and without trap doors.

But tall, tight-lipped Slevyas, master thief candidate, and fat, darting-eyed Fissif, thief second class, brevetted first class for this operation, with a rating of talented in double-dealing, were not in the least worried. Everything was proceeding according to plan. Each carried thonged in his pouch a much smaller pouch of jewels of the first water only, for Jengao, now breathing stentoriously inside and senseless from the slugging he'd suffered, must be allowed, nay, nursed and encouraged, to build up his business again and so ripen it for another plucking. Almost the first law of the Thieves' Guild was never kill the hen that laid brown eggs with a ruby in the yolk, or white eggs with a diamond in the white.

The two thieves also had the relief of knowing that, with

the satisfaction of a job well done, they were going straight home now, not to a wife, Aarth forbid! – or to parents and children, all gods forfend! – but to Thieves' House, headquarters and barracks of the all-mighty Guild which was father to them both and mother too, though no woman was allowed inside its ever-open portal on Cheap Street.

In addition there was the comforting knowledge that although each was armed only with his regulation silver-hilted thief's knife, a weapon seldom used except in rare intramural duels and brawls, in fact more a membership token than a weapon, they were nevertheless most strongly convoyed by three reliable and lethal bravos hired for the evening from the Slayers' Brotherhood, one moving well ahead of them as point, the other two well behind as rear guard and chief striking force, in fact almost out of sight – for it is never wise that such convoying be obvious, or so believed Krovas, Grandmaster of the Thieves' Guild.

And if all that were not enough to make Slevyas and Fissif feel safe and serene, there danced along soundlessly beside them in the shadow of the north curb, a small, malformed or at any rate somewhat large-headed shape that might have been a small dog, a somewhat undersized cat, or a very big rat. Occasionally it scuttled familiarly and even encouragingly a little way toward their snugly felt-slippered feet, though it always scurried swiftly back into the darker dark.

True, this last guard was not an absolutely unalloyed reassurance. At that very moment, scarcely twoscore paces yet from Jengao's, Fissif tautly walked for a bit on tiptoe and strained his pudgy lips upward to whisper softly in Slevyas' long-lobed ear, 'Damned if I like being dogged by that Familiar of Hristomilo, no matter what security he's supposed to afford us. Bad enough that Krovas employs or lets himself be cowed into employing a sorcerer of most dubious, if dire, reputation and aspect, but that—'

'Shut your trap!' Slevyas hissed still more softly.

Fissif obeyed with a shrug and occupied himself even more restlessly and keenly than was his wont in darting his gaze this way and that, but chiefly ahead.

Some distance in that direction, in fact just short of the Gold Street intersection, Cash was bridged by an enclosed second-story passageway connecting the two buildings which made up the premises of the famous stone-masons and sculptors Rokkermas and Slaarg. The firm's buildings themselves were fronted by very shallow porticos supported by unnecessarily large pillars of varied shape and decoration, advertisements more than structural members.

From just beyond the bridge there came two low, brief whistles, signal from the point bravo that he had inspected that area for ambushes and discovered nothing suspicious and that Gold Street was clear.

Fissif was by no means entirely satisfied by the safety signal. To tell the truth, the fat thief rather enjoyed being apprehensive and even fearful, at least up to a point. A sense of strident panic overlaid with writhing calm made him feel more excitingly alive than the occasional woman he enjoyed. So he scanned most closely through the thin, sooty smog the frontages and overhangs of Rokkermas and Slaarg as his and Slevyas' leisurely seeming yet unslow pace brought them steadily closer.

On this side the bridge was pierced by four small windows, between which were three large niches in which stood – another advertisement – three life-size plaster statues, somewhat eroded by years of weather and dyed varyingly tones of dark gray by as many years of smog. Approaching Jengao's before the burglary, Fissif had noted them with a swift but comprehensive overshoulder glance. Now it seemed to him that the statue to the right had indefinably changed. It was that of a man of medium height wearing cloak and hood, who gazed down with crossed arms and brooding aspect. No, not indefinably quite — the statue was a more uniform dark gray now, he fancied, cloak, hood, and face; it seemed somewhat sharper featured, less eroded; and he would almost swear it had grown shorter!

Just below the niche, moreover, there was a scattering of gray and raw white rubble which he didn't recall having been there earlier. He strained to remember if during the excitement of the burglary, with its lively leopard-slaying and slugging and all, the unsleeping watch-corner of his mind had recorded a distant crash, and now he believed it had. His quick imagination pictured the possibility of a hole or even door behind each statue, through which it might be given a strong push and so tumbled onto passersby, himself and Slevyas specifically, the right-hand statue having been crashed to test the device and then replaced with a near twin.

He would keep close watch on all three statues as he and Slevyas walked under. It would be easy to dodge if he saw one start to overbalance. Should he yank Slevyas out of harm's way when that happened? It was something to think about.

Without pause his restless attention fixed next on the porticos and pillars. The latter, thick and almost three yards tall, were placed at irregular intervals as well as being irregularly shaped and fluted, for Rokkermas and Slaarg were most modern and emphasized the unfinished look, randomness, and the unexpected.

Nevertheless it seemed to Fissif, his wariness wide awake now, that there was an intensification of unexpectedness, specifically that there was one more pillar under the porticos than when he had last passed by. He couldn't be sure which pillar was the newcomer, but he was almost certain there was one.

Share his suspicions with Slevyas? Yes, and get another hissed reproof and flash of contempt from the small, dull-seeming eyes.

The enclosed bridge was close now. Fissif glanced up at the right-hand statue and noted other differences from the one he'd recalled. Although shorter, it seemed to hold itself more strainingly erect, while the frown carved in its dark gray face was not so much one of philosophic brooding as sneering contempt, self-conscious cleverness, and conceit.

Still, none of the three statues toppled forward as he and Slevyas walked under the bridge. However, something else happened to Fissif at that moment.

One of the pillars winked at him.

The Gray Mouser – for so Mouse now named himself to himself and Ivrian – turned around in the right-hand niche, leaped up and caught hold of the cornice, silently vaulted to the flat roof, and crossed it precisely in time to see the two thieves emerge below.

Without hesitation he leaped forward and down, his body straight as a crossbow bolt, the soles of his ratskin boots aimed at the shorter thief's fat-buried shoulder blades, though leading him a little to allow for the yard he'd walk while the Mouser hurtled toward him.

In the instant that he leaped, the tall thief glanced up overshoulder and whipped out a knife, though making no move to push or pull Fissif out of the way of the human projectile speeding toward him. The Mouser shrugged in full flight. He'd just have to deal with the tall thief faster after knocking down the fat one.

More swiftly than one would have thought he could manage, Fissif whirled around then and thinly screamed, 'Slivikin!'

The ratskin boots took him high in the belly. It was like landing on a big cushion. Writhing aside from Slevyas' first thrust, the Mouser somersaulted forward, turning feet over head, and as the fat thief's skull hit a cobble with a dull *bong* he came to his feet with dirk in hand, ready to take on the tall one.

But there was no need. Slevyas, his small eyes glazed, was toppling too.

One of the pillars had sprung forward, trailing a voluminous robe. A big hood had fallen back from a youthful face and long-haired head. Brawny arms had emerged from the long, loose sleeves that had been the pillar's topmost section, while the big fist ending one of the arms had dealt Slevyas a shrewd knockout punch on the chin.

Fafhrd and the Gray Mouser faced each other across the two thieves sprawled senseless. They were poised for attack, yet for the moment neither moved.

Each discerned something inexplicably familiar in the other.

Fafhrd said, 'Our motives for being here seem identical.'

'Seem? Surely must be!' the Mouser answered curtly, fiercely eyeing this potential new foe, who was taller by a head than the tall thief.

'You said?'

'I said, "Seem? Surely must be!"'

'How civilized of you!' Fafhrd commented in pleased tones.

'Civilized?' the Mouser demanded suspiciously, gripping his dirk tighter.

'To care, in the eye of action, exactly what's said,' Fafhrd explained. Without letting the Mouser out of his vision, he glanced down. His gaze traveled from the belt and pouch of one fallen thief, to those of the other. Then he looked up at the Mouser with a broad, ingenuous smile.

'Sixty-sixty?' he suggested.

The Mouser hesitated, sheathed his dirk, and rapped out, 'A deal!' He knelt abruptly, his fingers on the drawstrings of Fissif's pouch. 'Loot you Slivikin,' he directed.

It was natural to suppose that the fat thief had been crying his companion's name at the end.

Without looking up from where he knelt, Fafhrd remarked, 'That ... ferret they had with them. Where did it go?'

'Ferret?' the Mouser answered briefly. 'It was a marmoset!'

'Marmoset,' Fafhrd mused. 'That's a small tropical monkey, isn't it? Well, might have been, but I got the strange impression that—'

The silent, two-pronged rush which almost overwhelmed them at that instant really surprised neither of them. Each had been expecting it, but the expectation had dropped out of conscious thought with the startlement of their encounter.

The three bravos racing down upon them in concerted attack, two from the west and one from the east, all with swords poised to thrust, had assumed that the two highjackers would be armed at most with knives and as timid or at least cautious in weapons-combat as the general run of thieves and counter-thieves. So it was they who were surprised and thrown into confusion when with the lightning speed of youth the Mouser and Fafhrd sprang up, whipped out fearsomely long swords, and faced them back to back.

The Mouser made a very small parry in carte so that the thrust of the bravo from the east went past his left side only a hair's breadth. He instantly riposted. His adversary, desperately springing back, parried in turn in carte. Hardly slowing, the tip of the Mouser's long, slim sword dropped under that parry with the delicacy of a princess curtsying and then leaped forward and a little upward, the Mouser making an impossibly long-looking lunge for one so small, and went between two scales of the bravo's armored jerkin and between his ribs and through his heart and out his back as if all were angelfood cake.

Meanwhile Fafhrd, facing the two bravos from the west, swept aside their low thrusts with somewhat larger, down-sweeping parries in seconde and low prime, then flipped up his sword, long as the Mouser's but heavier, so that it slashed through the neck of his right-hand adversary, half decapitating him. Then he, dropping back a swift step, readied a thrust for the other.

But there was no need. A narrow ribbon of bloodied steel, followed by a gray glove and arm, flashed past him from behind and transfixed the last bravo with the identical thrust the Mouser had used on the first.

The two young men wiped and sheathed their swords. Fafhrd brushed the palm of his open right hand down his robe and held it out. The Mouser pulled off right-hand gray glove and shook the other's big hand in his sinewy one. Without word exchanged, they knelt and finished looting the two unconscious thieves, securing the small bags of jewels. With an oily towel and then a dry one, the Mouser sketchily wiped from his face the greasy ash-soot mixture which had darkened it, next swiftly rolled up both towels and returned them to his own pouch. Then, after only a questioning eye-twitch east on the Mouser's part and a nod from Fafhrd, they swiftly walked on in the direction Slevyas and Fissif and their escort had been going.

After reconnoitering Gold Street, they crossed it and continued east on Cash at Fafhrd's gestured proposal.

'My woman's at the Golden Lamprey,' he explained.

'Let's pick her up and take her home to meet my girl,' the Mouser suggested.

'Home?' Fafhrd inquired politely, only the barest hint of question in his voice.

'Dim Lane,' the Mouser volunteered.

'Silver Eel?'

'Behind it. We'll have some drinks.'

'I'll pick up a jug. Never have too much juice.'

'True. I'll let you.'

Several squares farther on Fafhrd, after stealing a

number of looks at his new comrade, said with conviction, 'We've met before.'

The Mouser grinned at him. 'Beach by the Mountains of Hunger?'

'Right! When I was a pirate's ship-boy.'

'And I was a wizard's apprentice.'

Fafhrd stopped, again wiped right hand on robe, and held it out. 'Name's Fafhrd. Ef ay ef aitch ar dee.'

Again the Mouser shook it. 'Gray Mouser,' he said defiantly, as if challenging anyone to laugh at the sobriquet. 'Excuse me, but how exactly do you pronounce that? Faf-hrud?'

'Just Faf-erd.'

'Thank you.' They walked on.

'Gray Mouser, eh?' Fafhrd remarked. 'Well, you killed yourself a couple of rats tonight.'

'That I did.' The Mouser's chest swelled and he threw back his head. Then with a comic twitch of his nose and a sidewise half-grin he admitted, 'You'd have got your second man easily enough. I stole him from you to demonstrate my speed. Besides, I was excited.'

Fafhrd chuckled. 'You're telling me? How do you suppose I was feeling?'

Later, as they were crossing Pimp Street, he asked, 'Learn much magic from your wizard?'

Once more the Mouser threw back his head. He flared his nostrils and drew down the corners of his lips, preparing his mouth for boastful, mystifying speech. But once more he found himself twitching his nose and half grinning. What the deuce did this big fellow have that kept him from putting on his usual acts? 'Enough to tell me it's damned dangerous stuff. Though I still fool with it now and then.'

Fafhrd was asking himself a similar question. All his life he'd mistrusted small men, knowing his height awakened their instant jealousy. But this clever little chap was

133

somehow an exception. Quick thinker and brilliant swordsman too, no argument. He prayed to Kos that Vlana would like him.

On the northeast corner of Cash and Whore a slow-burning torch shaded by a broad gilded hoop cast a cone of light up into the thickening black night-smog and another cone down on the cobbles before the tavern door. Out of the shadows into the second cone stepped Vlana, handsome in a narrow black velvet dress and red stockings, her only ornaments a silver-sheathed and -hilted dagger and a silver-worked black pouch, both on a plain black belt.

Fafhrd introduced the Gray Mouser, who behaved with an almost fawning courtesy, obsequiously gallant. Vlana studied him boldly, then gave him a tentative smile.

Fafhrd opened under the torch the small pouch he'd taken off the tall thief. Vlana looked down into it. She put her arms around Fafhrd, hugged him tight, and kissed him soundly. Then she thrust the jewels into the pouch on her belt.

When that was done, he said, 'Look, I'm going to buy a jug. You tell her what happened, Mouser.'

When he came out of the Golden Lamprey he was carrying four jugs in the crook of his left arm and wiping his lips on the back of his right hand. Vlana was frowning. He grinned at her. The Mouser smacked his lips at the jugs. They continued east on Cash. Fafhrd realized that the frown was for more than the jugs and the prospect of stupidly drunken male revelry. The Mouser tactfully walked ahead, ostensibly to lead the way.

When his figure was little more than a blob in the thickening smog, Vlana whispered harshly, 'You had two members of the Thieves' Guild knocked out cold and you didn't cut their throats?'

'We slew three bravos,' Fafhrd protested by way of excuse.

134

'My quarrel is not with the Slayers' Brotherhood, but that abominable Guild. You swore to me that whenever you had the chance—'

'Vlana! I couldn't have the Gray Mouser thinking I was an amateur counter-thief consumed by hysteria and blood lust.'

'You already set great store by him, don't you?'

'He possibly saved my life tonight.'

'Well, he told me that *he'd* have slit their throats in a wink, if he'd known I wanted it that way.'

'He was only playing up to you from courtesy.'

'Perhaps and perhaps not. But *you* knew and you didn't—'

'Vlana, shut up!'

Her frown became a rageful glare, then suddenly she laughed wildly, smiled twitchingly as if she were about to cry, mastered herself and smiled more lovingly. 'Pardon me, darling,' she said. 'Sometimes you must think I'm going mad and sometimes I believe I am.'

'Well, don't,' he told her shortly. 'Think of the jewels we've won instead. And behave yourself with our new friends. Get some wine inside you and relax. I mean to enjoy myself tonight. I've earned it.'

She nodded and clutched his arm in agreement and for comfort and sanity. They hurried to catch up with the dim figure ahead.

The Mouser, turning left, led them a half square north on Cheap Street to where a narrower way went east again. The black mist in it looked solid.

'Dim Lane,' the Mouser explained.

Fafhrd nodded that he knew.

Vlana said, 'Dim's too weak – too *transparent* a word for it tonight,' with an uneven laugh in which there were still traces of hysteria and which ended in a fit of strangled coughing. When she could swallow again, she gasped out, 'Damn Lankhmar's night-smog! What a hell of a city!'

'It's the nearness here of the Great Salt Marsh,' Fafhrd explained.

And he did indeed have part of the answer. Lying low betwixt the Marsh, the Inner Sea, the River Hlal, and the flat southern grainfields watered by canals fed by the Hlal, Lankhmar with its innumerable smokes was the prey of fogs and sooty smogs. No wonder the citizens had adopted the black toga as their formal garb. Some averred the toga had originally been white or pale brown, but so swiftly soot-blackened, necessitating endless laundering, that a thrifty overlord had ratified and made official what nature or civilization's arts decreed.

About halfway to Carter Street, a tavern on the north side of the lane emerged from the murk. A gape-jawed serpentine shape of pale metal crested with soot hung high for a sign. Beneath it they passed a door curtained with begrimed leather, the slit in which spilled out noise, pulsing torchlight, and the reek of liquor.

Just beyond the Silver Eel the Mouser led them through an inky passageway outside the tavern's east wall. They had to go single file, feeling their way along rough, slimily bemisted brick and keeping close together.

'Mind the puddle,' the Mouser warned. 'It's deep as the Outer Sea.'

The passageway widened. Reflected torchlight filtering down through the dark mist allowed them to make out only the most general shape of their surroundings. To the right was more windowless, high wall. To the left, crowding close to the back of the Silver Eel, rose a dismal, rickety building of darkened brick and blackened, ancient wood. It looked utterly deserted to Fafhrd and Vlana until they had craned back their heads to gaze at the fourth-story attic under the ragged-guttered roof. There faint lines and points of yellow light shone around and through three tightly-latticed windows. Beyond, crossing the T of the space they were in, was a narrow alley.

'Bones Alley,' the Mouser told them in somewhat lofty tones. 'I call it Ordure Boulevard.'

'I can smell that,' Vlana said.

By now she and Fafhrd could see a long, narrow wooden outside stairway, steep yet sagging and without a rail, leading up to the lighted attic. The Mouser relieved Fafhrd of the jugs and went up it quite swiftly.

'Follow me when I've reached the top,' he called back. 'I think it'll take your weight, Fafhrd, but best one of you at a time.'

Fafhrd gently pushed Vlana ahead. With another hysteria-tinged laugh and a pause midway up for another fit of choked coughing, she mounted to the Mouser where he now stood in an open doorway, from which streamed yellow light that died swiftly in the night-smog. He was lightly resting a hand on a big, empty, wrought-iron lamp-hook firmly set in a stone section of the outside wall. He bowed aside, and she went in.

Fafhrd followed, placing his feet as close as he could to the wall, his hands ready to grab for support. The whole stairs creaked ominously and each step gave a little as he shifted his weight onto it. Near the top, one gave way with the muted crack of half-rotted wood. Gently as he could, he sprawled himself hand and knee on as many steps as he could reach to distribute his weight, and cursed sulfurously.

'Don't fret, the jugs are safe,' the Mouser called down gayly.

Fafhrd crawled the rest of the way, a somewhat sour look on his face, and did not get to his feet until he was inside the doorway. When he had done so, he almost gasped with surprise.

It was like rubbing the verdigris from a cheap brass ring and finding a rainbow-fired diamond of the first water set in it. Rich drapes, some twinkling with embroidery of silver and gold, covered the walls except where the shuttered windows were – and the shutters of those were gilded. Similar but darker fabrics hid the low ceiling, making a gorgeous canopy in which the flecks of gold and silver were like stars. Scattered about were plump cushions and low tables, on which burned a multitude of candles. On shelves against the walls were neatly stacked like small logs a vast reserve of candles, numerous scrolls, jugs, bottles, and enameled boxes. A low vanity table was backed by a mirror of honed silver and thickly scattered over with jewels and cosmetics. In a large fireplace was set a small metal stove, neatly blacked, with an ornate fire-pot. Also set beside the stove were a tidy pyramid of thin, resinous torches with frayed ends – fire-kindlers – and other pyramids of short-handled brooms and mops, small, short logs, and gleamingly black coal.

On a low dais by the fireplace was a wide, short-legged, high-backed couch covered with a cloth of gold. On it sat a thin, pale-faced, delicately handsome girl clad in a dress of thick violet silk worked with silver and belted with a silver chain. Her slippers were of white snow-serpent fur. Silver pins headed with amethysts held in place her high-piled black hair. Around her shoulders was drawn a white ermine wrap. She was leaning forward with uneasy-seeming graciousness and extending a narrow, white hand which shook a little to Vlana, who knelt before her and now gently took the proffered hand and bowed her head over it, her own glossy, straight, dark-brown hair making a canopy, and pressed the other girl's hand's back to her lips.

Fafhrd was happy to see his woman playing up properly to this definitely odd though delightful situation. Then looking at Vlana's long, red-stockinged leg stretched far behind her as she knelt on the other, he noted that the floor was everywhere strewn – to the point of double, treble, and quadruple overlaps – with thick-piled, close-woven, many-hued rugs of the finest imported from the

Eastern Lands. Before he knew it, his thumb had shot toward the Gray Mouser.

'You're the Rug Robber!' he proclaimed. 'You're the Carpet Crimp! – and the Candle Corsair too!' he continued, referring to two series of unsolved thefts which had been on the lips of all Lankhmar when he and Vlana had arrived a moon ago.

The Mouser shrugged impassive-faced at Fafhrd, then suddenly grinned, his slitted eyes a-twinkle, and broke into an impromptu dance which carried him whirling and jigging around the room and left him behind Fafhrd, where he deftly reached down the hooded and long-sleeved huge robe from the latter's stooping shoulders, shook it out, carefully folded it, and set it on a pillow.

After a long, uncertain pause, the girl in violet nervously patted with her free hand the cloth of gold beside her and Vlana seated herself there, carefully not too close, and the two women spoke together in low voices, Vlana taking the lead, though not obviously.

The Mouser took off his own gray, hooded cloak, folded it almost fussily, and laid it beside Fafhrd's. Then they unbelted their swords, and the Mouser set them atop folded robe and cloak.

Without those weapons and bulking garments, the two men looked suddenly like youths, both with clear, close-shaven faces, both slender despite the swelling muscles of Fafhrd's arms and calves, he with long red-gold hair falling down his back and about his shoulders, the Mouser with dark hair cut in bangs, the one in brown leather tunic worked with copper wire, the other in jerkin of coarsely woven gray silk.

They smiled at each other. The feeling each had of having turned boy all at once made their smiles for the first time a bit embarrassed. The Mouser cleared his throat and, bowing a little, but looking still at Fafhrd, extended a loosely spread-fingered arm toward the golden couch and said with a preliminary stammer, though otherwise smoothly enough, 'Fafhrd, my good friend, permit me to introduce you to my princess. Ivrian, my dear, receive Fafhrd graciously if you please, for tonight he and I fought back to back against three and we conquered.'

Fafhrd advanced, stooping a little, the crown of his red-gold hair brushing the bestarred canopy, and knelt before Ivrian exactly as Vlana had. The slender hand extended to him looked steady now, but was still quiveringly a-tremble, he discovered as soon as he touched it. He handled it as if it were silk woven of the white spider's gossamer, barely brushing it with his lips, and still felt nervous as he mumbled some compliments.

He did not sense, at least at the moment, that the Mouser was quite as nervous as he, if not more so, praying hard that Ivrian would not overdo her princess part and snub their guests, or collapse in trembling or tears or run to him or into the next room, for Fafhrd and Vlana were literally the first beings, human or animal, noble, freeman, or slave, that he had brought or allowed into the luxurious nest he had created for his aristocratic beloved – save the two love birds that twittered in a silver cage hanging to the other side of the fireplace from the dais.

Despite his shrewdness and new-found cynicism it never occurred to the Mouser that it was chiefly his charming but preposterous coddling of Ivrian that was keeping doll-like and even making more so the potentially brave and realistic girl who had fled with him from her father's torture chamber four moons ago.

But now as Ivrian smiled at last and Fafhrd gently returned her her hand and cautiously backed off, the Mouser relaxed with relief, fetched two silver cups and two silver mugs, wiped them needlessly with a silken towel, carefully selected a bottle of violet wine, then with a grin at Fafhrd uncorked instead one of the jugs the Northerner

140

had brought, and near-brimmed the four gleaming vessels and served them all four.

With another preliminary clearing of throat, but no trace of stammer this time, he toasted, 'To my greatest theft to date in Lankhmar, which willy-nilly I must share sixty-sixty with' – he couldn't resist the sudden impulse – 'with this great, long-haired, barbarian lout here!' And he downed a quarter of his mug of pleasantly burning wine fortified with brandy.

Fafhrd quaffed off half of his, then toasted back, 'To the most boastful and finical little civilized chap I've ever deigned to share loot with,' quaffed off the rest, and with a great smile that showed white teeth held out his empty mug.

The Mouser gave him a refill, topped off his own, then set that down to go to Ivrian and pour into her lap from their small pouch the gems he'd filched from Fissif. They gleamed in their new, enviable location like a small puddle of rainbow-hued quicksilver.

Ivrian jerked back a-tremble, almost spilling them, but Vlana gently caught her arm, steadying it, and leaned in over the jewels with a throaty gasp of wonder and admiration, slowly turned an envious gaze on the pale girl, and began rather urgently but smilingly to whisper to her. Fafhrd realized that Vlana was acting now, but acting well and effectively, since Ivrian was soon nodding eagerly and not long after that beginning to whisper back. At her direction, Vlana fetched a blue-enameled box inlaid with silver, and the two of them transferred the jewels from Ivrian's lap into its blue velvet interior. Then Ivrian placed the box close beside her and they chatted on.

As he worked through his second mug in smaller gulps, Fafhrd relaxed and began to get a deeper feeling of his surroundings. The dazzling wonder of the first glimpse of this throne room in a slum, its colorful luxury intensified by contrast with the dark and mud and slime and rotten stairs and Ordure Boulevard just outside, faded, and he began to note the rickettiness and rot under the grand overlay.

Black, rotten wood and dry, cracked wood too showed here and there between the drapes and also loosed their sick, ancient stinks. The whole floor sagged under the rugs, as much as a span at the center of the room. A large cockroach was climbing down a gold-worked drape, another toward the couch. Threads of night-smog were coming through the shutters, making evanescent black arabesques against the gilt. The stones of the large fireplace had been scrubbed and varnished, yet most of the mortar was gone from between them; some sagged, others were missing altogether.

The Mouser had been building a fire there in the stove. Now he pushed in all the way the yellow-flaring kindler he'd lit from the fire-pot, hooked the little black door shut over the mounting flames, and turned back into the room. As if he'd read Fafhrd's mind, he took up several cones of incense, set their peaks a-smolder at the fire-pot, and placed them about the room in gleaming, shallow, brass bowls – stepping hard on the one cockroach by the way and surreptitiously catching and crushing the other in the base of his flicked fist. Then he stuffed silken rags in the widest shutter-cracks, took up his silver mug again, and for a moment gave Fafhrd a very hard look, as if daring him to say just one word against the delightful yet faintly ridiculous doll's house he'd prepared for his princess.

Next moment he was smiling and lifting his mug to Fafhrd, who was doing the same. Need of refills brought them close together. Hardly moving his lips, the Mouser explained *sotto voce*, 'Ivrian's father was a duke. I slew him, by black magic, I believe, while he was having me done to death on the torture rack. A most cruel man, cruel to his daughter too, yet a duke, so that Ivrian is wholly unused to fending or caring for herself. I pride myself that I maintain her in grander state than ever her father did with all his serving men and maids.'

Suppressing the instant criticisms he felt of this attitude and program, Fafhrd nodded and said amiably, 'Surely you've thieved together a most charming little palace, quite worthy of Lankhmar's overlord Karstak Ovartamortes, or the King of Kings at Tisilinilit.'

From the couch Vlana called in her husky contralto, 'Gray Mouser, your princess would hear an account of tonight's adventure. And might we have more wine?'

Ivrian called, 'Yes, please, Mouse.'

Wincing almost imperceptibly at that earlier nickname, the Mouser looked to Fafhrd for the go-ahead, got the nod, and launched into his story. But first he served the girls wine. There wasn't enough for their cups, so he opened another jug and after a moment of thought uncorked all three, setting one by the couch, one by Fafhrd where he sprawled now on the pillowy carpets, and reserving one for himself. Ivrian looked wide-eyed apprehensive at this signal of heavy drinking ahead, Vlana cynical with a touch of anger, but neither voiced their criticism.

The Mouser told the tale of counter-thievery well, acting it out in part, and with only the most artistic of embellishments – the ferret-marmoset before escaping ran up his back and tried to scratch out his eyes – and he was interrupted only twice.

When he said, 'And so with a whish and a snick I bared Scalpel –' Fafhrd remarked, 'Oh, so you've nicknamed your sword as well as yourself?'

The Mouser drew himself up. 'Yes, and I call my dirk Cat's Claw. Any objections? Seem childish to you?'

'Not at all. I call my own sword Graywand. All weapons are in a fashion alive, civilized and nameworthy. Pray continue.'

And when he mentioned the beastie of uncertain nature

that had gamboled along with the thieves (and attacked his eyes!), Ivrian paled and said with a shudder, 'Mouse! That sounds like a witch's familiar!'

'Wizard's,' Vlana corrected. 'Those gutless Guild-villains have no truck with women, except as fee'd or forced vehicles for their lust. But Krovas, their current king, though superstitious, is noted for taking *all* precautions, and might well have a warlock in his service.'

'That seems most likely; it harrows me with dread,' the Mouser agreed with ominous gaze and sinister voice. He really didn't believe or feel what he said – he was about as harrowed as virgin prairie – in the least, but he eagerly accepted any and all atmospheric enhancements of his performance.

When he was done, the girls, eyes flashing and fond, toasted him and Fafhrd for their cunning and bravery. The Mouser bowed and eye-twinklingly smiled about, then sprawled him down with a weary sigh, wiping his forehead with a silken cloth and downing a large drink.

After asking Vlana's leave, Fafhrd told the adventurous tale of their escape from Cold Corner – he from his clan, she from an acting troupe – and of their progress to Lankhmar, where they lodged now in an actors' tenement near the Plaza of Dark Delights. Ivrian hugged herself to Vlana and shivered large-eyed at the witchy parts – at least as much in delight as fear of Fafhrd's tale, he thought. He told himself it was natural that a doll-girl should love ghost stories, though he wondered if her pleasure would have been as great if she had known that his ghost stories were truly true. She seemed to live in worlds of imagination – once more at least half the Mouser's doing, he was sure.

The only proper matter he omitted from his account was Vlana's fixed intent to get a monstrous revenge on the Thieves' Guild for torturing to death her accomplices and harrying her out of Lankhmar when she'd tried free-lance thieving in the city, with miming as a cover. Nor of course did he mention his own promise – foolish, he thought now – to help her in this bloody business.

After he'd done and got his applause, he found his throat dry despite his skald's training, but when he sought to wet it, he discovered that his mug was empty and his jug too, though he didn't feel in the least drunk; he had talked all the liquor out of him, he told himself, a little of the stuff escaping in each glowing word he'd spoken.

The Mouser was in like plight and not drunk either – though inclined to pause mysteriously and peer toward infinity before answering question or making remark. This time he suggested, after a particularly long infinity-gaze, that Fafhrd accompany him to the Eel while he purchased a fresh supply.

'But we've a lot of wine left in *our* jug,' Ivrian protested. 'Or at least a little,' she amended. It did sound empty when Vlana shook it. 'Besides, you've wine of all sorts here.'

'Not this sort, dearest, and first rule is never mix 'em,' the Mouser explained, wagging a finger. 'That way lies unhealth, aye, and madness.'

'My dear,' Vlana said, sympathetically patting Ivrian's wrist, 'at some time in any good party all the men who are really men simply have to go out. It's extremely stupid, but it's their nature and can't be dodged, believe me.'

'But, Mouse, I'm scared. Fafhrd's tale frightened me. So did yours – I'll hear that big-headed, black ratty familiar a-scratch at the shutters when you're gone, I know I will!'

It seemed to Fafhrd she was not afraid at all, only taking pleasure in frightening herself and in demonstrating her power over her beloved.

'Darlingest,' the Mouser said with a small hiccup, 'there is all the Inner Sea, all the Land of the Eight Cities, and to boot all the Trollstep Mountains in their sky-scraping grandeur between you and Fafhrd's frigid specters or – pardon me, my comrade, but it could be – hallucinations

145

admixed with coincidences. As for familiars, pish! They've never in the world been anything but the loathy, all-too-natural pets of stinking old women and womanish old men.'

'The Eel's but a step, Lady Ivrian,' Fafhrd said, 'and you'll have beside you my dear Vlana, who slew my chiefest enemy with a single cast of that dagger she now wears.'

With a glare at Fafhrd that lasted no longer than a wink, but conveyed 'What a way to reassure a frightened girl!' Vlana said merrily, 'Let the sillies go, my dear. 'Twill give us chance for a private chat, during which we'll take 'em apart from winefumey head to restless foot.'

So Ivrian let herself be persuaded and the Mouser and Fafhrd slipped off, quickly shutting the door behind them to keep out the night-smog. Their rather rapid steps down the stairs could clearly be heard from within. There were faint creakings and groanings of the ancient wood outside the wall, but no sound of another tread breaking or other mishap.

Waiting for the four jugs to be brought up from the cellar, the two newly met comrades ordered a mug each of the same fortified wine, or one near enough, and ensconced themselves at the least noisy end of the long serving counter in the tumultuous tavern. The Mouser deftly kicked a rat that thrust black head and shoulders from his hole.

After each had enthusiastically complimented the other on his girl, Fafhrd said diffidently, 'Just between ourselves, do you think there might be anything to your sweet Ivrian's notion that the small dark creature with Slivikin and the other Guild thief was a wizard's familiar, or at any rate the cunning pet of a sorcerer, trained to act as go-between and report disasters to his master or to Krovas or to both?'

The Mouser laughed lightly. 'You're building bugbears

146

– formless baby ones unlicked by logic – out of nothing, dear barbarian brother, if I may say so. *Imprimis*, we don't really know the beastie was connected with the Guild-thieves at all. May well have been a stray catling or a big bold rat – like this damned one!' He kicked again. 'But, *secundus*, granting it to be the creature of a wizard employed by Krovas, how could it make useful report? I don't believe in animals that talk – except for parrots and such birds, which only … parrot – or ones having an elaborate sign language men can share. Or perhaps you envisage the beastie dipping its paddy paw in a jug of ink and writing its report in big on a floor-spread parchment?

'Ho, there, you back of the counter! Where are my jugs? Rats eaten the boy who went for them days ago? Or he simply starved to death while on his cellar quest? Well, tell him to get a swifter move on and meanwhile brim us again!

'No, Fafhrd, even granting the beastie to be directly or indirectly a creature of Krovas, and that it raced back to Thieves' House after our affray, what could it tell them there? Only that something had gone wrong with the burglary at Jengao's. Which they'd soon suspect in any case from the delay in the thieves' and bravos' return.'

Fafhrd frowned and muttered stubbornly, 'The furry slinker might, nevertheless, convey our appearances to the Guild masters, and they might recognize us and come after us and attack us in our homes. Or Slivikin and his fat pal, revived from their bumps, might do likewise.'

'My dear friend,' the Mouser said condolingly, 'once more begging your indulgence, I fear this potent wine is addling your wits. If the Guild knew our looks or where we lodge, they'd have been nastily on our necks days, weeks, nay, months ago. Or conceivably you don't know that their penalty for free-lance or even unassigned thieving within the walls of Lankhmar and for three leagues outside them is nothing less than death, after torture if happily that can be achieved.'

'I know all about that and my plight is worse even than yours,' Fafhrd retorted, and after pledging the Mouser to secrecy told him the tale of Vlana's vendetta against the Guild and her deadly serious dreams of an all-encompassing revenge.

During the story the four jugs came up from the cellar, but the Mouser only ordered that their earthenware mugs be refilled.

Fafhrd finished, 'And so, in consequence of a promise given by an infatuated and unschooled boy in a southern angle of the Cold Waste, I find myself now as a sober – well, at other times – man being constantly asked to make war on a power as great as that of Karstak Ovartamortes, for as you may know, the Guild has locals in all other cities and major towns of this land, not to mention agreements including powers of extradition with robber and bandit organizations in other countries. I love Vlana dearly, make no mistake about that, and she is an experienced thief herself, without whose guidance I'd hardly have survived my first week in Lankhmar, but on this one topic she has a kink in her brains, a hard knot neither logic nor persuasion can even begin to loosen. And I, well, in the month I've been here I've learned that the only way to survive in civilization is to abide by its unwritten rules – far more important than its laws chiseled in stone – and break them only at peril, in deepest secrecy, and taking all precautions. As I did tonight – not my first highjacking, by the by.'

'Certes t'would be insanity to assault the Guild direct, your wisdom's perfect there,' the Mouser commented. 'If you cannot break your most handsome girl of this mad notion, or coax her from it – and I can see she's a fearless, self-willed one – then you must stoutly refuse e'en her least request in that direction.'

'Certes I must,' Fafhrd agreed, adding somewhat

accusingly, 'though I gather you told her you'd have willingly slit the throats of the two we struck senseless.'

'Courtesy merely, man! Would you have had me behave ungraciously to your girl? 'Tis measure of the value I was already setting then on your goodwill. But only a woman's man may cross her. As you must, in this instance.'

'Certes I must,' Fafhrd repeated with great emphasis and conviction. 'I'd be an idiot taking on the Guild. Of course if they should catch me they'd kill me in any case for free-lancing and highjacking. But wantonly to assault the Guild direct, kill one Guild-thief needlessly, only behave as if I might – lunacy entire!'

'You'd not only be a drunken, drooling idiot, you'd questionless be stinking in three nights at most from that emperor of diseases, Death. Malicious attacks on her person, blows directed at the organization, the Guild requites tenfold what she does other rule-breakings. All planned robberies and other thefts would be called off and the entire power of the Guild and its allies mobilized against you alone. I'd count your chances better to take on single-handed the host of the King of Kings rather than the Thieves' Guild's subtle minions. In view of your size, might, and wit you're a squad perhaps, or even a company, but hardly an army. So, no least giving-in to Vlana in this one matter.'

'Agreed!' Fafhrd said loudly, shaking the Mouser's iron-thewed hand in a near crusher grip.

'And now we should be getting back to the girls,' the Mouser said.

'After one more drink while we settle the score. Ho, boy!'

'Suits.' The Mouser dug into his pouch to pay, but Fafhrd protested vehemently. In the end they tossed coin for it, and Fafhrd won and with great satisfaction clinked out his silver smerduks on the stained and dinted counter, also marked with an infinitude of mug circles, as if it had been once the desk of a mad geometer. They pushed themselves to their feet, the Mouser giving the rathole one last light kick for luck.

At this, Fafhrd's thoughts looped back and he said, 'Grant the beastie can't paw-write, or talk by mouth or paw, it still could have followed us at distance, marked down your dwelling, and then returned to Thieves' House to lead its masters down on us like a hound!'

'Now you're speaking shrewd sense again,' the Mouser said. 'Ho, boy, a bucket of small beer to go! On the instant!' Noting Fafhrd's blank look, he explained, 'I'll spill it outside the Eel to kill our scent and all the way down the passageway. Yes, and splash it high on the walls too.'

Fafhrd nodded wisely. 'I thought I'd drunk my way past the addled point.'

Vlana and Ivrian, deep in in excited talk, both started at the pounding rush of footsteps up the stairs. Racing behemoths could hardly have made more noise. The creaking and groaning were prodigious and there were the crashes of two treads breaking, yet the pounding footsteps never faltered. The door flew open and their two men rushed in through a great mushroom top of night-smog which was neatly sliced off its black stem by the slam of the door.

'I told you we'd be back in a wink,' the Mouser cried gayly to Ivrian, while Fafhrd strode forward, unmindful of the creaking floor, crying, 'Dearest heart, I've missed you sorely,' and caught up Vlana despite her voiced protests and pushings-off and kissed and hugged her soundly before setting her back on the couch again.

Oddly, it was Ivrian who appeared to be angry at Fafhrd then, rather than Vlana, who was smiling fondly if somewhat dazedly.

'Fafhrd, sir,' she said boldly, her little fists set on her narrow hips, her tapered chin held high, her dark eyes blazing, 'my beloved Vlana has been telling me about the unspeakably atrocious things the Thieves' Guild did to her and to her dearest friends. Pardon my frank speaking to one I've only met, but I think it quite unmanly of you to refuse her the just revenge she desires and fully deserves. And that goes for you too, Mouse, who boasted to Vlana of what you would have done had you but known, who in like case did not scruple to slay my very own father – or reputed father – for his cruelties!'

It was clear to Fafhrd that while he and the Gray Mouser had idly boozed in the Eel, Vlana had been giving Ivrian a doubtless empurpled account of her grievances against the Guild and playing mercilessly on the naïve girl's bookish, romantic sympathies and high concept of knightly honor. It was also clear to him that Ivrian was more than a little drunk. A three-quarters empty flask of violet wine of far Kiraay sat on the low table next them.

Yet he could think of nothing to do but spread his big hands helplessly and bow his head, more than the low ceiling made necessary, under Ivrian's glare, now reinforced by that of Vlana. After all, they *were* in the right. He *had* promised.

So it was the Mouser who first tried to rebut.

'Come now, pet,' he cried lightly as he danced about the room, silk-stuffing more cracks against the thickening nightsmog and stirring up and feeding the fire in the stove, 'and you too, beauteous Lady Vlana. For the past month Fafhrd has been hitting the Guild-thieves where it hurts them most – in their purses a-dangle between their legs. His highjackings of the loot of their robberies have been like so many fierce kicks in their groins. Hurts worse, believe me, than robbing them of life with a swift, near painless sword slash or thrust. And tonight I helped him in his worthy purpose – and will eagerly do so again. Come, drink we up all.' Under his handling, one of the new jugs came uncorked with a pop and he darted about brimming silver cups and mugs.

'A merchant's revenge!' Ivrian retorted with scorn, not one whit appeased, but rather angered anew. 'Ye both are at heart true and gentle knights, I know, despite all current backsliding. At the least you must bring Vlana the head of Krovas!'

'What would she *do* with it? What *good* would it be except to spot the carpets?' the Mouser plaintively inquired, while Fafhrd, gathering his wits at last and going down on one knee, said slowly, 'Most respected Lady Ivrian, it is true I solemnly promised my beloved Vlana I would help her in her revenge, but that was while I was still in barbarous Cold Corner, where blood-feud is a commonplace, sanctioned by custom and accepted by all the clans and tribes and brother-hoods of the savage Northerners of the Cold Waste. In my naïveté I thought of Vlana's revenge as being of that sort. But here in civilization's midst, I discover all's different and rules and customs turned upside-down. Yet – Lankhmar or Cold Corner – one must seem to observe rule and custom to survive. Here cash is all-powerful, the idol placed highest, whether one sweat, thieve, grind others down, or scheme for it. Here feud and revenge are outside all rules and punished worse than violent lunacy. Think, Lady Ivrian, if Mouse and I should bring Vlana the head of Krovas, she and I would have to flee Lankhmar on the instant, every man's hand against us; while you infallibly would lose this fairyland Mouse has created for love of you and be forced to do likewise, be with him a beggar on the run for the rest of your natural lives.'

It was beautifully reasoned and put ... and no good whatsoever. While Fafhrd spoke, Ivrian snatched up her new-filled cup and drained it. Now she stood up straight as a soldier, her pale face flushed, and said scathingly to Fafhrd kneeling before her, '*You count the cost!* You speak to me of *things*' – she waved at the many-hued splendor around her – 'of mere property, however costly, when *honor* is at stake. You gave Vlana *your word*. Oh, is knighthood wholly dead? And that applies to you, too, Mouse, who swore you'd slit the miserable throats of two noisome Guild-thieves,'

'I didn't swear *to*,' the Mouser objected feebly, downing a big drink. 'I merely said *I would have*,' while Fafhrd could only shrug again and writhe inside and gulp a little easement from his silver mug. For Ivrian was speaking in the same guilt-showering tones and using the same unfair yet heart-cleaving womanly arguments as Mor his mother might have, or Mara, his deserted Snow Clan sweetheart and avowed wife, big-bellied by now with his child.

In a master stroke, Vlana tried gently to draw Ivrian down to her golden seat again. 'Softly, dearest,' she pleaded. 'You have spoken nobly for me and my cause, and believe me, I am most grateful. Your words revived in me great, fine feelings dead these many years. But of us here, only you are truly an aristocrat attuned to the highest proprieties. We other three are naught but thieves. Is it any wonder some of us put safety above honor and word-keeping, and most prudently avoid risking our lives? Yes, we are three thieves and I am outvoted. So please speak no more of honor and rash, dauntless bravery, but sit you down and—'

'You mean they're both *afraid* to challenge the Thieves' Guild, don't you?' Ivrian said, eyes wide and face twisted by loathing. 'I always thought my Mouse was a nobleman first and a thief second. Thieving's nothing. My father lived by cruel thievery done on rich wayfarers and neighbors less powerful than he, yet he was an aristocrat. Oh, you're *cowards*, both of you! *Poltroons!*' she finished, turning her eyes flashing with cold scorn first on the Mouser, then on Fafhrd.

The latter could stand it no longer. He sprang to his

feet, face flushed, fists clenched at his sides, quite unmindful of his down-clattered mug and the ominous creak his sudden action drew from the sagging floor.

'*I am not a coward!*' he cried. 'I'll dare Thieves' House and fetch you Krovas' head and toss it with blood a-drip at Vlana's feet. I swear that, witness me, Kos the god of dooms, by the brown bones of Nalgron my father and by his sword Graywand here at my side!'

He slapped his left hip, found nothing there but his tunic, and had to content himself with pointing tremble-armed at his belt and scabbarded sword where they lay atop his neatly folded robe – and then picking up, refilling splashily, and draining his mug.

The Gray Mouser began to laugh in high, delighted, tuneful peals. All stared at him. He came dancing up beside Fafhrd, and still smiling widely, asked, '*Why not?* Who speaks of fearing the Guild-thieves? Who becomes upset at the prospect of this ridiculously easy exploit, when all of us know that all of them, even Krovas and his ruling clique, are but pygmies in mind and skill compared to me or Fafhrd here? A wonderously simple, foolproof scheme has just occurred to me for penetrating Thieves' House, every closet and cranny. Stout Fafhrd and I will put it into effect at once. Are you with me, Northerner?'

'Of course I am,' Fafhrd responded gruffly, at the same time frantically wondering what madness had gripped the little fellow.

'Give me a few heartbeats to gather needed props, and we're off!' the Mouser cried. He snatched from a shelf and unfolded a stout sack, then raced about, thrusting into it coiled ropes, bandage rolls, rags, jars of ointment and unction and unguent, and other oddments.

'But you can't go *tonight*,' Ivrian protested, suddenly grown pale and uncertain-voiced. 'You're both ... in no condition to.'

'You're both *drunk*,' Vlana said harshly. 'Silly drunk –

and that way you'll get naught in Thieves' House but your deaths. Fafhrd, where's that heartless reason you employed to slay or ice-veined see slain a clutch of mighty rivals and win me at Cold Corner and in the chilly, sorcery-webbed depths of Trollstep Canyon? Revive it! And infuse some into your skipping gray friend.'

'Oh, no,' Fafhrd told her as he buckled on his sword. 'You wanted the head of Krovas heaved at your feet in a great splatter of blood, and that's what you're going to get, like it or not!'

'Softly, Fafhrd,' the Mouser interjected, coming to a sudden stop and drawing tight the sack's mouth by its strings. 'And softly you too, Lady Vlana, and my dear princess. Tonight I intend but a scouting expedition. No risks run, only the information gained needful for planning our murderous strike tomorrow or the day after. So no head-choppings whatsoever tonight, Fafhrd, you hear me? Whatever may hap, hist's the word. And don your hooded robe.'

Fafhrd shrugged, nodded, and obeyed.

Ivrian seemed somewhat relieved. Vlana too, though she said, 'Just the same you're both drunk.'

'All to the good!' the Mouser assured her with a mad smile. 'Drink may slow a man's sword-arm and soften his blows a bit, but it sets his wits ablaze and fires his imagination, and those are the qualities we'll need tonight. Besides,' he hurried on, cutting off some doubt Ivrian was about to voice, 'drunken men are supremely cautious! Have you ever seen a staggering sot pull himself together at sight of the guard and walk circumspectly and softly past?'

'Yes,' Vlana said, 'and fall flat on his face just as he comes abreast 'em.'

'Pish!' the Mouser retorted and, throwing back his head, grandly walked toward her along an imaginary straight line. Instantly he tripped over his own foot, plunged

155

forward, suddenly without touching floor did an incredible forward flip, heels over head, and landed erect and quite softly – toes, ankles, and knees bending just at the right moment to soak up impact – directly in front of the girls. The floor barely complained.

'You see?' he said, straightening up and unexpectedly reeling backward. He tripped over the pillow on which lay his cloak and sword, but by a wrenching twist and a lurch stayed upright and began rapidly to accouter himself.

Under cover of this action Fafhrd made quietly yet swiftly to fill once more his and the Mouser's mugs, but Vlana noted it and gave him such a glare that he set down mugs and uncorked jug so swiftly his robe swirled, then stepped back from the drinks table with a shrug of resignation and toward Vlana a grimacing nod.

The Mouser shouldered his sack and drew open the door. With a casual wave at the girls, but no word spoken, Fafhrd stepped out on the tiny porch. The night-smog had grown so thick he was almost lost to view. The Mouser waved four fingers at Ivrian, softly called, 'Bye-bye, Misling,' then followed Fafhrd.

'Good fortune go with you,' Vlana called heartily.

'Oh, be careful, Mouse,' Ivrian gasped.

The Mouser, his figure slight against the loom of Fafhrd's, silently drew shut the door.

Their arms automatically gone around each other, the girls waited for the inevitable creaking and groaning of the stairs. It delayed and delayed. The night-smog that had entered the room dissipated and still the silence was unbroken.

'What can they be doing out there?' Ivrian whispered. 'Plotting their course?'

Vlana, scowling, impatiently shook her head, then disentangled herself, tiptoed to the door, opened it, descended softly a few steps, which creaked most dolefully, then returned, shutting the door behind her.

'They're gone,' she said in wonder, her eyes wide, her hands spread a little to either side, palms up.

'I'm frightened!' Ivrian breathed and sped across the room to embrace the taller girl.

Vlana hugged her tight, then disengaged an arm to shoot the door's three heavy bolts.

In Bones Alley the Mouser returned to his pouch the knotted line by which they'd descended from the lamp hook. He suggested, 'How about stopping at the Silver Eel?'

'You mean and just *tell* the girls we've been to Thieves' House?' Fafhrd asked, not too indignantly.

'Oh, no,' the Mouser protested. 'But you missed your stirrup cup upstairs and so did I.'

At the word 'stirrup' he looked down at his ratskin boots and then crouching began a little gallop in one place, his boot-soles clopping softly on the cobbles. He flapped imaginary reins – 'Giddap!' – and quickened his gallop, but leaning sharply back pulled to a stop – 'Whoa!' – when with a crafty smile Fafhrd drew from his robe two full jugs.

'Palmed 'em, as 'twere, when I set down the mugs. Vlana sees a lot, but not all.'

'You're a prudent, far-sighted fellow, in addition to having some skill at sword taps,' the Mouser said admiringly. 'I'm proud to call you comrade.'

Each uncorked and drank a hearty slug. Then the Mouser led them west, they veering and stumbling only a little. Not so far as Cheap Street, however, but turning north into an even narrower and more noisome alley.

'Plague Court,' the Mouser said. Fafhrd nodded.

After several preliminary peepings and peerings, they staggered swiftly across wide, empty Crafts Street and into Plague Court again. For a wonder it was growing a little lighter. Looking upward, they saw stars. Yet there was no wind blowing from the north. The air was deathly still.

In their drunken preoccupation with the project at hand

and mere locomotion, they did not look behind them. There the night-smog was thicker than ever. A high-circling nighthawk would have seen the stuff converging from all sections of Lankhmar, north, east, south, west – from the Inner Sea, from the Great Salt Marsh, from the many-ditched grainlands, from the River Hlal – in swift-moving black rivers and rivulets, heaping, eddying, swirling, dark and reeking essence of Lankhmar from its branding irons, braziers, bonfires, bonefires, kitchen fires and warmth fires, kilns, forges, breweries, distilleries, junk and garbage fires innumerable, sweating alchemists' and sorcerers' dens, crematoriums, charcoal burners' turfed mounds, all those and many more … converging purposefully on Dim Lane and particularly on the Silver Eel and perhaps especially on the ricketty house behind it, untenanted except for attic. The closer to that center it got, the more substantial the smog became, eddy-strands and swirl-tatters tearing off and clinging to rough stone corners and scraggly-surfaced brick like black cobwebs.

But the Mouser and Fafhrd merely exclaimed in mild, muted amazement at the stars, muggily mused as to how much the improved visibility would increase the risk of their quest, and cautiously crossing the Street of the Thinkers, called Atheist Avenue by moralists, continued to Plague Court until it forked.

The Mouser chose the left branch, which trended northwest.

'Death Alley.'

Fafhrd nodded.

After a curve and recurve, Cheap Street swung into sight about thirty paces ahead. The Mouser stopped at once and lightly threw his arm against Fafhrd's chest.

Clearly in view across Cheap Street was a wide, low, open doorway, framed by grimy stone blocks. There led up to it two steps hollowed by the treadings of centuries. Orange-yellow light spilled out from bracketed torches inside. They couldn't see very far in because of Death Alley's angle. Yet as far as they *could* see, there was no porter or guard in sight, nor anyone at all, not even a watchdog on a chain. The effect was ominous.

'Now how do we get into the damn place?' Fafhrd demanded in a hoarse whisper. 'Scout Murder Alley for a back window that can be forced? You've pries in that sack, I trow. Or try the roof? You're a roof man, I know already. Teach me the art. I know trees and mountains, snow, ice, and bare rock. See this wall here?' He backed off from it, preparing to up it in a rush.

'Steady on, Fafhrd,' the Mouser said, keeping his hand against the big young man's chest. 'We'll hold the roof in reserve. Likewise all walls. And I'll take it on trust you're a master climber. As to how we get in, we walk straight through that doorway.' He frowned. 'Tap and hobble, rather. Come on, while I prepare us.'

As he drew the skeptically grimacing Fafhrd back down Death Alley until all Cheap Street was again cut off from view, he explained. 'We'll pretend to be beggars, members of *their* guild, which is but a branch of the Thieves' Guild and houses with it, or at any rate reports in to the Beggarmasters at Thieves' House. We'll be new members, who've gone out by day, so it'll not be expected that the Night Beggarmaster and any night watchmen know our looks.'

'But we don't look like beggars,' Fafhrd protested. 'Beggars have awful sores and limbs all a-twist or lacking altogether.'

'That's just what I'm going to take care of now,' the Mouser chuckled, drawing Scalpel. Ignoring Fafhrd's backward step and wary glance, the Mouser gazed puzzledly at the long tapering strip of steel he'd bared, then with a happy nod unclipped from his belt Scalpel's scabbard furbished with ratskin, sheathed the sword and swiftly wrapped it up, hilt and all, in a spiral, with the wide ribbon of a bandage roll dug from his sack.

'There!' he said, knotting the bandage ends. 'Now I've a tapping cane.'

'What's that?' Fafhrd demanded. 'And why?'

'Because I'll be blind, that's why.' He took a few shuffling steps, tapping the cobbles ahead with wrapped sword – gripping it by the quillons, or cross-guard, so that the grip and pommel were up his sleeve – and groping ahead with his other hand. 'That look all right to you?' he asked Fafhrd as he turned back. 'Feels perfect to me. Bat-blind, eh? Oh, don't fret, Fafhrd – the rag's but gauze. I can see through it fairly well. Besides, I don't have to convince anyone inside Thieves' House I'm actually blind. Most Guild-beggars fake it, as you must know. Now what to do with you? Can't have you blind also – too obvious, might wake suspicion.' He uncorked his jug and sucked inspiration. Fafhrd copied this action, on principle.

The Mouser smacked his lips and said, 'I've got it! Fafhrd, stand on your right leg and double up your left behind you at the knee. Hold! Don't fall on me! Avaunt! But steady yourself by my shoulder. That's right. Now get that left foot higher. We'll disguise your sword like mine, for a crutch cane – it's thicker and'll look just right. You can also steady yourself with your other hand on my shoulder as you hop – the halt leading the blind, always good for a tear, always good theater! But higher with that left foot! No, it just doesn't come off – I'll have to rope it. But first unclip your scabbard.'

Soon the Mouser had Graywand and its scabbard in the same state as Scalpel and was tying Fafhrd's left ankle to his thigh, drawing the rope cruelly tight, though Fafhrd's wine-anesthetized nerves hardly registered it. Balancing himself with his steel-corded crutch cane as the Mouser worked, he swigged from his jug and pondered deeply. Ever since joining forces with Vlana, he'd been interested

160

in the theater, and the atmosphere of the actors' tenement had fired that interest further, so that he was delighted at the prospect of acting a part in real life. Yet brilliant as the Mouser's plan undoubtedly was, there did seem to be drawbacks to it. He tried to formulate them.

'Mouser,' he said, 'I don't know as I like having our swords tied up, so we can't draw 'em in emergency.'

'We can still use 'em as clubs,' the Mouser countered, his breath hissing between his teeth as he drew the last knot hard. 'Besides, we'll have our knives. Say, pull your belt around until yours is behind your back, so your robe will hide it sure. I'll do the same with Cat's Claw. Beggars don't carry weapons, at least in view, and we must maintain dramatic consistency in every detail. Stop drinking now; you've had enough. I myself need only a couple swallows more to reach my finest pitch.'

'And I don't know as I like going hobbled into that den of cutthroats. I can hop amazingly fast, it's true, but not as fast as I can run. Is it really wise, think you?'

'You can slash yourself loose in an instant,' the Mouser hissed with a touch of impatience and anger. 'Aren't you willing to make the least sacrifice for art's sake?'

'Oh, very well,' Fafhrd said, draining his jug and tossing it aside. 'Yes, of course I am.'

'Your complexion's too hale,' the Mouser said, inspecting him critically. He touched up Fafhrd's features and hands with pale gray greasepaint, then added wrinkles with dark. 'And your garb's too tidy.' He scooped dirt from between the cobbles and smeared it on Fafhrd's robe, then tried to put a rip in it, but the material resisted. He shrugged and tucked his lightened sack under his belt.

'So's yours,' Fafhrd observed, and stooping on his right leg got a good handful of muck himself, ordure in it by its feel and stink. Heaving himself up with a mighty effort, he wiped the stuff off on the Mouser's cloak and gray silken jerkin too.

161

The small man got the odor and cursed, but, 'Dramatic consistency,' Fafhrd reminded him. 'It's well we stink. Beggars do – that's one reason folk give 'em coins: to get rid of 'em. And no one at Thieves' House will be eager to inspect us close. Now come on, while our fires are still high.' And grasping hold of the Mouser's shoulder, he propelled himself rapidly toward Cheap Street, setting his bandaged sword between cobbles well ahead and taking mighty hops.

'Slow down, idiot,' the Mouser cried softly, shuffling along with the speed almost of a skater to keep up, while tapping his (sword) cane like mad. 'A cripple's supposed to be *feeble* – that's what draws the sympathy.'

Fafhrd nodded wisely and slowed somewhat. The ominous empty doorway slid again into view. The Mouser tilted his jug to get the last of his wine, swallowed awhile, then choked sputteringly. Fafhrd snatched and drained the jug, then tossed it over shoulder to shatter noisily.

They hop-shuffled into Cheap Street, halting almost at once for a richly clad man and woman to pass. The richness of the man's garb was sober and he was on the fat and oldish side, though hard-featured. A merchant doubtless, and with money in the Thieves' Guild – protection money, at least – to take this route at this hour.

The richness of the woman's garb was garish though not tawdry and she was beautiful and young, and looked still younger. A competent courtesan, almost certainly.

The man started to veer around the noisome and filthy pair, his face averted, but the girl swung toward the Mouser, concern growing in her eyes with hothouse swiftness. 'Oh, you poor boy! Blind. What tragedy,' she said. 'Give us a gift for him, lover.'

'Keep away from those stinkards, Misra, and come along,' he retorted, the last of his speech vibrantly muffled, for he was holding his nose.

She made him no reply, but thrust white hand into his

ermine pouch and swiftly pressed a coin against the Mouser's palm and closed his fingers on it, then took his head between her palms and kissed him sweetly on the lips before letting herself be dragged on.

'Take good care of the little fellow, old man,' she called fondly back to Fafhrd while her companion grumbled muffled reproaches at her, of which only 'perverted bitch' was intelligible.

The Mouser stared at the coin in his palm, then sneaked a long look after his benefactress. There was a dazed wonder in his voice as he whispered to Fafhrd, 'Look. *Gold.* A golden coin and a beautiful woman's sympathy. Think you we should give over this rash project and for a profession take up beggary?'

'Buggery even, rather!' Fafhrd answered harsh and low. That 'old man' rankled. 'Onward we, bravely!'

They upped the two worn steps and went through the doorway, noting the exceptional thickness of the wall. Ahead was a long, straight, high-ceilinged corridor ending in a stairs and with doors spilling light at intervals and well-set torches adding their flare, but empty all its length.

They had just got through the doorway when cold steel chilled the neck and pricked a shoulder of each of them. From just above, two voices commanded in unison, 'Halt!'

Although fired – and fuddled – by fortified wine, they each had wit enough to freeze and then very cautiously look upward.

Two gaunt, scarred, exceptionally ugly faces, each topped by a gaudy scarf binding back hair, looked down at them from a big, deep niche just above the doorway and helping explain its lowness. Two bent, gnarly arms thrust down the swords that still pricked them.

'Gone out with the noon beggar-batch, eh?' one of them observed. 'Well, you'd better have a high take to justify your tardy return. The Night Beggarmaster's on a Whore Street furlough. Report above to Krovas. Gods, you stink!

Better clean up first, or Krovas will have you bathed in live steam. Begone!'

The Mouser and Fafhrd shuffled and hobbled forward at their most authentic. One niche-guard cried after them, 'Relax, boys! You don't have to put it on here.'

'Practice makes perfect,' the Mouser called back in a quavering voice. Fafhrd's finger-ends dug his shoulder warningly. They moved along somewhat more naturally, so far as Fafhrd's tied-up leg allowed.

'Gods, what an easy life the Guild-beggars have,' the other niche-guard observed to his mate. 'What slack discipline and low standards of skill! Perfect, my sacred butt! You'd think a child could see through those disguises.'

'Doubtless some children do,' his mate retorted. 'But their dear mothers and fathers only drop a tear and a coin or give a kick. Grown folk go blind, lost in their toil and dreams, unless they have a profession such as thieving which keeps them mindful of things as they really are.'

Resisting the impulse to ponder this sage philosophy, and glad they would not have to undergo a Beggarmaster's shrewd inspection – truly, thought Fafhrd, Kos of the Dooms seemed to be leading him direct to Krovas and perhaps head-chopping *would* be the order of the night – he and the Mouser went watchfully and slowly on. And now they began to hear voices, mostly curt and clipped ones, and other noises.

They passed some doorways they'd liked to have paused at, to study the activities inside, yet the most they dared do was slow down a bit more. Fortunately most of the doorways were wide, permitting a fairly long view.

Very interesting were some of those activities. In one room young boys were being trained to pick pouches and slit purses. They'd approach from behind an instructor, and if he heard scuff of bare foot or felt touch of dipping hand – or, worst, heard *clunk* of dropped leaden mock-coin

– that boy would be thwacked. Others seemed to be getting training in group-tactics: the jostle in front, the snatch from behind, the swift passing of lifted items from youthful thief to confederate.

In a second room, from which pushed air heavy with the reeks of metal and oil, older student thieves were doing laboratory work in lock picking. One group was being lectured by a grimy-handed graybeard, who was taking apart a most complex lock piece by weighty piece. Others appeared to be having their skill, speed, and ability to work soundlessly tested – they were probing with slender picks the keyholes in a half dozen doors set side-by-side in an otherwise purposeless partition, while a supervisor holding a sandglass watched them keenly.

In a third, thieves were eating at long tables. The odors were tempting, even to men full of booze. The Guild did well by its members.

In a fourth, the floor was padded in part and instruction was going on in slipping, dodging, ducking, tumbling, tripping, and otherwise foiling pursuit. These students were older too. A voice like a sergeant-major's rasped, 'Nah, nah, nah! You couldn't give your crippled grandmother the slip. I said duck, not genuflect to holy Aarth. Now this time—'

'Grif's used grease,' an instructor called.

'He has, eh? To the front, Grif!' the rasping voice replied as the Mouser and Fafhrd moved somewhat regretfully out of sight, for they realized much was to be learned here: tricks that might stand them in good stead even tonight. 'Listen, all of you!' the rasping voice continued, so far-carrying it followed them a surprisingly long way. 'Grease may be very well on a night job – by day its glisten shouts its user's profession to all Nehwon! But in any case it makes a thief overconfident. He comes to depend on it and then in a pinch he finds he's forgot to apply it. Also its aroma can betray him. Here we work

165

always dry-skinned – save for natural sweat! – as all of you were told first night. Bend over, Grif. Grasp your ankles. Straighten your knees.'

More thwacks, followed by yelps of pain, distant now, since the Mouser and Fafhrd were halfway up the end-stairs, Fafhrd vaulting somewhat laboriously as he grasped curving banister and swaddled sword.

The second floor duplicated the first, but was as luxurious as the other had been bare. Down the long corridor lamps and filagreed incense pots pendant from the ceiling alternated, diffusing a mild light and spicy smell. The walls were richly draped, the floor thick-carpeted. Yet this corridor was empty too and, moreover, *completely* silent. After a glance at each other, they started off boldly.

The first door, wide open, showed an untenanted room full of racks of garments, rich and plain, spotless and filthy, also wig stands, shelves of beards and such, and several wall mirrors faced by small tables crowded with cosmetics and with stools before them. A disguising room, clearly.

After a look and listen either way, the Mouser darted in and out to snatch up a large green flask from the nearest table. He unstoppered and sniffed it. A rotten-sweet gardenia-reek contended with the nose-sting of spirits of wine. The Mouser sloshed his and Fafhrd's fronts with this dubious perfume.

'Antidote to ordure,' he explained with the pomp of a physician, stoppering the flask. 'Don't want to be parboiled by Krovas. No, no, no.'

Two figures appeared at the far end of the corridor and came toward them. The Mouser hid the flask under his cloak, holding it between elbow and side, and he and Fafhrd continued onward – to turn back would look suspicious, both drunkenly judged.

The next three doorways they passed were shut by heavy doors. As they neared the fifth, the two approaching figures, coming on arm-in-arm, yet taking long strides, moving more swiftly than the hobble-shuffle, became distinct. Their clothing was that of noblemen, but their faces those of thieves. They were frowning with indignation and suspicion too at the Mouser and Fafhrd.

Just then – from somewhere between the two man-pairs, it sounded – a voice began to speak words in a strange tongue, using the rapid monotone priests employ in a routine service or some sorcerers in their incantations.

The two richly clad thieves slowed at the seventh doorway and looked in. Their progress ceased altogether. Their necks strained, their eyes widened. They visibly paled. Then of a sudden they hastened onward, almost running, and bypassed Fafhrd and the Mouser as if they were furniture. The incantatory voice drummed on without missing a beat.

The fifth doorway was shut, but the sixth was open. The Mouser peeked in with one eye, his nose brushing the jamb. Then he stepped forward and gazed inside with entranced expression, pushing the black rag up onto his forehead for better vision. Fafhrd joined him.

It was a large room, empty so far as could be told of human and animal life, but filled with most interesting things. From knee-height up, the entire far wall was a map of the city of Lankhmar and its immediate surrounds. Every building and street seemed depicted, down to the meanest hovel and narrowest court. There were signs of recent erasure and redrawing at many spots, and here and there little colored hieroglyphs of mysterious import.

The floor was marble, the ceiling blue as lapis lazuli. The side walls were thickly hung, by ring and padlock. One was covered with all manner of thieves' tools, from a huge thick pry-bar that looked as if it could unseat the universe, or at least the door of the overlord's treasure-vault, to a rod so slim it might be an elf-queen's wand and seemingly designed to telescope out and fish from distance

167

for precious gauds on milady's spindle-legged, ivory-topped vanity table; the other wall had on it all sorts of quaint, gold-gleaming and jewel-flashing objects, evidently mementos chosen for their oddity from the spoils of memorable burglaries, from a female mask of thin gold, breathlessly beautiful in its features and contours, but thickly set with rubies simulating the spots of the pox in its fever-stage, to a knife whose blade was wedge-shaped diamonds set side by side and this diamond cutting-edge looking razor-sharp.

All about were tables set chiefly with models of dwelling houses and other buildings, accurate to the last minutia, it looked, of ventilation hole under roof gutter and ground-level drain hole, of creviced wall and smooth. Many were cut away in partial or entire section to show the layout of rooms, closets, strongrooms, doorways, corridors, secret passages, smoke-ways, and air-ways in equal detail.

In the center of the room was a bare round-table of ebony and ivory squares. About it were set seven straight-backed but well-padded chairs, the one facing the map and away from the Mouser and Fafhrd being higher backed and wider armed than the others – a chief's chair, likely that of Krovas.

The Mouser tiptoed forward, irresistibly drawn, but Fafhrd's left hand clamped down on his shoulder like the iron mitten of a Mingol cataphract and drew him irresistibly back.

Scowling his disapproval, the Northerner brushed down the black rag over the Mouser's eyes again, and with his crutch-hand thumbed ahead; then set off in that direction in most carefully calculated, silent hops. With a shrug of disappointment the Mouser followed.

As soon as they had turned away from the doorway, but before they were out of sight, a neatly black-bearded, crop-haired head came like a serpent's around the side of the highest-backed chair and gazed after them from deep-sunken yet glinting eyes. Next a snake-supple, long hand followed the head out, crossed thin lips with ophidian fore-finger for silence, and then finger-beckoned the two pairs of dark-tunicked men who were standing to either side of the doorway, their backs to the corridor wall, each of the four gripping a curvy knife in one hand and a dark leather, lead-weighted bludgeon in the other.

When Fafhrd was halfway to the seventh doorway, from which the monotonous yet sinister recitation continued to well, there shot out through it a slender, whey-faced youth, his narrow hands clapped over his mouth, under terror-wide eyes, as if to shut in screams or vomit, and with a broom clamped in an armpit, so that he seemed a bit like a young warlock about to take to the air. He dashed past Fafhrd and the Mouser and away, his racing footsteps sounding rapid-dull on the carpeting and hollow-sharp on the stairs before dying away.

Fafhrd gazed back at the Mouser with a grimace and shrug, then squatting one-legged until the knee of his bound-up leg touched the floor, advanced half his face past the doorjamb. After a bit, without otherwise changing position, he beckoned the Mouser to approach. The latter slowly thrust half his face past the jamb, just above Fafhrd's.

What they saw was a room somewhat smaller than that of the great map and lit by central lamps that burned blue-white instead of customary yellow. The floor was marble, darkly colorful and complexly whorled. The dark walls were hung with astrological and anthropomantic charts and instruments of magic and shelved with cryptically labeled porcelain jars and also with vitreous flasks and glass pipes of the oddest shapes, some filled with colored fluids, but many gleamingly empty. At the foot of the walls, where the shadows were thickest, broken and discarded stuff was irregularly heaped, as if swept out of the way and forgot, and here and there opened a large rathole.

In the center of the room and brightly illuminated by contrast was a long table with thick top and many stout legs. The Mouser thought fleetingly of a centipede and then of the bar at the Eel, for the tabletop was densely stained and scarred by many a spilled elixir and many a deep black burn by fire or acid or both.

In the midst of the table an alembic was working. The lamp's flame – deep blue, this one – kept a-boil in the large crystal cucurbit a dark, viscid fluid with here and there diamond glints. From out of the thick, seething stuff, strands of a darker vapor streamed upward to crowd through the cucurbit's narrow mouth and stain – oddly, with bright scarlet – the transparent head and then, dead black now, flow down the narrow pipe from the head into a spherical crystal receiver, larger even than the cucurbit, and there curl and weave about like so many coils of living black cord – an endless, skinny, ebon serpent.

Behind the left end of the table stood a tall, yet hunchbacked man in black robe and hood, which shadowed more than hid a face of which the most prominent features were a long, thick, pointed nose with out-jutting, almost chinless mouth just below. His complexion was sallow-gray like clay and a short-haired, bristly, gray beard grew high on his wide cheeks. From under a receding forehead and bushy gray brows, wide-set eyes looked intently down at an age-browned scroll, which his disgustingly small clubhands, knuckles big, short backs gray-bristled, ceaselessly unrolled and rolled up again. The only move his eyes ever made, besides the short side-to-side one as he read the lines he was rapidly intoning, was an occasional farther sidewise glance at the alembic.

On the other end of the table, beady eyes darting from the sorcerer to the alembic and back again, crouched a small black beast, the first glimpse of which made Fafhrd dig fingers painfully into the Mouser's shoulder and the latter almost gasp, not from the pain. It was most like a rat, yet it had a higher forehead and closer-set eyes that either had ever seen in a rat, while its forepaws, which it constantly rubbed together in what seemed restless glee, looked like tiny copies of the sorcerer's clubhands.

Simultaneously yet independently, Fafhrd and the Mouser each became certain it was the beast which had gutter-escorted Slivikin and his mate, then fled, and each recalled what Ivrian had said about a witch's familiar and Vlana about the likelihood of Krovas employing a warlock.

What with the ugliness of the clubhanded man and beast and between them the ropy black vapor coiling and twisting in the great receiver and head, like a black umbilical cord, it was a most horrid sight. And the similarities, save for size, between the two creatures were even more disquieting in their implications.

The tempo of the incantation quickened, the blue-white flames brightened and hissed audibly, the fluid in the cucurbit grew thick as lava, great bubbles formed and loudly broke, the black rope in the receiver writhed like a nest of snakes; there was an increasing sense of invisible presences, the supernatural tension grew almost unendurable, and Fafhrd and the Mouser were hard put to keep silent the open-mouthed gasps by which they now breathed, and each feared his heartbeat could be heard cubits away.

Abruptly the incantation peaked and broke off, like a drum struck very hard, then instantly silenced by palm and fingers outspread against the head. With a bright flash and dull explosion, cracks innumerable appeared in the cucurbit; its crystal became white and opaque, yet it did not shatter or drip. The head lifted a span, hung there, fell back. While two black nooses appeared among the coils in the receiver and suddenly narrowed until they were only two big black knots.

The sorcerer grinned, rolling up the end of the

parchment with a snap, and shifted his gaze from the receiver to his familiar, while the latter chittered shrilly and bounded up and down in rapture.

'Silence, Slivikin! Comes now your time to race and strain and sweat,' the sorcerer cried, speaking pidgin Lankhamarese now, but so rapidly and in so squeakingly high-pitched a voice that Fafhrd and the Mouser could barely follow him. They did, however, both realize they had been completely mistaken as to the identity of Slivikin. In moment of disaster, the fat thief had called to the witch-beast for help rather than to his human comrade.

'Yes, master,' Slivikin squeaked back no less clearly, in an instant revising the Mouser's opinions about talking animals. He continued in the same fifelike, fawning tones, 'Harkening in obedience, Hristomilo.'

Now they knew the sorcerer's name too.

Hristomilo ordered in whiplash pipings, 'To your appointed work! See to it you summon an ample sufficiency of feasters! I want the bodies stripped to skeletons, so the bruises of the enchanted smog and all evidence of death by suffocation will be vanished utterly. But forget not the loot! On your mission, now – depart!'

Slivikin, who at every command had bobbed his head in manner reminiscent of his bouncing, now squealed, 'I'll see it done!' and gray-lightninglike leaped a long leap to the floor and down an inky rathole.

Hristomilo, rubbing together his disgusting clubhands much as Slivikin had his, cried chucklingly, 'What Slevyas lost, my magic has rewon!'

Fafhrd and the Mouser drew back out of the doorway, partly with the thought that since neither his incantation and his alembic, nor his familiar now required his unblinking attention, Hristomilo would surely look up and spot them; partly in revulsion from what they had seen and heard; and in poignant if useless pity for Slevyas, whoever he might be, and for the other unknown victims of the rat-

172

like and conceivably rat-related sorcerer's death-spells, poor strangers already dead and due to have their flesh eaten from their bones.

Fafhrd wrested the green bottle from the Mouser and, though almost gagging on the rotten-flowery reek, gulped a large, stinging mouthful. The Mouser couldn't quite bring himself to do the same, but was comforted by the spirits of wine he inhaled during this byplay.

Then he saw, beyond Fafhrd, standing before the doorway to the map room, a richly clad man with gold-hilted knife jewel-scabbarded at his side. His sunken-eyed face was prematurely wrinkled by responsibility, overwork, and authority, and framed by neatly cropped black hair and beard. Smiling, he silently beckoned them.

The Mouser and Fafhrd obeyed, the latter returning the green bottle to the former, who recapped it and thrust it under the left elbow with well-concealed irritation.

Each guessed their summoner was Krovas, the Guild's Grandmaster. Once again Fafhrd marveled, as he hobble-dehoyed along, reeling and belching, how Kos or the Fates were guiding him to his target tonight. The Mouser, more alert and more apprehensive too, was reminding himself that they had been directed by the niche-guards to report to Krovas, so that the situation, if not developing quite in accord with his own misty plans, was still not deviating disastrously.

Yet not even his alertness, nor Fafhrd's primeval instincts, gave him forewarning as they followed Krovas into the map room.

Two steps inside, each of them was shoulder-grabbed and bludgeon-menaced by a pair of ruffians further armed with knives tucked in their belts.

They judged it wise to make no resistance, on this one occasion at least bearing out the Mouser's mouthings about the supreme caution of drunken men.

'All secure, Grandmaster,' one of the ruffians rapped out.

Krovas swung the highest-backed chair around and sat down, eyeing them cooly yet searchingly.

'What brings two stinking, drunken beggar-Guildsmen into the top-restricted precincts of the masters?' he asked quietly.

The Mouser felt the sweat of relief bead his forehead. The disguises he had brilliantly conceived were still working, taking in even the head man, though he had spotted Fafhrd's tipsiness. Resuming his blind-man manner, he quavered, 'We were directed by the guard above the Cheap Street door to report to you in person, great Krovas, the Night Beggarmaster being on furlough for reasons of sexual hygiene. Tonight we've made good haul!' And fumbling in his purse, ignoring as far as possible the tightened grip on his shoulders he brought out the golden coin given him by the sentimental courtesan and displayed it tremble-handed.

'Spare me your inexpert acting,' Krovas said sharply. 'I'm not one of your marks. And take that rag off your eyes.'

The Mouser obeyed and stood to attention again insofar as his pinioning would permit, and smiling the more seeming carefree because of his reawakening uncertainties. Conceivably he wasn't doing quite as brilliantly as he'd thought.

Krovas leaned forward and said placidly yet piercingly, 'Granted you were so ordered – and most improperly so; that door-guard will suffer for his stupidity! – why were you spying into a room beyond this one when I spotted you?'

'We saw brave thieves flee from that room,' the Mouser answered pat. 'Fearing that some danger threatened the Guild, my comrade and I investigated, ready to scotch it.'

'But what we saw and heard only perplexed us, great sir,' Fafhrd appended quite smoothly.

'I didn't ask you, sot. Speak when you're spoken to,' Krovas snapped at him. Then, to the Mouser, 'You're an overweening rogue, most presumptuous for your rank.'

In a flash the Mouser decided that further insolence, rather than fawning, was what the situation required. 'That I am, sir,' he said smugly. 'For example, I have a master plan whereby you and the Guild might gain more wealth and power in three months than your predecessors have in three millennia.'

Krovas' face darkened. 'Boy!' he called. Through the curtains of an inner doorway, a youth, with dark complexion of a Kleshite and clad only in a black loincloth sprang to kneel before Krovas, who ordered, 'Summon first my sorcerer, next the thieves Slevyas and Fissif,' whereupon the dark youth dashed into the corridor.

Then Krovas, his face its normal pale again, leaned back in his great chair, lightly rested his sinewy arms on its great padded ones, and smilingly directed the Mouser, 'Speak your piece. Reveal to us this master plan.'

Forcing his mind *not* to work on the surprising news that Slevyas was not victim but thief and not sorcery-slain but alive and available – why did Krovas want him *now*? – the Mouser threw back his head and, shaping his lips in a faint sneer, began, 'You may laugh merrily at me, Grandmaster, but I'll warrant that in less than a score of heartbeats you'll be straining sober-faced to hear my least word. Like lightning, wit can strike anywhere, and the best of you in Lankhmar have age-honored blind spots for things obvious to us of outland birth. My master plan is but this: let Thieves' Guild under your iron autocracy seize supreme power in Lankhmar City, then in Lankhmar Land, next over all Nehwon, after which who knows what realms undreamt will know your suzerainty!'

The Mouser had spoken true in one respect: Krovas

was no longer smiling. He was leaning forward a little and his face was darkening again, but whether from interest or anger it was too soon to say.

The Mouser continued, 'For centuries the Guild's had more than the force and intelligence needed to make a *coup d'état* a nine-finger certainty; today there's not one hair's chance in a bush head of failure. It is the proper state of things that thieves rule other men. All Nature cries out for it. No need slay old Karstak Ovartamortes, merely overmaster, control, and so rule through him. You've already fee'd informers in every noble or wealthy house. Your post's better than the King of Kings'. You've a mercenary striking force permanently mobilized, should you have need of it, in the Slayers' Brotherhood. We Guild-beggars are your foragers. O great Krovas, the multitudes know that thievery rules Nehwon, nay, the universe, nay, more, the highest gods' abode! And the multitudes accept this, they balk only at the hypocrisy of the present arrangement, at the pretense that things are otherwise. Oh, give them their decent desire, great Krovas! Make it all open, honest and aboveboard, with thieves ruling in name as well as fact.'

The Mouser spoke with passion, for the moment believing all he said, even the contradictions. The four ruffians gaped at him with wonder and not a little awe. They slackened their holds on him and on Fafhrd too.

But leaning back in his great chair again and smiling thinly and ominously, Krovas said cooly, 'In *our* Guild intoxication is no excuse for folly, rather grounds for the extremest penalty. But I'm well aware you organized beggars operate under a laxer discipline. So I'll deign to explain to you, you wee drunken dreamer, that we thieves know well that, behind the scenes, we already rule Lankhmar, Nehwon, all life in sooth – for what is life but greed in action? But to make this an open thing would not only force us to take on ten thousand sorts of weary work others now do for us, it would also go against another of life's deep laws: illusion. Does the sweetmeats hawker show you his kitchen? Does a whore let average client watch her enamel-over her wrinkles and hoist her sagging breasts in cunning gauzy slings? Does a conjuror turn out for you his hidden pockets? Nature works by subtle, secret means – man's invisible seed, spider bite, the viewless spores of madness and of death, rocks that are born in earth's unknown bowels, the silent stars a-creep across the sky – and we thieves copy her.'

'That's good enough poetry, sir,' Fafhrd responded with undertone of angry derision, for he had himself been considerably impressed by the Mouser's master plan and was irked that Krovas should do insult to his new friend by disposing of it so lightly. 'Closet kingship may work well enough in easy times. But' – he paused histrionically – 'will it serve when Thieves' Guild is faced with an enemy determined to obliterate it forever, a plot to wipe it entirely from the earth?'

'What drunken babble's this?' Krovas demanded, sitting up straight. '*What* plot?'

''Tis a most *secret* one,' Fafhrd responded grinning, delighted to pay this haughty man in his own coin and thinking it quite just that the thief-king sweat a little before his head was removed for conveyance to Vlana. 'I know naught of it, except that many a master thief is marked down for the knife – and your head doomed to fall!'

Fafhrd merely sneered his face and folded his arms, the still slack grip of his captors readily permitting it, his (sword) crutch hanging against his body from his lightly gripping hand. Then he scowled as there came a sudden shooting pain in his numbed, bound-up left leg, which he had forgotten for a space.

Krovas raised a clenched fist and himself half out of his chair, in prelude to some fearsome command – likely that Fafhrd be tortured. The Mouser cut in hurriedly with,

'The Secret Seven, they're called, are its leaders. None in the outer circles of the conspiracy know their names, though rumor has it that they're secret Guild-thief renegades representing, one for each, the cities of Oool Hrusp, Kvarch Nar, Ilthmar, Horborixen, Tisilinilit, far Kriaay and Lankhmar's very self. It's thought they're moneyed by the merchants of the East, the priests of Wan, the sorcerers of the Steppes and half the Mingol leadership too, legended Quarmall, Aarth's Assassins in Sarheenmar, and also no lesser man than the King of Kings.'

Despite Krovas' contemptuous and then angry remarks, the ruffians holding the Mouser continued to harken to their captive with interest and respect, and they did not retighten their grip on him. His colorful revelations and melodramatic delivery held them, while Krovas' dry, cynical, philosophic observations largely went over their heads.

Hristomilo came gliding into the room then, his feet presumably taking swift, but very short steps, at any rate his black robe hung undisturbed to the marble floor despite his slithering speed.

There was a shock at his entrance. All eyes in the map room followed him, breaths were held, and the Mouser and Fafhrd felt the horny hands that gripped them shake just a little. Even Krovas' all-confident, world-weary expression became tense and guardedly uneasy. Clearly the sorcerer of the Thieves' Guild was more feared than loved by his chief employer and by the beneficiaries of his skills.

Outwardly oblivious to this reaction to his appearance, Hristomilo, smiling thin-lipped, halted close to one side of Krovas' chair and inclined his hood-shadowed rodent face in the ghost of a bow.

Krovas held palm toward the Mouser for silence. Then, wetting his lips, he asked Hristomilo sharply yet nervously, 'Do you know these two?'

Hristomilo nodded decisively. 'They just now peered a befuddled eye each at me,' he said, 'whilst I was about that business we spoke of. I'd have shooed them off, reported them, save such action might have broken my spell, put my words out of time with the alembic's workings. The one's a Northerner, the other's features have a southern cast – from Tovilyis or near, most like. Both younger than their now-looks. Free-lance bravos, I'd judge 'em, the sort the Brotherhood hires as extras when they get at once several big guard and escort jobs. Clumsily disguised now, of course, as beggars.'

Fafhrd by yawning, the Mouser by pitying headshake tried to convey that all this was so much poor guesswork.

'That's all I can tell you without reading their minds,' Hristomilo concluded. 'Shall I fetch my lights and mirrors?'

'Not yet.' Krovas turned face and shot a finger at the Mouser. 'How do you know these things you rant about? – Secret Seven and all. Straight simplest answer now – no rodomontades.'

The Mouser replied most glibly: 'There's a new courtesan dwells on Pimp Street – Tyarya her name, tall, beauteous, but hunchbacked, which oddly delights many of her clients. Now Tyarya loves me 'cause my maimed eyes match her twisted spine, or from simply pity of my blindness – *she* believes it! – and youth, or from some odd itch, like her clients' for her, which that combination arouses in her flesh.

'Now one of her patrons, a trader newly come from Klelg Nar – Mourph, he's called – was impressed by my intelligence, strength, boldness, and closemouthed tact, and those same qualities in my comrade too. Mourph sounded us out, finally asking if we hated the Thieves' Guild for its control of the Beggars' Guild. Sensing a chance to aid the Guild, we played up, and a week ago he recruited us into a cell of three in the outermost strands of the conspiracy web of the Seven.'

'You presumed to do all of this on your own?' Krovas demanded in freezing tones, sitting up straight and gripping hard the chair arms.

'Oh, no,' the Mouser denied guilelessly. 'We reported our every act to the Day Beggarmaster and he approved them, told us to spy our best and gather every scrap of fact and rumor we could about the Seven's conspiracy.'

'And he told me not a word about it!' Krovas rapped out. 'If true, I'll have Bannat's head for this! But you're lying, aren't you?'

As the Mouser gazed with wounded eyes at Krovas, meanwhile preparing a most virtuous denial, a portly man limped past the doorway with help of a gilded staff. He moved with silence and aplomb.

But Krovas saw him. 'Night Beggarmaster!' he called sharply. The limping man stopped, turned, came crippling majestically through the door. Krovas stabbed finger at the Mouser, then Fafhrd. 'Do you know these two, Flim?'

The Night Beggarmaster unhurriedly studied each for a space, then shook his head with its turban of cloth of gold. 'Never seen either before. What are they? Fink beggars?'

'But Flim wouldn't know us,' the Mouser explained desperately, feeling everything collapsing in on him and Fafhrd. 'All our contacts were with Bannat alone.'

Flim said quietly, 'Bannat's been abed with the swamp ague this past ten-day. Meanwhile *I* have been Day Beggarmaster as well as Night.'

At that moment Slevyas and Fissif came hurrying in behind Flim. The tall thief bore on his jaw a bluish lump. The fat thief's head was bandaged above his darting eyes. He pointed quickly at Fafhrd and the Mouser and cried, 'There are the two that slugged us, took our Jengao loot, and slew our escort.'

The Mouser lifted his elbow and the green bottle

crashed to shards at his feet on the hard marble. Gardenia-reek sprang swiftly through the air.

But more swiftly still the Mouser, shaking off the careless hold of his startled guards, sprang toward Krovas, clubbing his wrapped-up sword. If he could only overpower the King of Thieves and hold Cat's Claw at his throat, he'd be able to bargain for his and Fafhrd's lives. That is, unless the other thieves wanted their master killed, which wouldn't surprise him at all.

With startling speed Flim thrust out his gilded staff, tripping the Mouser, who went heels over head, midway seeking to change his involuntary somersault into a voluntary one.

Meanwhile Fafhrd lurched heavily against his left-hand captor, at the same time swinging bandaged Graywand strongly upward to strike his right-hand captor under the jaw. Regaining his one-legged balance with a mighty contortion, he hopped for the loot-wall behind him.

Slevyas made for the wall of thieves' tools, and with a muscle-cracking effort wrenched the great pry-bar from its padlocked ring.

Scrambling to his feet after a poor landing in front of Krovas' chair, the Mouser found it empty and the Thief King in a half-crouch behind it, gold-hilted dagger drawn, deep-sunk eyes coldly battle-wild. Spinning around, he saw Fafhrd's guards on the floor, the one sprawled senseless, the other starting to scramble up, while the great Northerner, his back against the wall of weird jewelry, menaced the whole room with wrapped-up Graywand and with his long knife, jerked from its scabbard behind him.

Likewise drawing Cat's Claw, the Mouser cried in trumpet voice of battle, 'Stand aside, all! He's gone mad! I'll hamstring his good leg for you!' And racing through the press and between his own two guards, who still appeared to hold him in some awe, he launched himself with flashing dirk at Fafhrd, praying that the Northerner, drunk now with battle as well as wine and poisonous perfume, would recognize him and guess his stratagem.

Graywand slashed well above his ducking head. His new friend not only guessed, but was playing up – and not just missing by accident, the Mouser hoped. Stooping low by the wall, he cut the lashings on Fafhrd's left leg. Graywand and Fafhrd's long knife continued to spare him. Springing up, he headed for the corridor, crying over-shoulder to Fafhrd, 'Come on!'

Hristomilo stood well out of his way, quietly observing. Fissif scuttled toward safety. Krovas stayed behind his chair, shouting, 'Stop them! Head them off!'

The three remaining ruffian guards, at last begining to recover their fighting-wits, gathered to oppose the Mouser. But menacing them with swift feints of his dirk, he slowed them and darted between – and then just in the nick of time knocked aside with a downsweep of wrapped-up Scalpel Flim's gilded staff, thrust once again to trip him.

All this gave Slevyas time to return from the toolswall and aim at the Mouser a great swinging blow with the massive pry-bar. But even as that blow started, a very long, bandaged sword on a very long arm thrust over the Mouser's shoulder and solidly and heavily poked Slevyas high on the chest, jolting him backward, so that the pry-bar's swing was short and whistled past harmlessly.

Then the Mouser found himself in the corridor and Fafhrd beside him, though for some weird reason still only hopping. The Mouser pointed toward the stairs. Fafhrd nodded, but delayed to reach high, still on one leg only, and rip off the nearest wall a dozen cubits of heavy drapes, which he threw across the corridor to baffle pursuit.

They reached the stairs and started up the next flight, the Mouser in advance. There were cries behind, some muffled.

'Stop hopping, Fafhrd!' the Mouser ordered queru-lously. 'You've got two legs again.'

'Yes, and the other's still dead,' Fafhrd complained. 'Ahh! Now feeling begins to return to it.'

A thrown knife whisked between them and dully clinked as it hit the wall point-first and stone-powder flew. Then they were around the bend.

Two more empty corridors, two more curving flights, and then they saw above them on the last landing a stout ladder mounting to a dark, square hole in the roof. A thief with hair bound back by a colorful handkerchief – it appeared to be a doorguards' identification – menaced the Mouser with drawn sword, but when he saw that there were two of them, both charging him determinedly with shining knives and strange staves of clubs, he turned and ran down the last empty corridor.

The Mouser, followed closely by Fafhrd, rapidly mounted the ladder and without pause vaulted up through the hatch into the star-crusted night.

He found himself near the unrailed edge of a slate roof which slanted enough to have made it look most fearsome to a novice roof-walker, but safe as houses to a veteran.

Crouched on the long peak of the roof was another kerchiefed thief holding a dark lantern. He was rapidly covering and uncovering, presumably in some code, the lantern's bull's eye, whence shot a faint green beam north to where a red point of light winked dimly in reply – as far away as the sea wall, it looked, or perhaps the masthead of a ship beyond, riding in the Inner Sea. Smuggler?

Seeing the Mouser, this one instantly drew sword and, swinging the lantern a little in his other hand, advanced menacingly. The Mouser eyed him warily – the dark lantern with its hot metal, concealed flame, and store of oil would be a tricky weapon.

But then Fafhrd had clambered out and was standing beside the Mouser, on both feet again at last. Their adversary backed slowly away toward the north end of the roof ridge. Fleetingly the Mouser wondered if there was another hatch there.

Turning back at a bumping sound, he saw Fafhrd prudently hoisting the ladder. Just as he got it free, a knife flashed up close past him out of the hatch. While following its flight, the Mouser frowned, involuntarily admiring the skill required to hurl a knife vertically with any accuracy.

It clattered down near them and slid off the roof. The Mouser loped south across the slates and was halfway from the hatch to that end of the roof when the faint chink came of the knife striking the cobbles of Murder Alley.

Fafhrd followed more slowly, in part perhaps from a lesser experience of roofs, in part because he still limped a bit to favor his left leg, and in part because he was carrying the heavy ladder balanced on his right shoulder.

'We won't need that,' the Mouser called back.

Without hesitation Fafhrd heaved it joyously over the edge. By the time it crashed in Murder Alley, the Mouser was leaping down two yards and across a gap of one to the next roof, of opposite and lesser pitch. Fafhrd landed beside him.

The Mouser led them at almost a run through a sooty forest of chimneys, chimney pots, ventilators with tails that made them always face the wind, black-legged cisterns, hatch covers, bird houses, and pigeon traps across five roofs, four progressively a little lower, the fifth regaining a yard of the altitude they'd lost – the spaces between the buildings easy to leap, none more than three yards, no ladder-bridge required, and only one roof with a some-what greater pitch than that of Thieves' House – until they reached the Street of the Thinkers at a point where it was crossed by a roofed passageway much like the one at Rokkermas and Slaarg's.

While they crossed it at a crouching lope, something hissed close past them and clattered ahead. As they leaped down from the roof of the bridge, three more somethings hissed over their heads to clatter beyond. One rebounded from a square chimney almost to the Mouser's feet. He picked it up, expecting a stone, and was surprised by the greater weight of a leaden ball big as two doubled-up fingers.

'They,' he said, jerking thumb overshoulder, 'lost no time in getting slingers on the roof. When roused, they're good.'

Southeast then through another black chimney-forest to a point on Cheap Street where upper stories overhung the street so much on either side that it was easy to leap the gap. During this roof-traverse, an advancing front of night-smog, dense enough to make them cough and wheeze, had engulfed them and for perhaps sixty heartbeats the Mouser had had to slow to a shuffle and feel his way, Fafhrd's hand on his shoulder. Just short of Cheap Street they had come abruptly and completely out of the smog and seen the stars again, while the black front had rolled off northward behind them.

'Now what the devil was that?' Fafhrd had asked and the Mouser had shrugged.

A nighthawk would have seen a vast thick hoop of black night-smog blowing out in all directions from a center near the Silver Eel, growing ever greater and greater in diameter and circumferences.

East of Cheap Street the two comrades soon made their way to the ground, landing back in Plague Court behind the narrow premises of Nattick Nimblefingers the Tailor.

Then at last they looked at each other and their trammeled swords and their filthy faces and clothing made dirtier still by roof-soot, and they laughed and laughed and laughed Fafhrd roaring still as he bent over to massage his left leg above and below knee. This hooting and wholly unaffected self-mockery continued while they unwrapped their swords – the Mouser as if his were a surprise package – and clipped their scabbards once more to their belts.

Their exertions had burned out of them the last mote and atomy of strong wine and even stronger stenchful perfume, but they felt no desire whatever for more drink, only the urge to get home and eat hugely and guzzle hot, bitter gahveh, and tell their lovely girls angth the tale of the their mad adventure.

They loped on side by side, at intervals glancing at each other and chuckling, though keeping a normally wary eye behind and before for pursuit or interception, despite their expecting neither.

Free of night-smog and drizzled with starlight, their cramped surroundings seemed much less stinking and oppressive than when they had set out. Even Ordure Boulevard had a freshness to it.

Only once for a brief space did they grow serious.

Fafhrd said, 'You were a drunken idiot-genius indeed tonight, even if I was a drunken clodhopper. Lashing up my leg! Tying up our swords so we couldn't use 'em save as clubs!'

The Mouser shrugged. 'Yet that sword-tying doubtless saved us from committing a number of murders tonight.'

Fafhrd retorted, a little hotly, 'Killing in fight isn't murder.'

Again the Mouser shrugged. 'Killing is murder, no matter what nice names you give. Just as eating is devouring, and drinking guzzling. Gods, I'm dry, famished, and fatigued! Come on, soft cushions, food, and steaming gahveh!'

They hastened up the long, creaking, broken-treaded stairs with an easy carefulness and when they were both on the porch, the Mouser shoved at the door to open it with surprise-swiftness.

It did not budge.

'Bolted,' he said to Fafhrd shortly. He noted now there was hardly any light at all coming through the cracks around the door, or noticeable through the lattices – at most, a faint orange-red glow. Then with sentimental grin and in a fond voice in which only the ghost of uneasiness lurked, he said, 'They've gone to sleep, the unworrying wenches!' He knocked loudly thrice and then cupping his lips shouted softly at the door crack, 'Hola, Ivrian! I'm home safe. Hail, Vlana! Your man's done you proud, felling Guide-thieves innumerable with one foot tied behind his back!'

There was no sound whatever from inside – that is, if one discounted a rustling so faint it was impossible to be sure of it.

Fafhrd was wrinkling his nostrils. 'I smell smoke.'

The Mouser banged on the door again. Still no response.

Fafhrd motioned him out of the way, hunching his big shoulder to crash the portal.

The Mouser shook his head and with a deft tap, slide, and tug removed a brick that a moment before had looked a firm-set part of the wall beside the door. He reached in all his arm. There was the scrape of a bolt being withdrawn, then another, then a third. He swiftly recovered his arm and the door swung fully inward at a touch.

But neither he nor Fafhrd rushed in at once, as both had intended to, for the indefinable scent of danger and the unknown came puffing out along with an increased reek of smoke and a slight sickening sweet scent that though female was no decent female perfume, and a musty-sour animal odor.

They could see the room faintly by the orange glow coming from the small oblong of the open door of the little, well-blacked stove. Yet the oblong did not sit properly upright but was unnaturally a-tilt; clearly the stove had been half overset and now leaned against a side wall of the fireplace, its small door fallen open in that direction.

By itself alone, that unnatural angle conveyed the entire impact of a universe overturned.

The orange glow showed the carpets oddly rucked up with here and there black circles a palm's breadth across, the neatly stacked candles scattered about below their shelves along with some of the jars and enameled boxes, and, above all, two black, low, irregular, longish heaps, the one by the fireplace, the other half on the golden couch, half at its foot.

From each head there stared at the Mouser and Fafhrd innumerable pairs of tiny, rather widely set, furnace-red eyes.

On the thickly carpeted floor on the other side of the fireplace was a silver cobweb – a fallen silver cage, but no love birds sang from it.

There was a faint scrape of metal as Fafhrd made sure Graywand was loose in his scabbard.

As if that tiny sound had beforehand been chosen as the signal for attack, each instantly whipped out sword and they advanced side by side into the room, warily at first, testing the floor with each step.

At the screech of the swords being drawn, the tiny furnace-red eyes had winked and shifted restlessly, and now with the two men's approach they swiftly scattered pattering, pair by red pair, each pair at the forward end of a small, low, slender, hairless-tailed black body, and each making for one of the black circles in the rugs, where they vanished.

Indubitably the black circles were ratholes newly gnawed up through the floor and rugs, while the red-eyed creatures were black rats.

Fafhrd and the Mouser sprang forward, slashing and chopping at them in a frenzy, cursing and human-snarling besides.

They sundered few. The rats fled with preternatural

swiftness, most of them disappearing down holes near the walls and the fireplace.

Also Fafhrd's first frantic chop went through the floor and on his third step with an ominous crack and splintering his leg plunged through the floor to his hip. The Mouser darted past him, unmindful of further crackings.

Fafhrd heaved out his trapped leg, not even noting the splinter-scratches it got and as unmindful as the Mouser of the continuing creakings. The rats were gone. He lunged after his comrade, who had thrust a bunch of kindlers into the stove, to make more light.

The horror was that, although the rats were all gone, the two longish heaps remained, although considerably diminished and, as now shown clearly by the yellow flames leaping from the tilted black door, changed in hue – no longer were the heaps red-beaded black, but a mixture of gleaming black and dark brown, a sickening purple-blue, violet and velvet black and ermine white, and the reds of stockings and blood and bloody flesh and bone.

Although hands and feet had been gnawed bone-naked, and bodies tunneled heart-deep, the two faces had been spared. That was not good, for they were the parts purple-blue from death by strangulation, lips drawn back, eyes bulging, all features contorted in agony. Only the black and very dark brown hair gleamed unchanged – that and the white, white teeth.

As each man stared down at his love, unable to look away despite the waves of horror and grief and rage washing higher and higher in him, each saw a tiny black strand uncurl from the black depression ringing each throat and drift off, dissipating, toward the open door behind them – two strands of night-smog.

With a crescendo of crackings the floor sagged fully three spans more in the center before arriving at a new temporary stability.

Edges of centrally tortured minds noted details: that Vlana's silver-hilted dagger skewered to the floor a rat, which, likely enough, overeager had approached too closely before the night-smog had done its magic work. That her belt and pouch were gone. That the blue-enameled box inlaid with silver, in which Ivrian had put the Mouser's share of the highjacked jewels, was gone too.

The Mouser and Fafhrd lifted to each other white, drawn faces which were quite mad, yet completely joined in understanding and purpose. No need to tell each other what must have happened here when the two nooses of black vapor had jerked tight in Hristomilo's receiver, or why Slivikin had bounced and squeaked in glee, or the significance of such phrases as 'an ample sufficiency of feasters,' or 'forget not the loot,' or 'that business we spoke of.' No need for Fafhrd to explain why he now stripped off his robe and hood, or why he jerked up Vlana's dagger, snapped the rat off it with a wrist-flick, and thrust it in his belt. No need for the Mouser to tell why he searched out a half dozen jars of oil and after smashing three of them in front of the flaming stove, paused, thought, and stuck the other three in the sack at his waist, adding to them the remaining kindlers and the fire-pot, brimmed with red coals, its top lashed down tight.

Then, still without word exchanged, the Mouser muffled his hand with a small rug and reaching into the fireplace deliberately tipped the flaming stove forward, so that it fell door-down on oil-soaked rugs. Yellow flames sprang up around him.

They turned and raced for the door. With louder crackings than any before, the floor collapsed. They desperately scrambled their way up a steep hill of sliding carpets and reached door and porch just before all behind them gave way and the flaming rugs and stove and all the firewood and candles and the golden couch and all the little tables and boxes and jars – and the unthinkably mutilated bodies of their first loves – cascaded into the dry, dusty, cobweb-choked room below, and the great flames of a cleansing or at least obliterating cremation began to flare upward.

They plunged down the stairs, which tore away from the wall and collapsed and dully crashed in the dark just as they reached the ground. They had to fight their way over the wreckage to get to Bones Alley.

By then flames were darting their bright lizard-tongues out of the shuttered attic windows and the boarded-up ones in the story just below. By the time they reached Plague Court, running side by side at top speed, the Silver Eel's fire-alarm was clanging cacophonously behind them.

They were still sprinting when they took the Death Alley fork. Then the Mouser grappled Fafhrd and forced him to a halt. The big man struck out, cursing insanely, and only desisted – his white face still a lunatic's – when the Mouser cried, panting, 'Only ten heartbeats to arm us!'

He pulled the sack from his belt and, keeping tight hold of its neck, crashed it on the cobbles – hard enough to smash not only the bottles of oil, but also the fire-pot, for the sack was soon flaming a little at its base.

Then he drew gleaming Scalpel and Fafhrd Graywand and they raced on, the Mouser swinging his sack in a great circle beside him to fan its flames. It was a veritable ball of fire burning his left hand as they dashed across Cheap Street and into Thieves' House, and the Mouser, leaping high, swung it up into the great niche above the doorway and let go of it.

The niche-guards screeched in surprise and pain at the fiery invader of their hidey-hole and had no time to do anything with their swords, or whatever weapons else they had, against the other two invaders.

Student thieves poured out of the doors ahead at the screeching and foot-pounding, and then poured back as they saw the fierce point of flames and the two demon-faced oncomers brandishing their long, shining swords.

One skinny little apprentice – he could hardly have been ten years old – lingered too long. Graywand thrust him pitilessly through as his big eyes bulged and his small mouth gaped in horror and plea to Fafhrd for mercy.

Now from ahead of them there came a weird, wailing call, hollow and hair-raising, and doors began to thud shut instead of spewing forth the armed guards they almost prayed would appear to be skewered by their swords. Also, despite the long, bracketed torches looking newly renewed, the corridor was dark.

The reason for this last became clear as they plunged up the stairs. Strands of night-smog were appearing in the well, materializing from nothing or the air.

The strands grew longer and more numerous and tangible. They touched and clung nastily. In the corridor above they were forming from wall to wall and from ceiling to floor, like a gigantic cobweb, and were becoming so substantial that the Mouser and Fafhrd had to slash them to get through, or so their two maniac minds believed. The black web muffled a little a repetition of the eerie, wailing call, which came from the seventh door ahead and this time ended in a gleeful chittering and cackling insane as the emotions of the two attackers.

Here too doors were thudding shut. In an ephemeral flash of rationality, it occurred to the Mouser that it was not he and Fafhrd the thieves feared, for they had not been seen yet, but rather Hristomilo and his magic, even though working in defense of Thieves' House.

Even the map room, whence counter-attack would most likely erupt, was closed off by a huge oaken, iron-studded door.

They were now twice slashing black, clinging, rope-thick spiderweb for every single step they drove themselves forward. Midway between the map and magic rooms, there was forming on the inky web, ghostly at first but swiftly growing more substantial, a black spider big as a wolf.

The Mouser slashed heavy cobweb before it, dropped back two steps, then hurled himself at it in a high leap. Scalpel thrust through it, striking amidst its eight new-formed jet eyes, and it collapsed like a daggered bladder, loosing a vile stink.

Then he and Fafhrd were looking into the magic room, the alchemist's chamber. It was much as they had seen it before, except some things were doubled, or multiplied even further.

On the long table two blue-boiled cucurbits bubbled and roiled, their heads shooting out a solid, writhing rope more swiftly than moves the black swamp-cobra, which can run down a man – and not into twin receivers, but into the open air of the room (if any of the air in Thieves' House could have been called open then) to weave a barrier between their swords and Hristomilo, who once more stood tall though hunch-backed over his sorcerous, brown parchment, though this time his exultant gaze was chiefly fixed on Fafhrd and the Mouser, with only an occasional downward glance at the text of the spell he drummingly intoned.

At the other end of the table, in the web-free space, there bounced not only Slivikin, but also a huge rat matching him in size in all members except the head.

From the ratholes at the foot of the walls, red eyes glittered and gleamed in pairs.

With a bellow of rage Fafhrd began slashing at the black barrier, but the ropes were replaced from the cucurbit heads as swiftly as he sliced them, while the cut ends, instead of drooping slackly, now began to strain hungrily toward him like constrictive snakes or strangle-vines.

He suddenly shifted Graywand to his left hand, drew his long knife and hurled it at the sorcerer. Flashing toward its mark, it cut through three strands, was deflected and slowed by a fourth and fifth, almost halted by a sixth, and ended hanging futilely in the curled grip of a seventh.

Hristomilo laughed cacklingly and grinned, showing his huge upper incisors, while Slivikin chittered in ecstasy and bounded the higher.

The Mouser hurled Cat's Claw with no better result – worse, indeed, since his action gave two darting smog-strands time to curl hamperingly around his sword-hand and stranglingly around his neck. Black rats came racing out of the big holes at the cluttered base of the walls.

Meanwhile other strands snaked around Fafhrd's ankles, knees and left arm, almost toppling him. But even as he fought for balance, he jerked Vlana's dagger from his belt and raised it over his shoulder, its silver hilt glowing, its blade brown with dried rat's-blood.

The grin left Hristomilo's face as he saw it. The sorcerer screamed strangely and importuningly then and drew back from his parchment and the table, and raised clawed clubhands to ward off doom.

Vlana's dagger sped unimpeded through the black web – its strands even seemed to part for it – and betwixt the sorcerer's warding hands, to bury itself to the hilt in his right eye.

He screamed thinly in dire agony and clawed at his face.

The black web writhed as if in death spasm.

The cucurbits shattered as one, spilling their lava on the scarred table, putting out the blue flames even as the thick wood of the table began to smoke a little at the lava's edge. Lava dropped with *plops* on the dark marble floor.

With a faint, final scream Hristomilo pitched forward, hands still clutched to his eyes above his jutting nose, silver dagger-hilt still protruding between his fingers.

The web grew faint, like wet ink washed with a gush of clear water.

The Mouser raced forward and transfixed Slivikin and the huge rat with one thrust of Scalpel before the beasts knew what was happening. They too died swiftly with thin screams, while all the other rats turned tail and fled back down their holes swift almost as black lightning.

Then the last trace of night-smog or sorcery-smoke vanished and Fafhrd and the Mouser found themselves standing alone with three dead bodies and a profound silence that seemed to fill not only this room but all Thieves' House. Even the cucurbit-lava had ceased to move, was hardening, and the wood of the table no longer smoked.

Their madness was gone and all their rage too – vented to the last red atomy and glutted to more than satiety. They had no more urge to kill Krovas or any other of the thieves than to swat flies. With horrified inner eye Fafhrd saw the pitiful face of the child-thief he'd skewered in his lunatic anger.

Only their grief remained with them, diminished not one whit, but rather growing greater – that and an ever more swiftly growing revulsion from all that was around them: the dead, the disordered magic room, all Thieves' House, all of the city of Lankhmar to its last stinking alleyway and smog-wreathed spire.

With a hiss of disgust the Mouser jerked Scalpel from the rodent cadavers, wiped it on the nearest cloth, and returned it to its scabbard. Fafhrd likewise sketchily cleansed and sheathed Graywand. Then the two men picked up their knife and dirk from where they'd dropped to the floor when the web had dematerialized, though neither so much as glanced at Vlana's dagger where it was buried. But on the sorcerer's table they did notice Vlana's black velvet, silver-worked pouch and belt, the latter half overrun by the hardened black lava, and Ivrian's blue-enameled box inlaid with silver. From these they took the gems of Jengao.

With no more word than they had exchanged back at the Mouser's burned nest behind the Eel, but with a continuing sense of their unity of purpose, their identity of intent, and of their comradeship, they made their way with shoulders bowed and with slow, weary steps which only very gradually quickened out of the magic room and down the thick-carpeted corridor, past the map room's wide door still barred with oak and iron, and past all the other shut, silent doors – clearly the entire Guild was terrified of Hristomilo, his spells, and his rats; down the echoing stairs, their footsteps speeding a little; down the bare-floored lower corridor past its closed, quiet doors, their footsteps resounding loudly no matter how softly they sought to tread; under the deserted, black-scorched guard-niche, and so out into Cheap Street, turning left and north because that was the nearest way to the Street of the Gods, and there turning right and east – not a waking soul in the wide street except for one skinny, bent-backed apprentice lad unhappily swabbing the flagstones in front of a wine shop in the dim pink light beginning to seep from the east, although there were many forms asleep, a-snore and a-dream in the gutters and under the dark porticos – yes, turning right and east down the Street of the Gods, for that way was the Marsh Gate, leading to Causey Road across the Great Salt Marsh, and the Marsh Gate was the nearest way out of the great and glamorous city that was now loathsome to them, indeed, not to be endured for one more stabbing, leaden heartbeat than was necessary – a city of beloved, unfaceable ghosts.

SWORDS
AGAINST DEATH

Book 2 in the Swords Series

CONTENTS

Gods and the Street of the Thinkers (called by theologians Atheists' Avenue), and backed by Murder Alley – the immense guild hall of the altogether-too-well organized Thieves of Lankhmar; skulkers of tremendous skill, cutpurses unparalleled, pickpockets nonpareil, picklocks without match, stealers extraordinary, even on occasion extraordinarily expert killers – though preferring to hire out such work to the Slayers' Brotherhood (another organization which Fafhrd and the Mouser detest). Of odd disguises and a black kitten. Of a tasty redhead named Ivlis and her maid. Of dust and death.

well-known dangers of stealing the eye of an idol, whether the idol be doll-tiny or mountain-huge. Ice, snows, volcanoes, lava – and seven most deadly killers.

Another old theme: the danger of those feathered reptiles, birds. Lankhmar upside-down, with the hawks freed and all her most beautiful women wearing gold and silver cages around their faces. Strange domestic arrangements – and re-arrangements – of the fat merchant Muulsh, his most tantalizing young wife Atya, and her maid.

How the Gray Mouser and Fafhrd were finally most unhappily rid of the ghosts of Ivrian and Vlana, and then became eternal servants, after a fashion and only part-time, of Sheelba of the Eyeless Face and Ningauble of the Seven Eyes. Of an utter madman with an utterly magnificent project. Of an ill-placed dwelling near Dim Lane, of the Shadowland and its most grim ruler. Also of dust and death. But also of rebirth, or, anyhow, re-lust.

Of one of the earliest services of Fafhrd and the Mouser to their wizardly employers Ningauble and Sheelba. Of a blight on existence. Of the showiest and spiciest shop in any of the many universes. Of the horrid Devourers and their abominable tactics and of how the Gray Mouser and Fafhrd, by sheerest luck, finally bested them. Of how, most delectably and properly, girls are for dessert. But unfortunately spiders too.

I: THE CIRCLE CURSE

A tall swordsman and a small one strode out the Marsh
Gate of Lankhmar and east along Causey Road. They
were youths by their skin and suppleness, men by their
expressions of deep-bitten grief and stony purpose.

The sleepy guardsmen in browned-iron cuirasses did
not question them. Only madmen and fools willingly leave
the grandest city in the world of Nehwon, especially at
dawn and afoot. Besides, these two looked extremely
dangerous.

Ahead the sky was bright pink, like the bubbling rim of
a great crystal goblet brimmed with effervescent red wine
for delight of the gods, while the paler pink glow rising
therefrom drove the last stars west. But before the sun
could glare one scarlet sliver above the horizon, a black
storm came racing out of the north over the Inner Sea – a
sea-squall making landfall. It grew almost as dark again as
night, except when the lightning stabbed and the thunder
shook his great iron shield. The stormwind carried the
salty tang of the sea commingled with the foul reek of the
marsh. It bent the green swords of the sea grass flat and
lashed into writhing the arms of the thorn and seahawk
trees. It pushed black swampwater a yard up the northern
side of the narrow, serpentine, flat-topped ridge that was
Causey Road. Then came pelting rain.

The two swordsmen made no comment to each other
and did not alter their movements, except to lift their

shoulders and faces a little and slant the latter north, as if they welcomed the storm's cleansing and sting and what tiny distraction it brought to some deep agony of mind and heart.

'Ho, Fafhrd!' a deep voice grated above the thunder's growl and the wind's roar and the rattle of the rain.

The tall swordsman turned his head sharply south.

'Hist, Gray Mouser!'

The small swordsman did likewise.

Close by the southern side of the road a rather large, rounded hut stood on five narrow posts. The posts had to be tall, for Causey Road ran high here yet the floor of the hut's low, rounded doorway looked straight at the tall swordsman's head.

This was nothing very strange, except that all men know that none dwell in the venomous Great Salt Marsh, save for giant worms, poison eels, water cobras, pale spindle-legged swamp rats, and the like.

Blue lightning glared, revealing with great clarity a hooded figure crouched inside the low doorway. Each fold and twist of the figure's draperies stood out as precisely as in an iron engraving closely viewed.

But the lightning showed nothing whatsoever inside the hood, only inky blackness.

Thunder crashed.

Then from the hood the grating voice recited the following lines, harshly and humorlessly hammering out the words, so that what was light verse became a dismal and doomful incantation:

> *Ho, Fafhrd tall!*
> *Hist, Mouser small!*
> *Why leave you the city*
> *Of marvelous parts?*
> *It were a great pity*
> *To wear out your hearts*

> *And wear out the soles of your feet,*
> *Treading all earth,*
> *Foregoing all mirth,*
> *Before you once more Lankhmar greet.*
> *Now return, now return, now!*

This doleful ditty was three-quarters done before the two swordsmen realized that they were striding along steadily all this while and the hut still abreast them. So it must be walking along with them on its posts, or legs rather. And now that they were aware of this, they could see those five thin wooden members swinging and knee-bending.

When the grating voice ceased to speak on that last great 'now', Fafhrd halted.

So did the Mouser.

So did the hut.

The two swordsmen turned toward the low doorway, facing it squarely.

Simultaneously with deafening thunderclap, a great bolt of lightning struck close behind them. It jolted their bodies, shocked their flesh thrillingly and painfully, and it illumined the hut and its dweller brighter than day, yet still revealed nothing inside the dweller's hood.

If the hood had been empty, the draperies at its back would have been shown clearly. But no, there was only that oval of ebon darkness, which even the levinbolt could not illumine.

As unmoved by this prodigy as by the thunder-stroke, Fafhrd bellowed above the storm toward the doorway, his voice sounding tiny to himself in his thunder-smitten ears, 'Hear me, witch, wizard, nightgaunt, whatever you are! I shall never in my life enter again the foul city which has stolen from me my dearest and only love, the incomparable and irreplaceable Vlana, for whom I shall forever grieve and for whose unspeakable death I shall forever feel guilt. The Thieves' Guild slew her for her free-lance thieving – and we slew the slayers, though it profited us nothing at all.'

'Likewise I shall never lift foot toward Lankhmar again,' the Gray Mouser took up from beside him in a voice like an angry trumpet, 'the loathy metropolis which horribly bereft me of my beloved Ivrian, even as Fafhrd was bereft and for similar reason, and left me loaded with an equal weight of sorrow and shame, which I shall bear forever, even past my perishing.' A salt spider big as a platter sailed close by his ear in the grip of the gale, kicking its thick, corpse-white legs, and veered off past the hut, but the Mouser did not start in the least and there was no break whatever in his words as he continued, 'Know, being of blackness, haunter of the dark, that we slew the foul wizard who murdered our loves and killed his two rodentine familiars and mauled and terrorized his employers at Thieves' House. But revenge is empty. It cannot bring back the dead. It cannot assuage by one atom the grief and guilt we shall feel forever for our darlings.'

'Indeed it cannot,' Fafhrd seconded loudly, 'for we were drunk when our darlings died, and for that there is no forgiveness. We highjacked a small treasure in gems from thieves of the Guild, but we lost the two jewels beyond price and without compare. And we shall never return to Lankhmar!'

Lightning shone from beyond the hut and thunder crackled. The storm was moving inland, south from the road.

The hood that held darkness drew back a little and slowly shook from side to side, once, twice, thrice. The harsh voice intoned, fainter because Fafhrd's and the Mouser's ears were still somewhat deafened and a-ring from that father of thunderstrokes:

Never and forever are neither for men,
You'll be returning again and again.

Then the hut was moving inland too on its five spindly legs. It turned around, so that its door faced away from them, and its speed increased, its legs moving nimbly as those of a cockroach, and was soon lost amongst the tangle of thorn and seahawk trees.

So ended the first encounter of the Mouser and his comrade Fafhrd with Sheelba of the Eyeless Face.

Later that day the two swordsmen waylaid an insufficiently guarded merchant Lankhmar-bound, depriving him of the best two of his four cart-horses – for thieving was first nature to them – and on these clumping mounts made their way out of the Great Salt Marsh and across the Sinking Land to the sinister hub-city of Ilthmar with its treacherous little inns and innumerable statues and bas-reliefs and other depictions of its rat-god. There they changed their clumsy horses for camels and were soon humping south across the desert, following the eastern shore of the turquoise Sea of the East. They crossed the River Tilth in dry season and continued on through the sands, bound for the Eastern Lands, where neither of them had previously traveled. They were searching for distraction in strangeness and intended first to visit Horborixen, citadel of the King of Kings and city second only to Lankhmar in size, antiquity, and baroque splendor.

For the next three years, the Years of Leviathan, the Roc, and the Dragon, they wandered the world of Nehwon south, east, north, and west, seeking forgetfulness of their first great loves and their first great guilts and finding neither. They ventured east past mystic Tisilinilit with its slender, opalescent spires, which always seemed newly crystallized out of its humid, pearly skies, to lands that were legends in Lankhmar and even Horborixen. One amongst many was the skeletally shrunken Empire of

Eevamarensee, a country so decadent, so far-grown into the future, that all the rats and men are bald and even the dogs and cats hairless.

Returning by a northerly route through the Great Steppes, they narrowly escaped capture and enslavement by the pitiless Mingols. In the Cold Waste they sought for Fafhrd's Snow Clan, only to discover that it had been last year overwhelmed by a lemming horde of Ice Gnomes and, according to best rumor, massacred to the last person, which would have included Fafhrd's mother Mor, his deserted girl-bride Mara, and his first issue if any.

For a space they served Lithquil, the Mad Duke of Ool Hrusp, devising for him sprightly mock-duels, simulated murders, and other entertainments. Then they coasted south through the Outer Sea aboard a Sarheenmar trader to tropic Klesh, where they adventured a while in the jungle fringes. Then north again, circling past secretest Quarmall, that shadow realm, to the Lakes of Pleea that are the headwaters of the Hlal and to the beggar-city of Tovilyis, where the Gray Mouser believed he had been birthed, but was not sure, and when they left that lowly metropolis he was no surer. Crossing by grain barge the Sea of the East, they prospected for gold a while in the Mountains of the Elder Ones, their last highjacked gems having been long since gambled away or spent. Unsuccessful in this quest, they wended their way west again toward the Inner Sea and Ilthmar.

They lived by thievery, robbery, bodyguarding, brief commissions as couriers and agents – commissions they always, or almost always, fulfilled punctiliously – and by showmanship, the Mouser entertaining by legerdemain, juggling, and buffoonery, while Fafhrd with his gift for tongues and training as a Singing Skald excelled at minstrelsy, translating the legends of his frigid homeland into many languages. They never worked as cooks, clerks, carpenters, tree-fellers, or common servants and they never, never, never enlisted as mercenary soldiers – their service to Lithquil having been of a more personal nature.

They acquired new scars and skills, comprehensions and compassions, cynicisms and secrecies – a laughter that lightly mocked and a cool poise that tightly crusted all inner miseries and most of the time hid the barbarian in Fafhrd and the slum boy in the Mouser. They became outwardly merry, uncaring, and cool, but their grief and guilt stayed with them, the ghosts of Ivrian and Vlana haunting their sleeping and their waking dreams, so that they had little commerce with other girls, and that more a discomfort than a joy. Their comradeship became firmer than a rock, stronger than steel, but all other human relations were fleeting. Melancholy was their commonest mood, though mostly hid even from each other.

Came noon of the Day of the Mouse in the Month of the Lion in the Year of the Dragon. They were taking their siestas in the cool of a cave near Ilthmar. Outside, heat shimmered above hard-baked ground and scanty brown grass, but here was most pleasant. Their horses, a gray mare and a chestnut gelding, found shade in the cavern's mouth. Fafhrd had sketchily inspected the place for serpents, but discovered none. He loathed the cold scaly ones of the south, so different from the hot-blooded, fur-bearing snakes of the Cold Waste. He went a little way into a narrow, rocky corridor leading from the back of the cave under the small mountain in which it was set, but returned when light failed and he had found neither reptiles nor end.

They rested comfortably on their uncurled bedrolls. Sleep would not come to them, so idle talk did. By slow stages this talk became serious. Finally the Gray Mouser summed up the last trinity of years.

'We have searched the wide world over and not found forgetfulness.'

'I dispute that,' Fafhrd countered. 'Not the latter part,

for I am still as ghost-locked as you, but we have not crossed the Outer Sea and hunted over the great continent legend will have in the west.'

'I believe we have,' the Mouser disputed. 'Not the former part, I'll agree, and what purpose in searching the sea? But when we went out farthest east and stood on the shore of that great ocean, deafened by its vast surf, I believe we stood on the western coast of the Outer Sea with nothing between us and Lankhmar but wild water.'

'What great ocean?' Fafhrd demanded. 'And what vast surf? It was a lake, a mere puddle with some ripples in it. I could readily see the opposite shore.'

'Then you were seeing mirages, friend of mine, and languishing in one of those moods when all Nehwon seems but a small bubble you could burst with flick of fingernail.'

'Perhaps,' Fafhrd agreed. 'Oh, how weary I am of this life.'

There was a little cough, no more than a clearing of throat, in the dark behind them. They did not otherwise move, but their hair stirred at its roots, so close and intimate had been that tiny noise, and so indicative of intelligence rather than mere animality, because of a measuredly attention-asking quality about it.

Then as one they turned head over shoulder and looked back at the black mouth of the rocky corridor. After a bit it seemed to each of them that he could see seven small, faint green glows swimming in the dark there and lazily changing position, like seven fireflies hovering, but with their light steadier and far more diffuse, as if each firefly wore a cloak made of several layers of gauze.

Then a voice sugary and unctuous, senescent though keen – a voice like a quavering flute – spoke from amidst those dimmest glows, saying, 'Oh my sons, begging the question of that hypothetical western continent, on which I do not propose to enlighten you, there is yet one place in

Nehwon you have not searched for forgetfulness since the cruel deaths of your beloved girls.'

'And what place may that be?' the Mouser asked softly after a long moment and with slightest stammer. 'And who are you?'

'The city of Lankhmar, my sons. Who I am, besides your spiritual father, is a private matter.'

'We have sworn a great oath against ever returning to Lankhmar,' Fafhrd growled after a bit, the growl low and just a shade defensive and perhaps even intimidated.

'Oaths are made to be kept only until their purpose be fulfilled,' the fluty voice responded. 'Every geas is lifted at last, every self-set rule repealed. Otherwise orderliness in life becomes a limitation to growth; discipline, chains; integrity, bondage and evil-doing. You have learned what you can from the world. You have graduated from that huge portion of Nehwon. It now remains that you take up your postgraduate studies in Lankhmar, highest university of civilized life here.'

The seven faint glows were growing still dimmer now and drawing together, as if retreating down the corridor.

'We won't go back to Lankhmar,' Fafhrd and the Mouser replied, speaking as one.

The seven glows faded altogether. So faintly the two men could barely hear it – yet hear it each did – the fluty voice inquired, 'Are you afraid?' Then they heard a grating of rock, a very faint sound, yet somehow ponderous.

So ended the first encounter of Fafhrd and his comrade with Ningauble of the Seven Eyes.

After a dozen heartbeats, the Gray Mouser drew his slim, arm-and-a-half-long sword, Scalpel, with which he was accustomed to draw blood with surgical precision, and followed its glittering tip into the rocky corridor. He strode very deliberately, with a measured determination. Fafhrd went after, but more cautiously with many a hesitation, holding the point of his heavier sword Graywand, which he yet handled most nimbly in strife, close to the stony floor and wagging it from side to side. The seven glows in their lazy swayings and bobbings had mightily suggested to him the heads of large cobras raised up to strike. He reasoned that cave cobras, if such existed, might well be phosphorescent like abyssal eels.

They had penetrated somewhat farther under the mountainside than Fafhrd had on his first inspection – their slow pace enabling their eyes to accommodate better to the relative darkness – when with a slight, high-pitched shiver, Scalpel jarred vertical rock. Waiting without a word where they stood, their cave vision improved to the point where it became indisputable, without any more sword-testing at all, that the corridor ended where they were, wanting hole big enough even for a speaking serpent to glide away, let alone a being rightfully capable of speech. The Mouser pressed and then Fafhrd threw his weight against the rock ahead at several points, but it held firm as purest mountain-heart. Nor had they missed any side tracks, even of the narrowest, or any pits or roof-holes on the way – a point they doubly checked going out.

Back at their bedrolls, their horses still tranquilly nibbling brown grass at the cavern's mouth, Fafhrd said abruptly, 'What we heard speak, it was an echo.'

'How have an echo without a voice?' the Mouser demanded with peevish impatience. 'As well have a tail without a cat. I mean, a living tail.'

'A small snow snake greatly resembles the animated tail of a white house cat,' Fafhrd replied imperturbably. 'Aye, and has just such a high, quavering cry.'

'Are you suggesting—?'

'Of course not. As I imagine you do, I think there was a door somewhere in the rock, fitted so well we could not discern the junctures. We heard it shut. But before that, he – she, it, they – went through it.'

'Then why babble of echoes and snow snakes?'

'It is well to consider all possibilities.'

'He – she and so forth – named us sons,' the Mouser mused.

'Some say the serpent is wisest, oldest, and even father of all,' Fafhrd observed judiciously.

'Snakes again! Well, one thing's certain: all hold it rash folly for a man to take advice of a serpent, let alone seven.'

'Yet he – consider the other pronouns spoken – had a point, Mouser. Mauger the indeterminate western continent, we have traveled all Nehwon in spiderweb wise. What's left but Lankhmar?'

'Damn your pronouns! We swore never to return. Have you forgotten that, Fafhrd?'

'No, but I'm dying of boredom. Times I have sworn never again to drink wine.'

'I would choke to death on Lankhmar! Her day-smokes, her night-smogs, her rats, her filth!'

'At the moment, Mouser, I care little whether I live or die, and where or when or how.'

'Now adverbs and conjunctions! Bah, you need a drink!'

'We seek a deeper forgetfulness. They say to lay a ghost, go where she died.'

'Aye, and be worse haunted!'

'I could not be worse haunted than now.'

'To let a serpent shame us by asking, were we afraid!'

'Are we, perhaps?'

And so the argument went, with the final forseeable result that Fafhrd and the Mouser cantered past Ilthmar to a stony stretch of shore that was a curiously abraded low precipice, and waited there a day and a night for the Sinking Land to emerge with anomalous aqueous convulsions from the waters joining the Sea of the East to the Inner Sea. They swiftly and warily crossed its flinty, steaming expanse – for it was a hot, sunny day – and so again rode Causey Road, but this time back toward Lankhmar.

Distant, twin thunderstorms played to either side – north over the Inner Sea and south above the Great Salt Marsh – as they approached that monstrous city and as its towers, spires, fanes, and great crenelated wall emerged from its huge, customary cap of smoke, being somewhat silhouetted by the light of the setting sun, which was turned to a dull silver disk by the high fog and the smoke.

Once the Mouser and Fafhrd thought they saw a rounded, flat-floored shape on tall, invisible legs moving amongst the seahawk trees and faintly heard a harsh voice crying, 'I told you. I told you. I told you,' but both Sheelba's wizardly hut and voice, if they were those, remained distant as the storms.

In such wise Fafhrd and the Gray Mouser returned flat against their oaths to the city they despised, yet hankered after. They did not find forgetfulness there, the ghosts of Ivrian and Vlana were not laid, yet perhaps solely because of passage of time, the two heroes were a little less troubled by them. Nor were their hates, as of the Thieves' Guild, rekindled, but rather faded. And in any case Lankhmar seemed no worse than any other place in Nehwon and more interesting than most. So they stayed there for a space, making it once more the headquarters of their adventurings.

II: THE JEWELS IN THE FOREST

It was the Year of the Behemoth, the Month of the Hedgehog, the Day of the Toad. A hot, late summer sun was sinking down toward evening over the somber, fertile land of Lankhmar. Peasants toiling in the endless grain-fields paused for a moment and lifted their earth-stained faces and noted that it would soon be time to commence lesser chores. Cattle cropping the stubble began to move in the general direction of home. Sweaty merchants and shopkeepers decided to wait a little longer before enjoying the pleasures of the bath. Thieves and astrologers moved restlessly in their sleep, sensing that the hours of night and work were drawing near.

At the southernmost limit of the land of Lankhmar, a day's ride beyond the village of Soreev, where the grain fields give way to rolling forests of maple and oak, two horsemen cantered leisurely along a narrow, dusty road. They presented a sharp contrast. The larger wore a tunic of unbleached linen, drawn tight at the waist by a very broad leather belt. A fold of linen cloak was looped over his head as a protection against the sun. A long sword with a pomegranate-shaped golden pommel was strapped to his side. Behind his right shoulder a quiver of arrows jutted up. Half sheathed in a saddlecase was a thick yew bow, unstrung. His great lean muscles, white skin, copper hair, green eyes, and above all the pleasant yet untamed expression of his massive countenance, all hinted at a land of origin colder, rougher, and more barbarous than that of Lankhmar.

Even as everything about the larger man suggested the wilderness, so the general appearance of the smaller man — and he was considerably smaller — spoke of the city. His dark face was that of a jester. Bright, black eyes, snub nose, and little lines of irony about the mouth. Hands of a conjurer. Something about the set of his wiry frame betokening exceptional competence in street fights and tavern brawls. He was clad from head to foot in garments of gray silk, soft and curiously loose of weave. His slim sword, cased in gray mouseskin, was slightly curved toward the tip. From his belt hung a sling and a pouch of missiles.

Despite their many dissimilarities, it was obvious that the two men were comrades, that they were united by a bond of subtle mutual understanding, woven of melancholy, humor, and many another strand. The smaller rode a dappled gray mare; the larger, a chestnut gelding.

They were nearing a point where the narrow road came to the end of a rise, made of a slight turn, and wound down into the next valley. Green walls of leaves pressed in on either side. The heat was considerable but not oppressive. It brought to mind thoughts of satyrs and centaurs dozing in hidden glades.

Then the gray mare, slightly in the lead, whinnied. The smaller man tightened his hold on the reins, his black eyes darting quick, alert glances, first to one side of the road and then to the other. There was a faint scraping sound, as of wood on wood.

Without warning the two men ducked down, clinging to the side harness of their horses. Simultaneously came the musical twang of bowstrings, like the prelude of some forest concert, and several arrows buzed angrily through the spaces that had just been vacated. Then the mare and the gelding were around the turn and galloping like the wind, their hooves striking up great puffs of dust.

From behind came excited shouts and answers as the pursuit got underway. There seemed to have been fully seven or eight men in the ambuscade – squat, sturdy rogues wearing chain-mail shirts and steel caps. Before the mare and the gelding had gone a stone's throw down the road, they were out and after, a black horse in the lead, a black-bearded rider second.

But those pursued were not wasting time. The larger man rose to a stand in his stirrups, whipping the yew bow from its case. With his left hand he bent it against the stirrup, with his right he drew the upper loop of the string into place. Then his left hand slipped down the bow to the grip and his right reached smoothly back over his shoulder for an arrow. Still guiding his horse with his knees, he rose even higher and turned in his saddle and sent an eagle-feathered shaft whirring. Meanwhile his comrade had placed a small leaden ball in his sling, whirled it twice about his head, so that it hummed stridently, and loosed his cast.

Arrow and missile sped and struck together. The one pierced the shoulder of the leading horseman and the other smote the second on his steel cap and tumbled him from his saddle. The pursuit halted abruptly in a tangle of plunging and rearing horses. The men who had caused this confusion pulled up at the next bend in the road and turned back to watch.

'By the Hedgehog,' said the smaller, grinning wickedly, 'but they will think twice before they play at ambuscades again!'

'Blundering fools,' said the larger. 'Haven't they even learned to shoot from their saddles? I tell you, Gray Mouser, it takes a barbarian to fight his horse properly.'

'Except for myself and a few other people,' replied the one who bore the feline nickname of Gray Mouser. 'But look, Fafhrd, the rogues retreat bearing their wounded, and one gallops far ahead. *Tcha*, but I dinted black beard's pate for him. He hangs over his nag like a bag of meal. If he'd have known who we were, he wouldn't have been so hot on the chase.'

There was some truth to this last boast. The names of the Gray Mouser and the Northerner Fafhrd were not unknown in the lands around Lankhmar and in proud Lankhmar, too. Their taste for strange adventure, their mysterious comings and goings, and their odd sense of humor were matters that puzzled almost all men alike.

Abruptly Fafhrd unstrung his bow and turned forward in his saddle.

'This should be the very valley we are seeking,' he said. 'See, there are the two hills, each with two close-set humps, of which the document speaks. Let's have another look at it, to test my guess.'

The Gray Mouser reached into his capacious leather pouch and withdrew a page of thick vellum, ancient and curiously greenish. Three edges were frayed and worn; the fourth showed a clean and recent cut. It was inscribed with the intricate hieroglyphs of Lankhmarian writing, done in the black ink of the squid. But it was not to these that the Mouser turned his attention, but to several faint lines of diminutive red script, written into the margin. These he read.

'Let kings stack their treasure houses ceiling-high, and merchants burst their vaults with hoarded coin, and fools envy them. I have a treasure that outvalues theirs. A diamond as big as a man's skull. Twelve rubies each as big as the skull of a cat. Seventeen emeralds each as big as the skull of a mole. And certain rods of crystal and bars of orichalcum. Let overlords swagger jewel-bedecked and queens load themselves with gems, and fools adore them. I have a treasure that will outlast theirs. A treasure house have I builded for it in the far southern forest, where the two hills hump double, like sleeping camels, a day's ride beyond the village of Soreev.

'A great treasure house with a high tower, fit for a king's dwelling – yet no king may dwell there. Immediately below the keystone of the chief dome my treasure lies hid, eternal as the glittering stars. It will outlast me and my name, I, Urgaan of Angarngi. It is my hold on the future. Let fools seek it. They shall win it not. For although my treasure house be empty as air, no deadly creature in rocky lair, no sentinel outside anywhere, no pitfall, poison, trap, or snare, above and below the whole place bare, of demon or devil not a hair, no serpent lethal-fanged yet fair, no skull with mortal eye a-glare, yet have I left a guardian there. Let the wise read this riddle and forbear.'

'The man's mind runs to skulls,' muttered the Mouser. 'He must have been a gravedigger or a necromancer.'

'Or an architect,' observed Fafhrd thoughtfully, 'in those past days when graven images of the skulls of men and animals served to bedeck temples.'

'Perhaps,' agreed the Mouser. 'Surely the writing and ink are old enough. They date at least as far back as the Century of the Wars with the East – five long lifespans.'

The Mouser was an accomplished forger, both of handwriting and of objects of art. He knew what he was talking about.

Satisfied that they were near the goal of their quest, the two comrades gazed through a break in the foliage down into the valley. It was shaped like the inside of a pod – shallow, long, and narrow. They were viewing it from one of the narrow ends. The two peculiarly humped hills formed the long sides. The whole of the valley was green with maple and oak, save for a small gap toward the

219

middle. That, thought the Mouser, might mark a peasant's dwelling and the cleared space around it.

Beyond the gap he could make out something dark and squarish rising a little above the treetops. He called his companion's attention to it, but they could not decide whether it was indeed a tower such as the document mentioned, or just a peculiar shadow, or perhaps even the dead, limbless trunk of a gigantic oak. It was too far away.

'Almost sufficient time has passed,' said Fafhrd, after a pause, 'for one of those rogues to have sneaked up through the forest for another shot at us. Evening draws near.'

They spoke to their horses and moved on slowly. They tried to keep their eyes fixed on the thing that looked like a tower, but since they were descending, it almost immediately dropped out of sight below the treetops. There would be no further chance of seeing it until they were quite close at hand.

The Mouser felt a subdued excitement running through his flesh. Soon they would discover if there was a treasure to be had or not. A diamond as big as a man's skull ... rubies ... emeralds ... He found an almost nostalgic delight in prolonging and savoring to the full this last, leisurely stage of their quest. The recent ambuscade served as a necessary spice.

He thought of how he had slit the interesting-looking vellum page from the ancient book on architecture that reposed in the library of the rapacious and overbearing lord Rannarsh. Of how, half in jest, he had sought out and interrogated several peddlers from the South. Of how he had found one who had recently passed through a village named Soreev. Of how that one had told him of a stone structure in the forest south of Soreev, called by the peasants the House of Angarngi and reputed to be long deserted. The peddler had seen a high tower rising above the trees. The Mouser recalled the man's wizened, cunning face and chuckled. And that brought to mind the greedy, sallow face of Lord Rannarsh, and a new thought occurred to him.

'Fafhrd,' he said, 'those rogues we just now put to flight – what did you take them for?'

The Northerner grunted humorous contempt.

'Run-of-the-manger ruffians. Waylayers of fat merchants. Pasture bravos. Bumpkin bandits!'

'Still, they were all well armed, and armed alike – as if they were in some rich man's service. And that one who rode far ahead. Mightn't he have been hastening to report failure to some master?'

'What is your thought?'

The Mouser did not reply for some moments.

'I was thinking,' he said, 'that Lord Rannarsh is a rich man and a greedy one, who slavers at the thought of jewels. And I was wondering if he ever read those faint lines of red lettering and made a copy of them, and if my theft of the original sharpened his interest.'

The Northerner shook his head.

'I doubt it. You are oversubtle. But if he did, and if he seeks to rival us in this treasure quest, he'd best watch each step twice – and choose servitors who can fight on horseback.'

They were moving so slowly that the hooves of the mare and the gelding hardly stirred up the dust. They had no fear of danger from the rear. A well-laid ambuscade might surprise them, but not a man or horse in motion. The narrow road wound along in a purposeless fashion. Leaves brushed their faces, and occasionally they had to swing their bodies out of the way of encroaching branches. The ripe scent of the late summer forest was intensified now that they were below the rim of the valley. Mingled with it were whiffs of wild berries and aromatic shrubs. Shadows imperceptibly lengthened.

'Nine chances out of ten,' murmured the Mouser dreamily, 'the treasure house of Urgaan of Angarngi was looted some hundred years ago, by men whose bodies are already dust.'

'It may be so,' agreed Fafhrd. 'Unlike men, rubies and emeralds do not rest quietly in their graves.'

This possibility, which they had discussed several times before, did not disturb them now, or make them impatient. Rather did it impart to their quest the pleasant melancholy of a lost hope. They drank in the rich air and let their horses munch random mouthfuls of leaves. A jay called shrilly from overhead and off in the forest a catbird was chattering, their sharp voices breaking in on the low buzzing and droning of the insects. Night was drawing near. The almost-horizontal rays of the sun gilded the treetops. Then Fafhrd's sharp ears caught the hollow lowing of a cow.

A few more turns brought them into the clearing they had spied. In line with their surmise, it proved to contain a peasant's cottage – a neat little low-eaved house of weathered wood, situated in the midst of an acre of grain. To one side was a bean patch; to the other, a woodpile which almost dwarfed the house. In front of the cottage stood a wiry old man, his skin as brown as his homespun tunic. He had evidently just heard the horses and turned around to look.

'Ho, father,' called the Mouser, 'it's a good day to be abroad in, and a good home you have here.'

The peasant considered these statements and then nodded his head in agreement.

'We are two weary travelers,' continued the Mouser.

Again the peasant nodded gravely.

'In return for two silver coins will you give us lodging for the night?'

The peasant rubbed his chin and then held up three fingers.

'Very well, you shall have three silver coins,' said the Mouser, slipping from his horse. Fafhrd followed suit.

Only after giving the old man a coin to seal the bargain did the Mouser question casually, 'Is there not an old, deserted place near your dwelling called the House of Angarngi?'

The peasant nodded.

'What's it like?'

The peasant shrugged his shoulders.

'Don't you know?'

The peasant shook his head.

'But haven't you ever seen the place?' The Mouser's voice carried a note of amazement he did not bother to conceal.

He was answered by another headshake.

'But father, it's only a few minutes' walk from your dwelling, isn't it?'

The peasant nodded tranquilly, as if the whole business were no matter for surprise.

A muscular young man, who had come from behind the cottage to take their horses, offered a suggestion.

'You can see tower from other side the house. I can point her out.'

At this the old man proved he was not completely speechless by saying in a dry, expressionless voice: 'Go ahead. Look at her all you want.'

And he stepped into the cottage. Fafhrd and the Mouser caught a glimpse of a child peering around the door, an old woman stirring a pot, and someone hunched in a big chair before a tiny fire.

The upper part of the tower proved to be barely visible through a break in the trees. The last rays of the sun touched it with deep red. It looked about four or five bowshots distant. And then, even as they watched, the sun dipped under and it became a featureless square of black stone.

'She's an old place,' explained the young man vaguely.

223

'I been all around her. Father, he's just never bothered to look.'

'You've been inside?' questioned the Mouser.

The young man scratched his head.

'No. She's just an old place. No good for anything.'

'There'll be a fairly long twilight,' said Fafhrd, his wide green eyes drawn to the tower as if by a lodestone. 'Long enough for us to have a closer look.'

'I'd show the way,' said the young man, 'save I got water to fetch.

'No matter,' replied Fafhrd. 'When's supper?'

'When the first stars show.'

They left him holding their horses and walked straight into the woods. Immediately it became much darker, as if twilight were almost over, rather than just begun. The vegetation proved to be somewhat thicker than they had anticipated. There were vines and thorns to be avoided. Irregular, pale patches of sky appeared and disappeared overhead.

The Mouser let Fafhrd lead the way. His mind was occupied with a queer sort of reverie about the peasants. It tickled his fancy to think how they had stolidly lived their toilsome lives, generation after generation, only a few steps from what might be one of the greatest treasure-troves in the world. It seemed incredible. How could people sleep so near jewels and not dream of them? But probably they never dreamed.

So the Gray Mouser was sharply aware of few things during the journey through the woods, save that Fafhrd seemed to be taking a long time – which was strange, since the barbarian was an accomplished woodsman.

Finally a deeper and more solid shadow loomed up through the trees, and in a moment they were standing in the margin of a small, boulder-studded clearing, most of which was occupied by the bulky structure they sought. Abruptly, even before his eyes took in the details of the

224

place, the Mouser's mind was filled with a hundred petty perturbations. Weren't they making a mistake in leaving their horses with those strange peasants? And mightn't those rogues have followed them to the cottage? And wasn't this the Day of the Toad, an unlucky day for entering deserted houses? And shouldn't they have a short spear along, in case they met a leopard? And wasn't that a whippoorwill he heard crying on his left hand, an augury of ill omen?

The treasure house of Urgaan of Angarngi was a peculiar structure. The main feature was a large, shallow dome, resting on walls that formed an octagon. In front, and merging into it, were two lesser domes. Between these gaped a great square doorway. The tower rose asymmetrically from the rear part of the chief dome. The eyes of the Mouser sought hurriedly through the dimming twilight for the cause of the salient peculiarity of the structure, and decided it lay in the utter simplicity. There were no pillars, no outjutting cornices, no friezes, no architectural ornaments of any sort, skull-embellished or otherwise. Save for the doorway and a few tiny windows set in unexpected places, the House of Angarngi was a compact mass of uniformly dark gray stones most closely joined.

But now Fafhrd was striding up the short flight of terraced steps that led toward the open door, and the Mouser followed him, although he would have liked to spy around a little longer. With every step he took forward he sensed an odd reluctance growing within him. His earlier mood of pleasant expectancy vanished as suddenly as if he'd stepped into quicksand. It seemed to him that the black doorway yawned like a toothless mouth. And then a little shudder went through him, for he saw the mouth had a tooth – a bit of ghostly white that jutted up from the floor. Fafhrd was reaching down toward the object.

'I wonder whose skull this may be?' said the Northerner calmly.

The Mouser regarded the thing, and the scattering of bones and fragments of bones beside it. His feeling of uneasiness was fast growing toward a climax, and he had the unpleasant conviction that, once it did reach a climax, something would happen. What was the answer to Fafhrd's question? What form of death had struck down that earlier intruder? It was very dark inside the treasure house. Didn't the manuscript mention something about a guardian? It was hard to think of a flesh-and-blood guardian persisting for three hundred years, but there were things that were immortal or nearly immortal. He could tell that Fafhrd was not in the least affected by any premonitory disquietude, and was quite capable of instituting an immediate search for the treasure. That must be prevented at all costs. He remembered that the Northerner loathed snakes.

'This cold, damp stone,' he observed casually. 'Just the place for scaly, cold-blooded snakes.'

'Nothing of the sort,' replied Fafhrd angrily. 'I'm willing to wager there's not a single serpent inside. Urgaan's note said, "No deadly creature in rocky lair," and to cap that, "no serpent lethal-fanged yet fair."'

'I am not thinking of guardian snakes Urgaan may have left here,' the Mouser explained, 'but only of serpents that may have wandered in for the night. Just as that skull you hold is not one set there by Urgaan "with mortal eye a-glare," but merely the brain-case of some unfortunate wayfarer who chanced to perish here.'

'I don't know,' Fafhrd said, calmly eyeing the skull. 'Its orbits might glow phosphorescently in absolute dark.'

A moment later he was agreeing it would be well to postpone the search until daylight returned, now that the treasure house was located. He carefully replaced the skull.

As they re-entered the woods, the Mouser heard a little inner voice whispering to him, *Just in time. Just in time.*

Then the sense of uneasiness departed as suddenly as it had come, and he began to feel somewhat ridiculous. This caused him to sing a bawdy ballad of his own invention, wherein demons and other supernatural agents were ridiculed obscenely. Fafhrd chimed in good-naturedly on the choruses.

It was not as dark as they expected when they reached the cottage. They saw to their horses, found they had been well cared for, and then fell to the savory mess of beans, porridge, and pot herbs that the peasant's wife ladled into oak bowls. Fresh milk to wash it down was provided in quaintly carved oak goblets. The meal was a satisfying one and the interior of the house was neat and clean, despite its stamped earthen floor and low beams, which Fafhrd had to duck.

There turned out to be six in the family, all told. The father, his equally thin and leathery wife, the older son, a young boy, a daughter, and a mumbling grandfather, whom extreme age confined to a chair before the fire. The last two were the most interesting of the lot.

The girl was in the gawkish age of mid-adolescence, but there was a wild, coltish grace in the way she moved her lanky legs and slim arms with their prominent elbows. She was very shy, and gave the impression that at any moment she might dart out the door and into the woods.

In order to amuse her and win her confidence, the Mouser began to perform small feats of legerdemain, plucking copper coins out of the ears of the astonished peasant, and bone needles from the nose of his giggling wife. He turned beans into buttons and back again into beans, swallowed a large fork, made a tiny wooden manikin jig on the palm of his hand, and utterly bewildered the cat by pulling what seemed to be a mouse out of its mouth.

The old folks gaped and grinned. The little boy became frantic with excitement. His sister watched everything with concentrated interest, and even smiled warmly when the Mouser presented her with a square of fine, green linen he had conjured from the air, although she was still too shy to speak.

Then Fafhrd roared sea-chanteys that rocked the roof and sang lusty songs that set the old grandfather gurgling with delight. Meanwhile the Mouser fetched a small wineskin from his saddlebags, concealed it under his cloak, and filled the oak goblets as if by magic. These rapidly fuddled the peasants, who were unused to so potent a beverage, and by the time Fafhrd had finished telling a bloodcurdling tale of the frozen north, they were all nodding, save the girl and the grandfather.

The latter looked up at the merry-making adventurers, his watery eyes filled with a kind of impish, senile glee, and mumbled, 'You two be right clever men. Maybe you be beast-dodgers.' But before this remark could be elucidated, his eyes had gone vacant again, and in a few moments he was snoring.

Soon all were asleep, Fafhrd and the Mouser keeping their weapons close at hand, but only variegated snores and occasional snaps from the dying embers disturbed the silence of the cottage.

The Day of the Cat dawned clear and cool. The Mouser stretched himself luxuriously and, catlike, flexed his muscles and sucked in the sweet, dewy air. He felt exceptionally cheerful and eager to be up and doing. Was not this *his* day, the day of the Gray Mouser, a day in which luck could not fail him?

His slight movements awakened Fafhrd and together they stole silently from the cottage so as not to disturb the peasants, who were oversleeping with the wine they had taken. They refreshed their faces and hands in the wet grass and visited their horses. Then they munched some bread, washed it down with drafts of cool well water flavored with wine, and made ready to depart.

This time their preparations were well thought out. The Mouser carried a mallet and a stout iron pry-bar, in case they had to attack masonry, and made certain that candles, flint, wedges, chisels, and several other small tools were in his pouch. Fafhrd borrowed a pick from the peasant's implements and tucked a coil of thin, strong rope in his belt. He also took his bow and quiver of arrows.

The forest was delightful at this early hour. Bird cries and chatterings came from overhead, and once they glimpsed a black, squirrel-like animal scampering along a bough. A couple of chipmunks scurried under a bush dotted with red berries. What had been shadow the evening before was now a variety of green-leafed beauty. The two adventurers trod softly.

They had hardly gone more than a bowshot into the woods when they heard a faint rustling behind them. The rustling came rapidly nearer, and suddenly the peasant girl burst into view. She stood breathless and poised, one hand touching a treetrunk, the other pressing some leaves, ready to fly away at the first sudden move. Fafhrd and the Mouser stood as stock-still as if she were a doe or a dryad. Finally she managed to conquer her shyness and speak.

'You go there?' she questioned, indicating the direction of the treasure house with a quick, ducking nod. Her dark eyes were serious.

'Yes, we go there,' answered Fafhrd, smiling.

'Don't.' This word was accompanied by a rapid headshake.

'But why shouldn't we, girl?' Fafhrd's voice was gentle and sonorous, like an integral part of the forest. It seemed to touch some spring within the girl that enabled her to feel more at ease. She gulped a big breath and began.

'Because I watch it from edge of the forest, but never go close. Never, never, never. I say to myself there be a magic circle I must not cross. And I say to myself there be a giant inside. Queer and fearsome giant.' Her words were coming rapidly now, like an undammed stream. 'All gray he be, like the stone of his house. All gray – eyes and hair and fingernails, too. And he has a stone club as big as a tree. And he be big, bigger than you, twice as big.' Here she nodded at Fafhrd. 'And with his club he kills, kills, kills. But only if you go close. Every day, almost, I play a game with him. I pretend to be going to cross the magic circle. And he watches from inside the door, where I can't see him, and he thinks I'm going to cross. And I dance through the forest all around the house, and he follows me, peering from the little windows. And I get closer and closer to the circle, closer and closer. But I never cross. And he be very angry and gnash his teeth, like rocks rubbing rocks, so that the house shakes. And I run, run, run away. But you mustn't go inside. Oh, you mustn't.'

She paused, as if startled by her own daring. Her eyes were fixed anxiously on Fafhrd. She seemed drawn toward him. The Northerner's reply carried no overtone of patronizing laughter.

'But you've never actually seen the gray giant, have you?'

'Oh, no. He be too cunning. But I say to myself he must be there inside. I know he be inside. And that's the same thing, isn't it? Grandfather knows about him. We used to talk about him, when I was little, Grandfather calls him the beast. But the others laugh at me, so I don't tell.'

Here was another astounding peasant-paradox, thought the Mouser with an inward grin. Imagination was such a rare commodity with them that this girl unhesitatingly took it for reality.

'Don't worry about us, girl. We'll be on the watch for your gray giant,' he started to say, but he had less success than Fafhrd in keeping his voice completely natural or else the cadence of his words didn't chime so well with the forest setting.

The girl uttered one more warning. 'Don't go inside, oh, please,' and turned and darted away.

The two adventurers looked at each other and smiled. Somehow the unexpected fairy tale with its conventional ogre and its charmingly naïve narrator added to the delight of the dewy morning. Without a comment they resumed their soft-stepping progress. And it was well that they went quietly for, when they had gotten within a stone's throw of the clearing, they heard low voices that seemed to be in grumbling argument. Immediately they cached the pick and pry-bar and mallet under a clump of bushes, and stole forward, taking advantage of the natural cover and watching where they planted their feet.

On the edge of the clearing stood half a dozen stocky men in black chain-mail shirts, bows on their backs, shortswords at their sides. They were immediately recognizable as the rogues who had laid the ambuscade. Two of them started for the treasure house, only to be recalled by a comrade. Whereupon the argument apparently started afresh.

'That red-haired one,' whispered the Mouser after an unhurried look. 'I can swear I've seen him in the stables of Lord Rannarsh. My guess was right. It seems we have a rival.'

'Why do they wait, and keep pointing at the house?' whispered Fafhrd. 'Is it because some of their comrades are already at work inside?'

The Mouser shook his head. 'That cannot be. See those picks and shovels and levers they have rested on the ground? No, they wait for someone – for a leader. Some of them want to examine the house before he arrives. Others counsel against it. And I will bet my head against a bowling ball that the leader is Rannarsh himself. He is much too greedy and suspicious to entrust a treasure quest to any henchmen.'

'What's to do?' murmured Fafhrd. 'We cannot enter the

house unseen, even if it were the wise course, which it isn't. Once in, we'd be trapped.'

'I've half a mind to loose my sling at them right now and teach them something about the art of ambuscade,' replied the Mouser, slitting his eyes grimly. 'Only then the survivors would flee into the house and hold us off until, mayhap, Rannarsh came, and more men with him.'

'We might circle part way around the clearing,' said Fafhrd, after a moment's pause, 'keeping to the woods. Then we can enter the clearing unseen and shelter ourselves behind one of the small domes. In that way we become masters of the doorway, and can prevent their taking cover inside. Thereafter I will address them suddenly and try to frighten them off, you meanwhile staying hid and giving substance to my threats by making enough racket for ten men.'

This seemed the handiest plan to both of them, and they managed the first part of it without a hitch. The Mouser crouched behind the small dome, his sword, sling, daggers, and a couple of sticks of wood laid ready for either noise-making or fight. Then Fafhrd strode briskly forward, his bow held carelessly in front of him, an arrow fitted to the string. It was done so casually that it was a few moments before Rannarsh's henchmen noticed him. Then they quickly reached for their own bows and as quickly desisted when they saw that the huge newcomer had the advantage of them. They scowled in irritated perplexity.

'Ho, rogues!' began Fafhrd. 'We allow you just as much time as it will take you to make yourselves scarce, and no more. Don't think to resist or come skulking back. My men are scattered through the woods. At a sign from me they will feather you with arrows.'

Meanwhile the Mouser had begun a low din and was slowly and artistically working it up in volume. Rapidly varying the pitch and intonation of his voice and making it echo first from some part of the building and then from the forest wall, he created the illusion of a squad of blood-thirsty bow-men. Nasty cries of 'Shall we let fly?' 'You take the redhead,' and 'Try for the belly shot; it's surest,' kept coming now from one point and now another, until it was all Fafhrd could do to refrain from laughing at the woebegone, startled glances the six rogues kept darting around. But his merriment was extinguished when, just as the rogues were starting to slink shamefacedly away, an arrow arched erratically out of the woods, passing a spear's length above his head.

'Curse that branch!' came a deep, guttural voice the Mouser recognized as issuing from the throat of Lord Rannarsh. Immediately after, it began to bark commands.

'At them, you fools! It's all a trick. There are only the two of them. Rush them!'

Fafhrd turned without warning and loosed point-blank at the voice, but did not silence it. Then he dodged back behind the small dome and ran with the Mouser for the woods.

The six rogues, wisely deciding that a charge with drawn swords would be overly heroic, followed suit, unslinging their bows as they went. One of them turned before he had reached sufficient cover, nocking an arrow. It was a mistake. A ball from the Mouser's sling took him low in the forehead, and he toppled forward and was still.

The sound of that hit and fall was the last heard in the clearing for quite a long time, save for the inevitable bird cries, some of which were genuine, and some of which were communications between Fafhrd and the Mouser. The conditions of the death-dealing contest were obvious. Once it had fairly begun, no one dared enter the clearing, since he would become a fatally easy mark; and the Mouser was sure that none of the five remaining rogues had taken shelter in the treasure house. Nor did either side dare withdraw all its men out of sight of the doorway, since that would allow someone to take a commanding position

233

in the top of the tower, providing the tower had a negotiable stair. Therefore it was a case of sneaking about near the edge of the clearing, circling and counter-circling, with a great deal of squatting in a good place and waiting for somebody to come along and be shot.

The Mouser and Fafhrd began by adopting the latter strategy, first moving about twenty paces nearer the point at which the rogues had disappeared. Evidently their patience was a little better than that of their opponents. For after about ten minutes of nerve-racking waiting, during which pointed seed pods had a queer way of looking like arrowheads, Fafhrd got the red-haired hench-man full in the throat just as he was bending his bow for a shot at the Mouser. That left four besides Rannarsh himself. Immediately the two adventurers changed their tactics and separated, the Mouser circling rapidly around the treasure house and Fafhrd drawing as far back from the open space as he dared.

Rannarsh's men must have decided on the same plan, for the Mouser almost bumped into a scar-faced rogue as soft-footed as himself. At such close range, bow and sling were both useless – in their normal function. Scarface attempted to jab the barbed arrow he held into the Mouser's eye. The Mouser weaved his body to one side, swung his sling like a whip, and felled the man senseless with a blow from the horn handle. Then he retreated a few paces, thanked the Day of the Cat that there had not been two of them, and took to the trees as being a safer, though slower method of progress. Keeping to the middle heights, he scurried along with the sure-footedness of a rope walker, swinging from branch to branch only when it was necessary, making sure he always had more than one way of retreat open.

He had completed three-quarters of his circuit when he heard the clash of swords a few trees ahead. He increased his speed and was soon looking down on a sweet little combat. Fafhrd, his back to a great oak, had his broadsword out and was holding off two of Rannarsh's henchmen, who were attacking with their shorter weapons. It was a tight spot and the Northerner realized it. He knew that ancient sagas told of heroes who could best four or more men at swordplay. He also knew that such sagas were lies, providing the hero's opponents were reasonably competent.

And Rannarsh's men were veterans. They attacked cautiously but incessantly, keeping their swords well in front of them and never slashing wildly. Their breath whistled through their nostrils, but they were grimly confident, knowing the Northerner dared not lunge strongly at one of them because it would lay him wide open to a thrust by the other. Their game was to get one on each side of him and then attack simultaneously.

Fafhrd's counter was to shift position quickly and attack the nearer one murderously before the other could get back in range. In that way he managed to keep them side by side, where he could hold their blades in check by swift feints and crosswise sweeps. Sweat beaded his face and blood dripped from a scratch on his left thigh. A fearsome grin showed his white teeth, which occasionally parted to let slip a base, primitive insult.

The Mouser took in the situation at a glance, descended rapidly to a lower bough, and poised himself, aiming a dagger at the back of one of Fafhrd's adversaries. He was, however, standing very close to the thick trunk, and around this trunk darted a horny hand tipped with a short sword. The third henchman had also thought it wise to take to the trees. Fortunately for the Mouser, the man was uncertain of his footing and therefore his thrust, although well aimed, came a shade slow. As it was the little gray-clad man only managed to dodge by dropping off.

Thereupon he startled his opponent with a modest acrobatic feat. He did not drop to the ground, knowing

235

that would put everyone at the mercy of the man in the tree. Instead, he grabbed hold of the branch on which he had been standing, swung himself smartly up again, and grappled. Steadying themselves now with one hand, now another, they drove for each other's throats, ramming with knees and elbows whenever they got a chance. At the first onset both dagger and sword were dropped, the latter sticking point-down in the ground directly between the two battling henchmen and startling them so that Fafhrd almost got home an attack.

The Mouser and his man surged and teetered along the branch away from the trunk, inflicting little damage on each other since it was hard to keep balance. Finally they slid off at the same time, but grabbed the branch with their hands. The puffing henchman aimed a vicious kick. The Mouser escaped it by yanking up his body and doubling up his legs. The latter he let fly violently, taking the henchman full in the chest, just where the ribs stop. The unfortunate retainer of Rannarsh-fell to the ground, where he had the wind knocked out of him a second time.

At the same moment one of Fafhrd's opponents tried a trick that might have turned out well. When his companion was pressing the Northerner closely, he snatched for the shortsword sticking in the ground, intending to hurl it underhanded as if it were a javelin. But Fafhrd, whose superior endurance was rapidly giving him an advantage in speed, anticipated the movement and simultaneously made a brilliant counterattack against the other man. There were two thrusts, both lightning-like, the first a feint at the belly, the second a slicing stab that sheared through the throat to the spine. Then he whirled around and, with a quick sweep, knocked both weapons out of the hands of the first man, who looked up in bewilderment and promptly collapsed into a sitting position, panting in utter exhaustion, though with enough breath left to cry, 'Mercy!'

To cap the situation, the Mouser dropped lightly down, as if out of the sky. Fafhrd automatically started to raise his sword, for a backhand swipe. Then he stared at the Mouser for as long a time as it took the man sitting on the ground to give three tremendous gasps. Then he began to laugh, first uncontrollable snickers and later thundering peals. It was a laughter in which the battle-begotten madness, completely sated anger, and relief at escape from death were equally mingled.

'Oh, by Glaggerk and by Kos!' he roared. 'By the Behemoth! Oh, by the Cold Waste and the guts of the Red God! Oh! Oh! Oh!' Again the insane bellowing burst out. 'Oh, by the Killer Whale and the Cold Woman and her spawn!' By degrees the laughter died away, choking in his throat. He rubbed his forehead with the palm of his hand and his face became starkly grave. Then he knelt beside the man he had just slain, and straightened his limbs, and closed his eyes, and began to weep in a dignified way that would have seemed ridiculous and hypocritical in anyone but a barbarian.

Meanwhile the Mouser's reactions were nowhere near as primitive. He felt worried, ironic, and slightly sick. He understood Fafhrd's emotions, but knew that he would not feel the full force of his own for some time yet, and by then they would be deadened and somewhat choked. He peered about anxiously, fearful of an anticlimactic attack that would find his companion helpless. He counted over the tally of their opponents. Yes, the six henchmen were all accounted for. But Rannarsh himself, where was Rannarsh? He fumbled in his pouch to make sure he had not lost his good-luck talismans and amulets. His lips moved rapidly as he murmured two or three prayers and cantrips. But all the while he held his sling ready, and his eyes never once ceased their quick shifting.

From the middle of a thick clump of bushes he heard a series of agonized gasps, as the man he had felled from the tree began to regain his wind. The henchman whom Fafhrd had disarmed, his face ashy pale from exhaustion rather than fright, was slowly edging back into the forest. The Mouser watched him carelessly, noting the comical way in which the steel cap had slipped down over his forehead and rested against the bridge of his nose. Meanwhile the gasps of the man in the bushes were taking on a less agonized quality. At almost the same instant, the two rose to their feet and stumbled off into the forest.

The Mouser listened to their blundering retreat. He was sure that there was nothing more to fear from them. *They* wouldn't come back. And then a little smile stole into his face, for he heard the sounds of a third person joining them in their flight. That would be Rannarsh, thought the Mouser, a man cowardly at heart and incapable of carrying on single-handed. It did not occur to him that the third person might be the man he had stunned with his sling handle.

Mostly just to be doing something, he followed them leisurely for a couple of bowshots into the forest. Their trail was impossible to miss, being marked by trampled bushes and thorns bearing tatters of cloth. It led in a beeline away from the clearing. Satisfied, he returned, going out of his way to regain the mallet, pick, and pry-bar.

He found Fafhrd tying a loose bandage around the scratch on his thigh. The Northerner's emotions had run their gamut and he was himself again. The dead man for whom he had been somberly grieving now meant no more to him than food for beetles and birds. Whereas for the Mouser it continued to be a somewhat frightening and sickening object.

'And now do we proceed with our interrupted business?' the Mouser asked.

Fafhrd nodded in a matter-of-fact manner and rose to his feet. Together they entered the rocky clearing. It came to them as a surprise how little time the fight had taken. True, the sun had moved somewhat higher, but the atmosphere was still that of early morning. The dew had not dried yet. The treasure house of Urgaan of Angarngi stood massive, featureless, grotesquely impressive.

'The peasant girl predicted the truth without knowing it,' said the Mouser with a smile. 'We played her game of "circle-the-clearing and don't-cross-the-magic-circle," didn't we?'

The treasure house had no fears for him today. He recalled his perturbations of the previous evening, but was unable to understand them. The very idea of a guardian seemed somewhat ridiculous. There were a hundred other ways of explaining the skeleton inside the doorway.

So this time it was the Mouser who skipped into the treasure house ahead of Fafhrd. The interior was disappointing, being empty of any furnishings and as bare and unornamented as the outside walls. Just a large, low room. To either side square doorways led to the smaller domes, while to the rear a long hallway was dimly apparent, and the beginnings of a stair leading to the upper part of the main dome.

With only a casual glance at the skull and the broken skeleton, the Mouser made his way toward the stair.

'Our document,' he said to Fafhrd, who was now beside him, 'speaks of the treasure as resting just below the keystone of the chief dome. Therefore we must seek in the room or rooms above.'

'True,' answered the Northerner, glancing around. 'But I wonder, Mouser, just what use this structure served. A man who builds a house solely to hide a treasure is shouting to the world that he *has* a treasure. Do you think it might have been a temple?'

The Mouse suddenly shrank back with a sibilant exclamation. Sprawled a little way up the stair was another skeleton, the major bones hanging together in lifelike fashion. The whole upper half of the skull was smashed to bony shards paler than those of a gray pot. 'Our hosts are overly ancient and indecently naked,' hissed the Mouser, angry with himself for being startled. Then he darted up the stairs to examine the grisly find. His sharp eyes picked out several objects among the bones. A rusty dagger, a tarnished gold ring that looped a knucklebone, a handful of horn buttons, and a slim, green-eaten copper cylinder. The last awakened his curiosity. He picked it up, dislodging hand-bones in the process, so that they fell apart, rattling dryly. He pried off the cap of the cylinder with his dagger point, and shook out a tightly rolled sheet of ancient parchment. This he gingerly unwound. Fafhrd and he scanned the lines of diminutive red lettering by the light from a small window on the landing above.

Mine is a secret treasure. Orichalcum have I, and crystal, and blood-red amber. Rubies and emeralds that demons would war for, and a diamond as big as the skull of a man. Yet none have seen them save I. I, Urgaan of Angarngi, scorn the flattery and the envy of fools. A fittingly lonely treasure house have I built for my jewels. There, hidden under the keystone, they may dream unperturbed until earth and sky wear away. A day's ride beyond the village of Soreev, in the valley of the two double-humped hills, lies that house, trebly-domed and single-towered. It is empty. Any fool may enter. Let him. I care not.

'The details differ slightly,' murmured the Mouser, 'but the phrases have the same ring as in our document.'

'The man must have been mad,' asserted Fafhrd, scowling. 'Or else why should he carefully hide a treasure and then, with equal care, leave directions for finding it?'

'We thought *our* document was a memorandum or an oversight,' said the Mouser thoughtfully. 'Such a notion can hardly explain *two* documents.' Lost in speculation, he turned toward the remaining section of the stair, only to find still another skull grinning at him from a shadowy angle. This time he was not startled, yet he experienced the same feeling that a fly must experience when, enmeshed in a spider's web, it sees the dangling, empty corpses of a dozen of its brothers. He began to speak rapidly.

'Nor can such a notion explain *three* or *four* or mayhap a *dozen* such documents. For how came these other questers here, unless each had found a written message? Urgaan of Angarngi may have been mad, but he sought deliberately to lure men here. One thing is certain: this house conceals – or did conceal – some deadly trap. Some guardian. Some giant beast, say. Or perhaps the very stones distill a poison. Perhaps hidden springs release sword blades which stab out through cracks in the walls and then return.'

'That cannot be,' answered Fafhrd. 'These men were killed by great, bashing blows. The ribs and spine of the first were splintered. The second had his skull cracked open. And that third one there. See! The bones of his lower body are smashed.'

The Mouser started to reply. Then his face broke into an unexpected smile. He could see the conclusion to which Fafhrd's arguments were unconsciously leading – and he knew that that conclusion was ridiculous. What thing would kill with great, bashing blows? What thing but the gray giant the peasant girl had told them about? The gray giant twice as tall as a man, with his great stone club – a giant fit only for fairy tales and fantasies.

And Fafhrd returned the Mouser's smile. It seemed to him that they were making a great deal of fuss about nothing. These skeletons were suggestive enough, to be sure, but did they not represent men who had died many, many years ago – centuries ago? What guardian could outlast three centuries? Why, that was a long enough time to weary the patience of a demon! And there were no such things as demons, anyhow. And there was no earthly use

241

in mucking around about ancient fears and horrors that were as dead as dust. The whole matter, thought Fafhrd, boiled down to something very simple. They had come to a deserted house to see if there was a treasure in it.

Agreed upon this point, the two comrades made their way up the remaining section of stair that led to the dimmer regions of the House of Angarngi. Despite their confidence, they moved cautiously and kept sharp watch on the shadows lying ahead. This was wise.

Just as they reached the top, a flash of steel spun out of the darkness. It nicked the Mouser in the shoulder as he twisted to one side. There was a metallic clash as it fell to the stone floor. The Mouser, gripped by a sudden spasm of anger and fright, ducked down and dashed rapidly through the door from which the weapon had come, straight at the danger, whatever it was.

'Dagger-tossing in the dark, eh, you slick-bellied worm?' Fafhrd heard the Mouser cry, and then he, too, had plunged through the door.

Lord Rannarsh cowered against the wall, his rich hunting garb dusty and disordered, his black, wavy hair pushed back from his forehead, his cruelly handsome face a sallow mask of hate and extreme terror. For the moment the latter emotion seemed to predominate and, oddly enough, it did not appear to be directed toward the men he had just assailed, but toward something else, something unapparent.

'O gods!' he cried. 'Let me go from here. The treasure is yours. Let me out of this place. Else I am doomed. The thing has played at cat and mouse with me. I cannot bear it. I cannot bear it!'

'So now we pipe a different tune, do we?' snarled the Mouser. 'First dagger-tossing, then fright and pleas!'

'Filthy coward tricks,' added Fafhrd. 'Skulking here safe while your henchmen died bravely.'

'Safe? Safe, you say? O gods!' Rannarsh almost

screamed. Then a subtle change became apparent in his rigid-muscled face. It was not that his terror decreased. If anything, that became greater. But there was added to it, over and above, a consciousness of desperate shame, a realization that he had demeaned himself ineradicably in the eyes of these two ruffians. His lips began to writhe, showing tight-clenched teeth. He extended his left hand in a gesture of supplication.

'Oh, mercy, have mercy,' he cried piteously, and his right hand twitched a second dagger from his belt and hurled it underhand at Fafhrd.

The Northerner knocked aside the weapon with a swift blow of his palm, then said deliberately, 'He is yours, Mouser. Kill the man.'

And now it was cat against cornered rat. Lord Rannarsh whipped a gleaming sword from its gold-worked scabbard and rushed in, cutting, thrusting, stabbing. The Mouser gave ground slightly, his slim blade flickering in a defensive counterattack that was wavering and elusive, yet deadly. He brought Rannarsh's rush to a standstill. His blade moved so quickly that it seemed to weave a net of steel around the man. Then it leaped forward three times in rapid succession. At the first thrust it bent nearly double against a concealed shirt of chain mail. The second thrust pierced the belly. The third transfixed the throat. Lord Rannarsh fell to the floor, spitting and gagging, his fingers clawing at his neck. There he died.

'An evil end,' said Fafhrd somberly, 'although he had fairer play than he deserved, and handled his sword well. Mouser, I like not this killing, although there was surely more justice to it than the others.'

The Mouser, wiping his weapon against his opponent's thigh, understood what Fafhrd meant. He felt no elation his victory, only a cold, queasy disgust. A moment before he had been raging, but now there was no anger left in him. He pulled open his gray jerkin and inspected the dagger wound in his left shoulder. A little blood was still welling from it and trickling down his arm.

'Lord Rannarsh was no coward,' he said slowly. 'He killed himself, or at least caused his own death, because we had seen him terrified and heard him cry in fright.'

And at these words, without any warning whatsoever, stark terror fell like an icy eclipse upon the hearts of the Gray Mouser and Fafhrd. It was as if Lord Rannarsh had left them a legacy of fear, which passed to them immediately upon his death. And the unmanning thing about it was that they had no premonitory apprehension, no hint of its approach. It did not take root and grow gradually greater. It came all at once, paralyzing, over-whelming. Worse still, there was no discernible cause. One moment they were looking down with something of indifference upon the twisted corpse of Lord Rannarsh. The next moment their legs were weak, their guts were cold, their spines were prickling, their teeth clicking, their hearts pounding, their hair lifting at the roots.

Fafhrd felt as if he had walked unsuspecting into the jaws of a gigantic serpent. His barbaric mind was stirred to the deeps. He thought of the grim god Kos brooding alone in the icy silence of the Cold Waste. He thought of the masked powers Fate and Chance, and of the game they play for the blood and brains of men. And he did not will these thoughts. Rather did the freezing fear seem to crystallize them, so that they dropped into his conscious-ness like snow flakes.

Slowly he regained control over his quaking limbs and twitching muscles. As if in a nightmare, he looked around him slowly, taking in the details of his surroundings. The room they were in was semicircular, forming half of the great dome. Two small windows, high in the curving ceiling, let in light.

An inner voice kept repeating, *Don't make a sudden move.*

Slowly. Slowly. Above all, don't run. The others did. That was why they died so quickly. Slowly. Slowly.

He saw the Mouser's face. It reflected his own terror. He wondered how much longer this would last, how much longer he could stand it without running amuck, how much longer he could passively endure this feeling of a great invisible paw reaching out over him, span by span, implacably.

The faint sound of footsteps came from the room below. Regular and unhurried footsteps. Now they were crossing into the rear hallway below. Now they were on the stairs. And now they had reached the landing, and were advancing up the second section of the stairs.

The man who entered the room was tall and frail and old and very gaunt. Scant locks of intensely black hair straggled down over his high-domed forehead. His sunken cheeks showed clearly the outlines of his long jawbone, and waxy skin was pulled tight over his small nose. Fanatical eyes burned in deep, bony sockets. He wore the simple, sleeveless robe of a holy man. A pouch hung from the cord round his waist.

He fixed his eyes upon Fafhrd and the Gray Mouser.

'I greet you, you men of blood,' he said in a hollow voice.

Then his gaze fell with displeasure upon the corpse of Rannarsh.

'More blood has been shed. It is not well.'

And with the bony forefinger of his left hand he traced in the air a curious triple square, the sign sacred to the Great God.

'Do not speak,' his calm, toneless voice continued, 'for I know your purposes. You have come to take treasure from this house. Others have sought to do the same. They have failed. You will fail. As for myself, I have no lust for treasure. For forty years I have lived on crusts and water, devoting my spirit to the Great God.' Again he traced the curious sign. 'The gems and ornaments of this world and the jewels and gauds of the world of demons cannot tempt or corrupt me. My purpose in coming here is to destroy an evil thing.

'I' – and here he touched his chest – 'I am Arvlan of Angarngi, the ninth lineal descendant of Urgaan of Angarngi. This I always knew, and sorrowed for, because Urgaan of Angarngi was a man of evil. But not until fifteen days ago, on the Day of the Spider, did I discover from ancient documents that Urgaan had built this house, and built it to be an eternal trap for the unwise and venturesome. He has left a guardian here, and that guardian has endured.

'Cunning was my accursed ancestor, Urgaan, cunning and evil. The most skillful architect in all Lankhmar was Urgaan, a man wise in the ways of stone and learned in geometrical lore. But he scorned the Great God. He longed for improper powers. He had commerce with demons, and won from them an unnatural treasure. But he had no use for it. For in seeking wealth and knowledge and power, he lost his ability to enjoy any good feeling or pleasure, even simple lust. So he hid his treasure, but hid it in such a way that it would wreak endless evil on the world, even as he felt men and one proud, contemptuous, cruel woman – as heartless as this fane – had wreaked evil upon him. It is my purpose and my right to destroy Urgaan's evil.

'Seek not to dissuade me, lest doom fall upon you. As for me, no harm can befall me. The hand of the Great God is poised above me, ready to ward off any danger that may threaten his faithful servant. His will is my will. Do not speak, men of blood! I go to destroy the treasure of Urgaan of Angarngi.'

And with these words, the gaunt holy man walked calmly on, with measured stride, like an apparition, and disappeared through the narrow doorway that led into the forward part of the great dome.

Fafhrd stared after him, his green eyes wide, feeling no desire to follow or to interfere. His terror had not left him, but it was transmuted. He was still aware of a dreadful threat, but it no longer seemed to be directed against him personally.

Meanwhile, a most curious notion had lodged in the mind of the Mouser. He felt that he had just now seen, not a venerable holy man, but a dim reflection of the centuries-dead Urgaan of Angarngi. Surely Urgaan had that same high-domed forehead, that same secret pride, that same air of command. And those locks of youthfully black hair, which contrasted so ill with the aged face also seemed part of a picture looming from the past. A picture dimmed and distorted by time, but retaining something of the power and individuality of the ancient original.

They heard the footsteps of the holy man proceed a little way into the other room. Then for the space of a dozen heartbeats there was complete silence. Then the floor began to tremble slightly under their feet, as if the earth were quaking, or as if a giant were treading near. Then there came a single quavering cry from the next room, cut off in the middle by a single sickening crash that made them lurch. Then, once again, utter silence.

Fafhrd and the Mouser looked at one another in blank amazement – not so much because of what they had just heard but because, almost at the moment of the crash, the pall of terror had lifted from them completely. They jerked out their swords and hurried into the next room.

It was a duplicate of the one they had quitted, save that instead of two small windows, there were three, one of them near the floor. Also, there was but a single door, the one through which they had just entered. All else was closely morticed stone – floor, walls, and hemi-domed ceiling.

Near the thick center wall, which bisected the dome, lay the body of the holy man. Only 'lay' was not the right word. Left shoulder and chest were mashed against the floor. Life was fled. Blood puddled around.

Fafhrd's and the Mouser's eyes searched wildly for a being other than themselves and the dead man and found none – no, not one gnat hovering amongst the dust motes revealed by the narrow shafts of sunlight shooting down through the windows. Their imaginations searched as wildly and as much in vain for a being that could strike such a man-killing blow and vanish through one of the three tiny orifices of the windows. A giant, striking serpent with a granite head ...

Set in the wall near the dead man was a stone about two feet square, jutting out a little from the rest. On this was boldly engraved, in antique Lankhmarian hieroglyph: 'Here rests the treasure of Urgaan of Angarngi.'

The sight of that stone was like a blow in the face to the two adventurers. It roused every ounce of obstinacy and reckless determination in them. What matter that an old man sprawled smashed beside it? They had their swords! What matter they now had proof some grim guardian resided in the treasure house? They could take care of themselves! Run away and leave that stone unmoved, with its insultingly provocative inscription? No, by Kos, and the Behemoth! They'd see themselves in Nehwon's hell first!

Fafhrd ran to fetch the pick and the other large tools, which had been dropped on the stairs when Lord Rannarsh tossed his first dagger. The Mouser looked more closely at the jutting stone. The cracks around it were wide and filled with a dark, tarry mixture. It gave out a slightly hollow sound when he tapped it with his sword hilt. He calculated that the wall was about six feet thick at this point – enough to contain a sizable cavity. He tapped experimentally along the wall in both directions, but the hollow ring quickly ceased. Evidently the cavity was a fairly small one. He noted that the crevices between all the other stones were very fine, showing no evidence of any cementing substance whatsoever. In fact, he couldn't be sure that they weren't false crevices, superficial cuts in the surface of solid rock. But that hardly seemed possible. He heard Fafhrd returning, but continued his examination.

The state of the Mouser's mind was peculiar. A dogged determination to get at the treasure overshadowed other emotions. The inexplicably sudden vanishing of his former terror had left certain parts of his mind benumbed. It was as if he had decided to hold his thoughts in leash until he had seen what the treasure cavity contained. He was content to keep his mind occupied with material details, and yet make no deductions from them.

His calmness gave him a feeling of at least temporary safety. His experiences had vaguely convinced him that the guardian, whatever it was, which had smashed the holy man and played cat and mouse with Rannarsh and themselves, did not strike without first inspiring a premonitory terror in its victims.

Fafhrd felt very much the same way, except that he was even more single-minded in his determination to solve the riddle of the inscribed stone.

They attacked the wide crevices with chisel and mallet. The dark tarry mixture came away fairly easily, first in hard lumps, later in slightly rubbery, gouged strips. After they had cleared it away to the depth of a finger, Fafhrd inserted the pick and managed to move the stone slightly. Thus the Mouser was enabled to gouge a little more deeply on that side. Then Fafhrd subjected the other side of the stone to the leverage of the pick. So the work proceeded, with alternate pryings and gougings.

They concentrated on each detail of the job with unnecessary intensity, mainly to keep their imaginations from being haunted by the image of a man more than two hundred years dead. A man with high-domed forehead, sunken cheeks, nose of a skull – that is, if the dead thing on the floor was a true type of the breed of Angarngi. A man who had somehow won a great treasure, and then hid it away from all eyes, seeking to obtain neither glory nor material profit from it. Who said he scorned the envy of fools, and who yet wrote many provocative notes in diminutive red lettering in order to inform fools of his treasure and make them envious. Who seemed to be reaching out across the dusty centuries, like a spider spinning a web to catch a fly on the other side of the world.

And yet, he was a skillful architect, the holy man had said. Could such an architect build a stone automaton twice as tall as a tall man? A gray stone automaton with a great club? Could he make a hiding place from which it could emerge, deal death, and then return? No, no, such notions were childish, not to be entertained! Stick to the job in hand. First find what lay behind the inscribed stone. Leave thoughts until afterward.

The stone was beginning to give more easily to the pressure of the pick. Soon they would be able to get a good purchase on it and pry it out.

Meanwhile an entirely new sensation was growing in the Mouser – not one of terror at all, but of physical revulsion. The air he breathed seemed thick and sickening. He found himself disliking the texture and consistency of the tarry mixture gouged from the cracks, which somehow he could only liken to wholly imaginary substances, such as the dung of dragons or the solidified vomit of the Behemoth. He avoided touching it with his fingers, and he kicked away the litter of chunks and strips that had gathered around his feet. The sensation of queasy loathing became difficult to endure.

He tried to fight it, but had no more success than if it had been seasickness, which in some ways it resembled. He felt unpleasantly dizzy. His mouth kept filling with saliva. The cold sweat of nausea beaded his forehead. He could tell that Fafhrd was unaffected, and he hesitated to mention the matter; it seemed ridiculously out of place, especially as it was unaccompanied by any fear or fright. Finally the stone itself began to have the same effect on him as the tarry mixture, filling him with a seemingly causeless, but none the less sickening revulsion. Then he could bear it no longer. With a vaguely apologetic nod to Fafhrd, he dropped his chisel and went to the low window for a breath of fresh air.

This did not seem to help matters much. He pushed his head through the window and gulped deeply. His mental processes were overshadowed by the general indifference of extreme nausea, and everything seemed very far away. Therefore when he saw that the peasant girl was standing in the middle of the clearing, it was some time before he began to consider the import of the fact. When he did, part of his sickness left him; or at least he was enabled to overpower it sufficiently to stare at her with gathering interest.

Her face was white, her fists were clenched, her arms held rigid at her sides. Even at the distance he could catch something of the mingled terror and determination with which her eyes were fixed on the great doorway. Toward this doorway she was forcing herself to move, one jerking step after another, as if she had to keep screwing her courage to a higher pitch. Suddenly the Mouser began to feel frightened, not for himself at all, but for the girl. Her terror was obviously intense, and yet she must be doing what she was doing – braving her 'queer and fearsome gray giant' – for his sake and Fafhrd's. At all costs, he thought, she must be prevented from coming closer. It was wrong that she be subjected for one moment longer to such a horribly intense terror.

His mind was confused by his abominable nausea, yet he knew what he must do. He hurried toward the stairs with shaky strides, waving Fafhrd another vague gesture. Just as he was going out of the room he chanced to turn up his eyes, and spied something peculiar on the ceiling. What it was he did not fully realize for some moments.

Fafhrd hardly noticed the Mouser's movements, much less his gestures. The block of stone was rapidly yielding to his efforts. He had previously experienced a faint suggestion of the Mouser's nausea, but perhaps because of his greater single-mindedness, it had not become seriously bothersome. And now his attention was wholly concentrated on the stone. Persistent prying had edged it out a palm's breadth from the wall. Seizing it firmly in his two powerful hands, he tugged it from one side to the other, back and forth. The dark, viscous stuff clung to it tenaciously, but with each sidewise jerk it moved forward a little.

The Mouser lurched hastily down the stairs, fighting vertigo. His feet kicked bones and sent them knocking against the walls. What was it he had seen on the ceiling? Somehow, it seemed to mean something. But he must get the girl out of the clearing. She mustn't come any closer to the house. She mustn't enter.

Fafhrd began to feel the weight of the stone, and knew that it was nearly clear. It was damnably heavy – almost a foot thick. Two carefully gauged heaves finished the job. The stone overbalanced. He stepped quickly back. The stone crashed ponderously on the floor. A rainbow glitter came from the cavity that had been revealed. Fafhrd eagerly thrust his head into it.

The Mouser staggered toward the doorway. It was a bloody smear he had seen on the ceiling. And just above the corpse of the holy man. But why should that be? He'd been smashed against the floor, hadn't he? Was it blood splashed up from his lethal clubbing? But then why smeared? No matter. The girl. He must get to the girl. He must. There she was, almost at the doorway. He could see her. He felt the stone floor vibrating slightly beneath his feet. But that was his dizziness, wasn't it?

Fafhrd felt the vibration, too. But any thought he might have had about it was lost in his wonder at what he saw. The cavity was filled to a level just below the surface of the opening, with a heavy metallic liquid that resembled mercury, except that it was night-black. Resting on this liquid was a more astonishing group of gems than Fafhrd had ever dreamed of.

In the center was a titan diamond, cut with a myriad of oddly angled facets. Around it were two irregular circles, the inner formed of twelve rubies, each a decahedron, the outer formed of seventeen emeralds, each an irregular octahedron. Lying between these gems, touching some of them, sometimes connecting them with each other, were thin, fragile-looking bars of crystal, amber, greenish tourmaline, and honey-pale orichalcum. All these objects did not seem to be floating in the metallic liquid so much as resting upon it, their weight pressing down the surface into shallow depressions, some cup-shaped, others trough-like. The rods glowed faintly, while each of the gems glittered with a light that Fafhrd's mind strangely conceived to be refracted starlight.

His gaze shifted to the mercurous heavy fluid, where it bulged up between, and he saw distorted reflections of stars and constellations which he recognized, stars and constellations which would be visible now in the sky overhead, were it not for the concealing brilliance of the sun. An awesome wonder engulfed him. His gaze shifted back to the gems. There was something tremendously meaningful about their complex arrangement, something that seemed to speak of overwhelming truths in an alien symbolism. More, there was a compelling impression of inner movement, or sluggish thought, of inorganic consciousness. It was like what the eyes see when they close at night – not utter blackness, but a shifting, fluid pattern of many-colored points of light. Feeling that he was reaching impiously into the core of a thinking mind, Fafhrd gripped with his right hand for the diamond as big as a man's skull.

The Mouser blundered through the doorway. There could be no mistaking it now. The close-morticed stones were trembling. That bloody smear, as if the ceiling had champed down upon the holy man, crushing him against the floor, or as if the floor had struck upward. But there was the girl, her terror-wide eyes fastened upon him, her mouth open for a scream that did not come. He must drag her away, out of the clearing.

But why should he feel that a fearful threat was now directed at himself as well? Why should he feel that something was poised above him, threatening? As he stumbled down the terraced steps, he looked over his shoulder and up. The tower. The tower! It was falling. It was falling toward him. It was dipping at him over the dome. But there were no fractures along its length. It was not breaking. It was not falling. It was bending.

Fafhrd's hand jerked back, clutching the great, strangely faceted jewel, so heavy that he had difficulty in keeping his hold upon it. Immediately the surface of the metallic, star-reflecting fluid was disturbed. It bobbled and shook. Surely the whole house was shaking, too. The other jewels began to dart about erratically, like water insects on the surface of a puddle. The various crystalline and metallic bars began to spin, their tips attracted now to one jewel and now to another, as if the jewels were lodestone and the bars iron needles. The whole surface of the fluid was in a whirling, jerking confusion that suggested a mind gone mad because of loss of its chief part.

For an agonizing instant the Mouser stared up amazement – frozen at the clublike top of the tower, ponderously hurling itself down upon him. Then he ducked and lunged forward at the girl, tackling her, rapidly rolling over and over with her. The tower top struck a sword's length behind them, with a thump that jolted them momentarily off the ground. Then it jerked itself up from the pitlike depression it had made.

Fafhrd tore his gaze away from the incredible, alien beauty of the jewel-confused cavity. His right hand was burning. The diamond was hot. No, it was cold beyond belief. By Kos, the room was changing shape! The ceiling was bulging downward at a point. He made for the door, then stopped dead in his tracks. The door was closing like a stony mouth. He turned and took a few steps over the quaking floor toward the small, low window. It snapped shut, like a sphincter. He tried to drop the diamond. It clung painfully to the inside of his hand. With a snap of his wrist he whipped it away from him. It hit the floor and began to bounce about, glaring like a living star.

The Mouser and the peasant girl rolled toward the edge of the clearing. The tower made two more tremendous bashes at them, but both went yards wide, like the blows of a blind madman. Now they were out of range. The Mouser lay sprawled on his side, watching a stone house that hunched and heaved like a beast, and a tower that bent double as it thumped grave-deep pits into the ground. It crashed into a group of boulders and its top broke off, but the jaggedly fractured end continued to beat the boulders in wanton anger, smashing them into fragments. The Mouser felt a compulsive urge to take out his dagger and stab himself in the heart. A man had to die when he saw something like that.

Fafhrd clung to sanity because he was threatened from a new direction at every minute and because he could say to himself, 'I know. I know. The house is a beast, and the jewels are its mind. Now that mind is mad. I know. I know.' Walls, ceiling, and floor quaked and heaved, but their movements did not seem to be directed especially at him. Occasional crashes almost deafened him. He staggered over rocky swells, dodging stony advances that were

255

half bulges and half blows, but that lacked the speed and directness of the tower's first smash at the Mouser. The corpse of the holy man was jolted about in grotesque mechanical reanimation.

Only the great diamond seemed aware of Fafhrd. Exhibiting a fretful intelligence, it kept bounding at him viciously, sometimes leaping as high as his head. He involuntarily made for the door as his only hope. It was champing up and down with convulsive regularity. Watching his chance, he dived at it just as it was opening, and writhed through. The diamond followed him, striking at his legs. The carcass of Rannarsh was flung sprawling in his path. He jumped over it, then slid, lurched, stumbled, fell down stairs in earthquake, where dry bones danced. Surely the beast must die, the house must crash and crush him flat. The diamond leaped for his skull, missed, hurtled through the air, and struck a wall. Thereupon it burst into a great puff of iridescent dust.

Immediately the rhythm of the shaking of the house began to increase. Fafhrd raced across the heaving floor, escaped by inches the killing embrace of the great doorway, plunged across the clearing – passing a dozen feet from the spot where the tower was beating boulders into crushed rock – and then leaped over two pits in the ground. His face was rigid and white. His eyes were vacant. He blundered bull-like into two or three trees, and only came to a halt because he knocked himself flat against one of them.

The house had ceased most of its random movements, and the whole of it was shaking like a huge dark jelly. Suddenly its forward part heaved up like a behemoth in death agony. The two smaller domes were jerked ponderously a dozen feet off the ground, as if they were the paws. The tower whipped into convulsive rigidity. The main dome contracted sharply, like a stupendous lung. For a moment it hung there, poised. Then it crashed to the ground in a heap of gigantic stone shards. The earth shook. The forest resounded. Battered atmosphere whipped branches and leaves. Then all was still. Only from the fractures in the stone a tarry, black liquid was slowing oozing, and here and there iridescent puffs of air suggested jewel-dust.

Along a narrow, dusty road two horsemen were cantering slowly toward the village of Soreev in the southernmost limits of the land of Lankhmar. They presented a somewhat battered appearance. The limbs of the larger, who was mounted on a chestnut gelding showed several bruises, and there was a bandage around his thigh and another around the palm of his right hand. The smaller man, the one mounted on a gray mare, seemed to have suffered an equal number of injuries.

'Do you know where we're headed?' said the latter, breaking a long silence. 'We're headed for a city. And in that city are endless houses of stone, stone towers without numbers, streets paved with stone, domes, arches, stairs. *Tcha*, if I feel then as I feel now, I'll never go within a bowshot of Lankhmar's walls.'

His large companion smiled.

'What now, little man? Don't tell me you're afraid of – earthquakes?'

III: THIEVES' HOUSE

'What's the use of knowing the name of a skull? One would never have occasion to talk to it,' said the fat thief loudly. 'What interests me is that it has rubies for eyes.'

'Yet it is written here that its name is Ohmphal,' replied the black-bearded thief in the quieter tones of authority.

'Let me see,' said the bold, red-haired wench, leaning over his shoulder. She needed to be bold; all women were immemorially forbidden to enter Thieves' House. Together the three of them read the tiny hieroglyphs.

ITEM: *the skull Ohmphal, of the Master Thief Ohmphal, with great ruby eyes, and one pair of jeweled hands.* HISTORY OF ITEM: *the skull Ohmphal was stolen from the Thieves' Guild by the priests of Votishal and placed by them in the crypt of their accursed temple.* INSTRUCTIONS: *the skull Ohmphal is to be recovered at the earliest opportunity, that it may be given proper veneration in the Thieves' Sepulcher.* DIFFICULTIES: *the lock of the door leading to the crypt is reputed to be beyond the cunning of any thief to pick.* WARNINGS: *within the crypt is rumored to be a guardian beast of terrible ferocity.*

'Those crabbed letters are devilish hard to read,' said the red-haired wench, frowning.

'And no wonder, for they were written centuries ago,' said the black-bearded thief.

The fat thief said, 'I never heard tell of a Thieves'

Sepulcher, save the junkyard, the incinerator, and the Inner Sea.'

'Times and customs change,' the black-bearded thief philosophized. 'Periods of reverence alternate with periods of realism.'

'Why is it called the skull Ohmphal?' the fat thief wondered. 'Why not the skull *of* Ohmphal?'

The black-bearded thief shrugged.

'Where did you find this parchment?' the red-haired wench asked him.

'Beneath the false bottom of a moldering chest in our storerooms,' he replied.

'By the gods who are not,' chuckled the fat thief, still poring over the parchment, 'the Thieves' Guild must have been superstitious in those ancient days. To think of wasting jewels on a mere skull. If we ever get hold of Master Ohmphal, we'll venerate him – by changing his ruby eyes into good hard money.'

'Aye!' said the black-bearded thief. 'And it was just that matter I wanted to talk to you about, Fissif – the getting hold of Ohmphal.'

'Oh, but there are – difficulties, as you, Krovas our master, must surely know,' said the fat thief, quickly singing another tune. 'Even today, after the passage of centuries, men still shudder when they speak of the crypt of Votishal, with its lock and its beast. There is no one in the Thieves' Guild who can—'

'No one in the Thieves' Guild, that's true!' interrupted the black-bearded thief sharply. 'But' – and here his voice began to go low – 'there are those outside the Thieves' Guild who can. Have you heard that there is recently returned here to Lankhmar a certain rogue and picklock known as the Gray Mouser? And with him a huge barbarian who goes by the name of Fafhrd, but is sometimes called the Beast-Slayer? We have a score as you well know, to settle with both of them. They slew our sorcerer, Hristomilo. That pair commonly hunts alone – yet if you were to approach them with this tempting suggestion …'

'But, Master,' interposed the fat thief, 'in that case, they would demand at least two-thirds of the profits.'

'Exactly!' said the black-bearded thief, with a sudden flash of cold humor. The red-haired wench caught his meaning, and laughed aloud. 'Exactly! And that is just the reason why I have chosen you, Fissif, the smoothest of double-crossers, to undertake this business.'

The ten remaining days of the Month of the Serpent had passed, and the first fifteen days of the Month of the Owl, since those three had conferred. And the fifteenth day had darkened into night. Chill fog, like a dark shroud, hugged ancient stony Lankhmar, chief city of the land of Lankhmar. This night the fog had come earlier than usual, flowing down the twisting streets and mazy alleyways. And it was getting thicker.

In one street rather narrower and more silent than the rest – Cheap Street, its name – a square yellow torchlight shone from a wide doorway in a vast and rambling house of stone. There was something ominous in a single open door in a street where all other doors were barred against the darkness and the damp. People avoided this street at night. And there was reason for their fear. The house had a bad reputation. People said it was the den in which the thieves of Lankhmar gathered to plot and palaver and settle their private bickerings, the headquarters from which Krovas, the reputed Master Thief, issued his orders – in short, the home of the formidable Thieves' Guild of Lankhmar.

But now a man came hurrying along this street, every now and then looking apprehensively over his shoulder. He was a fat man, and he hobbled a little, as if he had recently ridden hard and far. He carried a tarnished and ancient-looking copper box of about the size to contain a human head. He paused in the doorway and uttered a certain password – seemingly to the empty air, for the long hall ahead of him was empty. But a voice from a point inside and above the doorway answered, 'Pass, Fissif. Krovas awaits you in his room.' And the fat one said, 'They follow me close – you know the two I mean.' And the voice replied, 'We are ready for them.' And the fat one hurried down the hall.

For a considerable time, then, there was nothing but silence and the thickening fog. Finally a faint warning whistle came from somewhere down the street. It was repeated closer by and answered from inside the doorway.

Then, from the same direction as the first whistle, came the tread of feet, growing louder. It sounded as if there were only one person, but the effulgence of the light from the door showed that there was also a little man, who walked softly, a little man clad in close-fitting garments of gray – tunic, jerkin, mouseskin cap and cloak.

His companion was rangy and copper-haired, obviously a northern barbarian from the distant lands of the Cold Waste. His tunic was rich brown, his cloak green. There was considerable leather about him – wrist-bands, head-band, boots, and a wide tight-laced belt. Fog had wet the leather and misted the brass studding it. As they entered the square of light before the doorway, a frown furrowed his broad wide forehead. His green eyes glanced quickly from side to side. Putting his hand on the little man's shoulder, he whispered:

'I don't like the looks of this, Gray Mouser.'

'*Tcha!* The place always looks like this, as you well know,' retorted the Gray Mouser sharply, his mobile lips sneering and dark eyes blazing. 'They just do it to scare the populace. Come on, Fafhrd! We're not going to let that misbegotten, double-dealing Fissif escape after the way he cheated us.'

'I know all that, my angry little weasel,' the barbarian replied, tugging the Mouser back. 'And the idea of Fissif escaping displeases me. But putting my bare neck in a trap displeases me more. Remember, they whistled.'

'*Tcha!* They always whistle. They like to be mysterious. I know these thieves. Fafhrd. I know them well. And you yourself have twice entered Thieves' House and escaped. Come on!'

'But I don't know *all* of Thieves' House,' Fafhrd protested. 'There's a modicum of danger.'

'Modicum! *They* don't know all of Thieves' House, their own place. It's a maze of the unknown, a labyrinth of forgotten history. *Come on!*'

'I don't know. It awakens evil memories of my lost Vlana.'

'And of my lost Ivrian! But must we let them win because of that?'

The big man shrugged his shoulders and started forward.

'On second thought,' whispered the Mouser, 'there may be something to what you say.' And he slipped a dirk from his belt.

Fafhrd showed white teeth in grin and slowly pulled a big-pommeled longsword from its well-oiled scabbard.

'A rotten weapon for infighting,' murmured the Mouser in a comradely sardonical way.

Warily now they approached the door, each taking a side and sticking close to the wall. Holding the grip of his sword low, the point high, ready to strike in any direction, Fafhrd entered. The Mouser was a little ahead of him. Out of the corner of his eye Fafhrd saw something snakelike dropping down at the Mouser's head from above, and struck at it quickly with his sword. This flipped it toward him and he caught it with his free hand. It was a strangler's noose. He gave it a sudden sidewise heave and the man gripping the other end toppled out from a ledge above. For an instant he seemed to hang suspended in the air, a dark-skinned rogue with long black hair and a greasy tunic of red leather worked with gold thread. As Fafhrd deliberately raised his sword, he saw that the Mouser was lunging across the corridor at him, dirk in hand. For a moment he thought the Mouser had gone mad. But the Mouser's dirk missed him by a hairbreadth and another blade whipped past his back.

The Mouser had seen a trapdoor open in the floor beside Fafhrd and a bald-headed thief shoot up, sword in hand. After deflecting the blow aimed at his companion, the Mouse slammed the trapdoor back and had the satisfaction of catching with it the blade of the sword and two left-hand fingers of the ducking thief. All three were broken and the muted yowl from below was impressive. Fafhrd's man, spitted on the longsword, was quite dead.

From the street came several whistles and the sound of men moving in.

'They've cut us off!' snapped the Mouser. 'Our best chance lies ahead. We'll make for Krovas' room. Fissif may be there. Follow me!'

And he darted down the corridor and up a winding stair, Fafhrd behind him. At the second level they left the stair and raced for a doorway from which yellow light shone.

It puzzled the Mouser that they had met with no interference. His sharp ears no longer caught sounds of pursuit. On the threshold he pulled up quickly, so that Fafhrd collided with him.

It was a large room with several alcoves. Like the rest of the building, the floor and walls were of smooth dark stone, unembellished. It was lit by four earthenware lamps set at random on a heavy cyprus table. Behind the table sat a richly robed, black-bearded man, seemingly staring down in extreme astonishment at a copper box and a litter of smaller objects, his hands gripping the table edge. But they had no time to consider his odd motionlessness and still odder complexion, for their attention was immediately riveted on the red-haired wench who stood beside him.

As she sprang back like a startled cat, Fafhrd pointed at what she held under one arm and cried, 'Look, Mouser, the skull! The skull and the hands!'

Clasped in her slim arm was indeed a brownish, ancient-looking skull, curiously banded with gold from whose eye sockets great rubies sparkled and whose teeth were diamonds and blackened pearls. And in her white hand were gripped two neat packets of brown bones, tipped with a golden gleam and reddish sparkle. Even as Fafhrd spoke she turned and ran toward the largest alcove, her lithe legs outlined against silken garments. Fafhrd and the Mouser rushed after her. They saw she was heading for a small low doorway. Entering the alcove her free hand shot out and gripped a cord hanging from the ceiling. Not pausing, swinging at the hips, she gave it a tug. Folds of thick, weighted velvet fell down behind her. The Mouser and Fafhrd plunged into them and floundered. It was the Mouser who got through first, wriggling under. He saw an oblong of faint light narrowing ahead of him, sprang for it, grabbed at the block of stone sinking into the low doorway, then jerked his hand back with a curse and sucked at bruised fingers. The stone panel closed with a slight grating noise.

Fafhrd lifted the thick folds of velvet on his broad shoulders as if they were a great cloak. Light from the main rooms flooded into the alcove and revealed a closely mortised stone wall of uniform appearance. The Mouser started to dig the point of his dirk into a crack, then desisted.

'Pah! I know these doors! They're either worked from the other side or else by distant levers. She's gotten clear away and the skull with her.'

He continued to suck the fingers that had come so near

to being crushed, wondering superstitiously if his breaking of the trapdoor thief's fingers had been a kind of omen.

'We forget Krovas,' said Fafhrd suddenly, lifting the drapes with his hand and looking back over his shoulder.

But the black-bearded man had not taken any notice of the commotion. As they approached him slowly they saw that his face was bluish-purple under the swarthy skin, and that his eyes bulged not from astonishment, but from strangulation. Fafhrd lifted the oily, well-combed beard and saw cruel indentations on the throat, seeming more like those of claws than fingers. The Mouser examined the things on the table. There were a number of jeweler's instruments, their ivory handles stained deep yellow from long use. He scooped up some small objects.

'Krovas had already pried three of the finger-jewels loose and several of the teeth,' he remarked, showing Fafhrd three rubies and a number of pearls and diamonds, which glittered on his palm.

Fafhrd nodded and again lifted Krovas' beard, frowning at the indentations, which were beginning to deepen in color.

'I wonder who the woman is?' said the Mouser. 'No thief is permitted to bring a woman here on pain of death. But the Master Thief has special powers and perhaps can take chances.'

'He has taken one too many,' muttered Fafhrd.

Then the Mouser awoke to their situation. He had half-formulated a plan of effecting an escape from the Thieves' House by capturing and threatening Krovas. But a dead man cannot be effectively intimidated. As he started to speak to Fafhrd they caught the murmur of several voices and the sound of approaching footsteps. Without deliberation they retired into the alcove, the Mouser cutting a small slit in the drapes at eye level and Fafhrd doing the same.

They heard someone say, 'Yes, the two of them got

clean away, damn their luck! We found the alley door open.'

The first thief to enter was paunchy, white-faced, and obviously frightened. The Gray Mouser and Fafhrd immediately recognized him as Fissif. Pushing him along roughly was a tall, expressionless fellow with heavy arms and big hands. The Mouser knew him, too – Slevyas the Tight-lipped, recently promoted to be Krovas' chief lieutenant. About a dozen others filed into the room and took up positions near the walls. Veteran thieves all, with a considerable sprinkling of scars, pock-marks, and other mutilations, including two black-patched eye sockets. They were somewhat wary and ill at ease, held daggers and shortswords ready, and all stared intently at the strangled man.

'So Krovas is truly dead,' said Slevyas, shoving Fissif forward. 'At least that much of your story is true.'

'Dead as a fish,' echoed a thief who had moved closer to the table. 'Now we've got us a better master. We'll have no more of black-beard and his red-haired wench.'

'Hide your teeth, rat, before I break them!' Slevyas whipped out the words coldly.

'But you are our master now,' replied the thief in a surprised voice.

'Yes, I'm the master of all of you, unquestioned master, and my first piece of advice is this: to criticize a dead thief may not be irreverent – but it is certainly a waste of time. Now, Fissif, where's the jeweled skull? We all know it's more valuable than a year's pickpocketing, and that the Thieves' Guild needs gold. So, no nonsense!'

The Mouser peering cautiously from his slit, grinned at the look of fear on Fissif's fat-jowled face.

'The skull, Master?' said Fissif in a quavering sepulchral tone. 'Why, it's flown back to the grave from which we three filched it. Surely if those bony hands could strangle Krovas, as I saw with my own eyes, the skull could fly.'

266

Slevyas slapped Fissif across the face.

'You lie, you quaking bag of mush! I will tell you what happened. You plotted with those two rogues, the Gray Mouser and Fafhrd. You thought no one would suspect you because you double-crossed them according to instructions. But you planned a double-double-cross. You helped them escape the trap we had set, let them kill Krovas, and then assured their escape by starting a panic with your tale of dead fingers killing Krovas. You thought you could brazen it out.'

'But Master,' Fissif pleaded, 'with my own eyes I saw the skeletal fingers leap to his throat. They were angry with him because he had pried forth some of the jewels that were their nails and—'

Another slap changed his statement to a whining grunt.

'A fool's story,' sneered a scrawny thief. 'How could the bones hold together?'

'They were laced on brass wires,' returned Fissif in meek tones.

'Nah! And I suppose the hands, after strangling Krovas, picked up the skull and carried it away with them?' suggested another thief. Several sniggered. Slevyas silenced them with a look, then indicated Fissif with his thumb.

'Pinion him,' he ordered.

Two thieves sidled up to Fissif, who offered no resistance. They twisted his arms behind his back.

'We'll do this thing decently,' said Slevyas, seating himself on the table. 'Thieves' trial. Everything in order. Briefly this is a matter for the Thieves' Jury to consider. Fissif, cut-purse of the first rank, was commissioned to loot the sacred grave at the temple of Votishal of one skull and one pair of hands. Because of certain unusual difficulties involved, Fissif was ordered to league himself with two outsiders of special talent, to wit, the northern barbarian Fafhrd and the notorious Gray Mouser.'

The Mouser made a courteous and formal bow behind the drapes, then glued his eye once more to the slit.

'The loot obtained, Fissif was to steal it from the two others – and at the earliest possible moment, to avoid their stealing it from him.'

The Mouser thought he heard Fafhrd smother a curse and grit his teeth.

'If possible, Fissif was to slay them,' concluded Slevyas. 'In any case he was to bring the loot direct to Krovas. So much for Fissif's instructions, as detailed to me by Krovas. Now tell your story, Fissif, but – mind you – no old-wives' tales.'

'Brother thieves,' began Fissif in a heavy mournful voice. This was greeted by several derisive cries. Slevyas rapped carelessly for order.

'I followed out those instructions just as they were given me,' continued Fissif. 'I sought out Fafhrd and the Gray Mouser, and interested them in the plan. I agreed to share the loot equally with them, a third to each man.'

Fafhrd, squinting at Fissif through the drape, nodded his head solemnly. Fissif then made several uncomplimentary remarks about Fafhrd and the Mouser, evidently hoping thereby to convince his listeners that he had not plotted with them. The other thieves only smiled grimly.

'And when it came to the actual filching of the loot from the temple,' Fissif went on, gaining confidence from the sound of his own voice, 'it turned out I had little need of their help.'

Again Fafhrd smothered a curse. He could hardly endure listening in silence to such outrageous lies. But the Mouser enjoyed it after a fashion.

'This is an unwise time to brag,' interjected Slevyas. 'You know very well that the Mouser's cunning was needed in picking the great triple lock, and that the guardian beast could not easily have been slain but for the Northerner.'

Fafhrd was somewhat mollified by this. Fissif became humble again and bowed his head in assent. The thieves began gradually to close in on him.

'And so,' he finished in a kind of panic, 'I took up the loot while they slept, and spurred on to Lankhmar. I dared not slay them, for fear the killing of one would awaken the other. I brought the loot direct to Krovas, who complimented me and began to pry out the gems. There lies the copper box which held the skull and hands.' He pointed at the table. 'And as for what happened afterward—' he paused, wet his lips, looked around fearfully, then added in a small despairing voice, 'It happened just as I told you before.'

The thieves, snarling disbelief, closed in, but Slevyas halted them with a peremptory rap. He seemed to be considering something.

Another thief darted into the room, saluted Slevyas. 'Master,' he panted, 'Moolsh, stationed on the roof opposite the alley door, has just reported that, though open all night, no one either entered or left. The two intruders may still be here!'

Slevyas' start as he received the news was almost imperceptible. He stared at his informant. Then slowly and as if drawn by instinct, his impassive face turned until his pale, small eyes rested upon the heavy drapes curtaining the alcove. As he was about to give an order, the drapes bellied out as if with a great gust of wind. They swung forward and up until almost level with the ceiling, and he glimpsed two figures racing forward. The tall, copper-haired barbarian was aiming a blow at him.

With a suppleness which belied his large frame, Slevyas half-ducked, half-dropped, and the great longsword bit deep into the table against which he had been resting. From the floor he saw his underlings springing back in confusion, one staggered by a blow. Fissif, quicker-nerved than the rest because he knew his life was at stake in more ways than one, snatched and hurled a dagger. It was an imperfect throw, traveling pommel-forward. But it was accurate. Slevyas saw it take the tall barbarian on the side of the head as he rushed through the doorway, seeming to stagger him. Then Slevyas was on his feet, sword drawn and organizing pursuit. In a few moments the room was empty, save for dead Krovas staring at an empty copper box in a cruel mockery of astonishment.

The Gray Mouser knew the layout of the Thieves' House – not as well as the palm of his hand, but well enough – and he led Fafhrd around stony angles, sprang up and down small sets of steps, two or three each, which made it difficult to determine which level they were on. The Mouser had drawn his slim sword Scalpel for the first time and used it to knock over the candles they passed, and to make swipes at the wall torches, hoping thereby to confuse the pursuit, whose whistles sounded sharply from behind them. Twice Fafhrd stumbled and recovered himself.

Two half-dressed apprentice thieves stuck their heads out of a door. The Mouser slammed it in their inquiring excited faces, then sprang down a curving stairway. He was heading for a third exit he surmised would be poorly guarded.

'If we are separated, let our rendezvous be the Silver Eel,' he said in a quick aside to Fafhrd, mentioning a tavern they frequented.

The Northerner nodded. His head was beginning to feel less dizzy now, though it still pained him considerably. He did not, however, gauge accurately the height of the low arch under which the Mouser sped after descending the equivalent of two levels, and it gave his head as hard a clip as had the dagger. Everything went dark and whirling before his eyes. He heard the Mouser saying, 'This way now! We follow the left-hand wall,' and trying to keep a tight hold on his consciousness, he plunged into the narrow corridor down which the Mouser was pointing. He thought the Mouser was following him.

But the Mouser had waited a moment too long. True, the main pursuit was still out of sight, but a watchman whose duty it was to patrol this passage, hearing the whistles, had returned hurriedly from a friendly game of dice. The Mouser ducked as the artfully-cast noose settled around his neck, but not quite soon enough. It tightened cruelly against ear, cheek, and jawbone, and brought him down. In the next instant Scalpel severed the cord, but that gave the watchman time to get out his sword. For a few perilous moments the Mouser fought him from the floor, warding off a flashing point that came close enough to his nose to make him cross-eyed. Watching his chance, he scrambled to his feet, rushed his man back a dozen paces with a whirlwind attack in which Scalpel seemed to become three or four swords, and ended the man's cries for help with a slicing thrust through the neck.

The delay was sufficient. As the Mouser wrenched away the noose from his cheek and mouth, where it had gagged him during the fight, he saw the first of Slevyas' crowd dart out under the archway. Abruptly the Mouser made off down the main corridor, away from the path of escape Fafhrd had taken. A half dozen plans flashed through his mind. There came a triumphant outcry as Slevyas' crowd sighted him, then a number of whistles from ahead. He decided his best chance was to make for the roof, and whirled into a cross corridor. He was hopeful that Fafhrd had escaped, though the Northerner's behavior bothered him. He was supremely confident that he, the Gray Mouser could elude ten times as many thieves as now careened and skidded through the mazy corridors of the Thieves' House. He lengthened his skipping stride, and his soft-shod feet fairly flew over the well-worn stone.

Fafhrd, lost in pitch darkness for he didn't know how long, steadied himself against what felt like a table and

271

tried to remember how he had gotten so grievously far astray. But his skull throbbed and kept tightening with pain, and the incidents he recalled were jumbled up, with gaps in between. There was a matter of sprawling down a stair and of pushing against a wall of carven stone which had given way silently and let him tumble through. At one point he had been violently sick and at another he must have been unconscious for some time, for he recalled pushing himself up from a prone position and crawling for some distance on hands and knees through a jumble of casks and bales of rotten cloth. That he had banged his head at least once more he was certain; pushing his fingers through his tangled, sweaty locks he could detect as many as three distinct lumps in his scalp. His chief emotion was a dull and persistent anger directed at the heavy masses of stone around him. His primitive imagination half-invested them with a conscious intent to oppose him and block him off whichever way he moved. He knew that he had somehow confused the Mouser's simple directions. Just which wall was it the little gray man had told him to follow? And just where was the Mouser? In some fearful mix-up likely.

If only the air weren't so hot and dry, he felt he'd be able to think things out better. Nothing seemed to agree. Even the quality of the air didn't fit with his impression that he had been descending most of the way, as if into a deep cellar. It should have been cold and damp, but it wasn't. It was dry and warm. He slid his hand along the wooden surface on which it was resting, and soft dust piled up between his fingers. That, along with the impenetrable darkness and total silence, would seem to indicate he was in a region of the Thieves' House long disused. He brooded for a moment over his memories of the stone crypt from which he and the Mouser and Fissif had filched the jeweled skull. The fine dust, rising to his nostrils, made him sneeze, and that started him moving again. His groping hand found a wall. He tried to recall the direction from which he had originally approached the table, but was unable to, and so started out at random. He moved along slowly, feeling his way, hand and foot.

His caution saved him. One of the stones seemed to give slightly under his exploring foot and he jerked back. Abruptly there came a rasping sound followed by a clank and two muffled thuds. The air in front of his face was disturbed. He waited a moment, then groped forward cautiously through the blackness. His hand encountered a strip of rusty metal at shoulder level. Feeling along it gingerly he found it protruded from a crevice in the left wall, and ending in a point a few inches from a wall he now discovered to be on his right. Further groping revealed a similar blade below the first. He now realized that the thudding sounds had been caused by counter-weights, which, released by pressure on the stone, had automatically propelled the blades through the crevice. Another step forward and he would have been spitted. He reached for his long-sword, found it was not in the scabbard, so took the scabbard instead and with it broke off the two blades close to the wall. Then he turned and retraced his steps to the dust-covered table.

But a slow tracing of the wall beyond the table led him back to the corridor of the sword blades. He shook his aching head and cursed angrily because he had no light nor way of making fire. How then? Had he originally entered this blind alley by way of the corridor, missing the deadly stone by pure luck? That seemed to be the only answer, so with a growl he started off again down the corridor of the sword blades, arms outstretched and hands brushing the two walls, so that he might know when he came to an intersection, and footing it most gingerly. After a little it occurred to him that he might have fallen into the chamber behind from some entrance partway up the wall, but stubbornness kept him from turning back a second time.

The next thing his exploring foot encountered was an emptiness, which turned out to be the beginning of a flight of stone steps leading down. At that point he gave up trying to remember just how he had gotten where he was. About twenty steps down his nostrils caught a musty, arid odor welling up from below. Another twenty steps and he began comparing it to the odor found in certain ancient desert tombs of the Eastern Lands. There was an almost imperceptible spiciness to it, a dead spiciness. His skin felt hot and dry. He drew his long knife from his belt and moved silently, slowly.

At the fifty-third step the stair ended and the side walls retreated. From the feel of the air, he thought he must be in a large chamber. He advanced a little way, his boots scuffling a thick carpet of fine dust. There was a dry flapping and faint rattling in the air above his head. Twice something small and hard brushed his cheek. He remembered bat-infested caves into which he had previously ventured. But these tiny noises, though in many ways similar, were not quite like those of bats. The short hairs prickled on the back of his neck. He strained his eyes, but saw only the meaningless pattern of points of light that comes with inky darkness.

Again one of the things brushed his face and this time he was ready for it. His big hands grabbed swiftly – and then nearly dropped what they clutched, for it was dry and weightless, a mere framework of tiny brittle bones which cracked under his fingers. His finger and thumb encountered a minute animal skull.

His mind fought down the idea of bats which were skeletons and yet flapped to and fro in a great tomb-like chamber. Surely this creature must have died hanging to the roof above his head, and his entrance dislodged it. But he did not grasp again at the faint rattling noises in the air.

Then he began to sense sounds of another sort — diminutive shrill squeaks almost too high for the ear to catch. Whatever they were, real or imagined, there was that about them which bred panic, and Fafhrd found himself shouting: 'Speak to me! What are you whining and tittering about? Reveal yourselves!'

At this, echoes cried faintly back to him, and he knew for certain he was in a large chamber. Then there was silence, even the sounds in the air receding. And after the silence had endured for twenty or more beats of Fafhrd's pounding heart, it was broken in a way Fafhrd did not like.

A faint, high, listless voice came from somewhere ahead of him, saying, 'The man is a Northerner, brothers, a long-haired, uncouth barbarian from the Cold Waste.'

From a spot a little way to one side a similar voice responded, 'In our days we met many of his breed at the docks. We soused them with drink, and stole gold dust from their pouches. We were mighty thieves in our day, matchless in craft and cunning.'

And a third—'See, he has lost his sword, and look brothers, he has crushed a bat and holds it in his hand.'

Fafhrd's shout to the effect that this was all nonsense and mummery died before it reached his lips, for it suddenly occurred to him to wonder how these creatures could tell his appearance and even see what he held in his hand, when it was pitch dark. Fafhrd knew well that even the cat and the owl are blind in complete darkness. A crawling terror took hold of him.

'But the skull of a bat is not the skull of a man,' came what seemed to be the first voice. 'He is one of the three who recovered our brother's skull from the temple of Votishal. Yet he has not brought the skull with him.'

'For centuries our brother's bejeweled head has languished lonely under the accursed fane of Vitishal,' spoke a fourth. 'And now that those above have stolen him back, they do not mean to return him to us. They would tear out his glittering eyes and sell them for greasy coins. They are puny thieves, godless and greedy. They have forgotten us, their ancient brothers, and are evil entirely.'

There was something horribly dead and far away about the voices, as if they formed in a void. Something emotionless and yet strangely sad and strangely menacing, halfway between a faint, hopeless sigh and a fainter, icy laugh. Fafhrd clenched his hands tight, so that the tiny skeleton crackled to splinters, which he brushed away spasmodically. He tried to rally his courage and move forward, but could not.

'It is not fitting that such ignoble fate befall our brother,' came the first voice, which held the barest suggestion of authority over the others. 'Hearken now, Northerner, to our words, and hearken well.'

'See, brothers,' broke in the second, 'the Northerner is afraid, and wipes his mouth with his great hand, and gnaws his knuckle in uncertainty and fear.'

Fafhrd began to tremble at hearing his actions so minutely described. Long-buried terrors arose in his mind. He remembered his earliest thoughts of death, how as a boy he had first witnessed the terrible funeral rites of the Cold Waste and joined in muted prayers to Kos and the nameless god of doom. Then, for the first time, he thought he could distinguish something in the darkness. It might only have been a peculiar formation of the meaningless patter of dimly glittering points of light, but he distinguished a number of tiny sparklings on a level with his own head, all in pairs about a thumb's-length apart. Some were deep red, and some green, and some pale-blue like sapphires. He vividly recalled the ruby eyes of the skull stolen from Votishal, the skull Fissif averred had strangled Krovas with bony hands. The points of light were gathering together and moving toward him, very slowly.

'Northerner,' continued the first voice, 'know that we are the ancient master thieves of Lankhmar, and that we needs must have the lost brain, which is his skull, of our brother Ohmphal. You must bring it to us before the stars of midnight next shine overhead. Else you will be sought out and your life drawn from you.'

The pairs of colored lights were still closing in, and now Fafhrd thought he could hear the sound of dry, grating footsteps in the dust. He recalled the deep purple indentations on the throat of Krovas.

'You must bring the skull without fail,' echoed the second voice.

'Before next midnight,' came another.

'The jewels must be in the skull; not one must be held back from us.'

'Ohmphal our brother shall return.'

'If you fail us,' whispered the first voice, 'we shall come for the skull – and for you.'

And then they seemed to be all around him, crying out 'Ohmphal – Ohmphal,' in those detestable voices which were still not one whit louder or less far away. Fafhrd thrust out his hands convulsively, touched something hard and smooth and dry. And with that he shook and started like a frightened horse, turned and ran off at full speed, came to a painful, stumbling stop against the stone steps, and raced up them three at a time, stumbling and bruising his elbows against the walls.

The fat thief Fissif wandered about disconsolately in a large low cellar-chamber dimly lighted, littered with odds and ends and piled with empty casks and bales of rotten cloth. He chewed a mildly soporific nut which stained his lips blue and dribbled down his flabby jaws; at regular intervals he sighed in self-pity. He realized his prospects in the Thieves' Guild were rather dubious, even though Slevyas had granted him a kind of reprieve. He recalled the fishy look in Slevyas' eye and shivered. He did not like the loneliness of the cellar-chamber, but anything was preferable to the contemptuous, threatening glances of his brother thieves.

The sound of dragging footsteps caused him to swallow one of his monotonous sighs – his chew along with it – and duck behind a table. There appeared from the shadows a startling apparition. Fissif recognized it as the Northerner, Fafhrd, but it was a very sorry-looking Fafhrd, face pale and grimy, clothes and hair bedraggled and smeared with a grayish dust. He moved like a man bewildered or deep in thought. Fissif, realizing that there indeed was a golden opportunity, picked up a sizable tapestry-weight that was lying at hand, and stole softly after the brooding figure.

Fafhrd had just about convinced himself that the strange voices from which he had fled were only the figments of his brain, fostered by fever and headache. After all, he reasoned, a blow on the head often made a person see colored lights and hear ringing noises; he must have been almost witless to get lost in the dark so readily – the ease with which he'd retraced his path this time proved that. The thing to do now was concentrate on escaping from this musty den. He mustn't dream. There was a houseful of thieves on the lookout for him, and he might expect to meet one at any turn.

As he shook his head to clear it, and gazed up alertly, there descended on his thick skull the sixth blow it had received that night. But this one was harder.

Slevyas' reaction to the news of Fafhrd's capture was not exactly what Fissif had expected. He did not smile. He did not look up from the platter of cold meats set before him. He merely took a small swallow of pale-yellow wine and went on eating.

'The jeweled skull?' he questioned curtly, between mouthfuls.

Fissif explained that it was possible the Northerner had hidden or lost it somewhere in the lower reaches of the cellars. A careful search would answer the question. 'Perhaps the Gray Mouser was carrying it ...'

'You killed the Northerner?' asked Slevyas after a pause.

'Not quite,' answered Fissif proudly. 'But I joggled his brains for him.'

Fissif expected a compliment at this, or at least a friendly nod, but received instead a cold, appraising stare, the import of which was difficult to determine. Slevyas thoroughly masticated a mouthful of meat, swallowed it, then took a deliberate swallow of wine. All the while his eyes did not leave Fissif.

Finally he said, 'Had you killed him, you would at this instant be put to torture. Understand, fat-belly, that I do not trust you. Too many things point to your complicity. If you had plotted with him, you would have killed him to prevent your treason being revealed. Perhaps you did try to kill him. Fortunate for you his skull is thick.'

The matter-of-fact tone stifled Fissif's protest. Slevyas drained the last of his cup, leaned back, and signed for the apprentices to take the dishes away.

'Has the Northerner regained his senses?' he asked abruptly.

Fissif nodded, and added, 'He seemed to be in a fever. Struggled against his bonds and muttered words. Something about "next midnight." He repeated that three times. The rest was in an outlandish tongue.'

A scrawny, rat-eared thief entered. 'Master,' he said, bowing obsequiously, 'we have found the Gray Mouser. He sits at the Silver Eel Tavern. Several of ours watch the place. Shall he be captured or slain?'

'Has he the skull with him? Or a box that might hide it?'

'No, Master,' responded the thief lugubriously, bowing even lower than before.

Slevyas sat for a moment in thought, then motioned an apprentice to bring parchment and the black ink of the squid. He wrote a few lines, then threw a question to Fissif.

'What were the words the Northerner muttered?'

'"Next midnight," Master,' answered Fissif, becoming obsequious himself.

'They will fit nicely,' said Slevyas, smiling thinly as if at an irony only he could perceive. His pen moved on over the stiff parchment.

The Gray Mouser sat with his back to the wall behind a tankard-dented, wine-stained table at the Silver Eel, nervously rolling between finger and thumb one of the rubies he had taken from under the eyes of dead Krovas. His small cup of wine spiced with bitter herbs was still half full. His glance flitted restlessly around the almost empty rooms and back and forth between the four small window spaces, high in the wall, that let in the chill fog. He gazed narrowly at the fat, leather-aproned innkeeper who snored dismally on a stool beside the short stair leading up to the door. He listened with half an ear to the disjointed, somnolent mumbling of the two soldiers across the room, who clutched large tankards and, heads leaned together in drunken confidentialness, tried to tell each other of ancient stratagems and mighty marches.

Why didn't Fafhrd come? This was no time for the huge fellow to be late, yet since the Mouser's arrival at the Silver Eel the candles had melted down half an inch. The Mouser no longer found pleasure in recalling the perilous stages of his escape from Thieves' House – the dash up the stairs, the leaping from roof to roof, the short fight among the chimneys. By the Gods of Trouble! Would he have to go back to that den, now filled with ready knives and open eyes, to begin search for his companion? He snapped his fingers so that the jewel between them shot high toward the sooty ceiling, a little track of sparkling red which his other hand snatched back as it descended, like a lizard trapping a fly. Again he stared suspiciously at the slumped, open-mouthed innkeeper.

From the corner of his eye he saw the small steel

messenger streaking down toward him from a fog-dim rectangle of window. Instinctively he jerked to one side. But there was no need. The dagger buried its point in the tabletop an arm's length to one side. For what seemed a long time the Mouser stood ready to jump again. The hollow *chunking* noise of the impact had not awakened the innkeeper nor disturbed the soldiers, one of whom now snored, too. Then the Mouser's left hand reached out and rocked the dagger loose. He slipped the small roll of parchment from the forte of the blade and, his gaze still walking guard on the windows, read in snatches the harshly-drawn runes of Lankhmar.

Their import was this: *If you do not bring the jeweled skull to what was Krovas' and is now Slevyas' chamber by next midnight, we will begin to kill the Northerner.*

Again next night the fog crept into Lankhmar. Sounds were muffled and torches ringed with smoky halos. But it was not yet late, although midnight was nearing and the streets were filled with hurrying shopkeepers and crafts-men, and drinkers happily laughing from their first cups, and sailors new on leave ogling the shopgirls.

In the street next that on which stood Thieves' House – the Street of the Silk Merchants, it was called – the crowd was thinning. The merchants were shutting shop. Occa-sionally they exchanged the noisy greetings of business rivals and plied shrewd questions pertaining to the state of trade. Several of them looked curiously at a narrow stone building, over-shadowed by the dark mass of Thieves' House, and from whose slitlike upper windows warm light shone. There dwelt, with servants and hired bodyguard, one Ivlis, a handsome red-haired wench who sometimes danced for the overlord, and who was treated with respect, not so much for that reason, but because it was said that she was the mistress of the master of the Thieves' Guild, to whom the silk merchants paid tribute. But that very day rumor had whispered that the old master was dead and a new one taken his place. There was speculation among the silk merchants as to whether Ivlis was now out of favor and had shut herself up in fear.

A little old woman came hobbling along, her crooked cane feeling for the cracks between the slick cobblestones. Because she had a black cloak huddled around her and a black cowl over her head – and so seemed a part of the dark fog – one of the merchants almost collided with her in the shadows. He helped her around a slimy puddle and grinned commiseratingly when she complained in a quavering voice about the condition of the street and the manifold dangers to which an old woman was exposed. She went off mumbling to herself in a rather senile fashion, 'Come on now, it's just a little farther, just a little farther. But take care. Old bones are brittle, brittle.'

A loutish apprentice dyer came ambling along, bumped into her rudely, and walked on without looking back to see whether she had fallen. But he had not taken two steps before a well-planted kick jarred his spine. He whirled around clumsily but he saw only the bent old form tottering off, cane tapping uncertainly. Eyes and mouth wide open, he moved back several steps, scratching his head in bewilderment not unmixed with superstitious wonder. Later that night he gave half his wages to his old mother.

The old woman paused before the house of Ivlis, peered up at the lighted windows several times as if she were in doubt and her eyesight bad, then climbed up laboriously to the door and feebly waggled her cane against it. After a pause she rapped again, and cried out in a fretful, high voice: 'Let me in. Let me in. I bear news from the gods to the dweller in this house. You inside there, let me in!'

Finally a wicket opened and a gruff, deep voice said. 'Go on your way, old witch. None enters here tonight.'

But the old woman took no notice of this and repeated

stubbornly, 'Let me in, I say. I read the future. It's cold in the street and the fog freezes my old throat. Let me in. This noon a bat came flapping and told me portentously of events destined for the dweller in this house. My old eyes can see the shadows of things which are not yet. Let me in, I say.'

The slim figure of a woman was silhouetted in the window above the door. After a little it moved away.

The interchange of words between the old woman and the guard went on for some time. Then a soft, husky voice called down the stairwell, 'Let the wise woman in. She's alone, isn't she? Then I will talk with her.'

The door opened, though not very wide, and the black-cloaked form tottered in. The door was immediately closed and barred.

The Gray Mouser looked around at the three body-guards standing in the darkened hall, strapping fellows with two shortswords each. They were certainly not of the Thieves' Guild. They seemed ill at ease. He did not forget to wheeze asthmatically, holding his bent side, and thank with a simpering, senile leer the one who had opened the door.

The guard drew back with an ill-concealed expression of disgust. The Mouser was not a pretty sight, his face covered with cunningly blended grease and gray ashes, studded with hideous warts of putty, and half covered with wispy gray hair straggling down from the dried scalp of a real witch — so Laavyan the wig-seller had averred — that covered his pate.

Slowly the Mouser began to ascend the stair, leaning heavily on the cane and stopping every few steps as if to recover his breath. It was not easy for him to go at such a snail-like pace, with midnight so near. But he had already failed three times in attempts to enter this well-guarded house, and he knew that the slightest unnatural action might betray him. Before he was halfway up, the husky

283

voice gave a command and a dark-haired serving woman, in a black silk tunic, hurried down, her bare feet making little noise on the stone.

'You're very kind to an old woman,' he wheezed, patting the smooth hand which gripped his elbow. They began to move up a little faster. The Mouser's inner core of thought was concentrated on the jeweled skull. He could almost see it wavering in the darkness of the stairwell, a pale brown ovoid. That skull was the key to the Thieves' House and Fafhrd's safety. Not that Slevyas would be likely to release Fafhrd, even if the skull was brought. But having the skull, the Mouser knew he would be in a position to bargain. Without it, he would have to storm Slevyas' lair with every thief forewarned and ready for him. Last night luck and circumstance had fought on his side. It would not happen again. As these thoughts were passing through the Mouser's mind he grumbled and whined vaguely about the height of the stair and the stiffness of old joints.

The maid led him into a room strewn with thick-piled rugs and hung with silken tapestry. From the ceiling depended on heavy brassy chains a large-bowled copper lamp, intricately engraved, unlighted. A soft illumination and a pleasant aromatic odor came from pale-green candles set on little tables which also held jars of perfume, small fat-bellied pots of unguent, and the like.

Standing in the center of the room was the red-haired wench he had seen take the skull from Krovas' chamber. Her robe was of white silk. Her gleaming hair, redder than auburn, was held high with golden-headed pins. He had time now to study her face, noting the hardness of her yellow-green eyes and tight jaw, contrasted with her full soft lips and pale creamy skin. He recognized anxiety in the tense lines of her body.

'You read the future, hag?' Her question was more like a command.

'By hand and hair I read it,' replied the Mouser, putting an eerie note into his quavering falsetto. 'By palm and heart and eye.' He tottered toward her. 'Yes, and small creatures talk to me and tell me secrets.' With that he suddenly drew from under his cloak a small black kitten and almost thrust it into her face. She recoiled in surprise and cried out, but he could see that the action had, in her estimation, established him as a genuine witch.

Ivlis dismissed the maid and the Mouser hastened to follow up his advantage before Ivlis' mood of awe vanished. He spoke of doom and destiny, of omens and portents, of money and love and voyages over water. He played upon the superstitions he knew to be current among the dancing girls of Lankhmar. He impressed her by speaking of 'a dark man with a black beard, either recently dead or at death's door,' not mentioning the name of Krovas for fear too much accuracy would awaken her suspicion. He wove facts, guesses, and impressive generalities into an intricate web.

The morbid fascination of staring into the forbidden future took hold of her and she leaned forward, breathing rapidly, twisting her slim fingers together, sucking her under lip. Her hurried questions mainly concerned 'a cruel, cold-faced, large man,' in whom the Mouser recognized Slevyas, and whether or not she should leave Lankhmar.

The Mouser kept up a steady stream of words, only pausing occasionally to cough, wheeze, or cackle for added realism. At times he almost believed that he was indeed a witch, and that the things he spoke were dark unholy truths.

But thoughts of Fafhrd and the skull were uppermost in his mind, and he knew that midnight was close at hand. He learned much of Ivlis: for one thing, that she hated Slevyas almost more than she feared him. But the information he most wanted eluded him.

285

Then the Mouser saw something which stirred him on to greater efforts. Behind Ivlis a gap in the silken hangings showed the wall, and he noted that one of the large paneling stones seemed to be out of place. Suddenly he realized that the stone was of the same size, shape, and quality as that in Krovas' room. This, then, must be, he thought optimistically, the other end of the passage down which Ivlis had escaped. He determined that it would be his means of entry to the Thieves' House, whether he brought the skull or not.

Fearing to waste more time, the Mouser sprang his trick. He paused abruptly, pinched the kitten's tail to make it mew, then sniffed several times, made a hideous face, and said, 'Bones! I smell a dead man's bones!'

Ivlis caught her breath and looked up quickly at the large lamp hanging from the ceiling, the lamp which was unlit. The Mouser guessed what that glance meant.

But either his own satisfaction betrayed him or else Ivlis guessed she had been tricked into betraying herself, for she gazed at him sharply. The superstitious excitement drained from her face and the hardness came back into her eyes.

'You're a man!' she spat at him suddenly. Then with fury, 'Slevyas sent you!'

With that she jerked one of the dagger-long pins from her hair and flung herself at him, striking at his eyes as he dodged. He caught her wrist with his left hand, clapped his right over her mouth. The struggle was brief and almost completely noiseless because of the thick carpeting on which they rolled. When she had been carefully trussed and gagged with strips torn from the silken hangings, the Mouser first closed the door to the stair, then pulled open the stone panel, finding the narrow passageway he had expected. Ivlis glared at him, every look a vituperation, and struggled futilely. But he knew there was no time for explanations. Hitching up his incongruous garments, he sprang nimbly for the lamp, caught the upper edge. The

286

chains held and he raised himself until his eyes could see over the edge. Cradled inside were the dull brown gem-glittering skull and the jewel-tipped bones.

The upper bowl of the crystal water clock was almost empty. Fafhrd stolidly watched the twinkling drops form and fall into the lower bowl. He was on the floor with his back to the wall. His legs were tied from knee to ankle, his arms laced behind him with an equally unnecessary amount of cordage, so that he felt quite numb. To either side of him squatted an armed thief.

When the upper bowl emptied it would be midnight.

Occasionally his gaze shifted to the dark, disfigured faces which ringed the table on which the clock and certain curious instruments of torture rested. The faces were those of the aristocrats of the Thieves' Guild, men with crafty eyes and lean cheeks, who vied with one another as to the richness and greasiness of their finery. Flickering torches threw highlights of soiled reds and purples, tarnished cloth of silver and gold. But behind their masklike expressions Fafhrd sensed uncertainty. Only Slevyas, sitting in the chair of dead Krovas, seemed truly calm and self-possessed. His voice was almost casual as he interrogated a lesser thief who knelt abjectly before him.

'Are you indeed as great a coward as you would make us think?' he asked. 'Would you have us believe you were afraid of an empty cellar?'

'Master, I am no coward,' pleaded the thief. 'I followed the Northerner's footprints in the dust along the narrow corridor and almost to the bottom of the ancient stair, forgotten until today. But no man alive could hear without terror those strange, high voices, those bony rattlings. The dry air choked my throat, a wind blew out my torch. Things tittered at me. Master, I would attempt to filch a jewel from inside a wakeful cobra's coil if you should

287

command it. But down into that place of darkness I could not force myself.'

Fafhrd saw Slevyas' lips tighten and waited for him to pronounce sentence on the miserable thief, but remarks by the notables sitting around the table interrupted.

'There may be some truth to his tale,' said one. 'After all, who knows what may be in these cellars the Northerner's blundering discovered?'

'Until last night we never knew they existed,' echoed another. 'In the trackless dust of centuries strange things may lurk.[3]

'Last night,' added a third, 'we scoffed at Fissif's tale. Yet on the throat of Krovas we found the marks of claws or of naked bone.'

It was as if a miasma of fear had welled up from the cellars far below. Voices were solemn. The lesser thieves who stood near the walls, bearing torches and weapons, were obviously gripped by superstitious dread. Again Slevyas hesitated, although unlike the others he seemed perplexed rather than frightened. In the hush the monotonous splashes of the falling drops sounded loudly. Fafhrd decided to fish in troubled waters.

'I will tell you myself of what I found in the cellars,' he said in a deep voice. 'But first tell me where you thieves bury your dead.'

Appraising eyes turned upon him. This was the first time he had spoken since he came to his senses. His question was not answered, but he was allowed to speak. Even Slevyas, although he frowned at Fafhrd's words and fingered a thumbscrew, did not object. And Fafhrd's words were something to hear. They had a cavernous quality which suggested the northland and the Cold Waste, a dramatic ring like that in the voice of a skald. He told in detail of his descent into the dark regions below. Indeed, he added new details for effect, and made the whole experience seem like some frightening epic. The lesser thieves, unused to this kind of talk, gaped at him. Those around the table sat very still. He spun out his story as long as he dared, playing for time.

During the pauses in his speech the dripping of the water clock was no longer to be heard. Then Fafhrd's ear caught a small grating sound, as of stone on stone. His listeners did not seem to notice it, but Fafhrd recognized it as the opening of the stone panel in the alcove, before which the black drapes still hung.

He had reached the climax of his revelations.

'There, in those forgotten cellars,' his voice told, going a note deeper, 'are the living bones of the ancient Thieves of Lankhmar. Long have they lain there, hating you who have forgotten them. The jeweled skull was that of their brother, Ohmphal. Did not Krovas tell you that the plans for stealing the skull were handed down from the dim past? It was intended that Ohmphal be restored to his brothers. Instead, Krovas desecrated the skull, tearing out the jewels. Because of that indignity, the bony hands found supernatural power with which to slay him. I know not where the skull is now. But if it has not already returned to them, those below will come for it even now, tonight. And they will not be merciful.'

And then Fafhrd's words froze in his throat. His final argument, which had to do with his own release, remained unspoken. For, suspended in the air immediately in front of the black draperies of the alcove, was the skull of Ohmphal, its jeweled eyes glittering with light that was more than reflection. The eyes of the thieves followed those of Fafhrd, and the air whistled with intaken breaths of fear, fear so intense that it momentarily precluded panic. A fear such as they felt toward their living master, but magnified many times.

And then a high wailing voice spoke from the skull, 'Move not, oh you craven thieves of today! Tremble and be silent. It is your ancient master who speaks. Behold, I am Ohmphal!'

The effect of that voice was peculiar. Most of the thieves shrank back, gritting their teeth and clenching their hands to control trembling. But the sweat of relief trickled down Fafhrd's head, for he recognized the Mouser. And in fat Fissif's face puzzlement mingled with fear.

'First,' continued the voice from the skull, 'I shall strangle the Northman as an example to you. Cut his bonds and bring him to me. Be quick, lest I and my brothers slay you all.'

With twitching hands the thieves to the right and left of Fafhrd slit his lashings. He tensed his great muscles, trying to work out the paralyzing numbness. They pulled him to his feet and pushed him forward, stumbling, toward the skull.

Abruptly the black draperies were shaken by a commotion behind them. There came a shrill, almost animal scream of rage. The skull of Ohmphal slid down the black velvet and rolled out into the room, the thieves leaping out of its way and squealing as if for fear it came to bite their ankles with poisoned teeth. From the hole in its base fell a candle which flickered out. The draperies swung to one side and two struggling figures reeled into the room. For a moment even Fafhrd thought he was going mad at such an utterly unexpected sight as a fight between an old hag in black, with skirts tucked above her sturdy knees, and a red-haired wench with a dagger. Then the hag's cowl and wig were torn off and he recognized, under a complexion of grease and ashes, the Mouser's face. Fissif sprang forward past Fafhrd, his dagger out. The Northerner, awakening to action, caught him by the shoulder, hurled him against the wall, then snatched a sword from the fingers of a nerveless thief and staggered forward himself, muscles still numb.

Meanwhile Ivlis, becoming aware of the assembled thieves, suddenly stopped trying to skewer the Mouser. Fafhrd and the Mouser turned toward the alcove, where escape lay, and were almost bowled over by the sudden outrush of Ivlis' three bodyguards, come to rescue their mistress. The bodyguards immediately attacked Fafhrd and the Mouser, since they were nearest, chasing them back across the room, striking also at the thieves with their short heavy swords.

This incident further startled the thieves, yet gave them time to recover a little from their supernatural fear. Slevyas, sensing the essentials of the situation, fairly drove a group of underlings to block the alcove, galvanizing them into action with flat-edged thwacks of his sword blade. Then came chaos and pandemonium. Swords clashed and skirled together. Daggers flashed. Men were knocked down by panicky, meaningless rushes. Heads were thumped and blood flowed. Torches were swung and hurled like clubs, fell to the floor and singed the fallen, making them howl. Thief fought thief in the confusion, the notables who had sat at the table forming a unit for self-protection. Slevyas mustered a small body of followers and rushed Fafhrd. The Mouser tripped Slevyas, but the latter whirled around on his knees and ripped the black cloak with his longsword, almost skewering the small man. Fafhrd laid around him with a chair, bowling over those who opposed him; then spilled the table over on its side, the water clock crashing to splinters.

Gradually Slevyas regained control of the thieves. He knew they were at a disadvantage in the confusion, so his first move was to call them off, mustering them in two groups, one in the alcove, from which the drapes had been torn away, the other around the door. Fafhrd and the Mouser crouched behind the overturned table in the opposite angle of the room, its thick top serving as a barricade. The Mouser was somewhat surprised to find Ivlis crouching beside him.

'I saw you try to kill Slevyas,' she whispered grimly. 'In any case we are compelled to join forces.'

With Ivlis was one of the bodyguards. The other two lay dead or insensible, along with the dozen thieves who were scattered around the floor among the fallen torches which cast a faint flickering eerie light on the scene. Wounded thieves moaned, and crawled or were dragged out into the corridor by their comrades. Slevyas was shouting for mannets and more torches.

'We'll have to make a rush,' whispered Fafhrd through closed teeth with which he was knotting a bandage around a gash in his arm. And then he suddenly raised his head and sniffed. Somehow, through that confusion and the faint sweetish smell of blood had come an odor that made his flesh prickle and creep, an odor at once alien and familiar; a fainter odor, hot, dry and dusty. For a moment the thieves fell silent and Fafhrd thought he heard the sound of distant marching, the clicking of bony feet.

Then a thief cried, 'Master, Master, the skull, the skull! It moves! It clamps its teeth!'

There was a confused sound of men drawing back, then Slevyas' curse. The Mouser, peering around the tabletop, saw Slevyas kick the jeweled skull toward the center of the room.

'Fools,' he cried to his cowering followers, 'do you still believe those lies, those old-wives' whispers? Do you think dead bones can walk? I and no other am your master! And may all dead thieves be damned eternally!'

With that he brought his sword down whistling. The skull of Ohmphal shattered like an eggshell. A whining cry of fear came from the thieves. The room grew darker as though it were filling with dust.

'Now follow me!' cried Slevyas. 'Death to the intruders!'

But the thieves shrank back, darker shadows in the gloom. Fafhrd, sensing opportunity and mastering his growing fear, rushed out at Slevyas. The Mouser followed him. Fafhrd intended to kill him with his third blow. First a swipe at Slevyas' longer sword to deflect it, next a quick blow at the side to bring him off guard, then finally a back-handed slash at the head.

But Slevyas was a better swordsman than that. He parried the third cut so that it whistled harmlessly over his head, then thrust at the Northerner's throat. That thrust brought Fafhrd's supple muscles to full life; true, the blade grazed his neck, but his parry, striking Slevyas' sword near the hilt, numbed the master thief's hand. Fafhrd knew he had him then and drove him back with a mercilessly intense onslaught. He did not notice how the room was darkening. He did not wonder why Slevyas' desperate calls for assistance went unanswered; why the thieves were crowding toward the alcove, and why the wounded were crawling back into the room from the corridor. Toward that doorway he drove Slevyas, so that the man was silhouetted against it. Finally as Slevyas reached the doorway, he disarmed him with a blow which sent the thief's sword spinning, and put his own point to Slevyas' throat.

'Yield!' he cried.

Only then he realized the hateful dusty odor was thick in his nostrils, that the room was in utter silence, that from the corridor came a hot wind and the sound of marching bones clicking against the stone pavement. He saw Slevyas look over his shoulder, and he saw a fear like death in Slevyas' face. Then came a sudden intense darkness, like a puff of inky smoke. But before it came he saw bony arms clasp Slevyas' throat, and, as the Mouser dragged him back, he saw the doorway crowded with black skeletal forms whose eyes glittered green and red and sapphire. Then utter darkness, hideous with the screams of the thieves as they fought to crowd into the narrow tunnel in the alcove. And over and above the screams sounded thin high voices, like those of bats, cold as eternity. One cry he heard clearly.

'Slayer of Ohmphal, this is the vengeance of Ohmphal's brothers.'

Then Fafhrd felt the Mouser dragging him forward again, toward the corridor door. When he could see properly, he found they were fleeing through an empty Thieves' House – he, the Mouser, Ivlis, and the lone bodyguard.

Ivlis' maidservant, having barred the other end of the corridor in terror at the approaching sounds, crouched trembling in the rugs on the other side, listening in unwilling, sick horror – unable to flee – to the muffled screams and pleas and to the faint moaning sounds which bore a note of terrible triumph. The small black kitten arched its back, hair on end, and spat and hissed. Presently all sounds ceased.

Thereafter it was noted in Lankhmar that thieves were fewer. And it was rumored that the Thieves' Guild conducted strange rites at full moon, descending into deep cellars and worshipping some sort of ancient gods. It was even said that they gave these gods, whoever they were, one-third of all they stole.

But Fafhrd, drinking with the Mouser and Ivlis and a wench from Tovilyis in an upper room at the Silver Eel, complained that the fates were unfair.

'All that trouble and nothing to show for it! The gods have a lasting grudge against us.'

The Mouser smiled, reached into his pouch, and laid three rubies on the table.

'Ohmphal's fingertips,' he said briefly.

'How can you dare keep them?' questioned Ivlis. 'Are you not afraid of brown bones at midnight?' She shuddered and eyed the Mouser with a certain solicitude.

He returned her gaze and replied, though the ghost of his Ivrian rebuked him, 'My taste runs to pink bones, fittingly clothed.'

IV: THE BLEAK SHORE

'So you think a man can cheat death and outwit doom?' said the small, pale man, whose bulging forehead was shadowed by a black cowl.

The Gray Mouser, holding the dice box ready for a throw, paused and quickly looked sideways at the questioner.

'I said that a cunning man can cheat death for a long time.'

The Silver Eel bustled with pleasantly raucous excitement. Fighting men predominated and the clank of swordsmen's harness mingled with the thump of tankards, providing a deep obbligato to the shrill laughter of the women. Swaggering guardsmen elbowed the insolent bravos of the young lords. Grinning slaves bearing open wine jars dodged nimbly between. In one corner a slave girl was dancing, the jingle of her silver anklet bells inaudible in the din. Outside the small, tight-shuttered windows a dry, whistling wind from the south filled the air with dust that eddied between the cobblestones and hazed the stars. But here all was jovial confusion.

The Gray Mouser was one of a dozen at the gaming table. He was dressed all in gray – jerkin, silken shirt, and mouseskin cap – but his dark, flashing eyes and cryptic smile made him seem more alive than any of the others, save for the huge copper-haired barbarian next to him, who laughed immoderately and drank tankards of the sour wine of Lankhmar as if it were beer.

'They say you're a skilled swordsman and have come close to death many times,' continued the small, pale man in the black robe, his thin lips barely parting as he spoke the words.

But the Mouser had made his throw, and the odd dice of Lankhmar had stopped with the matching symbols of the eel and serpent uppermost, and he was raking in triangular golden coins. The barbarian answered for him.

'Yes, the gray one handles a sword daintily enough – almost as well as myself. He's also a great cheat at dice.'

'Are you, then, Fafhrd?' asked the other. 'And do you, too, truly think a man can cheat death, be he ever so cunning a cheat at dice?'

The barbarian showed his white teeth in a grin and peered puzzledly at the small, pale man whose somber appearance and manner contrasted so strangely with the revelers thronging the low-ceilinged tavern fumy with wine.

'You guess right again,' he said in a bantering tone. 'I am Fafhrd, a Northerner, ready to pit my wits against any doom.' He nudged his companion. 'Look, Mouser, what do you think of this little black-coated mouse who's sneaked in through a crack in the floor and wants to talk with you and me about death?'

The man in black did not seem to notice the jesting insult. Again his bloodless lips hardly moved, yet his words were unaffected by the surrounding clamor, and impinged on the ears of Fafhrd and the Gray Mouser with peculiar clarity.

'It is said you two came close to death in the Forbidden City of the Black Idols, and in the stone trap of Angarngi, and on the misty island in the Sea of Monsters. It is also said that you have walked with doom on the Cold Waste and through the Mazes of Klesh. But who may be sure of these things, and whether death and doom were truly near? Who knows but what you are both braggarts who have boasted once too often? Now I have heard tell that death sometimes calls to a man in a voice only he can hear. Then he must rise and leave his friends and go to whatever place death shall bid him, and there meet his doom. Has death ever called to you in such a fashion?'

Fafhrd might have laughed, but did not. The Mouser had a witty rejoinder on the tip of his tongue, but instead he heard himself saying: 'In what words might death call?'

'That would depend,' said the small man. 'He might look at two such as you and say the Bleak Shore. Nothing more than that. The Bleak Shore. And when he said it three times you would have to go.'

This time Fafhrd tried to laugh, but the laugh never came. Both of them could only meet the gaze of the small man with the white, bulging forehead, stare stupidly into his cold, cavernous eyes. Around them the tavern roared with mirth at some jest. A drunken guardsman was bellowing a song. The gamblers called impatiently to the Mouser to stake his next wager. A giggling woman in red and gold stumbled past the small, pale man, almost brushing away the black cowl that covered his pate. But he did not move. And Fafhrd and the Gray Mouser continued to stare – fascinatedly, helplessly – into his chill, black eyes, which now seemed to them twin tunnels leading into a far and evil distance. Something deeper than fear gripped them in iron paralysis. The tavern became faint and soundless, as if viewed through many thicknesses of glass. They saw only the eyes and what lay beyond the eyes, something desolate, dreary, and deadly.

'The Bleak Shore,' he repeated.

Then those in the tavern saw Fafhrd and the Gray Mouser rise and without sign or word of leave-taking walk together to the low oaken door. A guardsman cursed as the huge Northerner blindly shoved him out of the way.

There were a few shouted questions and mocking comments – the Mouser had been winning – but these were quickly hushed, for all perceived something strange and alien in the manner of the two. Of the small, pale, black-robed man none took notice. They saw the door open. They heard the dry moaning of the wind and a hollow flapping that probably came from the awnings. They saw an eddy of dust swirl up from the threshold. Then the door was closed and Fafhrd and the Mouser were gone.

No one saw them on their way to the great stone docks that bank the east side of the River Hlal from one end of Lankhmar to the other. No one saw Fafhrd's north-rigged, red-sailed sloop cast off and slip out into the current that slides down to the squally Inner Sea. The night was dark and the dust kept men indoors. But the next day they were gone, and the ship with them, and its Mingol crew of four – these being slave prisoners, sworn to life service, whom Fafhrd and the Mouser had brought back from an otherwise unsuccessful foray against the Forbidden City of the Black Idols.

About a fortnight later a tale came back to Lankhmar from Earth's End, the little harbor town that lies farthest of all towns to the west, on the very margin of the shipless Outer Sea; a tale of how a north-rigged sloop had come into port to take on an unusually large amount of food and water – unusually large because there were only six in the crew; a sullen, white-skinned Northern barbarian; an unsmiling little man in gray; and four squat, stolid, black-haired Mingols. Afterward the sloop had sailed straight into the sunset. The people of Earth's End had watched the red sail until nightfall, shaking their heads at its audacious progress. When this tale was repeated in Lankhmar, there were others who shook their heads, and some who spoke significantly of the peculiar behavior of the two companions on the night of their departure. And as the weeks dragged on into months and the months slowly succeeded one another, there were many who talked of Fafhrd and the Gray Mouser as two dead men.

Then Ourph the Mingol appeared and told his curious story to the dockmen of Lankhmar. There was some difference of opinion as to the validity of the story, for although Ourph spoke the soft language of Lankhmar moderately well, he was an outsider, and, after he was gone, no one could prove that he was or was not one of the four Mingols who had sailed with the north-rigged sloop. Moreover, his story did not answer several puzzling questions, which is one of the reasons that many thought it untrue.

'They were mad,' said Ourph, 'or else under a curse, those two men, the great one and the small one. I suspected it when they spared our lives under the very walls of the Forbidden City. I knew it for certain when they sailed west and west and west, never reefing, never changing course, always keeping the star of the ice fields on our right hand. They talked little, they slept little, they laughed not at all. Ola, they were cursed! As for us four – Teevs, Larlt, Ouwenyis, and I – we were ignored but not abused. We had our amulets to keep off evil magics. We were sworn slaves to the death. We were men of the Forbidden City. We made no mutiny.

'For many days we sailed. The sea was stormless and empty around us, and small, very small; it looked as if it bent down out of sight to the north and the south and the awful west, as if the sea ended an hour's sail from where we were. And then it began to look that way to the east, too. But the great Northerner's hand rested on the steering oar like a curse, and the small gray one's hand was as firm. We four sat mostly in the bow, for there was little enough sail-tending, and diced our destinies at night and morning, and gambled for our amulets and clothes – we would have played for our hides and bones, were we not slaves.

'To keep track of the days, I tied a cord around my right

thumb and moved it over a finger each day until it passed from right little finger to left little finger and came to my left thumb. Then I put it on Teev's right thumb. When it came to his left thumb he gave it to Larlt. So we numbered the days and knew them. And each day the sky became emptier and the sea smaller, until it seemed that the end of the sea was but a bowshot away from our stem and sides and stern. Teevs said that we were upon an enchanted patch of water that was being drawn through the air toward the red star that is Hell. Surely Teevs may have been right. There cannot be so much water to the west. I have crossed the Inner Sea and the Sea of Monsters – and I say so.

'It was when the cord was around Larlt's left ring finger that the great storm came at us from the south-west. For three days it blew stronger and stronger, smiting the water into great seething waves; crags and gullies piled mast-high with foam. No other men have seen such waves nor should see them; they are not churned for us or for our oceans. Then I had further proof that our masters were under a curse. They took no notice of the storm; they let it reef their sails for them. They took no notice when Teevs was washed overboard, when we were half swamped and filled to the gunwales with spume, our bailing buckets foaming like tankards of beer. They stood in the stern, both braced against the steering oar, both drenched by the following waves, staring straight ahead, seeming to hold converse with creatures that only the bewitched can hear. Ola! They were accursed! Some evil demon was preserving their lives for a dark reason of his own. How else came we safe through the storm?

'For when the cord was on Larlt's left thumb, the towering waves and briny foam gave way to a great black sea swell that the whistling wind rippled but did not whiten. When the dawn came and we first saw it, Ouwenyis cried out that we were riding by magics upon a

300

sea of black sand; and Larlt averred that we were fallen during the storm into the ocean of sulfurous oil that some say lies under the earth – for Larlt has seen the black, bubbling lakes of the Far East; and I remembered what Teevs had said and wondered if our patch of water had not been carried through the thin air and plunged into a wholly different sea on a wholly different world. But the small gray one heard our talk and dipped a bucket over the side and soused us with it, so that we knew our hull was still in water and that the water was salt – wherever that water might be.

'And then he bid us patch the sails and make the sloop shipshape. By midday we were flying west at a speed even greater than we had made during the storm, but so long were the swells and so swift did they move with us that we could only climb five or six in a whole day. By the Black Idols, but they were long!

'And so the cord moved across Ouwenyis' fingers. But the clouds were as leaden dark above us as was the strange sea heavy around our hull, and we knew not if the light that came through them was that of the sun or of some wizard moon, and when we caught sight of the stars they seemed strange. And still the white hand of the Northerner lay heavy on the steering oar, and still he and the gray one stared straight ahead. But on the third day of our flight across that black expanse the Northerner broke silence. A mirthless, terrible smile twisted his lips, and I heard him mutter "the Bleak Shore." Nothing more than that. The gray one nodded, as if there were some portentous magic in the words. Four times I heard the words pass the Northerner's lips, so that they were imprinted on my memory.

'The days grew darker and colder, and the clouds slid lower and lower, threatening, like the roof of a great cavern. And when the cord was on Ouwenyis' pointing finger we saw a leaden and motionless extent ahead of us, looking like the swells, but rising above them, and we knew that we were come to the Bleak Shore.

'Higher and higher that shore rose, until we could distinguish the towering basalt crags, rounded like the sea swell, studded here and there with gray boulders, whitened in spots as if by the droppings of gigantic birds – yet we saw no birds, large or small. Above the cliffs were dark clouds, and below them was a strip of pale sand, nothing more. Then the Northerner bent the steering oar and sent us straight in, as though he intended our destruction; but at the last moment he passed us at mast length by a rounded reef that hardly rose above the crest of the swell and found us harbor room. We sent the anchor over and rode safe.

'Then the Northerner and the gray one, moving like men in a dream, accoutered themselves, a shirt of light chain mail and a rounded, uncrested helmet for each – both helmets and shirts white with salt from the foam and spray of the storm. And they bound their swords to their sides, and wrapped great cloaks about them, and took a little food and a little water, and bade us unship the small boat. And I rowed them ashore and they stepped out onto the beach and walked toward the cliffs. Then, although I was much frightened, I cried out after them, "Where are you going? Shall we follow? What shall we do?" For several moments there was no reply. Then, without turning his head, the gray one answered, his voice a low, hoarse, yet far-carrying whisper. And he said, "Do not follow. We are dead men. Go back if you can."

'And I shuddered and bowed my head to his words and rowed out to the ship. Ouwenyis and Larlt and I watched them climb the high, rounded crags. The two figures grew smaller and smaller, until the Northerner was no more than a tiny, slim beetle and his gray companion almost invisible, save when they crossed a whitened space. Then a wind came down from the crags and blew the swell away

302

from the shore, and we knew we could make sail. But we stayed – for were we not sworn slaves? And am I not a Mingol?

'As evening darkened, the wind blew stronger, and our desire to depart – if only to drown in the unknown sea – became greater. For we did not like the strangely rounded basalt crags of the Bleak Shore; we did not like it that we saw no gulls or hawks or birds of any kind in the leaden air, no seaweed on the beach. And we all three began to catch glimpses of something shimmering at the summit of the cliffs. Yet it was not until the third hour of night that we upped anchor and left the Bleak Shore behind.

'There was another great storm after we were out several days, and perhaps it hurled us back into the seas we know. Ouwenyis was washed overboard and Larlt went mad from thirst, and toward the end I knew not myself what was happening. Only I was cast up on the southern coast near Quarmall and, after many difficulties, am come here to Lankhmar. But my dreams are haunted by those black cliffs and by visions of the whitening bones of my masters, and their grinning skulls staring empty-eyed at something strange and deadly.'

Unconscious of the fatigue that stiffened his muscles, the Gray Mouser wormed his way past the last boulder, finding shallow handholds and footholds at the juncture of the granite and black basalt, and finally stood erect on the top of the rounded crags that walled the Bleak Shore. He was aware that Fafhrd stood at his side, a vague, hulking figure in whitened chain-mail vest and helmet. But he saw Fafhrd vaguely, as if through many thicknesses of glass. The only things he saw clearly – and it seemed he had been looking at them for an eternity – were two cavernous, tunnel-like black eyes, and beyond them something desolate and deadly, which had once been across the Outer Sea but was now close at hand. So it had been, ever since he had risen from the gaming table in the low-ceilinged tavern in Lankhmar. Vaguely he remembered the staring people of Earth's End, the foam, and fury of the storm, the curve of the black sea swell, and the look of terror on the face of Ourph the Mingol; these memories, too, came to him as if through many thicknesses of glass. Dimly he realized that he and his companion were under a curse, and that they were now come to the source of that curse.

For the flat landscape that spread out before them was without sign of life. In front of them the basalt dipped down to form a large hollow of black sand – tiny particles of iron ore. In the sand were half embedded more than two score of what seemed to the Gray Mouser to be inky-black, oval boulders of various sizes. But they were too perfectly rounded, too regular in form to be boulders, and slowly it was borne in on the Mouser's consciousness that they were not boulders, but monstrous black eggs, a few small, some so large that a man could not have clasped his arms around them, one big as a tent.

Scattered over the sand were bones, large and small. The Mouser recognized the tusked skull of a boar, and two smaller ones – wolves. There was the skeleton of some great predatory cat. Beside it lay the bones of a horse, and beyond them the rib case of a man or ape. The bones lay all around the huge black eggs – a whitely gleaming circle.

From somewhere a toneless voice sounded, thin but clear, in accents of command, saying: 'For warriors, a warrior's doom.'

The Mouser knew the voice, for it had been echoing in his ears for weeks, ever since it had first come from the lips of a pale little man with a bulging forehead, wearing a black robe and sitting near him in a tavern in Lankhmar. And a more whispering voice came to him from within, saying, *He seeks always to repeat past experience, which has always been in his favor.*

Then he saw that what lay before him was not utterly lifeless. Movement of a sort had come to the Bleak Shore. A crack had appeared in one of the great black eggs, and then in another, and the cracks were branching, widening as bits of shell fell to the black, sandy floor.

The Mouser knew that this was happening in answer to the first voice, the thin one. He knew this was the end to which the thin voice had called him across the Outer Sea. Powerless to move farther, he dully watched the slow progress of this monstrous birth. Under the darkening leaden sky he watched twin deaths hatching out for him and his companion.

The first hint of their nature came in the form of a long, swordlike claw which struck out through a crack, widening it farther. Fragments of shell fell more swiftly.

The two creatures which emerged in the gathering dusk held enormity even for the Mouser's drugged mind. Shambling things, erect like men but taller, with reptilian heads boned and crested like helmets, feet clawed like a lizard's, shoulders topped with bony spikes, forelimbs each terminating in a single yard-long claw. In the semidarkness they seemed like hideous caricatures of fighting men, armored and bearing swords. Dusk did not hide the yellow of their blinking eyes.

Then the voice called again: 'For warriors, a warrior's doom.'

At those words the bonds of paralysis dropped from the Mouser. For an instant he thought he was waking from a dream. But then he saw the new-hatched creatures racing toward them, a shrill, eager screeching issuing from their long muzzles. From beside him he heard a quick, rasping sound as Fafhrd's sword whipped from its scabbard. Then the Mouser drew his own blade, and a moment later it crashed against a steel-like claw which thrust at his throat. Simultaneously, Fafhrd parried a like blow from the other monster.

What followed was nightmare. Claws that were swords slashed and stabbed. Not so swiftly that they could not be parried, though there were four against two. Counter-thrusts glanced off impenetrable bony armor. Both crea-tures suddenly wheeled, striking at the Mouser. Fafhrd drove in from the side, saving him. Slowly the two companions were driven back toward where the crag sheered off. The beasts seemed tireless, creatures of bone and metal rather than flesh. The Mouser foresaw the end. He and Fafhrd might hold them off for a while longer, but eventually fatigue would supervene; their parries would become slower, weaker; the beasts would have them.

As if in anticipation of this, the Mouser felt a claw nick his wrist. It was then that he remembered the dark, cavernous eyes that had drawn them across the Outer Sea, the voice that had loosed doom upon them. He was gripped with a strange, mad rage – not against the beasts but their master. He seemed to see the black, dead eyes staring at him from the black sand. Then he lost control of his actions. When the two monsters next attempted a double attack on Fafhrd he did not turn to help, but instead dodged past and dashed down into the hollow, toward the embedded eggs.

Left to face the monsters alone. Fafhrd fought like a madman himself, his great sword whistling as his last resources of energy jolted his muscles. He hardly noticed when one of the beasts turned back to pursue his comrade.

The Mouser stood among the eggs, facing one of a glossier hue and smaller than most. Vindictively he brought his sword crashing down upon it. The blow numbed his hand, but the egg shattered.

Then the Mouser knew the source of the evil of the Bleak Shore, lying here and sending its spirit abroad, lying here and calling men to doom. Behind him he heard the scrabbling steps and eager screeching of the monster chosen for his destruction. But he did not turn. Instead, he raised his sword and brought it down whirring on the half-embryonic creature gloating in secret over the creatures he had called to death, down on the bulging forehead of the small pale man with the thin lips.

Then he waited for the finishing blow of the claw. It did not come. Turning, he saw the monster sprawled on the black sand. Around him, the deadly eggs were crumbling to dust. Silhouetted against the lesser darkness of the sky, he saw Fafhrd stumbling toward him, sobbing out vague words of relief and wonder in a deep, throaty voice. Death was gone from the Bleak Shore, the curse cut off at the root. From out of the night sounded the exultant cry of a sea bird, and Fafhrd and the Mouser thought of the long, trackless road leading back to Lankhmar.

V: THE HOWLING TOWER

The sound was not loud, yet it seemed to fill the whole vast, darkening plain, and the palely luminous, hollow sky: a wailing and howling, so faint and monotonous that it might have been inaudible save for the pulsing rise and fall; an ancient, ominous sound that was somehow in harmony with the wild, sparsely vegetated landscape and the barbaric garb of the three men who sheltered in a little dip in the ground, lying close to a dying fire.

'Wolves, perhaps,' Fafhrd said. 'I have heard them howl that way on the Cold Waste when they hunted me down. But a whole ocean sunders us from the Cold Waste and there's a difference between the sounds, Gray Mouser.'

The Mouser pulled his gray woolen cloak closer around him. Then he and Fafhrd looked at the third man, who had not spoken. The third man was meanly clad, and his cloak was ragged and the scabbard of his short sword was frayed. With surprise, they saw that his eyes stared, white circled, from his pinched, leathery face and that he trembled.

'You've been over these plains many times before,' Fafhrd said to him, speaking the guttural language of the guide. 'That's why we've asked you to show us the way. You must know this country well.' The last words pointed the question.

The guide gulped, nodded jerkily. 'I've heard it before, not so loud,' he said in a quick, vague voice. 'Not at this time of year. Men have been known to vanish. There are stories. They say men hear it in their dreams and are lured away – not a good sound.'

'No wolf's a good wolf,' rumbled Fafhrd amusedly.

It was still light enough for the Mouser to catch the obstinate guarded look on the guide's face as he went on talking.

'I never saw a wolf in these parts, nor spoke with a man who killed one.' He paused, then rambled off abstractedly. 'They tell of an old tower somewhere out on the plains. They say the sound is strongest there. I have not seen it. They say—'

Abruptly he stopped. He was not trembling now, seemed withdrawn into himself. The Mouser prodded him with a few tempting questions, but the answers were little more than mouth noises, neither affirmative nor negative.

The fire glowed through white ashes, died. A little wind rustled the scant grasses. The sound had ceased now, or else it had sunk so deeply into their minds that it was no longer audible. The Mouser, peering sleepily over the humped horizon of Fafhrd's great cloaked body, turned his thoughts to faroff, many-taverned Lankhmar, leagues and leagues away across alien lands and a whole uncharted ocean. The limitless darkness pressed down.

Next morning the guide was gone. Fafhrd laughed and made light of the occurrence as he stood stretching and snuffing the cool, clear air.

'Foh! I could tell these plains were not to his liking, for all his talk of having crossed them seven times. A bundle of superstitious fears! You saw how he quaked when the little wolves began to howl. My word on it, he's run back to his friends we left at the last water.'

The Mouser, fruitlessly scanning the empty horizon, nodded without conviction. He felt through his pouch.

'Well, at least he's not robbed us – except for the two gold pieces we gave him to bind the bargain.'

Fafhrd's laughter pealed and he thumped the Mouser between the shoulder blades. The Mouser caught him by the wrist, threw him with a twist and a roll, and they wrestled on the ground until the Mouser was pinned.

'Come on,' grinned Fafhrd, springing up. 'It won't be the first time we've traveled strange country alone.'

They tramped far that day. The springiness of the Mouser's wiry body enabled him to keep up with Fafhrd's long strides. Toward evening a whirring arrow from Fafhrd's bow brought down a sort of small antelope with delicately ridged horns. A little earlier they had found an unsullied waterhole and filled their skin bags. When the late summer sunset came, they made camp and munched carefully broiled lion and crisped bits of fat.

The Mouser sucked his lips and fingers clean, then strolled to the top of a nearby hummock to survey the line of their next day's march. The haze that had curtailed vision during the afternoon was gone now, and he could peer far over the rolling, swelling grasslands through the cool, tangy air. At that moment the road to Lankhmar did not seem so long, or so weary. Then his sharp eyes spied an irregularity in the horizon toward which they were tending. Too distinct for trees, too evenly shaped for rock; and he had seen no trees or rock in this country. It stood out sharp and tiny against the pale sky. No, it was built by man; a tower of some sort.

At that moment the sound returned. It seemed to come from everywhere at once; as if the sky itself were wailing faintly, as as if the wide, solid ground were baying mournfully. It was louder this time, and there was in it a strange confusion of sadness and threat, grief and menace.

Fafhrd jumped to his feet and waved his arms strongly, and the Mouser heard him bellow out in a great, jovial voice, 'Come, little wolves, come and share our fire and singe your cold noses. I will send my bronze-beaked birds winging to welcome you, and my friend will show you how

310

a slung stone can buzz like a bee. We will teach you the mysteries of sword and axe. Come, little wolves, and be guests of Fafhrd and the Gray Mouser! Come, little wolves – or biggest of them all!'

The huge laugh with which he ended this challenge drowned out the alien sound and it seemed slow in reasserting itself, as though laughter were a stronger thing. The Mouser felt cheered and it was with a light heart that he told Fafhrd of what he had seen, and reminded him of what the guide had said about the noise and the tower.

Fafhrd only laughed again and guessed, 'Perhaps the sad, furry ones have a den there. We shall find out tomorrow, since we go that way. I would like to kill a wolf.'

The big man was in a jolly mood and would not talk with the Mouser about serious or melancholy things. Instead, he sang drinking songs and repeated old tavern jokes, chuckling hugely and claiming that they made him feel as drunk as wine. He kept up such an incessant clamor that the Mouser could not tell whether the strange howling had ceased, though he rather imagined he heard it once or twice. Certainly it was gone by the time they wrapped themselves up for sleep in the wraithlike starlight.

Next morning Fafhrd was gone. Even before the Mouser had halooed for him and scanned the nearby terrain, he knew that his foolish, self-ridiculed fears had become certainties. He could still see the tower, although in the flat, yellow light of morning it seemed to have receded, as though it were seeking to evade him. He even fancied he saw a tiny moving figure nearer to the tower than to him. That, he knew, was only imagination. The distance was too great. Nevertheless, he wasted little time in chewing and swallowing some cold meat, which still had a savory taste, in wrapping up some more for his pouch, and in taking a gulp of water. Then he set out at a long, springy lope, a pace he knew he could hold for hours.

At the bottom of the next swell in the plain he found

slightly softer ground, cast up and down it for Fafhrd's footprints and found them. They were wide-spaced, made by a man running.

Toward midday he found a waterhole, lay down to drink and rest a little. A short way back he had again seen Fafhrd's prints. Now he noted another set in the soft earth; not Fafhrd's, but roughly parallel to his. They were at least a day older, wide-spaced, too, but a little wobbly. From their size and shape they might very well have been made by the guide's sandals; the middle of the print showed faintly the mark of thongs such as he had worn about the instep.

The Mouser loped doggedly on. His pouch, rolled cloak, water bag, and weapons were beginning to feel a burden. The tower was appreciably closer, although the sun haze masked any details. He calculated he had covered almost half the distance.

The slight successive swells in the prairieland seemed as endless as those in a dream. He noticed them not so much by sight as by the infinitesimal hindrance and easing they gave his lope. The little low clumps of bush and brush by which he measured his progress were all the same. The infrequent gullies were no wider than could be taken in a stride. Once a coiled greenish serpent raised its flat head from the rock on which it was sunning and observed his passing. Occasionally grasshoppers whirred out of his path. He ran with his feet close to the ground to conserve energy, yet there was a strong, forward leap to his stride, for he was used to matching that of a taller man. His nostrils flared wide, sucking and expelling air. The wide mouth was set. There was a grim, fixed look to the black eyes above the browned cheeks. He knew that even at his best he would be hard put to equal the speed in Fafhrd's rangy, long-muscled frame.

Clouds sailed in from the north, casting great, hurrying shadows over the landscape, finally blotting out the sun altogether. He could see the tower better now. It was of a dark color, with black specks that might be small windows.

It was while he was pausing atop a rise for a breathing spell that the sound re-commenced, taking him unaware, sending a shiver over his flesh. It might have been the low clouds that gave it greater power and an eerie, echoing quality. It might have been his being alone that made it seem less sorrowful and more menacing. But it was undeniably louder, and its rhythmic swells came like great gusts of wind.

The Mouser had counted on reaching the tower by sunset. But the early appearance of the sound upset his calculations and did not bode well for Fafhrd. His judgment told him he could cover the rest of the distance at something like top speed. Instantly he came to a decision. He tossed his big pouch, waterskin, bundled cloak, sword, and harness into a clump of bushes; kept only his light inner jerkin, long dagger, and sling. Thus lightened, he spurted ahead, feet flying. The low clouds darkened. A few drops of rain spattered. He kept his eyes on the ground, watching for inequalities and slippery spots. The sound seemed to intensify and gain new unearthliness of timbre with every bounding stride he took forward.

Away from the tower the plain had been empty and vast, but here it was desolate. The sagging or tumbled wooden outbuildings, the domestic grains and herbs run wild and dying out, the lines of stunted and toppled trees, the suggestion of fences and paths and ruts – all combined to give the impression that human life had once been here but had long since departed. Only the great stone tower, with its obstinate solidity, and with sound pouring from it or seeming to pour from it, was alive.

The Mouser, pretty well winded though not shaky, now changed his course and ran in an oblique direction to take advantage of the cover provided by a thin line of trees and wind-blown scrub. Such caution was second nature with him. All his instincts clamored against the possibility of meeting a wolf or hound pack on open ground.

He had worked his way past and partway around the tower before he came to the conclusion that there was no line of concealment leading all the way up to the base. It stood a little aloof from the ruins around it.

The Mouser paused in the shelter afforded by a weather-silvered, buckled outbuilding; automatically searched about until he found a couple of small stones whose weight suited his sling. His sturdy chest still worked like a bellows, drinking air. Then he peered around a corner at the tower and stood there crouched a little, frowning.

It was not as high as he had thought; five stories or perhaps six. The narrow windows were irregularly placed, and did not give any clear idea of inner configuration. The stones were large and rudely hewn; seemed firmly set, save for those of the battlement, which had shifted somewhat. Almost facing him was the dark, uninformative rectangle of a doorway.

There was no rushing such a place, was the Mouser's thought; no sense in rushing a place that had no sign of defenders. There was no way of getting at it unseen; a watcher on the battlements would have noted his approach long ago. One could only walk up to it, tensely alert for unexpected attacks. And so the Mouser did that.

Before he had covered half the distance his sinews were taut and straining. He was mortally certain that he was being watched by something more than unfriendly. A day's running had made him a little light-headed, and his senses were abnormally clear. Against the unending hypnotic background of the howling he heard the splatters of the separate raindrops, not yet become a shower. He noted the size and shape of each dark stone around the darker doorway. He smelled the characteristic odor of stone, wood, soil, but yet no heavy animal smell. For the thousandth time he tried to picture some possible source for the sound. A dozen hound packs in a cavern underground? That was close, but not close enough. Something eluded him. And now the dark walls were very near, and he strained his eyes to penetrate the gloom of the doorway.

The remote grating sound might not have been enough of a warning, for he was almost in a trance. It may have been the sudden, very slight increase of darkness over his head that twanged the taut bowstrings of his muscles and sent him lunging with cat-like rapidity into the tower – instinctively, without pausing to glance up. Certainly he had not an instant to spare, for he felt an unyielding surface graze his escaping body and flick his heels. A spurt of wind rushed past him from behind, and the jar of a mighty impact staggered him. He spun around to see a great square of stone half obscuring the doorway. A few moments before it had formed part of the battlement.

Looking at it as it lay there denting the ground, he grinned for the first time that day and almost laughed in relief.

The silence was profound, startling. It occurred to the Mouser that the howling had ceased utterly. He glanced around the barren, circular interior, then started up the curving stone stair that hugged the wall. His grin was dangerous now, businesslike. On the first level above he found Fafhrd and – after a fashion – the guide. But he found a puzzle, too.

Like that below, the room occupied the full circumference of the tower. Light from the scattered, slit-like windows dimly revealed the chests lining the walls and the dried herbs and desiccated birds, small mammals, and reptiles hanging from the ceiling, suggesting an apothecary's shop. There was litter everywhere, but it was a tidy litter, seeming to have a tortuously logical arrangement all its own. On a table was a hodge-podge of stoppered bottles and jars, mortars, and pestles, odd instruments of horn, glass, and bone, and a brazier in which charcoal smoldered. There was also a plate of gnawed bones and beside it a brass-bound book of parchment, spread open by a dagger set across the pages.

Fafhrd lay face-up on a bed of skins laced to a low wooden framework. He was pale and breathed heavily, looked as if he had been drugged. He did not respond when the Mouser shook him gently and whispered his name, then shook him hard and shouted it. But the thing that baffled the Mouser was the multitude of linen bandages wound around Fafhrd's limbs and chest and throat, for they were unstained and, when he parted them, there were no wounds beneath. They were obviously not bonds.

And lying beside Fafhrd, so close that his big hand touched the hilt, was Fafhrd's great sword, unsheathed.

It was only then that the Mouser saw the guide, huddled in a dark corner behind the couch. He was similarly bandaged. But the bandages were stiff with rusty stains, and it was easy to see that he was dead.

The Mouser tried again to wake Fafhrd, but the big man's face stayed a marble mask. The Mouser did not feel that Fafhrd was actually there, and the feeling frightened and angered him.

As he stood nervously puzzling he became aware of slow steps descending the stone stair. Slowly they circled the tower. The sound of heavy breathing was heard, coming in regular spaced gasps. The Mouser crouched behind the tables, his eyes glued on the black hole in the ceiling through which the stair vanished.

The man who emerged was old and small and bent, dressed in garments as tattered and uncouth and musty-looking as the contents of the room. He was partly bald, with a matted tangle of gray hair around his large ears. When the Mouser sprang up and menaced him with a drawn dagger he did not attempt to flee, but went into what seemed an ecstasy of fear – trembling, babbling throaty sounds, and darting his arms about meaninglessly.

The Mouser thrust a stubby candle into the brazier, held it to the old man's face. He had never seen eyes so wide with terror – they jutted out like little white balls – nor lips so thin and unfeelingly cruel.

The first intelligible words that issued from the lips were hoarse and choked; the voice of a man who has not spoken for a long time.

'You are dead. You are dead!' he cackled at the Mouser, pointing a shaky finger. 'You should not be here. I killed you. Why else have I kept the great stone cunningly balanced, so that a touch would send it over? I knew you did not come because the sound lured you. You came to hurt me and to help your friend. So I killed you. I saw the stone fall. I saw you under the stone. You could not have escaped it. You are dead.'

And he tottered toward the Mouser, brushing at him as though he could dissipate the Mouser like smoke. But when his hands touched solid flesh he squealed and stumbled away.

The Mouser followed him, moving his knife suggestively. 'You are right as to why I came,' he said. 'Give me back my friend. Rouse him.'

To his surprise, the old man did not cringe, but abruptly stood his ground. The look of terror in the unblinking eyes underwent a subtle change. The terror was still there, but there was something more. Bewilderment vanished and something else took its place. He walked past the Mouser and sat down on a stool by the table.

'I am not much afraid of you,' he muttered, looking sideways. 'But there are those of whom I am very much afraid. And I fear you only because you will try to hinder me from protecting myself against them or taking the measures I know I must take.' He became plaintive. 'You must not hinder me. You must not.'

The Mouser frowned. The ghastly look of terror – and something more – that warped the old man's face seemed a permanent thing, and the strange words he spoke did not sound like lies.

'Nevertheless, you must rouse my friend.'

The old man did not answer this. Instead, after one quick glance at the Mouser, he stared vacantly at the wall, shaking his head, and began to talk.

'I do not fear you. Yet I know the depths of fear. You do not. Have you lived alone with *that sound* for years on years, knowing what it meant? I have.

'Fear was born into me. It was in my mother's bones and blood. And in my father's and in my brothers'. There was too much magic and loneliness in this, our home, and in my people. When I was a child they all feared and hated me – even the slaves and the great hounds that before me slavered and growled and snapped.

'But my fears were stronger than theirs, for did they not die one by one in such a way that no suspicion fell upon me until the end? I knew it was one against many, and I took no chances. When it began, they always thought I would be the next to go!' He cackled at this. 'They thought I was small and weak and foolish. But did not my brothers die as if strangled by their own hands? Did not my mother sicken and languish? Did not my father give a great cry and leap from the tower's top?

'The hounds were the last to go. They hated me most – even more than my father hated me – and the smallest of them could have torn out my throat. They were hungry because there was no one left to feed them. But I lured them into the deep cellar, pretending to flee from them; and when they were all inside I slipped out and barred the door. For many a night thereafter they bayed and howled at me, but I knew I was safe. Gradually the baying grew less and less as they killed each other, but the survivors gained new life from the bodies of the slain. They lasted a long time. Eventually there was only one single thin voice left to howl vengefully at me. Each night I went to sleep, telling myself, "Tomorrow there will be silence." But each morning I was awakened by the cry. Then I forced myself to take a torch and go down and peer through the wicket in the door of the cellar. But though I watched for a long time there was no movement, save that of the flickering shadows, and I saw nothing but white bones and tatters of skin. And I told myself that the sound would soon go away.'

The old man's thin lips were twisted into a pitiful and miserable expression that sent a chill over the Mouser.

'But the sound lived on, and after a long while it began to grow louder again. Then I knew that my cunning had been in vain. I had killed their bodies, but not their ghosts, and soon they would gain enough power to return and slay me, as they had always intended. So I studied more carefully my father's books of magic and sought to destroy their ghosts utterly or to curse them to such faroff places that they could never reach me. For a while I seemed to be succeeding, but the scales turned and they began to get the better of me. Closer and closer they came, and sometimes I seemed to catch my father's and brothers' voices, almost lost among the howling.

'It was on a night when they must have been very close that an exhausted traveller came running to the tower. There was a strange look in his eyes, and I thanked the beneficent god who had sent him to my door, for I knew what I must do. I gave him food and drink, and in his drink I mingled a liquid that enforced sleep and sent his naked ghost winging out of his body. *They* must have captured and torn it, for presently the man bled and died. But it satisfied them somewhat, for their howling went a long way off, and it was a long time before it began to creep back. Thereafter the gods were good and always sent me a guest before the sound came too close. I learned to bandage those I drugged so that they would last longer, and their deaths would satisfy the howling ones more fully.'

The old man paused then, and shook his head queerly and made a vague, reproachful, clucking noise with his tongue.

'But what troubles me now,' he said, 'is that they have become greedier, or perhaps they have seen through my cunning. For they are less easy to satisfy, and press at me closely and never go far away. Sometimes I wake in the night, hearing them snuffing about, and feeling their muzzles at my throat. I must have more men to fight them for me. I must. He' – pointing at the stiff body of the guide – 'was nothing to them. They took no more notice of him than a dry bone. That one' – his finger wavered over to Fafhrd – 'is big and strong. He should hold them back for a long time.'

It was dark outside now, and the only light came from the guttering candle. The Mouser glared at the old man where he sat perched on the stool like some ungainly plucked fowl. Then he looked to where Fafhrd lay, watched the great chest rise and fall, saw the strong, pallid jaw jutting up over high wrappings. And at that, a terrible anger and an unnerving, boundless irritation took hold of him and he hurled himself upon the old man.

But at the instant he started his long dagger on the downward stroke the sound gushed back. It seemed to overflow from some pit of darkness, and to inundate the tower and plain so that the walls vibrated and dust puffed out from the dead things hanging from the ceiling.

The Mouser stopped the blade a hand's breadth from the throat of the old man, whose head, twisted back, jiggled in terror. For the return of the sound forcibly set the question: Could anyone but the old man save Fafhrd now? The Mouser wavered between alternatives, pushed the old man away, knelt by Fafhrd's side, shook him, spoke to him. There was no response. Then he heard the voice of the old man. It was shaky and half drowned by the sound, but it carried an almost gloating note of confidence.

'Your friend's body is poised on the brink of life. If you handle it roughly it may overbalance. If you strip off the bandages he will only die the quicker. You cannot help him.' Then, reading the Mouser's question, 'No, there is no antidote.' Then hastily, as if he feared to take away all hope, 'But he will not be defenseless against them. He is strong. His ghost may be strong, too. He may be able to weary them out. If he lives until midnight he may return.'

The Mouser turned and looked up at him. Again the old man seemed to read something in the Mouser's merciless eyes, for he said, 'My death by your hand will not satisfy those who howl. If you kill me, you will not save your friend, but doom him. Being cheated of my ghost, they will rend his utterly.'

The wizened body trembled in an ecstasy of excitement and terror. The hands fluttered. The head bobbed back and forth, as if with the palsy. It was hard to read anything in that twitching, saucer-eyed face. The Mouser slowly got to his feet.

'Perhaps not,' said the Mouser. 'Perhaps as you say, your death will doom him.' He spoke slowly and in a loud, measured tone. 'Nevertheless, I shall take the chance of killing you right now unless you suggest something better.'

'Wait,' said the old man, pushing at the Mouser's dagger and drawing a pricked hand away. 'Wait. There is a way you could help him. Somewhere out there' – he made a sweeping, upward gesture with his hand – 'your friend's ghost is battling them. I have more of the drug left. I will give you some. Then you can fight them side by side. Together you may defeat them. But you must be quick. Look! Even now they are at him!'

The old man pointed at Fafhrd. The bandage on the

321

barbarian's left arm was no longer unstained. There was a growing splotch of red on the left wrist – the very place where a hound might take hold. Watching it, the Mouser felt his insides grow sick and cold. The old man was pushing something into his hand. 'Drink this. Drink this now,' he was saying.

The Mouser looked down. It was a small glass vial. The deep purple of the liquid corresponded with the hue of a dried trickle he had seen at the corner of Fafhrd's mouth. Like a man bewitched, he plucked out the stopper, raised it slowly to his lips, paused.

'Swiftly! Swiftly!' urged the old man, almost dancing with impatience. 'About half is enough to take you to your friend. The time is short. Drink! Drink!'

But the Mouser did not. Struck by a sudden, new thought, he eyed the old man over his upraised hand. And the old man must have instantly read the import of that thought, for he snatched up the dagger lying on the book and lunged at the Mouser with unexpected rapidity. Almost the thrust went home, but the Mouser recovered his wits and struck sideways with his free fist at the old man's hand so that the dagger clattered across the floor. Then, with a rapid, careful movement, the Mouser set the vial on the table. The old man darted after him, snatching at it, seeking to upset it, but the Mouser's iron grip closed on his wrists. He was forced to the floor, his arms pinioned, his head pushed back.

'Yes,' said the Mouser, 'I shall drink. Have no fear on that score. But you shall drink, too.'

The old man gave a strangled scream and struggled convulsively. 'No! No!' he cried. 'Kill me! Kill me with your knife! But not the drink! Not the drink!' The Mouser, kneeling on his arms to pinion them, pried at his jaw. Suddenly he became quiet and stared up, a peculiar lucidity in his white-circled, pinpoint-pupiled eyes. 'It's no use. I sought to trick you,' he said. 'I gave the last of the drug to your friend. The stuff you hold is poison. We shall both die miserably, and your friend will be irrevocably doomed.'

But when he saw that the Mouser did not heed this, he began once more to struggle like a maniac. The Mouser was inexorable. Although the base of his thumb was bitten deep, he forced the old man's jaws apart, held his nose and poured the thick purple liquor down. The face of the old man grew red and the veins stood out. When the gulp came it was like a death rattle. Then the Mouser drank off the rest – it was salty like blood and had a sickeningly sweet odor – and waited.

He was torn with revulsion at what he had done. Never had he inflicted such terror on man or woman before. He would much rather have killed. The look on the old man's face was grotesquely similar to that of a child under torture. Only that poor aged wretch, thought the Mouser, knew the full meaning of the howling that even now dinned menacingly in their ears. The Mouser almost let him reach the dagger toward which he was weakly squirming. But he thought of Fafhrd and gripped the old man tight.

Gradually the room filled with haze and began to swing and slowly spin. The Mouser grew dizzy. It was as if the sound were dissolving the walls. Something was wrenching at his body and prying at his mind. Then came utter blackness, whirled and shaken by a pandemonium of howling.

But there was no sound at all on the vast alien plain to which the blackness suddenly gave way. Only sight and a sense of great cold. A cloudless, sourceless moonlight revealed endless sweeps of smooth black rock and sharply edged the featureless horizon.

He was conscious of a thing that stood by him and seemed to be trying to hide behind him. Then, at a small distance, he noted a pale form which he instinctively knew to be Fafhrd. And around the pale form seethed a pack of black, shadowy animal shapes, leaping and retreating,

323

worrying at the pale form, their eyes glowing like the moonlight, but brighter, their long muzzles soundlessly snarling. The thing beside him seemed to shrink closer. And then the Mouser rushed forward toward his friend.

The shadow pack turned on him and he braced himself to meet their onslaught. But the leader leaped past his shoulder, and the rest divided and flowed by him like a turbulent black stream. Then he realized that the thing which had sought to hide behind him was no longer there. He turned and saw that the black shapes pursued another small pale form.

It fled fast, but they followed faster. Over sweep after sweep of rock the hunt continued. He seemed to see taller, man-shaped figures among the pack. Slowly they dwindled in size, became tiny, vague. And still the Mouser felt the horrible hate and fear that flowed from them.

Then the sourceless moonlight faded, and only the cold remained, and that, too, dissipated, leaving nothing.

When he awoke, Fafhrd's face was looking down at him, and Fafhrd was saying, 'Lie still, little man. Lie still. No, I'm not badly hurt. A torn hand. Not bad. No worse than your own.'

But the Mouser shook his head impatiently and pushed his aching shoulder off the couch. Sunlight was knifing in through the narrow windows, revealing the dustiness of the air. Then he saw the body of the old man.

'Yes,' Fafhrd said as the Mouser lay back weakly. 'His fears are ended now. They've done with him. I should hate him. But who can hate such tattered flesh? When I came to the tower he gave me the drink. There was something wrong in my head. I believed what he said. He told me it would make me a god. I drank, and it sent me to a cold waste in hell. But now it's done with and we're still in Nehwon.'

The Mouser, eyeing the thoroughly and unmistakably dead things that dangled from the ceiling, felt content.

VI: THE SUNKEN LAND

'I was born with luck as a twin!' roared Fafhrd jovially, leaping up so swiftly that the cranky sloop rocked a little in spite of its outriggers. 'I catch a fish in the middle of the ocean. I rip up its belly. And look, little man, what I find!'

The Gray Mouser drew back from the fish-bloodied hand thrust almost into his face, wrinkled his nose with sneering fastidiousness, raised his left eyebrow and peered. The object did not seem very small even on Fafhrd's broad palm, and although slimed-over a little, was indubitably gold. It was both a ring and a key, the key part set at a right angle, so that it would lie along the finger when worn. There were carvings of some sort. Instinctively the Gray Mouser did not like the object. It somehow focused the vague uneasiness he had felt now for several days.

To begin with, he did not like the huge, salty Outer Sea, and only Fafhrd's bold enthusiasm and his own longing for the land of Lankhmar had impelled him to embark on this long, admittedly risky voyage across uncharted deeps. He did not like the fact that a school of fish was making the water boil at such a great distance from any land. Even the uniformly stormless weather and favorable winds disturbed him, seeming to indicate correspondingly great misfortunes held in store, like a growing thundercloud in quiet air. Too much good luck was always dangerous. And now this ring, acquired without effort by an astonishingly lucky chance.

They peered at it more closely, Fafhrd slowly turning it around. The carving on the ring part, as far as one could make out, represented a sea monster dragging down a ship. It was highly stylized, however, and there was little detail. One might be mistaken. What puzzled the Mouser most, since he had traveled to far places and knew much of the world, was that he did not recognize the style.

But in Fafhrd it roused strange memories. Recollections of certain legends told around flickering driftwood fires through the long Northern nights; tales of great seafarings and distant raids made in ancient days; firelight glimpses of certain bits of loot taken by some unaccountably distant ancestor and considered too traditionally significant to barter or sell or even give away; ominously vague warnings used to frighten little boys who were inclined to swim or sail too far out. For a moment his green eyes clouded and his wind-burned face became serious, but only for a moment.

'A pretty enough thing, you'll agree,' he said, laughing. 'Whose door do you think it unlocks? Some king's mistress, I'd say. It's big enough for a king's finger.' He tossed it up, caught it, and wiped it on the rough cloth of his tunic.

'I wouldn't wear it,' said the Mouser. 'It was probably eaten from a drowned man's hand and sucked poison from the sea ooze. Throw it back.'

'And fish for a bigger one?' asked Fafhrd, grinning. 'No, I'm content with this.' He thrust it down on the middle finger of his left hand, doubled up his fist, and surveyed it critically. 'Good for bashing people with, too,' he remarked.

Then, seeing a big fish flash out of the water and almost flop into the cockpit, he snatched up his bow, fitted to the string a featherless arrow whose head was barbed and heavily weighted, and stared down over the side, one foot extended along the outrigger. A light, waxed line was attached to the arrow.

The Mouser watched him, not without envy. Fafhrd, big rangy man that he was, seemed to acquire an altogether new litheness and sureness of movement whenever they were on shipboard. He became as nimble as the Mouser was on shore. The Mouser was no landlubber and could swim as well as Fafhrd, but he always felt a trifle uneasy when there was only water in sight, day in and day out, just as Fafhrd felt uneasy in cities, though relishing taverns and street fights. On shipboard the Mouser became cautious and apprehensive; he made a point of watching for slow leaks, creeping fires, tainted food and rotten cordage. He disapproved of Fafhrd's constant trying out of new rigs and waiting until the last moment before reefing sail. It irked him a little that he couldn't quite call it foolhardy.

Fafhrd continued to scan intently the swelling, sliding waters. His long, copper-red hair was shoved back over his ears and knotted securely. He was clothed in rough brownish tunic and trousers. Light leather slippers, easily kicked off, were on his feet. Belt, longsword, and other weapons were, of course, wrapped away in oiled cloth against corrosion and rust. And there were no jewels or ornaments, save for the ring.

The Mouser's gaze shifted past him to where clouds were piling up a little on the horizon off the bow to starboard. He wondered, almost with relief, whether this mightn't be the dirty weather due them. He pulled his thin gray tunic closer at his throat and shifted the tiller a little. The sun, near setting, projected his crouching shadow against the brownish sail.

Fafhrd's bow twanged and the arrow plummeted. Line hissed from the reel he held in his arrow hand. He checked it with his thumb. It slackened a trifle, then jerked off toward the stern. Fafhrd's foot slid along the outrigger until it stopped against the pontoon, a good three arm's-lengths from the side. He let the other foot slide after it and lay there effortlessly braced, sea drenching his legs, playing the fish carefully, laughing and grunting satisfiedly.

'And what was your luck this time?' the Mouser asked afterward, as Fafhrd served them smoking-hot, white tender flesh boiled over the firebox in the snug cabin forward. 'Did you get a bracelet and necklace to match the ring?'

Fafhrd grinned with his mouth full and did not answer, as if there were nothing in the world to do but eat. But when they stretched themselves out later in the starry, cloud-broken darkness alive with a racing wind from starboard that drove their craft along at an increasing speed, he began to talk.

'I think they called the land Simorgya. It sank under the sea ages ago. Yet even then my people had gone raiding against it, though it was a long sail out and a weary beat homeward. My memory is uncertain. I only heard scraps of talk about it when I was a little child. But I did see a few trinkets carved somewhat like this ring; just a very few. The legends, I think, told that the men of far Simorgya were mighty magicians, claiming power over wind and waves and the creatures below. Yet the sea gulped them down for all that. Now they're there.' He rotated his hand until his thumb pointed at the bottom of the boat. 'My people, the legends say, went raiding against them one summer, and none of the boats returned, save one, which came back after hope had been lost, its men almost dead from thirst. They told of sailing on and on, and never reaching Simorgya, never sighting its rocky coast and squat, many-windowed towers. Only the empty sea. More raiders went out the next summer and the next, yet none ever found Simorgya.'

'But in that case,' questioned the Mouser sharply, 'may we not even now be sailing over that sunken land? May not that very fish you caught have swum in and out of the windows of those towers?'

'Who can say?' answered Fafhrd, a little dreamily. 'The ocean's big. If we're where we think we are – that is, almost home – it might be the case. Or not. I do not know if there ever really was a Simorgya. The legend-makers are great liars. In any case, that fish could hardly have been so ancient as to have eaten the flesh of a man of Simorgya.'

'Nevertheless,' said the Mouser in a small, flat voice, 'I'd throw the ring away.'

Fafhrd chuckled. His imagination was stirred, so that he saw the fabled land of Simorgya, not lightless and covered with great drifts of sea ooze, but as it once might have been, alive with ancient industry and commerce, strong with alien wizardry. Then the picture changed and he saw a long, narrow, twenty-oared galley, such as his people made, driving ahead into a stormy sea. There was the glint of gold and steel about the captain on the poop, and the muscles of the steersman cracked as he strained at the steering oar. The faces of the warrior-rowers were exultantly eager, dominated by the urge to rape the unknown. The whole ship was like a thirsty spearhead. He marveled at the vividness of the picture. Old longings vibrated faintly in his flesh. He felt the ring, ran his finger over the carving of the ship and monster, and again chuckled.

The Mouser fetched a stubby, heavy-wicked candle from the cabin and fixed it in a small horn lantern that was proof against the wind. Hanging at the stern it pushed back the darkness a little, not much. Until midnight it was the Mouser's watch. After a while Fafhrd slumbered.

He awoke with the feeling that the weather had changed and quick work was wanted. The Mouser was calling him. The sloop had heeled over so that the starboard pontoon rode the crests of the waves. There was chilly spray in the wind. The lantern swung wildly. Only astern were stars visible. The Mouser brought the sloop into the wind, and

Fafhrd took a triple reef in the sail, while waves hammered the bow, an occasional light crest breaking over.

When they were on their course again, he did not immediately join the Mouser, but stood wondering, for almost the first time, how the sloop would stand heavy seas. It was not the sort of boat he would have built in his Northern homeland, but it was the best that could be gotten under the circumstances. He had caulked and tarred it meticulously, replaced any wood that looked too weak, substituted a triangular sail for the square one, and increased the height of the bow a trifle. To offset a tendency to capsize, he had added outriggers a little astern of the mast, getting the strongest, truest wood for the long crosspieces, carefully steaming them into the proper shape. It was a good job, he knew, but that didn't change the fact that the boat had a clumsy skeleton and many hidden weaknesses. He sniffed the raw, salt air and peered to windward through narrowed eyes, trying to gauge the weather. The Mouser was saying something, he realized and he turned his head to listen.

'Throw the ring away before she blows a hurricane!'

He smiled and made a wide gesture that meant 'No.' Then he turned back to gaze at the wild glimmering chaos of darkness and waves to windward. Thoughts of the boat and the weather dropped away, and he was content to drink in the awesome, age-old scene, swaying to keep balance, feeling each movement of the boat and at the same time sensing, almost as if it were something akin to himself, the godless force of the elements.

It was then the thing happened that took away his power to react and held him, as it were, in a spell. Out of the surging wall of darkness emerged the dragon-headed prow of a galley. He saw the black wood of the sides, the light wood of the oars, the glint of wet metal. It was so like the ship of his imaginings that he was struck dumb with wonder as to whether it was only another vision, or whether he had had a foreglimpse of it by second sight, or whether he had actually summoned it across the deeps by his thoughts. It loomed higher, higher, higher.

The Mouser cried out and pushed over the tiller, his body arched with the mighty effort. Almost too late the sloop came out of the path of the dragon-headed prow. And still Fafhrd stared as at an apparition. He did not hear the Mouser's warning shout as the sloop's sail filled from the other side and slammed across with a rush. The boom caught him in the back of the knees and hurled him outward, but not into the sea, for his feet found the narrow pontoon and he balanced there precariously. In that instant an oar of the galley swung down at him and he toppled sideways, instinctively grasping the blade as he fell. The sea drenched him and wrenched at him, but he clung tightly and began to pull himself up the oar, hand over hand.

His legs were numb from the blows; he feared he would be unable to swim. And he was still bewitched by what he saw. For the moment he forgot the Mouser and the sloop entirely. He shook off the greedy waves, reached the side of the galley, caught hold of the oar-hole. Then he looked back and saw, in a kind of stupid surprise, the disappearing stern of the sloop and the Mouser's gray-capped face, revealed by a close swing of the lantern, staring at him in blank helplessness.

What happened next ended whatever spell had held him. A hand that carried steel struck. He twisted to one side and caught the wrist, then grasped the side of the galley, got his foot in the oarhole, on top of the oar, and heaved. The man dropped the knife too late, clawed at the side, failed to get a secure hold, and was dragged overboard, spitting and snapping his jaws in futile panic. Fafhrd, instinctively taking the offensive, sprang down onto the oarbench, which was the last of ten and half under the poop deck. His questioning eyes spied a rack of swords and he whirled one out, menacing the two shadowy figures hastening toward him, one from the forward oar-benches, one from the poop. They attacked with a rush, but silently, which was strange. The spray-wet weapons sparkled as they clashed.

Fafhrd fought warily, on guard for a blow from above, timing his lunges to the roll of the galley. He dodged a swashing blow and parried an unexpected back-handed slash from the same weapon. Stale, sour wine fumes puffed into his face. Someone dragged out an oar and thrust it like a huge lance; it came between Fafhrd and the two swordsmen, crashing heavily into the sword rack. Fafhrd glimpsed a rat-like, beady-eyed, toothy face peering up at him from the deeper darkness under the poop. One of the swordsmen lunged wildly, slipped and fell. The other gave ground, then gathered himself for a rush. But he paused with his sword in midair, looking over Fafhrd's head as if at a new adversary. The crest of a great wave struck him in the chest, obscuring him.

Fafhrd felt the weight of the water on his shoulders and clutched at the poop for support. The deck was at a perilous tilt. Water gushed up through the opposite oarholes. In the confusion, he realized, the galley had gotten into the troughs, and was beginning to take the seas broadside. She wasn't built to stand that. He vaulted up out of another breaking wave onto the poop and added his strength to that of the lone struggling steersman. Together they strained at the great oar, which seemed to be set in stone instead of water. Inch by inch, they fought their way across the narrow deck. None the less, the galley seemed doomed.

Then something – a momentary lessening of the wind and waves or perhaps a lucky pull by a forward oarsman – decided the issue. As slowly and laboriously as a water-logged hulk the galley lifted and began to edge back into the proper course. Fafhrd and steersman strained prodigiously to hold each foot gained. Only when the galley was riding safe before the wind did they look up. Fafhrd saw two swords leveled steadily a his chest. He calculated his chances and did not move.

It was not easy to believe that fire had been preserved through that tremendous wetting, but one of the swordsmen nevertheless carried a sputtering tarry torch. By its light Fafhrd saw that they were Northerners akin to himself. Big raw-boned fellows, so blond, they seemed almost to lack eyebrows. They wore metal-studded war gear and close-fitting bronze helmets. Their expressions were frozen halfway between a glare and a grin. Again he smelled stale wine. His glance strayed forward. Three oarsmen were bailing with bucket and hand crane.

Somebody was striding toward the poop – the leader, if one could guess from gold and jewels and an air of assurance. He sprang up the short ladder, his limbs supple as a cat's. He seemed younger than the rest and his features were almost delicate. Fine, silky blond hair was plastered wetly against his cheeks. But there was feline rapacity in his tight, smiling lips, and there was craziness in his jewel-blue eyes. Fafhrd hardened his own face against their inspection. One question kept nagging him. Why, even at the height of the confusion, had there been no cries, no shout, no bellowed orders? Since he had come aboard, there had not been a word uttered.

The young leader seemed to come to a conclusion about Fafhrd, for his thin smile widened a trifle and he motioned toward the oar deck. Then Fafhrd broke silence and said in a voice that sounded unnatural and hoarse, 'What do you intend? Weight well the fact that I saved your ship.'

He tensed himself, noting with some satisfaction that the steersman stayed close beside him, as if their shared task had forged a bond between them. The smile left the leader's face. He laid his finger to his lips and then impatiently repeated his first gesture. This time Fafhrd understood. He was to replace the oarsman he had pulled overboard. He could not but admit there was a certain ironic justice to the idea. It was borne in on him that swift death would be his lot if he renewed the fight at such a disadvantage; slow death, if he leaped overboard in the mad hope of finding the sloop in the howling, heaving darkness. The arms holding the swords became taut. He curtly nodded his head in submission. At least they were his own people.

With his first feel of the heavy, rebellious water against the blade of his oar, a new feeling took hold of Fafhrd – a feeling with which he was not unfamiliar. He seemed to become part of the ship, to share its purposes, whatever they might be. It was the age-old spirit of the oarbench. When his muscles had warmed to the task and his nerves became accustomed to the rhythm, he found himself stealing glances at the men around him, as if he had known them before; trying to penetrate and share the eager, set look on their faces.

Something huddled in many folds of ragged cloth shuffled out from the little cabin far back under the poop and held a leather flask to the lips of the opposite oarsman. The creature looked absurdly squat among such tall men. When it turned Fafhrd recognized the beady eyes he had glimpsed before and, as it came nearer, distinguished under the heavy cowl the wrinkled, subtle, ocher face of an aged Mingol.

'So you're the new one,' the Mingol croaked jeeringly. 'I liked your swordplay. Drink deep now, for Lavas Laerk may decide to sacrifice you to the sea gods before morning. But mind you, don't dribble any.'

Fafhrd sucked greedily, then almost coughed and spat when a rush of strong wine seared his throat. After a while the Mingol jerked the flask away.

'Now you know what Lavas Laerk feeds his oarsmen.

334

There are few crews in this world or the next that row on wine.' He chuckled, then said, 'But you're wondering why I talk aloud. Well, young Lavas Laerk may put a vow of silence on all his men, but he may not do the same to me, who is only a slave. For I tend the fire – how carefully you know – and serve out the wine and cook the meat, and recite incantations for the good of the ship. There are certain things that neither Lavas Laerk nor any other man, nor any other demon, may demand of me.'

'But what does Lavas Laerk—'

The Mingol's leathery palm clapped over Fafhrd's mouth and shut off the whispered question.

'Sh! Do you care so little for life? Remember, you are Lavas Laerk's henchman. But I will tell you what you would know.' He sat down on the wet bench beside Fafhrd, looking like a bundle of black rags someone had dropped there. 'Lavas Laerk has sworn to raid far Simorgya, and he has put a vow of silence upon himself and his men until they sight the coast. Sh! Sh! I know they say Simorgya is under the waves, or that there never was such a place. But Lavas Laerk swore a great oath before his mother, whom he hates worse than he hates his friends, and he killed a man who thought to question his decision. So it's Simorgya we seek, if only to steal pearls from the oysters and ravish the fishes. Lean down and row more easily for a space, and I will tell you a secret that's no secret and make a prophecy that's no prophecy.' He crowded closer. 'Lavas Laerk hates all men who are sober, for he believes – and rightly – that only drunken men are even a little like himself. Tonight the crew will row well, though it's a day since they've had meat. Tonight the wine will make them see at least the glow of the visions that Lavas Laerk sees. But next morning there will be aching backs and sick guts and pain-hammered skulls. And then there will be mutiny and not even Lavas Laerk's madness will save him.'

Fafhrd wondered why the Mingol shuddered, coughed weakly and made a gargling sound. He reached over and a warm fluid drenched his naked hand. Then Lavas Laerk pulled his dirk from the Mingol's neck and the Mingol rolled forward off the bench.

No word was spoken, but knowledge that some abominable deed had been committed passed from oarsman to oarsman through the stormy darkness until it reached the bench in the bow. Then gradually there began a kind of pent-up commotion, which increased markedly as there slowly percolated forward an awareness of the specially heinous nature of the deed – the murder of the slave who tended the fire and whose magical powers, though often scoffed at, were entwined with the destiny of the ship itself. Still no completely intelligible words, but low grunts and snarls and mutterings, the scrape of oars being drawn in and rested, a growing murmur in which consternation and fear and danger were mixed, and which washed back and forth between bow and poop like a wave in a tub. Half caught up by it, Fafhrd readied himself for a spring, though whether at the apprehensively motionless figure of Lavas Laerk or back toward the comparative safety of the poop cabin, he could not say. Certainly Lavas Laerk was doomed; or rather he would have been doomed, had not the steersman screamed from the poop in a great shaky voice, 'Land ho! Simorgya! Simorgya!'

That wild cry, like a clawed skeletal hand, seized upon the agitation of the crew and wrenched it to an almost unbearable climax. A shuddering inhalation of breath swept the ship. Then came shouts of wonder, cries of fear, curses that were half prayers. Two oarsmen started to fight together for no other reason than that the sudden, painful upgush of feeling demanded action of some sort, any sort. Another pushed wildly at his oar, screeching at the rest to follow his example and reverse the galley's course and so escape. Fafhrd vaulted up on his bench and stared ahead.

336

It loomed up vast as a mountain and perilously close. A great black blot vaguely outlined by the lesser darkness of the night, partly obscured by trailings of mist and scud, yet showing in various places and at varying distances squares of dim light which by their regular arrangement could be nothing but windows. And with each pounding heartbeat the roar of surf and the thunder of breaking waves grew louder.

All at once it was upon them. Fafhrd saw a great overhanging crag slide by, so close it snapped the last oar on the opposite side. As the galley lifted on a wave he looked awestruck into three windows in the crag – if it was a crag and not a half submerged tower – but saw nothing save a ghostly yellow luminescence. Then he heard Lavas Laerk bellowing commands in a harsh, high-pitched voice. A few of the men worked frantically at the oars, but it was too late for that, although the galley seemed to have gotten behind some protecting wall of rock into slightly calmer water. A terrible rasping noise went the length of the keel. Timbers groaned and cracked. A last wave lifted them and a great grinding crash sent men reeling and tumbling. Then the galley stopped moving altogether and the only sound was the roar of the surf, until Lavas Laerk cried exultantly, 'Serve out weapons and wine! Make ready for a raid!'

The words seemed incredible in this more than dangerous situation, with the galley broken beyond repair, gutted by the rocks. Yet the men rallied and seemed even to catch something of the wild eagerness of their master, who had proved to them that the world was no more sane then he.

Fafhrd watched them fetch torch after torch from the poop cabin, until the whole stern of the wreck smoked and flared. He watched them snatch and suck at the wineskins and heft the swords and dirks given out, comparing them and cleaving at the air to get the feel. Then some of them grabbed hold of him and hustled him to the sword rack, saying, 'Here, Red Hair, you must have a weapon, too.' Fafhrd went along unresisting, yet he felt that something would prevent them from arming one who so late had been their enemy. And he was right in this, for Lavas Laerk stopped the lieutenant who was about to hand Fafhrd a sword, and stared with growing intentness at Fafhrd's left hand.

Puzzled, Fafhrd raised it, and Lavas Laerk cried, 'Seize him!' and at the same instant jerked something from Fafhrd's middle finger. Then Fafhrd remembered. It was the ring.

'There can be no doubt about the workmanship,' said Lavas Laerk, peering cunningly at Fafhrd, his bright blue eyes giving the impression of being out of focus or slightly crossed. 'This man is a Simorgyan spy, or perhaps a Simorgyan demon who has taken the form of a Northerner to allay our suspicions. He climbed out of the sea in the teeth of a roaring storm, did he not? What man among you saw any boat?'

'I saw a boat,' ventured the steersman hurriedly. 'A queer sloop with a triangular sail—' But Lavas Laerk shut him up with a sideways glance.

Fafhrd felt the point of a dirk at his back and checked his tightening muscles.

'Shall we kill him?' The question came from close behind Fafhrd's ear.

Lavas Laerk smiled crookedly up at the darkness and paused, as if listening to the advice of some invisible storm wraith. Then he shook his head. 'Let him live for the present. He can show us where loot is hid. Guard him with naked swords.'

Whereupon they all left the galley, clambering down ropes hung from the prow onto rocks which the surf alternately covered and uncovered. One or two laughed and jumped. A dropped torch hissed out in the brine. There was much shouting. Someone began to sing in a drunken voice that had an edge like a rusty knife. Then Lavas Laerk got them into a sort of order and they marched away, half of them carrying torches, a few still hugging wineskins, sliding and slipping, cursing the sharp rocks and barnacles which cut them when they fell, hurling exaggerated threats at the darkness ahead, where strange windows glowed. Behind them the long galley lay like a dead beetle, the oars sprawled out all askew from the ports.

They had marched for some little distance, and the sound of the breakers was less thunderous, when their torchlight helped reveal a portal in a great wall of black rock that might or might not have been a castle rather than a caverned cliff. The portal was square and high as an oar. Three worn stone steps drifted with wet sand led up to it. Dimly they could discern on the pillars, and on the heavy lintel overhead, carvings partly obliterated by slime and incrustations of some sort, but unmistakably Simorgyan in their obscure symbolism.

The crew, staring silently now, drew closer together. The ragged procession became a tight knot. Then Lavas Laerk called mockingly, 'Where are your guards, Simorgya? Where are your fighting men?' and walked straight up the stone steps. After a moment of uncertainty, the knot broke and the men followed him.

On the massive threshold Fafhrd involuntarily halted, dumbstruck by realization of the source of the faint yellow light he had earlier noticed in the high windows. For the source was everywhere: ceiling, walls, and slimy floor all glowed with a wavering phosphorescence. Even the carvings glimmered. Mixed awe and repugnance gripped him. But the men pressed around and against him, and carried him forward. Wine and leadership had dulled their sensibilities and as they strode down the long corridor they seemed little aware of the abysmal scene.

At first some held their weapons ready to meet a

possible foray or ambush, but soon they lowered them negligently, and even sucked at the wineskins and jested. A hulking oarsman, whose blond beard was patched with yellow scud from the surf, struck up a chantey and others joined in, until the dank walls roared. Deeper and deeper they penetrated into the cave or castle, along the wide, winding, ooze-carpeted corridor.

Fafhrd was carried along by a current. When he moved too slowly, the others jostled him and he quickened his pace, but it was all involuntary. Only his eyes responded to his will, turning from side to side, drinking in details with fearful curiosity: the endless series of vague carvings, wherein sea monsters and unwholesome manlike figures and vaguely anthropomorphic giant skates or rays seemed to come alive and stir as the phosphorescence fluctuated; a group of highest windows or openings of some sort, from which dark slippery weeds trailed down; the pools of water here and there; the still-alive, gasping fish which the others trod or kicked aside; the clumps of bearded shells clinging to the corners; the impression of things scuttling out of the way ahead. Louder and louder the thought drummed in his skull: surely the others must realize where they were. Surely they must know the phosphorescence was that of the sea. Surely they must know that this was the retreat of the more secret creatures of the deep. Surely, surely they must know that Simorgya had indeed sunk under the sea and only risen up yesterday – or yester-hour.

But on they marched after Lavas Laerk, and still sang and shouted and swilled wine in quick gulps, throwing back their heads and lifting up the sacks as they strode. And Fafhrd could not speak. His shoulder muscles were contracted as if the weight of the sea were already pressing them down. His mind was engulfed and oppressed by the ominous presence of sunken Simorgya. Memories of the legends. Thoughts of the black centuries during which sea life had slowly crept and wriggled and swum through the

340

mazes of rooms and corridors until it had a lair in every crack and cranny and Simorgya was one with the mysteries of the ocean. In a deep grotto that opened on the corridor he made out a thick table of stone, with a great stone chair behind it; and though he could not be sure, he thought he distinguished an octopus shape slouched there in a travesty of a human occupant, tentacles coiling the chair, unblinking eyes staring glisteningly.

Gradually the flare of the smoky torches paled, as the phosphorescence grew stronger. And when the men broke off singing, the sound of the surf was no longer audible.

Then Lavas Laerk, from around a sharp turn in the corridor, uttered a triumphant cry. The others hastened after, stumbling, lurching, calling out eagerly.

'Oh, Simorgya!' cried Lavas Laerk. 'We have found your treasure house!'

The room in which the corridor ended was square and considerably lower-ceilinged than the corridor. Standing here and there were a number of black, soggy-looking, heavily-bound chests. The stuff underfoot was muckier. There were more pools of water. The phosphorescence was stronger.

A blond-bearded oarsman leaped ahead as the others hesitated. He wrenched at the cover of the nearest chest. A corner came away in his hands, the wood soft as cheese, the seeming metal a black, smeary ooze. He grasped at it again and pulled off most of the top, revealing a layer of dully-gleaming gold and slime-misted gems. Over that jeweled surface a crablike creature scuttled, escaping through a hole in the back.

With a great, greedy shout, the others rushed at the chests, jerking, gouging, even smiting with their swords at the spongy wood. Two, fighting as to which should break open a chest, fell against it and it went to pieces under them, leaving them struggling in jewels and muck.

All this while Lavas Laerk stood on the same spot from

which he had uttered his first taunting cry. To Fafhrd, who stood forgotten beside him, it seemed that Lavas Laerk was distraught that his quest should come to any end, that Lavas Laerk was desperately searching for something further, something more than jewels and gold to sate his mad willfulness. Then he noted that Lavas Laerk was looking at something intently – a square, slime-filmed, but apparently golden door across the room from the mouth of the corridor; upon it was the carving of some strange, undulant blanket-like sea monster. He heard Lavas Laerk laugh throatily and watched him stride unswervingly toward the door. He saw that Lavas Laerk had something in his hand. With a shock of surprise he recognized it as the ring Lavas Laerk had taken from him. He saw Lavas Laerk shove at the door without budging it. He saw Lavas Laerk fumble with the ring and fit the key part into the golden door and turn it. He saw the door give a little to Lavas Laerk's next push.

Then he realized – and the realization came with an impact like a rushing wall of water – that nothing had happened accidentally, that everything from the moment his arrow struck the fish had been intended by someone or something – something that wanted a door unlocked – and he turned and fled down the corridor as if a tidal wave were sucking at his heels.

The corridor, without torchlight, was pale and shifty as a nightmare. The phosphorescence seemed to crawl as if alive, revealing previously unspied creatures in every niche. Fafhrd stumbled, sprawled at full length, raced on. His fastest bursts of speed seemed slow, as in a bad dream. He tried to look only ahead, but still glimpsed from the corners of his eyes every detail he had seen before: the trailing weeds, the monstrous carvings, the bearded shells, the somberly staring octopus eyes. He noted without surprise that his feet and body glowed wherever the slime had splashed or smeared. He saw a small square of darkness in the omnipresent phosphorescence and sprinted toward it. It grew in size. It was the cavern's portal. He plunged across the threshold into the night. He heard a voice calling his name.

It was the Gray Mouser's voice. It came from the opposite direction to the wrecked galley. He ran toward it across treacherous ledges. Starlight, now come back, showed a black gulf before his feet. He leaped, landed with a shaking impact on another rock surface, dashed forward without falling. He saw the top of a mast above an edge of darkness and almost bowled over the small figure that was staring raptly in the direction from which he had just fled. The Mouser seized him by the shoulder, dragged him to the edge, pulled him over. They clove the water together and swam out to the sloop anchored in the rock-sheltered lee. The Mouser started to heave at the anchor but Fafhrd slashed the line with a knife snatched from the Mouser's belt and jerked up the sail in swift, swishing rushes.

Slowly the sloop began to move. Gradually the ripples became wavelets, the wavelets became smacking waves. Then they slipped past a black, foam-edged sword of rock and were in the open sea. Still Fafhrd did not speak, but crowded on all canvas and did all else possible to coax speed from the storm-battered sloop. Resigned to mystification, the Mouser helped him.

They had not been long underway when the blow fell. The Mouser, looking sternward, gave a hoarse incredulous cry. The wave swiftly overtaking them was higher than the mast. And something was sucking the sloop back. The Mouser raised his arms shieldingly. Then the sloop began to climb; up, up, up until it reached the top, overbalanced, and plummeted down on the opposite side. The first wave was followed by a second and a third, and a fourth, each almost as high. A larger boat would surely have been swamped. Finally the waves gave way to a choppy, foaming, unpredictable chaos, in which every ounce of effort and a thousand quick decisions were needed to keep the sloop afloat.

When the pale foredawn came, they were back on the homeward course again, a small improvised sail taking the place of the one ripped in the aftermath of the storm, enough water bailed from the hold to make the sloop seaworthy. Fafhrd, dazedly watching for the sunrise, felt weak as a woman. He only half heard the Mouser tell, in snatches, of how he had lost the galley in the storm, but followed what he guessed to be its general course until the storm cleared, and had sighted the strange island and landed there, mistakenly believing it to be the galley's home port.

The Mouser then brought thin, bitter wine and salt fish, but Fafhrd pushed them away and said, 'One thing I must know. I never looked back. You were staring earnestly at something behind me. What was it?'

The Mouser shrugged his shoulders. 'I don't know. The distance was too great and the light was queer. What I thought I saw was rather foolish. I'd have given a good deal to have been closer.' He frowned, shrugged his shoulders again. 'Well, what I thought I saw was this: a crowd of men wearing big black cloaks – they looked like Northerners – came rushing out of an opening of some sort. There was something odd about them: the light by which I saw them didn't seem to have any source. Then they waved the big black cloaks around as if they were fighting with them or doing some sort of dance … I told you it was very foolish … and then they got down on their hands and knees and covered themselves up with the cloaks and crawled back into the place from which they had come. Now tell me I'm a liar.'

Fafhrd shook his head. 'Only those weren't cloaks,' he said.

The Mouser began to sense that there was much more

344

to it than he had even guessed. 'What were they, then?' he asked.

'I don't know,' said Fafhrd.

'But then what was the place, I mean the island that almost sucked us down when it sank?'

'Simorgya,' said Fafhrd and lifted his head and began to grin in a cruel, chilly, wild-eyed way that took the Mouser aback. 'Simorgya,' repeated Fafhrd, and pulled himself to the side of the boat and glared down at the rushing water. 'Simorgya. And now it's sunk again. And may it soak there forever and rot in its own corruption, till all's muck!' He trembled spasmodically with the passion of his curse, then sank back. Along the rim of the east a ruddy smudge began to show.

VII: THE SEVEN BLACK PRIESTS

Eyes like red lava peered from a face black as dead lava down the sheer mountainside at the snowy ledge that narrowed off into chilly darkness barely touched by dawn. The black priest's heart pounded its rib cage. Never in his life nor his priest-father's before him had intruders come by this narrow way that led from the Outer Sea across the mountains known as the Bones of the Old Ones. Never in three long returns of the Year of the Monsters, never in four sailings of the ship to tropic Klesh to get them wives, had any but he and his fellow-priests trod the way below. Yet he had always guarded it as faithfully and warily as if it were the nightly assault-route of blasphemy-bent spearmen and bowmen.

There it came again – and unmistakably! – the rumble of singing. To judge from the tone, the man must have a chest like a bear's. As if he had drilled for this nightly (and he had) the black priest laid aside his conical hat and stepped out of his fur-lined shoes and slipped off his fur-lined robe, revealing his skinny-limbed, sag-bellied, well-greased frame.

Moving back in the stony niche, he selected a narrow stick from a closely-shielded fire and laid it across a pit in the rock. Its unsputtering flame revealed that the pit was filled to a hand's breadth of the top with a powder that glittered like smashed jewels. He judged it would take some thirty slow breaths for the stick to burn through at the middle.

He silently returned to the edge of the niche, which was the height of three tall men – seven times his own height – above the snowy ledge. And now, far along that ledge, he could dimly distinguish a figure – no, two. He drew a long knife from his loincloth and, crouching forward, poised himself on his hands and toes. He breathed a prayer to his strange and improbable god. Somewhere above, ice or rocks creaked and snapped faintly, as if the mountain too were flexing its muscles in murderous anticipation.

'Give us the next verse, Fafhrd,' merrily called the foremost of the two snow-treaders. 'You've had thirty paces to compose it, and our adventure took no longer. Or is the poetic hoot owl frozen at last in your throat?'

The Mouser grinned as he strode along with seeming recklessness, the sword Scalpel swinging at his side. His high-collared gray cloak and hood, pulled close around him, shadowed his swart features but could not conceal their impudence.

Fafhrd's garments, salvaged from their sloop wrecked on the chilly coast, were all wools and furs. A great golden clasp gleamed dully on his chest and a golden band, tilted awry, confined his snarled reddish hair. His white-skinned face, with green eyes wide set, had a calm bold look to it, though the brow was furrowed in thought. From over his right shoulder protruded a bow, while from over his left shoulder gleamed the sapphire eyes of a brazen dragon-head that was the pommel of a longsword slung on his back.

His brow cleared and, as if some more genial mountain than the frozen one they traveled along had given tongue, he sang:

> *Oh, Lavas Laerk*
> *Had a face like a dirk*

347

> *And of swordsmen twenty-and-three,*
> *And his greased black ship*
> *Through the waves did slip—*
> *'Twas the sleekest craft at sea;*
> *Yet it helped him naught*
> *When he was caught*
> *By magic, the Mouser, and me.*
> *And now he feeds fishes*
> *The daintiest dishes,*
> *But—*

The words broke off and the Gray Mouser heard the hissing scuff of leather on snow. Whirling around, he saw Fafhrd hurtled over the side of the cliff and he had a moment to wonder whether the huge Northerner, maddened by his own doggerel, had decided to illustrate dramatically Lavas Laerk's plunge to the bottomless deeps.

The next moment Fafhrd caught himself with elbows and hands on the margin of the ledge. Simultaneously, a black and gleaming form hit the spot he had just desperately vacated, broke its fall with bent arms and hunched shoulders, spun over in a somersault, and lunged at the Mouser with a knife that flashed like a splinter of the moon. The knife was about to take the Mouser in the belly when Fafhrd, supporting his weight on one forearm, twitched the attacker back by an ankle. At this the small black one hissed low and horribly, turned again, and lunged at Fafhrd. But now the Mouser was roused at last from the shocked daze that he assured himself could never grip him in a less hatefully cold country. He dove forward at the small black one, diverting his thrust – there were sparks as the weapon struck stone within a finger's width of Fafhrd's arm – and skidding his greased form off the ledge beyond Fafhrd. The small black one swooped out of sight as silently as a bat.

Fafhrd, dangling his great frame over the abyss, finished his verse:

But the daintiest dish is he.

'Hush, Fafhrd,' the Mouser hissed, stooped as he listened intently. 'I think I heard him hit.'

Fafhrd absentmindedly eased himself up to a seat. 'Not if that chasm is half as deep as the last time we saw its bottom, you didn't,' he assured his comrade.

'But what was he?' the Mouser asked frowningly. 'He looked like a man of Klesh.'

'Yes, with the jungle of Klesh as far from here as the moon,' Fafhrd reminded him with a chuckle. 'Some maddened hermit frostbitten black, no doubt. There are strange skulkers in these little hills, they say.'

The Mouser peered up the dizzy mile-high cliff and spotted the nearby niche. 'I wonder if there are more of him?' he questioned uneasily.

'Madmen commonly go alone,' Fafhrd asserted, getting up. 'Come, small nagger, we'd best be on our way if you want a hot breakfast. If the old tales are true, we should be reaching the Cold Waste by sunup – and there we'll find a little wood at least.'

At that instant a great glow sprang from the niche from which the small attacker had dropped. It pulsed, turning from violet to green to yellow to red.

'What makes that?' Fafhrd mused, his interest roused at last. 'The old tales say nothing of firevents in the Bones of the Old Ones. Now if I were to give you a boost, Mouser, I think you could reach that knob and then make your own way—'

'Oh no,' the Mouser interrupted, tugging at the big man and silently cursing himself for starting the question-asking. 'I want my breakfast cooked over more wholesome

349

flames. And I would be well away from here before other eyes see the glow.'

'None will see it, small dodger of mysteries,' Fafhrd said chucklingly, letting himself be urged away along the path. 'Look, even now it dies.'

But at least one other eye had seen the pulsing glow – an eye as large as a squid's and bright as the Dog Star.

'Ha, Fafhrd!' the Gray Mouser cried gaily some hours later in the full-broken dawn. 'There's an omen to warm our frozen hearts! A green hill winks at us frosty men – gives us the glad eye like a malachite-smeared dusky courtesan of Klesh!'

'She's as hot as a courtesan of Klesh, too,' the huge Northernier supplemented, rounding the brown crag's bulging shoulder n his turn, 'for she's melted all the snow.'

It was true. Although the far horizon shone white and green with the snows and glacial ice of the Cold Waste, the saucer-like depression in the foreground held a small unfrozen lake. And while the air was still chilly around them, so that their breath drifted away in small white clouds, the brown ledge they trod was bare.

Up from the nearer shore of the lake rose the hill to which the Mouser had referred, the hill from which one star-small point still reflected the new-risen sun's rays at them blindingly.

'That is, if it is a hill,' Fafhrd added softly. 'And in any case, whether a courtesan of Klesh or hill, she has several faces.'

The point was well taken. The hill's green flanks were formed of crags and hummocks which the imagination could shape into monstrous faces – all the eyes closed save the one that twinkled at them. The faces melted downward like wax into huge stony rivulets – or might they be elephantine trunks? – that plunged into the unruffled acid-seeming water. Here and there among the green were patches of dark red rock that might be blood, or mouths.

Clashing nastily in color, the hill's rounded summit seemed to be composed of a fleshily pink marble. It too persisted in resembling a face – that of a sleeping ogre. It was crossed by a stretch of vividly red rock that might be the ogre's lips. From a slit in the red rock, a faint vapor rose.

The hill had more than a volcanic look. It seemed like an upwelling from a more savage, primal, fiercer consciousness than any that even Fafhrd and the Gray Mouser knew, an upwelling frozen in the act of invading a younger, weaker world – frozen yet eternally watchful and waiting and yearning.

And then the illusion was gone – or four-faces-out-of-five gone and the fifth wavering. The hill was just a hill again – an odd volcanic freak of the Cold Waste – a green hill with a glitter.

Fafhrd let out a gusty sigh. He surveyed the farther shore of the lake. It was hillocky and matted with a dark vegetation that unpleasantly resembled fur. At one point there rose from it a stubby pillar of rock almost like an altar. Beyond the hairy bushes, which were here and there flecked with red-leafed ones, stretched the ice and snow, broken only occasionally by great rocks and rare clumps of dwarfed trees.

But something else was foremost in the Mouser's thoughts.

'The eye, Fafhrd. The glad, glittering eye!' he whispered, dropping his voice as though they were in a crowded street and some informer or rival thief might overhear. 'Only once before have I seen such a gleam, and that was by moonlight, across a king's treasure chamber. That time I did not come away with a huge diamond. A guardian serpent prevented it. I killed the wriggler, but its hiss brought other guards.

'But this time there's only a little hill to climb. And if at this distance the gem gleams so bright, Fafhrd' – his hand dropped and gripped his companion's leg, at the sensitive point just above the knee, for emphasis – 'think how big!'

The Northerner, frowning faintly at the violent squeeze as well as at his doubts and misgivings, nevertheless sucked an icy breath in appreciative greed.

'And we poor shipwrecked marauders,' continued the Mouser raptly, 'will be able to tell the gaping and envious thieves of Lankhmar that we not only crossed the Bones of the Old Ones, but picked them on the way.'

And he went skipping gaily down the skimpy ledge that merged into the narrow, lake-edged, rocky saddle that joined this greater mountain with the green one. Fafhrd followed more slowly, gazing steadily at the green hill, waiting for it to turn back into faces again, or to turn to no faces at all. It did neither. It occurred to him that it might have been partly shaped by human hands and, after that, the notion of a diamond-eyed idol seemed less implausible. At the far end of the saddle, just at the base of the green hill, he caught up with the Mouser, who was studying a flat, dark rock covered with gashes which a moment's glance told Fafhrd must be artificial.

'The runes of tropic Klesh!' the Northerner muttered. 'What should such hieroglyphs be doing so far from their jungle?'

'Chiseled, no doubt, by some hermit frost bitten black, whose madness taught him the Kleshic language,' the Mouser observed sardonically. 'Or have you already forgotten last night's knifer?'

Fafhrd shook his head curtly. Together they pored over the deep-chopped letters, bringing to bear knowledge gained from the perusing of ancient treasure-maps and the deciphering of code-messages carried by intercepted spies.

'The seven black …' Fafhrd read laboriously.

'… priests,' the Mouser finished for him. 'They're in it, whoever they may be. And a god or beast or devil – that writing hieroglyph means any one of the three, depending on the surrounding words, which I don't understand. It's very ancient writing. And the seven black priests are to serve the writhing hieroglyph, or to bind it – again either might be meant, or both.'

'And so long as the priesthood endures,' Fafhrd took up, 'that long will the god-beast-devil lie quietly ... or sleep ... or stay dead ... or not come up ...'

Abruptly the Mouser bounded straight into the air, fanning his feet. 'This rock is hot,' he complained.

Fafhrd understood. Even through the thick walrus-soles of his boots he was beginning to feel the unnatural warmth.

'Hotter than the floor of hell,' the Mouser observed, hopping first on one foot and then the other. 'Well, what now, Fafhrd? Shall we go up, or not?'

Fafhrd answered him with a sudden shout of laughter. 'You decided that, little man, long ago! Was it *I* who started to talk about huge diamonds?'

So up they went, choosing that point where a gigantic trunk, or tentacle, or melted chin strained from the encasing granite. It was not an easy climb, even at the beginning, for the green stone was everywhere rounded off, showing no marks of chisel or axe – which rather dampened Fafhrd's vague theory that this was a hill half-formed by human-wielded tools.

Upward the two of them edged and strained, their breath blowing out in bigger white clouds although the rock was uncomfortably hot under their hands. After an inch-by-inch climb up a slippery surface, where hands and feet and elbows and knees and even toasted chin must all help, they stood at last on the lower lip of one of the green hill's mouths. Here it seemed their ascent must end, for the great cheek above was smooth and sloped outward a spear's length above them.

But Fafhrd took from the Mouser's back a rope that had

once guyed the mast of their shipwrecked sloop, made a noose in it, and cast it up toward the forehead above, where a stubby horn or feeler projected. It caught and held. Fafhrd put his weight on it to test it, then looked inquiringly at his companion.

'What have you in mind?' the Mouser asked, clinging affectionately to the rock-face. 'This whole climb begins to seem mere foolishness.'

'But what of the jewel?' Fafhrd replied in pleasant mockery. 'So big, Mouser, so big!'

'Likely just a bit of quartz,' the Mouser said sourly. 'I have lost my hunger for it.'

'But as for me,' Fafhrd cried, 'I have only now worked up a good appetite.'

And he swung out into emptiness, around the green cheek and into thin, brilliant sunlight.

It seemed to him as if the still lake and the green hill were rocking, instead of himself. He came to rest below the face's monstrously pouchy eyelid. He climbed up hand over hand, found good footing on the ledge that was the eyelid pouch, and twitched the end of the rope back to the Mouser, whom he could no longer see. On the third cast it did not swing back. He squatted on the ledge, bracing himself securely to guy the rope. It went tight in his hands. Very soon the Mouser stepped onto the ledge beside him.

The gaiety was back in the small thief's face, but it was a fragile gaiety, as though he wanted to get this done with quickly. They edged their way along the great eye-pouch until they were directly below the fancied pupil. It was rather above Fafhrd's head, but the Mouser, nimbly hitching himself up on Fafhrd's shoulders peered in readily.

Fafhrd, bracing himself against the green wall, waited impatiently. It seemed as if the Mouser would never speak. 'Well?' he asked finally, when his shoulders had begun to ache from the Mouser's weight.

'Oh, it's a diamond, all right.' The Mouser sounded oddly uninterested. 'Yes, it's big. My fingers can just about span it. And it's cut like a smooth sphere – a sort of diamond eye. But I don't know about getting it out. It's set very deep. Should I try? Don't bellow so, Fafhrd, you'll blow us both off! I suppose we might as well take it, since we've come so far. But it won't be easy. My knife can't … yes, it can! I thought it was rock around the gem. But it's tarry stuff. Squidgy. There! I'm coming down.'

Fafhrd had a glimpse of something smooth, globular and dazzling, with an ugly, ragged, tarry circlet clinging to it. Then it seemed that someone flicked his elbow lightly. He looked down. Momentarily he had the strangest feeling of being in the green steamy jungle of Klesh. For protruding from the brown fur of his cloak was a wickedly barbed little dart, thickly smeared with a substance as black and tarry as that disfiguring the diamond eye.

He quickly dropped flat on the ledge, crying out to the Mouser to do the same. Then he carefully tugged loose the dart, finding to his relief that, although it had nicked the thick hide of his cloak beneath the fur, it had not touched flesh.

'I think I see him,' called the Mouser, peering down cautiously over the protected ledge. 'A little fellow with a very long blowgun and dressed in furs and a conical hat. Crouching there in those dark bushes across the lake. Black, I think, like our knifer last night. A Kleshian, I'd say, unless he's one more of your frostbitten hermits. Now he lifts the gun to his lips. Watch yourself!'

A second dart pinged against the rock above them, then dropped down close by Fafhrd's hand. He jerked it away sharply.

There was a whirring sound, ending in a muted snap. The Mouser had decided to get a blow in. It is not easy to swing a sling while lying prone on a ledge, but the

355

Mouser's missile crackled into the furry bushes close to the black blowgunner, who immediately ducked out of sight.

It was easy enough then to decide on a plan of action, for few were available. While the Mouser raked the bushes across the lake with sling shots, Fafhrd went down the rope. Despite the Mouser's protection, he fervently prayed that his cloak be thick enough. He knew from experience that the darts of Klesh are nasty things. At irregular intervals came the whirr of the Mouser's casts, cheering him on.

Reaching the green hill's base, he strung his bow and called up to the Mouser that he was ready in his turn to cover the retreat. His eyes searched the furry cliffs across the lake, and twice when he saw movement he sent an arrow from his precious store of twenty. Then the Mouser was beside him and they were racing off along the hot mountain edge toward where the cryptically ancient glacial ice gleamed green. Often they looked back across the lake at the dubious furry bushes spotted here and there with blood-red ones, and twice or thrice they thought they saw movement in them – movement coming their way. Whenever this happened, they sent an arrow or a stone whirring, though with what effect they could not tell.

'The seven black priests—' Fafhrd muttered.

'The six,' the Mouser corrected. 'We killed one of them last night.'

'Well, the six then,' Fafhrd conceded. 'They seem angry with us.'

'As why shouldn't they be?' the Mouser demanded. 'We stole their idol's only eye. Such an act annoys priests tremendously.'

'It seemed to have more eyes than that one,' Fafhrd asserted thoughtfully, 'if only it had opened them.'

'Thank Aarth it didn't!' the Mouser hissed. 'And 'ware that dart!'

Fafhrd hit the dirt – or rather the rock – instantly, and the black dart skirred on the ice ahead.

'I think they're unreasonably angry,' Fafhrd asserted, scrambling to his feet.

'Priests always are,' the Mouser said philosophically, with a sidewise shudder at the dart's black-crusted point.

'At any rate, we're rid of them,' Fafhrd said with relief, as he and the Mouser loped onto the ice. The Mouser leered at him sardonically, but Fafhrd didn't notice.

All day they trudged rapidly across the green ice, seeking their way southward by the sun, which got hardly a hand's breadth above the horizon. Toward night the Mouser brought down two low-winging arctic birds with three casts of his sling, while Fafhrd's long-seeing eyes spied a black cave-mouth in an outcropping of rock under a great snowy slope. Luckily there was a clump of dwarfed trees, uprooted and killed by moving ice, near the cave's mouth, and soon the two adventurers were gnawing tough, close-grained brown bird and watching the flickering little fire in the cave's entrance.

Fafhrd stretched hugely and said, 'Farewell to all black priests! That's another bother done with.' He reached out a large, long-fingered hand. 'Mouser, let me see that glass eye you dug from the green hill.'

The Mouser without comment reached into his pouch and handed Fafhrd the brilliant tar-circled globule. Fafhrd held it between his big hands and viewed it thoughtfully. The firelight shone through it and spread from it, highlighting the cave with red, baleful beams. Fafhrd stared unblinkingly at the gem, until the Mouser became very conscious of the great silence around them, broken only by the tiny but frequent crackling of the fire and the large but infrequent cracking of the ice outside. He felt weary to death, yet somehow couldn't consider sleep.

Finally Fafhrd said, in a faint unnatural voice, 'The earth we walk on once lived – a great hot beast, breathing out fire and spewing molten rock. Its constant yearning was to spit red-hot stuff at the stars. This was before all men.'

'What's that?' the Mouser queried, stirring from his half-trance.

'Now men have come, the earth has gone to sleep,' Fafhrd continued in the same hollow voice, not looking at the Mouser. 'But in its dream it thinks of life, and stirs, and tries to shape itself into the form of men.'

'What's that, Fafhrd?' the Mouser repeated uneasily. But Fafhrd answered him with sudden snores. The Mouser carefully teased the gem from his comrade's fingers. Its tarry rim was soft and slippery – repugnantly so, almost as if it were a kind of black tissue. The Mouser put the thing back in his pouch. A long time passed. Then the Mouser touched his companion's fur-clad shoulder. Fafhrd woke with a swift shudder. 'What is it, small one?' he demanded.

'Morning,' the Mouser told him briefly, pointing over the ashes of the fire at the lightening sky.

As they stooped their way out of the cave, there was a faint roaring sound. Looking over the snow-rim and up the slope, Fafhrd saw hurtling down toward them a vast white globe that grew in size in the very brief time while he watched. He and the Mouser barely managed to dive back into the cavern before the earth shook and the noise became ear-splitting and everything went momentarily dark as the huge snowball thundered over the cave-mouth. They both smelled the cold sour ashes blown into their faces from the dead fire by the globe's passing, and the Mouser coughed.

But Fafhrd instantly lunged out of the cave, swiftly stringing his great bow and fitting to it an arrow long as his arm. He sighted up the slope. At the slope's summit, tiny as bugs beyond the wickedly-barbed arrowhead, were a half-dozen conical-hatted figures, sharply silhouetted against the yellow-purple dawn.

They seemed busy as bugs too, fussing furiously with a white globe as tall as themselves.

Fafhrd let out half a breath, paused, and loosed his arrow. The tiny figures continued for several breaths to worry the stubborn globe. Then the one nearest it sprang convulsively and sprawled atop it. The globe began to roll down the slope, carrying the arrow-pierced black priest with it and gathering snow as it went. Soon he was hidden in the ever-thickening crust, but not before his flailing limbs had changed the globe's course, so that it missed the cave-mouth by a spear's length.

As the thundering died, the Mouser peered out cautiously.

'I shot the second avalanche aside,' Fafhrd remarked casually. 'Let's be moving.'

The Mouser would have led the way around the hill – a long and winding course looking treacherous with snow and slippery rock – but Fafhrd said, 'No, straight over the top, where their snowballs have cleared a path for us. They're much too cunning to expect us to take that path.'

However, he kept an arrow nocked to his bow as they made their way up the rocky slope, and moved quite cautiously as they surmounted the naked crest. A white landscape green-spotted with glacial ice opened before them, but no dark specks moved up it and there were no hiding places nearby. Fafhrd unstrung his bow and laughed.

'They seem to have scampered off,' he said. 'Doubtless they're running back to their little green hill to warm themselves. At any rate, we're rid of them.'

'Yes, just as we were yesterday,' the Mouser commented dryly. 'The fall of the knifer didn't seem to worry them at all, but doubtless they're scared witless because you put an arrow into another of their party.'

'Well, at all events,' Fafhrd said curtly, 'granting that

there were seven black priests to begin with, there are now but five.'

And he led the way down the other side of the hill, taking big reckless strides. The Mouser followed slowly, a stone rocking in his dangled sling and his gaze questing restlessly to every side. When they came to snow, he studied it, but there were no tracks as far as he could see to either side. By the time he reached the foot of the hill, Fafhrd was a sling's cast ahead. To make up the distance, the Mouser began a soft-footed, easy lope, yet he did not desist from his watchfulness. His attention was attracted by a squat hummock of snow just ahead of Fafhrd. Shadows might have told him whether there was anything crouched behind it, but the yellow-purple haze hid the sun, so he kept on watching the hummock, meanwhile speeding up his pace. He reached the hummock and saw there was no one behind it almost at the moment he caught up with Fafhrd.

The hummock exploded into a scatter of snow-chunks and a black sag-bellied figure erupted out of it at Fafhrd, ebony arm extended for a knife-slash at the Northerner's neck. Almost simultaneously the Mouser lunged forward, whirling his sling backhanded. The stone, still in the leather loop, caught the slasher high in the face. The curved knife missed by inches. The slasher fell. Fafhrd looked around with mild interest.

The attacker's forehead was so deeply indented that there could be no question of his condition, yet the Mouser stared down at him for a long time. 'A man of Klesh, all right,' he said broodingly, 'but fatter. Armored against the cold. Strange they should have come so far to serve their god.' He looked up and without raising his arm from his side, sharply twirled his sling – much as a bravo might in some alley as a warning to skulkers.

'Four to go,' he said and Fafhrd nodded slowly and soberly.

All day they trod across the Cold Waste – watchfully, but without further incident. A wind came up and the cold bit. The Mouser pulled in his hood so that it covered his mouth and nose, while even Fafhrd hugged his cloak closer around him.

As the sky was darkening to umber and indigo, Fafhrd suddenly stopped and strung his bow and let fly. For a moment the Mouser, who was a bit bothered by his comrade's bemused air, thought that the Northerner was shooting at mere snow. Then the snow leaped, kicking four gray hooves, and the Mouser realized Fafhrd had brought down white-furred meat. He licked his numb lips greedily as Fafhrd swiftly bled and gutted the animal and slung it over his shoulder.

A little way ahead was an outcropping of black rock. Fafhrd studied it for a moment, then took an axe from his belt and struck the rock a careful blow with the back of the head. The Mouser eagerly gathered in the corner of his cloak the large and small chunks that flaked off. He could feel their oiliness and he felt warmed by the mere thought of the rich flame they would make.

Just beyond the outcropping was a low cliff and at its base a cave-mouth slightly sheltered by a tall rock perhaps two spears' lengths in front of it. The Mouser felt a great glow of anticipated content as he followed Fafhrd toward the inviting dark orifice. He had greatly feared, being numb with cold, aching with fatigue, famished, that they might have to camp out and content themselves with the bones of yesternight's birds. Now in an astonishingly short space they had found food, fuel, shelter. So wonderfully convenient ...

And then, as Fafhrd rounded the sheltering rock and strode toward the cave-mouth, the thought came to the Mouser: *Much too convenient.* Without further thought, he dropped the coal and sprang at his comrade, hurling the huge fellow flat on his face.

A dart hissed close over him and clicked faintly against the sheltering rock. Again without pause the Mouser darted into the cave-mouth, whipping his sword Scalpel from its sheath. As he entered the cave he zigged a bit to the left, then zagged suddenly to the right and flattened himself against the rocky wall there, slashing prudently at the darkness as he tried to pierce it with his gaze.

Across from him, on the other side of the mouth, the cave bent back in an elbow, the end of which, to the Mouser's amazement, was not dark but dimly lit by a pulsing light that seemed neither that of fire nor the outer twilight. If anything, it resembled the unnatural glow they had seen back in the Bones of the Old Ones.

But unnatural or not, it had the advantage of silhouetting the Mouser's antagonist. The squat fellow was now gripping a curved knife rather than a blowgun. As the Mouser sprang at him, he scuttled back along the elbow and dodged around the corner from behind which the pulsing glow came. To the Mouser's further amazement, he felt not only a growing warmth as he pursued but also moistness in the air. He rounded the corner. The black priest, who'd stopped just beyond it, lunged at him. But the Mouser was prepared for this and Scalpel took his adversary neatly in the chest, just off center, transfixing him, while the curved knife slashed only steamy air.

For a moment the fanatic priest tried to work his way up along the thin blade and so get within striking distance of the Mouser. Then the nefarious glare died in the priest's eyes and he slumped, while the Mouser distastefully whipped out the blade.

The priest tottered back into the steamy glow, which the Mouser now saw came from a small pit just beyond. With a blood-choking gargling moan the black one stepped back into the pit and vanished. There was a scuff of flesh against rock, a pause, and then a faint splash, and then no sound at all, except for the soft, distant bubbling and seething

362

that the Mouser now realized came steadily from the pit – that is, until Fafhrd came clumping up belatedly.

'Three to go,' the Mouser informed him casually. 'The fourth is cooking at the bottom of that pit. But I want broiled dinner tonight, not boiled, and besides, I haven't a long enough fork. So fetch in the black stones I dropped.'

Fafhrd objected at first, eyeing the steam-and-fire vent almost superstitiously, and urged that they seek other lodging. But the Mouser argued that to spend the night in the now-empty, easily scanned cave was far better than to risk ambush in the outer dark. To the Mouser's relief Fafhrd agreed after peering down the pit for possible handholds that might help a live or boiled attacker. The small man had no desire to leave this pleasantly steamy spot.

The fire was built against the outer wall of the cave and near the mouth, so that no one could creep in without being revealed by its flames. After they had polished off some grilled liver and a number of tough, seared chops and had tossed the bones into the hot fire, where they sputtered merrily, Fafhrd settled back against the rocky wall and asked the Mouser to let him look at the diamond eye.

The Mouser complied with some reluctance, once again experiencing repugnance for the frostily-gleaming stone's tarry circlet. He had the feeling that Fafhrd was going to do something unwise with the stone – what, he didn't know. But the Northerner merely glanced at it for a moment, almost puzzledly, and then thrust it away in *his* pouch. The Mouser started to object, but Fafhrd curtly replied that it was their common property. The Mouser could not but agree.

They had decided to stand watch by turns, Fafhrd first. The Mouser snuggled his cloak around him, and tucked under his head a pillow made of pouch and folded hood. The coal fire flamed, the strange glow from the pit pulsed wanly. The Mouser found it decidedly pleasant to be between the dry heat of the former and the moist warmth of the latter, both spiced by the chill air from outside. He watched the play of shadows through half-closed eyes. Fafhrd, sitting between the Mouser and the flames, bulked reassuringly large, wide-eyed, and alert. The Mouser's last thought as he drowsed off was that he was rather glad that Fafhrd had the diamond. It made his own pillow that much less bumpy.

He woke hearing an odd soft voice. The fire had burned low. For a frightening moment he thought that a stranger had somehow come into the cave – perhaps muttering hypnotic words to put a sleepspell on his comrade. Then he realized that the voice was the one Fafhrd had used last night, and that the Northerner was staring into the diamond eye as if he were seeing limitless visions there, and rocking it slowly to and fro. The rocking made the glittering beams from the gem synchronize with the pulsing glow in a way the Mouser didn't like.

'Nehwon's blood,' Fafhrd was murmuring, his voice almost a chant, 'still pulses strongly under its wrinkled rocky skin, and still bleeds hot and raw from wounds in the mountains. But it needs the blood of heroes before it can shape itself into the form of men.'

The Mouser jumped up, grabbed Fafhrd by the shoulder and shook him gently.

'Those who truly worship Nehwon,' Fafhrd went on entrancedly, as if nothing had happened, 'guard its mountain-wounds and wait and pray for the great day of fulfillment when Nehwon shall wake again, this time in man's form, and rid itself of the vermin called men.'

The Mouser's shaking became violent and Fafhrd woke with a start – only to assert that he had been awake all the time and that the Mouser had been having a nightmare. He laughed at the Mouser's counter-assertions and would not budge from his own. Nor would he give up the

364

diamond, but tucked it deep in his pouch, gave two huge yawns and fell asleep while the Mouser was still expostulating.

The Mouser did not find his watch a pleasant one. In place of his former trust in this rocky nook, he now scented danger in every direction and peered as often at the steamy pit as at the black entrance beyond the glowing coals, entertaining himself with vivid visions of a cooked priest somehow writhing his way up. Meanwhile the more logical part of his mind dwelled on an unpleasantly consistent theory that the hot inner layer of Nehwon was indeed jealous of man, and that the green hill was one of those spots where inner Nehwon was seeking to escape its rocky jacket and form itself into all-conquering man-shaped giants of living stone. The black Kleshite priests would be Nehwon-worshippers eager for the destruction of all other men. And the diamond eye, far from being a bit of valuable and harmless loot, was somehow alive and seeking to enchant Fafhrd with its glittering gaze, and lead him to an obscure doom.

Three times the Mouser tried to get the gem away from his comrade, the third time by slitting the bottom of the Northerner's pouch. But though the Mouser knew himself the most cunning cutpurse in Lankhmar, though perhaps a trifle out of practice, Fafhrd each time hugged the pouch tighter to him and muttered peevishly in his sleep and unerringly brushed away the Mouser's questing hand. The Mouser thought of taking the diamond eye by force, but was stopped by the unreasoning conviction that this would touch off murderous resistance in the Northerner. Indeed, he had strong misgivings as to the state in which his comrade would awake.

But when the cave-mouth finally lightened, Fafhrd roused himself with a shake and a morning yawn-and-growl as stentorious and genial as any the Mouser had ever winced at. Fafhrd acted with such chipper, clear-headed enthusiasm that the Mouser's fears were quite blown away, or at least driven deep into the back of his mind. The two adventurers had a cold-meat breakfast, and carefully wrapped up and packed away the legs and shoulders that had been roasted during the night.

Then while Fafhrd covered him with arrow nocked to taut bowstring, the Mouser darted out and sprang to cover behind the outside of the stone sheltering the entrance. Bobbing up here and there for quick glances over its top, he scanned the cliff above the cave for any sign of ambushers. Holding his sling at the ready, he covered Fafhrd while the latter rushed forth. After a bit they satisfied themselves that there were at least no nearby lurkers in the pale dawn, and Fafhrd led off with a swinging stride. The Mouser followed briskly enough, but after a little while became possessed with a doubt. It seemed to him that Fafhrd was not leading them straight along their course, but swinging rather sharply off toward the left. It was hard to be at all sure, for the sun had still not broken through and the sky was filled with purplish and yellowish scarf-like clouds, while the Mouser could not tell for certain just which way they had come yesterday, since things are very different looking back than looking forward.

Nevertheless he voiced his doubts after a while, but Fafhrd replied with such good-humored assurance, 'The Cold Waste was my childhood playground, as familiar to me as Lankhmar's mazy alleys or the swampways of the Great Salt Marsh to you,' that the Mouser was almost completely satisfied. Besides, the day was windless, which pleased the Mouser no end, because of his worship of warmth.

After a good half-day's trudging they mounted a snowy rise and the Mouser's eyebrows rose incredulously at the landscape ahead: a tilted plain of green ice smooth as glass. Its upper edge, which lay somewhat to their right, was broken by jagged pinnacles, like the crest of a great smooth wave. Its lower slope stretched down for a vast distance to their left, finally losing itself in what looked like a white mist, while straight ahead there seemed to be no end.

The plain was so green that it looked like a giddily enchanted ocean, tilted at the command of some mighty magician. The Mouser felt sure it would reflect the stars on a clear night.

He was somewhat horrified, though hardly surprised, when his comrade coolly proposed that they walk straight across it. The Northerner's shrewd gaze had spotted a section just ahead of them where the slope leveled off briefly before sweeping down again. Along this level ribbon, Fafhrd asserted, they could walk with ease – and then the Northerner set out without waiting for a reply.

With a fatalistic shrug the Mouser followed, walking at first as if on eggs and with many an uneasy glance at the great downward slope. He wished he had bronze-cleated boots – even ones worn flat like Fafhrd's – or some sort of spurs to fix to his own slippery shoes, so that he'd have a better chance of stopping himself if he did start to slide. After a while he grew more confident and took longer and swifter, if still most gingerly steps, and the gap Fafhrd had put between them was closed.

They had walked for perhaps three bowshots across the plain, and still had no sight of an end to it, when a flicker of movement in the corner of his right eye made the Mouser look around.

Swiftly and silently sliding down toward them from some hiding place in the ragged crest, came the remaining black priests, three abreast. They kept their footing like expert skiers – and indeed they seemed to be wearing skis of some sort. Two of them carried spears improvised by thrusting dagger grips into the muzzles of their long blowguns, while the midmost had as lance a narrow, needle-sharp icicle or ice-shard at least eight feet long.

No time now for slings and arrows, and of what use to sword-skewer one who has already spear-skewered you? Besides, an icy slope is no place for dainty near-stationary maneuvering. Without a word to Fafhrd, so certain he was that the Northerner would do the same, the Mouser took off down the dreaded leftward slope.

It was as if he had cast himself into the arms of a demon of speed. Ice whirred softly under his boots; quiet air became cold wind whipping his garments and chilling his cheeks.

But not enough speed. The skiing black priests had a headstart. The Mouser hoped the level stretch would wreck them, but they merely sailed out from it with squat majesty and came down without losing footing – and hardly two spears' lengths behind. Daggers and ice-lance gleamed wickedly.

The Mouser drew Scalpel and after trying fruitlessly to pole himself along to greater velocity with it, squatted down so as to offer the least resistance to the air. Still the black priests gained. Fafhrd beside him dug in his dragon-pommeled long-sword so that ice-dust spouted up fountain-wise, and shot off in a great swing sideward. The priest bearing the ice-lance swerved after him.

Meanwhile the two other priests caught up with the Mouser. He arched his hurtling body away from the spear-thrust of the first and knocked that of the second aside with Scalpel, and for the next few moments there was fought the strangest sort of duel – almost as if they weren't moving at all, since they were all moving at the same speed. At one point the Mouser was sliding down backward, parrying the nasty blowgun-spears with his shorter weapon.

But two against one always helps, and this time might have proved fatal, if Fafhrd had not just then caromed back from his great sideward swing full of speed from some slope he alone had seen, and whirled his sword. He passed just behind the two priests and then their heads were skidding along separately from their bodies, though all at the same speed.

Yet it would have been all up with Fafhrd, for the last black priest, perhaps helped by the weight of his ice-lance, came hurtling after Fafhrd at even greater speed and would have skewered him except the Mouser deflected the ice-lance upward, with Scalpel held in two hands, and the icy point merely ruffled Fafhrd's streaming red hair.

The next moment they all plunged into the white-icy mist. The last glimpse the Mouser had of Fafhrd was of his speeding head alone, cutting a wake in the neck-high mist. Then the Mouser's eyes were beneath the mist's surface.

It was most strange to the Mouser to skim swiftly through milky stuff, ice-crystals stinging his cheeks, not knowing each instant if an unknown barrier might wreck him. He heard a grunt that sounded like Fafhrd's, and on top of that a tingling crash, which might have been the ice-spear shattering, followed by a sighing, tortured moan. Next came the feeling of reaching bottom, followed by an upward swoop, and then the Mouser broke out of the mist into the purple-yellow day and skidded into a soft snowbank and began to laugh wildly with relief. It was some moments before he noticed that Fafhrd, also shaking with laughter, was likewise half buried in the snow beside him.

When Fafhrd looked at the Mouser, the latter shrugged inquiringly at the mist behind them. The Northerner nodded confirmingly.

'The last priest dead. None to go!' the Mouser proclaimed happily, stretching in the snow as if it were a featherbed. His chief idea was to find the nearest cave – he was sure there would be one – and enjoy a great rest.

But Fafhrd turned out to be full of other ideas and a

seething energy. Nothing would do but they must press on swiftly until dusk, and he presented to the Mouser such alluring pictures of getting out of the Cold Waste by tomorrow, or even nightfall, that the small man soon found himself trotting along after the big one, though he couldn't help wondering from time to time how Fafhrd could be so supremely sure of his direction in this chaos of ice, snow, and churning, unpleasantly-tinted clouds. The whole Cold Waste couldn't have been his playground, surely, the Mouser told himself, with an inward shudder at child Fafhrd's notion of proper places to play.

Twilight overtook them before they reached the forests Fafhrd had promised, and at the Mouser's urgent insistence they began to hunt for a place to pass the night. This time a cave wasn't so easily come by. It was quite dark before Fafhrd spotted a rocky notch with a clump of stunted trees growing in front of it that promised at least fuel and passable shelter.

However, it appeared that the wood would hardly be needed, for just short of the tree-clump was a black rock outcropping resembling the one that had given them coal last night.

But just as Fafhrd joyfully lifted his axe, the outcropping came to life and lunged at his belly with a dagger.

Only Fafhrd's exuberant and undiminished energy saved his life. He arched his belly aside with a supple swiftness that amazed even the Mouser, and drove the axe deep into his attacker's head. The squat black body thrashed its limbs convulsively and swiftly grew stiff. Fafhrd's deep laughter rumbled like thunder. 'Shall we call him the none black priest, Mouser?' he inquired.

But the Mouser saw no cause for amusement. All his uneasiness returned. If they had missed their count on one of the black priests – say the one who had spun down in the snowball or the one supposedly slain in the mist – why mightn't they have missed their count on another? Besides, how could they have been so convinced, simply from an ancient inscription, that there had been only seven black priests? And once you admitted there might have been eight, why mightn't there be nine, or ten, or twenty?

However, Fafhrd merely chuckled at these worries and chopped wood and built a roaring fire in the rocky notch. And although the Mouser knew the fire would advertise their presence for miles around, he was so grateful for its warmth that he found himself unable to criticize Fafhrd at all severely. And when they had warmed and eaten their roast meat from the morning, such a delicious tiredness came over the Mouser that he tucked his cloak around him and headed straight for sleep. However, Fafhrd chose that moment to drag out and inspect by firelight the diamond eye, which made the Mouser open his own a slit.

This time Fafhrd did not seem inclined to go into a trance. He grinned in a lively and greedy fashion as he turned the gem this way and that, as though to admire the beams flashing from it while mentally appraising its value in square Lankhmarian goldpieces.

Although reassured, the Mouser was annoyed. 'Put it away, Fafhrd,' he snapped sleepily.

Fafhrd stopped turning the gem and one of its beams blinked directly at the Mouser. The latter shivered, for he had for a moment the sharp conviction that the gem was looking at him with evil intelligence.

But Fafhrd obediently tucked the gem away with a laugh-and-a-yawn and cloaked himself up for sleep. Gradually the Mouser's eerie feelings and realistic fears were both lulled as he watched the dancing flames, and he drowsed off.

The Mouser's next conscious sensations were of being tossed roughly down onto thick grass that felt unpleasantly like fur. His head ached splittingly and there was a pulsing yellow-purple glow, shot through with blinding gleams. It

371

was a few moments before he realized that all these lights were outside his skull rather than inside it.

He lifted his head to look around and agonizing pain shot through it. However, he persisted and shortly found out where he was.

He was lying on the hillocky, dark-vegetated shore across the acid-seeming lake from the green hill. The night sky was live with northern lights, while from the mouthlike slit – now open wider – in the green hill's pinkish top, a red smoke came in puffs like a man eagerly panting and heaving. All the hill's green flank-faces seemed monstrously alive in the mixed lights, their mouths twitching and their eyes flashing – as if every one of them held an eye-diamond. Only a few feet away from the Mouser, Fafhrd stood stiffly behind the stubby pillar of rock, which was indeed a carved altar of some sort, topped by a great bowl. The Northerner was chanting something in a grunty language the Mouser didn't know and had never heard Fafhrd use.

The Mouser struggled to a sitting position. Gingerly feeling his skull, he found a large lump over his right ear. At the same time Fafhrd struck sparks – apparently with stone and steel – above the bowl, and a pillar of purple flame shot up from it, and the Mouser saw that Fafhrd's eyes were tight shut and that in his hand he held the diamond eye.

Then the Mouser realized that the diamond eye had been far wiser than the black priests who had served its mountain idol. They, like many priests, had been much too fanatical and not nearly as clever as the god they served. While they had sought to rescue the filched eye and destroy the blasphemous thieves who had stolen it, the eye had taken care of itself very nicely. It had enchanted Fafhrd and deceived him into taking a circling course that would lead him and the Mouser back to the vengeful green hill. It had even speeded up the last stage of the journey, forcing Fafhrd to move by night, carrying the Mouser with him after stunning him in his sleep with a dangerously heavy blow.

Also, the diamond eye must have been more foresighted and purposeful than its priests. It must have some important end in view, over and beyond that of getting itself returned to its mountain-idol. Otherwise, why should it have instructed Fafhrd to preserve the Mouser carefully and bring him along? The diamond eye must have some use for both of them. Through the Mouser's aching brain reverberated the phrase he remembered Fafhrd muttering two nights before: 'But it needs the blood of heroes before it can shape itself into the form of man.'

As all these thoughts were seething painfully in the Mouser's brain, he saw Fafhrd coming toward him with diamond eye in one hand and drawn longsword in the other, but a winning smile on his blind face.

'Come, Mouser,' Fafhrd said gently, 'it is time we crossed the lake and climbed the hill and received the kiss and sweet suck of the topmost lips and mingled our blood with the hot blood of Nehwon. In that way we will live on in the stony rock-giants about to be born, and know with them the joy of crushing cities and trampling armies and stamping on all cultivated fields.'

These mad phrases stung the Mouser into action, unintimidated by the pulsing lights of sky and hill. He jerked Scalpel from its scabbard and sprang at Fafhrd, engaging the longsword and making a particularly clever disarming thrust-and-twist guaranteed to send the longsword spinning from Fafhrd's hand – especially since the Northerner still had his eyes closed tight.

Instead, Fafhrd's heavy blade evaded the Mouser's swift one as easily as one avoids a baby's slap, and, smiling sorrowfully, sent a rippling thrust at the Mouser's throat that the latter could escape only with the most fantastic and frantic of backward leaps.

The leap took him in the direction of the lake. Instantly Fafhrd closed in, attacking with scornful poise. His large face was a mask of blond contempt. His far heavier sword moved as deftly as Scalpel, weaving a gleaming arabesque of attack that forced the Mouser back, back, back.

And all the while Fafhrd's eyes stayed tight shut. Only when driven to the brink of the lake did the Mouser realize the reason. The diamond eye in Fafhrd's left hand was doing all the seeing for the Northerner. It followed every movement of Scalpel with a snaky intentness.

So, as he danced on the slippery black rim above the wildly-reflecting lake, with the skies throbbing yellow-purple above him and the green hill panting behind, the Mouser suddenly ignored Fafhrd's threatening blade and ducked and slashed unexpectedly at the diamond eye.

Fafhrd's cut whistled a finger's breadth above the Mouser's head.

The diamond eye, struck by Scalpel, exploded in a white burst.

The black furry ground beneath their feet heaved as if in despairing torment.

The green hill erupted with a vindictive red blast that sent the Mouser staggering and that shot a gush of molten rock twice the hill's height toward the bruised night-sky.

The Mouser grabbed hold of his bewilderedly-staring companion and rushed him away from the green hill and the lake.

A dozen heartbeats after they left the spot, the erupting molten rock drenched the altar and splashed wide. Some of the red gouts came even as far as the Mouser and Fafhrd, shooting fiery darts over their shoulders as they scampered. One or two gouts hit and the Mouser had to beat out a small fire they started in Fafhrd's cloak.

Looking back as he ran, the Mouser got a last glimpse of the green hill. Although still spouting fire and dribbling red streams, it seemed otherwise very solid and still, as though all its potentialities for life were vanished for a time, or forever.

When they finally stopped running, Fafhrd looked stupidly down at his left hand and said, 'Mouser, I've cut my thumb. It's bleeding.'

'So's the green hill,' the Mouser commented, looking back. 'And bleeding to death, I'm happy to say.'

VIII: CLAWS FROM THE NIGHT

Fear hovered in the moonlight over Lankhmar. Fear
flowed like mist through the twisting thoroughfares and
mazy alleyways, trickling even into that most intricately
curved and crevice-like street where a sootily flickering
lantern marked the doorway to the tavern of the Silver
Eel.

It was a subtle fear, not the sort inspired by a besieging
army, or warring nobles, or revolting slaves, or a mad
overlord bent on wanton slaughter, or an enemy fleet
sailing from the Inner Sea into the estuary of the Hlal. But
it was none the less potent. It clutched the soft throats of
the chattering women now entering the low doorway of
the Silver Eel, making their laughter more sudden and
shrill. It touched the women's escorts too, making them
speak louder and rattle their swords more than necessary.

This was a party of young aristocrats seeking excitement
in a place known to be disreputable and somewhat
dangerous. Their garments were rich and fantastic, after
the fashion of the decadent Lankhmar nobility. But there
was one thing that seemed almost too crazily faddish even
in exotic Lankhmar. The head of each woman was
enclosed in a small, delicately-wrought silver bird cage.

Again the door opened, this time to emit two men who
swiftly walked away. The one was tall and hulking, and
seemed to be concealing some object under his great cloak.
The other was small and lithe, clad from crown to toe in a

soft gray that merged with the diffused moonlight. He was carrying a fishpole over his shoulder.

'I wonder what Fafhrd and the Gray Mouser are up to now,' murmured a hanger-on, peering curiously over his shoulder. The landlord shrugged.

'No good, I'll warrant,' pressed the hanger-on. 'I saw the thing under Fafhrd's cloak move, as if alive. Today, in Lankhmar, that is most suspicious. You see what I mean? And then the fishpole.'

'Peace,' said the landlord. 'They are two honest rogues, even though much in need of money, if what they owe me for wine is any indication. Say nothing against them.'

But he looked a trifle puzzled and perturbed as he went inside again, impatiently pushing the hanger-on ahead of him.

It was three months since the fear had come to Lankhmar, and at the beginning it had been a very different sort of thing – hardly fear at all. Just an overly numerous series of thefts of cheap trinkets and costly gems, with women the chief sufferers. Bright and shining objects, no matter what their nature, were given the preference.

Gossip had it that a band of exceptionally light-fingered and haphazard pilferers was making a speciality of the tiring rooms of great ladies, though the whipping of maids and body-slaves failed to uncover any of the expected confederates. Then someone advanced the theory that it was the work of cunning children too young to judge well the value of objects.

But gradually the character of the thefts began to change. Fewer worthless baubles were taken. More and more often, valuable gems were plucked from a jumble of glass and gilt, giving the odd impression that the marauders were only by practice developing a sense of discrimination.

At about this time people began to suspect that the ancient and almost reputable Thieves' Guild of Lankhmar had invented a new stratagem, and there was talk of torturing a few suspected leaders or waiting for a west wind and burning the Street of the Silk Merchants.

But since the Thieves' Guild was a conservative and hide-bound organization wedded to traditional methods of thievery, suspicion shifted somewhat when it became increasingly evident that a mentality of incredible daring and ingenuity was at work.

Valuables disappeared in broad daylight, even from chambers locked and carefully guarded, or from sheer-walled roof-gardens. A lady secure in her home chanced to lay a bracelet on an inaccessible windowledge; it vanished while she chatted with a friend. A lord's daughter, walking in a private garden, felt someone reach down from a thickly-leafed tree and snatch a diamond pin from her hair; the tree was immediately climbed by nimble servitors, but nothing was found.

Then a hysterical maid ran to her mistress with the information that she had just seen a large bird, black in colour, making off through a window with an emerald ring clutched securely in its talons.

This story at first met with angry disbelief. It was concluded that the girl herself must have stolen the ring. She was whipped almost to death amid general approval.

The next day a large black bird swooped down on the niece of the Overlord and ripped a jewel from her ear.

Much supporting evidence was immediately forthcoming. People told of seeing birds of unusual appearance at odd times and places. It was recalled that in each of the thefts an aerial route had been left open. The victims began to remember things that had seemed inconsequential at the time – the beat of wings, the rustle of feathers, bird tracks and droppings, hovering shadows and the like.

All Lankhmar buzzed with amazed speculation. It was believed, however, that the thefts would cease, now that the authors were known and suitable precautions taken.

No special significance was attached to the injured ear of the Overlord's niece. Both these judgments proved wrong.

Two days later, the notorious courtesan Lessnya was beset by a large black bird while crossing a wide square. Forewarned, Lessnya struck at the bird with a gilt wand she was carrying, shouting to scare it off.

To the horror of the onlookers, the bird eluded the wild blows, set its talons in her white shoulder, and pecked her right eye viciously. Thereupon it gave a shuddering squawk, flapped its wings, and took off amid a flurry of black feathers, gripping a jade brooch in its claws.

Within the next three days, five more women were robbed in the same way; three of these were mutilated.

Lankhmar was frightened. Such unwholesomely purposeful behavior on the part of birds roused all sorts of superstitious fear. Bowmen armed with triple-pronged fowling-arrows were stationed on the roofs. Timid women stayed indoors, or wore cloaks to hide their jewels. Shutters were kept closed at night despite the summer heat. Considerable numbers of innocent pigeons and gulls were shot or poisoned. Cocky young nobles summoned their falconers and went hawking after the marauders.

But they had difficulty in locating any; and on the few occasions they did, their falcons found themselves opposed by adversaries who flew swiftly and fought back successfully. More than one mews mourned the death of a favorite fighting bird. All efforts to trace the winged thieves failed.

These activities did have one tangible result: most of the attacks and thefts thereafter occurred during the hours of darkness.

Then a woman died painfully three hours after having been clawed around the neck, and black robed physicians averred that there must have been a virulent poison in the wounding talons.

Panic grew and wild theories were advanced. The

priests of the Great God maintained that it was a divine rebuke to feminine vanity, and made dire prophecies about an imminent revolt of all animals against sinful man. Astrologers dropped dark and disturbing hints. A frantic mob burned a rookery belonging to a wealthy grain merchant, and then milled through the streets, stoning all birds and killing three of the sacred black swans before being dispersed.

Still the attacks continued. And Lankhmar, with her usual resiliency, began to adjust herself somewhat to this bizarre and inexplicable siege from the sky. Rich women made a fashion of their fear by adopting silver networks to protect their features. Several with made jokes about how, in a topsy-turvy world, the birds were loose and the women wore the cages. The courtesan Lessnya had her jeweler contrive a lustrous eye of hollow gold, which men said added to her exotic beauty.

Then Fafhrd and the Gray Mouser appeared in Lankhmar. Few guessed where the huge Northern barbarian and his small, dexterous companion had been or why they had returned at this particular time. Nor did Fafhrd or the Gray Mouser offer any explanations.

They busied themselves with inquiries at the Silver Eel and elsewhere, drinking much wine but avoiding brawls. Through certain devious channels of information the Mouser learned that the fabulously wealthy but socially unacceptable moneylender Muulsh had bought a famous ruby from the King of the East – then hard-pressed for cash – and was going to give it to his wife. Whereupon the Mouser and Fafhrd made further inquiries and certain secret preparations, and slipped away together from the tavern of the Silver Eel on a moonlit night, bearing objects of a mysterious nature which awakened doubts and suspicions in the mind of the landlord and others.

For there was no denying that the thing Fafhrd carried

under his great cloak moved as if alive and was the size of a large bird.

Moonlight did not soften the harsh angular lines of the great stone house of Muulsh, the moneylender. Square, flat-roofed, small-windowed, three stories high, it stood a little distance from the similar houses of the wealthy grain merchants like a rejected hanger-on.

Close to it flowed the waters of the Hlal, angrily churning past this portion of the city, which thrust out like an elbow into the mighty stream. Abutting and o'ertopping it on the side nearest the river loomed a lightless, tower-like structure, one of the several accursed and abandoned temples of Lankhmar, shut up in ancient times for reasons now known only to certain priests and necromancers.

Crowding close on the other side were the dark, solid forms of warehouses. There was an impression of tight-lipped power about this house of Muulsh – of great wealth and weighty secrets closely guarded.

But the Gray Mouser, peering down through one of the usual Lankhmar roof-windows into the tiring room of Muulsh's wife, was seeing a very different aspect of Muulsh's character. The notoriously heartless money-lender, quailing under a connubial tongue-lashing, looked like nothing so much as a fawning lapdog – except perhaps an anxious and solicitous hen.

'You worm! You slug! You gross, fat beast!' his slender young wife railed at him, almost chanting the words. 'You've ruined my life with your stinking money-grubbing! Not one noblewoman will even speak to me. Not one lord or grain merchant so much as dares flirt with me. Everywhere I am ostracized. And all because your fingers are greasy and vile from handling coins!'

'But, Atya,' he murmured timidly, 'I've always thought you had friends to visit. Almost every day you go off for hours on end – though without telling me where you've been.'

'You insensitive clod!' she cried. 'Is it any wonder that I slip away to some lonely nook to weep and seek bitter consolation in private? You will never understand the delicacy of my emotions. Why did I ever marry you? I wouldn't have, you may be sure – except that you forced my poor father into it when he was in difficulties. You bought me! It's the only way you know of getting anything.

'And then when my poor father died, you had the effrontery to buy this house, his house, the house I was born in. You did it to complete my humiliation. To take me back where everybody knew me and could say, "There goes the wife of that utterly impossible moneylender" – if they use such a polite word as wife! All you want is to torture and degrade me, drag me down to your own unutterable level. Oh, you obscene pig!'

And she made a tattoo with her gilded heels on the gleaming parquetry of the floor. Clad in yellow silk tunic and pantaloons, she was very pretty in a small, slight way. Her small-chinned, bright-eyed face was oddly attractive under its canopy of gleamingly smooth black hair. Her swift movements had the quality of restless fluttering. At the moment her every gesture conveyed anger and unbearable irritation, but there was also a kind of studied ease about her manner that suggested to the Mouser, who was hugely enjoying everything, a scene that had been played and replayed many times.

The room suited her well, with its silken hangings and fragile furniture. Low tables, scattered about, were crowded with jars of cosmetics, bowls of sweetmeats, and all sorts of frivolous bric-a-brac. The flames of slim tapers swayed in the warm breeze from the open windows.

On delicate chains were suspended a full dozen cages of canaries, nightingales, love birds, and other tiny warblers, some drowsing, others chirruping sleepily. Here and there were strewn small fluffy rugs. All in all, a very downy nest amidst the stoniness of Lankhmar.

Muulsh was somewhat as she had described him – fat, ugly, and perhaps twenty years older than she. His gaudy tunic fitted him like a sack. The look of mingled apprehension and desire he fixed upon his wife was irresistibly comic.

'Oh, Atya, my little dove, do not be angry with me. I try so hard to please you, and I love you so very much,' he cried, and tried to lay his hand on her arm. She eluded him. He hurried clumsily after her, immediately bumping into one of the bird cages, which hung at an inconvenient height. She turned on him in a miniature fury.

'Disturb my pets, will you, you brute! There, there, my dears, don't be frightened. It's just the old she-elephant.'

'Damn your pets!' he cursed impulsively, holding his forehead. Then he recollected himself and dodged back-ward, as if in fear of being thwacked with a slipper.

'Oh! So in addition to all your other crude affronts, we are also to be damned?' she said, her voice suddenly icy.

'No, no, my beloved Atya. I forgot myself. I love you very much, and your feathered pets as well. I meant no harm.'

'Of course you meant no harm! You merely want to torment us to death. You want to degrade and—'

'But, Atya,' he interrupted placatingly, 'I don't think I've really degraded you. Remember, even before I married you, your family never mingled with Lankhmar society.'

That remark was a mistake, as the eavesdropping Mouser, choking back his laughter, could plainly see. Muulsh must have realized it too, for as Atya went white and reached for a heavy crystal bottle, he retreated and cried out, 'I've brought you a present.'

'I can imagine what it's like,' she sneered disdainfully, relaxing a trifle but still holding the bottle poised. 'Some trinket a lady would give her maid. Or flashy rags fit only for a harlot.'

'Oh, no, my dear. This is a gift for an empress.'

'I don't believe you. It's because of your foul taste and filthy manners that Lankhmar won't accept me.' Her fine, decadently weak features contracted in a pout, her charming bosom still rising and falling from anger. '"She's the concubine of Muulsh the moneylender," they say, and snigger at me. Snigger!'

'They've no right to. I can buy the lot of them! Just wait until they see you wearing my gift. It's a jewel that the wife of the Overlord would give her eyeteeth to possess!'

At mention of the word 'jewel' the Mouser sensed a subtle shiver of anticipation run through the room. More than that, he saw one of the silken hangings stir in a way that the lazy breeze could hardly account for.

He edged cautiously forward, craning his neck and peered down sideways into the space between the hangings and the wall. Then slowly a smile of elfish amusement appeared on his compact, snub-nosed face.

Crouched in the faintly amber luminescence that filtered through the draperies were two scrawny men, naked except for dark breechcloths. Each carried a bag big enough to fit loosely over a human head. From these bags leaked a faint soporific scent that the Mouser had noticed before without being able to place.

The Mouser's smile deepened. Noiselessly he drew forward the slim fishpole at his side and inspected the line and the stickily-smeared claws that served for a hook.

'Show me the jewel!' said Atya.

'I shall, my dear. At once,' answered Muulsh. 'But don't you think we'd first best close the sky-window and the other ones?'

'We'll do nothing of the kind!' snapped Atya. 'Must I stifle just because a lot of old women have given way to a silly fear?'

384

'But, my dove, it's not a silly fear. All Lankhmar is afraid. And rightly.'

He moved as though to call a slave. Atya stamped her foot pettishly. 'Stop, you fat coward! I refuse to give way to childish frights. I won't believe any of those fantastic stories, no matter how many great ladies swear to them. Don't you dare have the windows closed. Show me the jewel at once, or – or I'll never be nice to you again.'

She seemed close to hysteria. Muulsh sighed and resigned himself.

'Very well, my sweet.'

He walked over to an inlaid table by the door, clumsily ducking past several bird cages, and fumbled at a small casket. Four pairs of eyes followed him intently. When he returned there was something in his hand that glittered. He set it down on the center of the table.

'There,' he said, stepping back. 'I told you it was fit for an empress, and it is.'

For a space there was breathless silence in the room. The two thieves behind the draperies edged forward hungrily, quietly loosening the drawstrings of the bags, their feet caressing the polished floor like cats' paws.

The Mouser slid the slim fishing rod through the sky-window, avoiding the silver chains of the cages, until the pendant claw was poised directly above the center of the table, like a spider preparing to drop on an unsuspecting large red beetle.

Atya stared. A new dignity and self-respect crept into Muulsh's expression. The jewel gleamed like a fat, lucent, quivering drop of blood.

The two thieves crouched to spring. The Mouser joggled the rod slightly, gauging his aim before he dropped the claw. Atya reached out an eager hand and moved toward the table.

But all these intended actions were simultaneously interrupted.

There was a beat and whirr of powerful wings. An inky bird a little larger than a crow flapped through a side window and skidded down into the room, like a fragment of blackness detached from the outer night. Its talons made arm-long scratches as it hit the table. Then it arched its neck, gave a loud, shuddering squawk, and launched itself toward Atya.

The room whirled with chaotic movements. The gummed claw halted midway in its drop. The two thieves fought ungracefully to keep their balance and avoid being seen. Muulsh waved his arms and shouted, 'Shoo! Shoo!' Atya collapsed.

The black bird swept close past Atya, its wings brushing and striking the silver cages, and beat out into the night.

Again there was momentary silence in the room. The gentle songbirds had been quite stilled by the incursion of their raptorial brother. The rod vanished through the sky-window. The two thieves scuttled behind the draperies and noiselessly edged toward a door. Their looks of bafflement and fright were giving way to professional chagrin.

Atya rose to her knees, dainty hands pressed to her face. A shudder tightened around Muulsh's fleshy neck and he moved toward her.

'Did it – did it hurt you? Your face. It struck at you.'

Atya dropped her hands, revealing an unmaimed countenance. She stared at her husband. Then all at once the stare changed to a glare, like a pot suddenly come to a boil.

'You big useless hen!' she cried out. 'For all you cared, it might have pecked out both my eyes! Why didn't you do something? Yelling "Shoo! Shoo!" when it struck at me! And the jewel gone forever now! Oh, you miserable capon!'

She rose to her feet, taking off one of her slippers with a wildly determined air. Muulsh retreated, protesting and bumped into a whole cluster of bird cages.

*

386

Only Fafhrd's tossed-aside cloak marked the spot where the Gray Mouser had left him. Hastening to the roof-edge, he made out Fafhrd's large form some distance away across the roofs of the adjoining warehouses. The barbarian was staring at the moonlit sky. The Mouser gathered up the cloak, leaped the narrow gap, and followed.

When the Mouser reached him, Fafhrd was grinning with great satisfaction so that his big white teeth showed. The size of his supple, brawny frame and the amount of metal-studded leather he wore in the form of armbands and broad belt were as much out of tune with civilized Lankhmar as were his long, copper hair, handsomely rugged features, and pale Northern skin, ghostly in the moonlight. Firmly clutching his heavy hawking-glove at the wrist was a white-capped eagle, which ruffled its feathers and made a disagreeable gargling noise in its throat at the Mouser's approach.

'Now tell me I can't hawk by full moon!' he cried out in great good humor. 'I don't know what happened in the room, or what luck you had, but as for the black bird that went in and came out – Lo! It is here!'

He pushed at a limp bundle of black feathers with his foot.

The Mouser hissed the names of several gods in quick succession, then asked, 'But the jewel?'

'I don't know about that,' said Fafhrd, brushing the matter aside. 'Ah, but you should have seen it, little man! A wondrous fight!' His voice regained its enthusiasm. 'The other one flew swift and cunningly but Kooskra here rose like the north wind up a mountain pass. For a while I lost them in the fray. There seemed to be something of a fight. Then Kooskra brought him down.'

The Mouser had dropped to his knees and was gingerly examining Kooskra's quarry. He slipped a small knife from his belt.

'And to think,' continued Fafhrd, as he adjusted a

leather hood over the eagle's head, 'that they told me these birds were demons or fierce phantasms of darkness! Faugh! They're only ungainly, night-flying crows.'

'You talk too loudly,' said the Mouser. Then he looked up. 'But there's no gainsaying that tonight the eagle beat the fishpole. See what I found in this one's gullet. He kept it to the end.'

Fafhrd snatched the ruby from the Mouser with his free hand and held it up to the moon.

'King's ransom!' he cried. 'Mouser, our fortune's made! I see it all. We shall follow these birds as they rob and let Kooskra rape them of their booty.' He laughed aloud.

This time there was no warning beat of wings – only a gliding shadow which grazed Fafhrd's upraised hand and slid silently away. It almost came to rest on the roof, then flapped powerfully upward.

'Blood of Kos!' cursed Fafhrd, waking from his dumbfounded amazement. 'Mouser, he's taken it!' Then, 'At him, Kooskra! At him!' as he swiftly unhooded the eagle.

But this time it was apparent from the first that something was wrong. The beat of the eagle's wings was slow, and he seemed to have difficulty gaining height. Nevertheless he drew near the quarry. The black bird veered suddenly, swooped, and rose again. The eagle followed closely, though his flight was still unsteady.

Wordlessly Fafhrd and the Mouser watched the birds approach the massive, high-reared tower of the deserted temple, until their feathered forms were silhouetted against its palely glowing, ancient surface.

Kooskra seemed then to recover full power. He gained a superior position, hovered while his quarry frantically darted and wheeled, then plummeted down.

'Got him, by Kos!' breathed Fafhrd, thumping his knee with his fist.

But it was not so. Kooskra struck at thin air. At the last

moment the black bird had slipped aside and taken cover in one of the high-set windows of the tower.

And now it was certain beyond doubt that something was wrong with Kooskra. He sought to beat about the embrasure sheltering his quarry, but lost height. Abruptly he turned and flew out from the wall. His wings moved in an irregular and convulsive way. Fafhrd's fingers tightened apprehensively on the Mouser's shoulder.

As Kooskra reached a point above them, he gave a great wild scream that shook the soft Lankhmar night. Then he fell, like a dead leaf, circling and spinning. Only once again did he seem to make an effort to command his wings, and then to no avail.

He landed heavily a short distance from them. When Fafhrd reached the spot, Kooskra was dead.

The barbarian knelt there, absently smoothing the feathers, staring up at the tower. Puzzlement, anger, and some sorrow lined his face.

'Fly north, old bird,' he murmured in a deep, small voice. 'Fly into nothingness, Kooskra.' Then he spoke to the Mouser. 'I find no wounds. Nothing touched him on this flight, I'll swear.'

'It happened when he brought down the other,' said the Mouser soberly. 'You did not look at the talons of that ugly fowl. They were smeared with a greenish stuff. Through some small gouge it entered him. Death was in him while he sat on your wrist, and it worked faster when he flew at the black bird.'

Fafhrd nodded, still staring at the tower. 'We've lost a fortune and a faithful killer tonight. But the night's not done. I have a curiosity about these death-dealing shadows.'

'What are you thinking?' asked the Mouser.

'That a man might easily hurl a grapnel and a line over a corner of that tower, and that I have such a line wound around my waist. We used it to mount Muulsh's roof, and

I shall use it again. Don't waste your words, little man. Muulsh? What have we to fear from him? He saw a bird take the jewel. Why should he send guards to search the roofs?

'Yes, I know the bird will fly away when I go after him. But he may drop the jewel, or you may get in a lucky cast with your sling. Besides, I have a special notion about these matters. Poison claws? I'll wear my gloves and cloak, and carry a naked dagger. Come on, little man. We'll not argue. That corner away from Muulsh's and the river should do the trick. The one where the tiny broken spire rises. We come, oh tower!' And he shook his fist.

The Mouser hummed a fragment of song under his breath and kept glancing around apprehensively, as he steadied the line by which Fafhrd was mounting the wall of the tower-temple. He felt decidedly ill at ease, what with Fafhrd on a fool's errand, and the night's luck probably run out, and the ancient temple silent and desolate.

It was forbidden on pain of death to enter such places, and no man knew what evil things might lurk there, fattening on loneliness. Besides all that, the moonlight was too revealing; he winced at the thought of what excellent targets he and Fafhrd made against the wall.

In his ears droned the low but mighty clamor of the waters of the Hlal, which swished and eddied past the base of the opposite wall. Once it seemed to him that the temple itself vibrated as though the Hlal were gnawing at its vitals.

Before his feet yawned the dark, six-foot chasm separating the warehouse from the temple. It allowed a sidewise glimpse of the walled temple-garden, overgrown with pale weeds and clogged with decay.

And now as he glanced in that direction he saw something that made him raise his eyebrows and sent a shiver crawling over his scalp. For across the moonlit space stole a manlike but unwholesomely bulky figure.

The Mouser's impression was that the strange body lacked the characteristic human curves and taperings of limb, that its face lacked features, that it was unpleasantly froglike. It seemed to be colored a uniform dull brown.

It vanished in the direction of the temple. What was it, the Mouser could not for the moment conjecture.

Intent on warning Fafhrd, he looked up, but the barbarian was already swinging into the embrasure at a dizzy height above. Disliking to shout, he paused undecided, half of a mind to skin up the line and join his comrade. All the while he kept humming a fragment of song – one used by thieves and supposed to enforce slumber on the inmates of a house being robbed. He wished fervently that the moon would get under a cloud.

Then, as if his fear had fathered a reality, something roughly grazed his ear and hit with a deadened thump against the temple wall. He knew what that meant – a ball of wet clay projected by a sling.

As he let his body collapse, two similar missiles followed the first. Close range, he could tell from the impact, and designed to kill rather than stun. He scanned the moonlit roof, but could see nothing. Before his knees touched the roof he had decided what he must do if he were to help Fafhrd at all. There was one quick way of retreat and he took it.

He grasped the long slack of the rope and dove into the chasm between the buildings, as three more balls of clay flattened against the wall.

As Fafhrd warily swung into the embrasure and found solid footing, he realized what had been bothering him about the character of the weatherworn carvings on the ancient wall: in one way or another they all seemed to be concerned with birds – raptorial birds in particular – and with human beings having grotesque avian features: beaked heads, batlike wings, and taloned limbs.

There was a whole border of such creatures around the

embrasure, and the projecting stone ornament over which the grapnel was caught represented the head of a hawk. This unpleasant coincidence loosened the stout gates of fear within him and a faint sense of awe and horror trickled into his mind, extinguishing a part of his anger at Kooskra's repellent death. But at the same time it served to confirm certain vague notions that had come to him earlier.

He looked around. The black bird seemed to have retreated into the interior of the tower, where tenuous moonlight revealed an obscurely littered stone floor and a door half open on a rectangle of blackness. Whipping out a long knife, he trod softly inward, shifting his weight slowly from one foot to the other to feel for possible weaknesses in the centuries-old masonry.

It grew darker and then a little lighter, as his straining eyes accustomed themselves to the dimness. The stone beneath his feet became slippery. And in stronger and stronger waves there was borne to his nostrils the pungent, musty smell of a mews.

There was an intermittent soft rustling, too. He told himself it was only natural that birds of some sort – perhaps pigeons – should nest in this deserted structure, but a darker train of reasoning insisted that his previous speculations were right.

He passed a projecting panel of stone and came into the chief upper chamber of the tower.

Moonlight striking through two gaps in the ceiling high above vaguely revealed alcoved walls, which widened away from him toward the left. The sound of the Hlal was muted and deepened here, as though it rose up more through the stones than through the air. He was very close, now, to the half-open door.

He noted a tiny grilled opening in it, like that of a cell. Rising against the wall at the broad end of the room was what seemed to be an altar of some sort, embellished by indistinct sculptures. And on either side of it, in regular terraces like those of the altar itself, were tier on tier of small black blots.

Then he heard a raucous, falsetto cry, 'Man! Man! Kill! Kill!' and saw a portion of the black blots launch themselves from the tiers, expanding in size as they spread their wings and converged upon him.

And largely because his fear had been expecting this, he jerked up his cloak to protect his naked head and whirled his knife at them in sweeping strokes. This close he could see them better: inky-feathered, cruelly taloned birds, each a brother to the two Kooskra had fought, squawking, squawking, striking at him like fighting cocks able to fly.

At first he thought he could readily beat them off, but it was like fighting an eddying storm of shadows. Perhaps he struck two or three. He could not tell. And it made no difference. He felt talons grasp and prick his left wrist.

Then, because it seemed the only thing to do, he leaped through the half-open door, slammed it behind him, knifed off the bird that clung like death to his wrist, found the pricks by touch, nicked them with his knife, and sucked the poison that might have been on the talons.

His shoulder pressed against the door, he listened to their baffled flapping and angry croaking. From here escape would be difficult; this inner room was indeed nothing but a cell, lightless save for the trace of moonlight that filtered through the grilled hole in the door. He could conjecture no ready way of regaining the embrasure and descending – they would have him completely at their mercy as he clung to the line.

He wanted to bellow a warning to the Mouser, but was afraid that his shouts, probably unintelligible at the distance, would only summon the Mouser into the same trap. In a rage of uncertainty he stamped vindictively the body of the bird he had slain.

Gradually his fears and anger calmed somewhat. The

birds seemed to have retreated. No longer did they swoop futilely against the door or cling screaming to the grillwork in the opening.

Through this aperture he could gain a fair view of the shadowy altar and the ladder-like perches. The black occupants were restless, edging back and forth, crowding one another, flurrying excitedly from perch to perch. The air was heavy with their smell.

And then he heard again the raucous, falsetto voice, only this time there was more than one.

'Jewels, jewels. Bright, bright.'

'Sparkling ones. Shining ones.'

'Ear to tear. Eye to peck.'

'Cheek to scratch. Neck to claw.'

And this time there was no doubting that it was the birds themselves who spoke. Fafhrd stared, fascinated. He had heard birds talk before – cursing parrots and slit-tongued ravens. Here there was the same monotony of tone and impression of mindlessness, the same vituperative repetitions. Indeed he had known parrots able to mimic human voices much more accurately.

But the phrases themselves were so devilishly apt that he momentarily feared they would cease to be mere isolated chatterings and become an intelligent discourse, with question and answer fitting. And he could not forget that undeniably purposeful command, 'Man! Man! Kill! Kill!'

As he listened spellbound to their cruel chorus, a figure stole past the grilled opening toward the altar. It was manlike only in its general form, featureless, with a uniform, leathery brown surface, like a heavy-hided, hairless bear. He saw the birds launch themselves at this strange figure too, and swarm around it, squawking and striking.

But it paid them no attention whatever, as though it were immune to beaks and poisoned claws. It strode unhurriedly with upraised head toward the altar. There the shifting moonlight from a gap above now struck almost vertically, making a pallid puddle on the floor before the altar itself, and Fafhrd saw the creature fumble at a large casket and begin to lift out small things that gleamed and glittered, unmindful of the birds which swirled around in ever greater number.

Then the creature moved so that the moonlight fell full upon it, and Fafhrd saw that it was a man clad in an ungainly suit of thick leather, with two long thin slits for eyeholes. He was clumsily but methodically transferring the contents of the casket to a leather bag he carried. And Fafhrd realized that the casket had been the cache for the many jewels and trinkets the birds had stolen.

The leather-armored form completed its task and strode off the way it had come, still surrounded by the small black storm-cloud of perplexedly squawking birds.

But as the figure came opposite Fafhrd the birds suddenly dropped away from it and flew back toward the altar, as if in obedience to a command that had come to them through the general din. The leather-armored form stopped dead and glanced searchingly around, the long eye-slits giving it an appearance of cryptic menace.

Then it started forward again. But simultaneously a noose dropped and tightened like a drawstring around the leather bag that formed its head.

The figure began to struggle and to stagger erratically, pawing at its neck with its leather-cased hand. Then it flailed both arms around in a ponderous, desperate way, so that the bag it still held came open and spurted jewels and jeweled metal. Finally a cunning jerk of the lasso sprawled it on the floor.

Fafhrd chose this moment to make a break for freedom. He relied on confusion and surprise. But in this he was not wise. Perhaps a trace of poison in his veins had touched his mind a little.

He almost reached the passage leading to the embrasure

before a second noose tightened cruelly around his own throat. His running feet went out from under him and his skull thumped the floor as he fell. The noose tightened further until he felt he was suffocating in a sea of black feathers wherein all the jewels of the world flashed blindingly.

As consciousness painfully pounded its way back into his skull, he heard a voice crying out frightenedly and jerkily:

'In the name of the Great God, who are you? What are you?'

Then a second voice answering – high, sweet, swift, bird-like, imperious, icy: 'I am the winged priestess, mistress of the hawks. I am the clawed queen, the feathered princess, incarnation of She who has ruled here forever, despite priests' interdict and Overlord's command. I am she who visits suitable injury on the haughty and voluptuous women of Lankhmar. I am she who sends messengers to take the tribute that was once laid freely though tremblingly upon my altar.'

Then the first voice spoke, in great apprehension, though not weakly: 'But you cannot mean to doom me in so hideous a way. I will keep your secrets well. I am only a thief.'

Then the second voice again, 'You are indeed a thief, for you sought to ravish the altar-treasure of Winged Tyaa, and for that crime the birds of Tyaa mete out punishment as they see fit. If they think you deserve mercy they will not kill; only peck out an eye – or, perhaps, two.'

There was a trilling and chirruping quality to the voice so that Fafhrd's tortured brain kept picturing some impossibly monstrous songbird. He sought to struggle to his feet, but found he was bound tightly to a chair. His arms and legs were numb, his left arm in addition ached and burned.

Then the soft moonlight ceased to be so much of a shooting pain, and he saw he was still in the same chamber, near the grilled door, facing the altar. Beside him was another chair, and in it sat the leather-armored man, similarly bound. But the leather hood had been removed, revealing the shaven skull and pockmarked, heavy-featured face of a man whom Fafhrd recognized – Stravas, a well-known cutpurse.

'Tyaa, Tyaa,' squawked the birds. 'Eyes to peck. Nose to rip.'

The eyes of Stravas were dark creases of fear between his shaved brows and thick cheeks. He spoke again toward the altar.

'I am a thief. Yes. But so are you. The gods of this temple are banned and forbidden. The Great God himself cursed them. Centuries ago they left this place. Whatever else you may be, you are an interloper. Somehow, perhaps by magic, you taught the birds to steal, knowing that many of them by nature like to pilfer shining things. What they steal, you take.

'You are no better than I, who guessed your secret and contrived a way to rob you in turn. You are no priestess, meting out death for sacrilege. Where are your worshippers? Where is your priesthood? Where are your benefactions? You are a thief!'

He strained tautly forward against his bonds, as if wanting to hurl himself toward the doom that might answer his reckless speech. Then Fafhrd saw, standing behind Stravas, a figure that made him doubt if his senses had rightly returned. For it was that of another leather-masked man.

But, as he blinked hard and peered again, he saw that the mask was only a small visor and that otherwise the man was clothed as a falconer, with heavy jerkin and huge gauntlets. From the broad leather belt hung a shortsword and a coiled lasso. Twisting around, Fafhrd glimpsed the outlines of a similar figure beside his own chair.

Then the voice from the altar answered, somewhat

more strident and shrill, but still musical and horribly bird-like. And as it answered, the birds chorused, 'Tyaa! Tyaa!'

'Now indeed you will die, and in tatters. And that one beside you, whose impious eagle slew Kivies and was by him slain, shall die too. But you will die knowing that Tyaa is Tyaa, and that her priestess and incarnate self is no interloper.'

And now Fafhrd looked straight at the alter – an action which he had unconsciously avoided up until this moment because of an overpowering superstitious awe and a queer revulsion.

The downward-striking shaft of moonlight had moved a little further toward the altar, revealing two stone figures which jutted out from it on either side, like gargoyles. Their carved faces were the faces of women but the menacingly bent arms ended in claws, and folded wings thrust over the shoulders. Whatever ancient craftsman had formed them, he had worked with devilish skill, for they gave the impression of being about to spread their stony wings and launch forward into the air.

On the altar itself, between the winged women, but further back and out of the moonlight, perched a large black shape with pendant crescents of blackness that might have been wings. Fafhrd stared at it, licking his lips, his poison-dulled mind unable to cope with the possibilities it conjured up.

But at the same time, although he was hardly aware of what they were doing, his long-fingered supple hands were beginning to work at the tight lashings that confined his wrists.

'Know, fool,' came the voice from the black shape, 'that gods do not cease to be when banned by false priests, or flee when cursed by a false and presumptuous god. Though priest and worshipper depart, they linger. I was small and I had no wings when I first climbed to this place, yet I felt their presence in the very stones. And I knew that my heart was sister to them.'

At that moment Fafhrd heard the Mouser calling his name, faintly and muffledly, but unmistakably. It seemed to come from the lower interior regions of the temple, mingling with the faint, deep-throated roar of the Hlal. The shape on the altar gave a trilling call and made a gesture, so that one of the pendant crescents moved.

A single black bird skimmed down to perch on the wrist of the falconer behind Stravas. Then the falconer moved away. His footsteps sounded as though he were descending a stair. The other falconer hastened to the embrasure through which Fafhrd had entered, and there was the sound of knife sawing rope. Then he returned.

'It seems that Tyaa does not lack worshippers tonight,' chittered the shape on the altar. 'And some day all the luxurious women of Lankhmar will mount terrified but unresisting to this place, to sacrifice portions of their beauty to Tyaa.'

It appeared to Fafhrd's sharpening eyesight that the blackness of the shape was too smooth for feathers, yet he could not be sure. He continued to work at the lashings, feeling those on his right wrist loosen.

'Beauty to spoil. Beauty to spoil,' hoarsely chanted the birds. 'Kiss with beak. Pet with claw.'

'When I was small,' continued the voice, 'I only dreamed of such things, stealing away secretly when I could from my father's house to this holy place. Yet even at that time the spirit of Tyaa was in me, making me feared and avoided by others.

'Then one day I found a young wounded bird hiding here, and I nursed it back to health. It was a descendant of one of the ancient birds of Tyaa, who, when the temple was defiled and shut up, flew away to the Mountains of Darkness to await the time when Tyaa would call them back. Sensing by occult means that Tyaa had been reborn

399

in me, it had returned. It knew me, and slowly – because we were small and alone – we remembered some of the ancient rituals and regained the power of conversing together.

'Then as year followed year, the others straggled back from the Mountains of Darkness, one by one. And these mated. And our ceremonies grew in perfection. It became difficult for me to be a priestess of Tyaa, without the outer world uncovering my secret. There was food to get, blood and flesh. There were long hours of instruction.

'Yet I persevered. And all the while those of my station in the outer world hated me more and more, sensing my power, and they affronted me and sought to humiliate me.

'A thousand times a day the honor of Tyaa was trampled in the dust. I was cheated of the privileges of my birth and station, and forced to consort with the uncouth and vulgar. Yet I submitted, and acted as if I were one of them, mocking their witlessness and frivolity and vanity. I bided my time, feeling within me the ever-strengthening spirit of Tyaa.'

'Tyaa! Tyaa!' echoed the birds.

'And then I searched for and found helpers in my quest: two descendants of the ancient Falconers of Tyaa, whose families had cherished the old worship and the old traditions. They knew me and did me homage. They are my priesthood.'

Fafhrd sensed the falconer beside him bow reverently low. He felt as if he were witnessing some malign shadow-show. Apprehension for the Mouser was like a lead weight pressing down on his confused thoughts. Irrelevantly, he noted a pearl-crusted brooch and a sapphire bracelet on the dirtied floor a little way from his chair. The jewels still lay where they had spilled from Stravas' bag.

'Four months ago,' persisted the voice, 'in the waning of the Moon of the Owl, I felt that Tyaa had grown to full

400

stature in me, and that the time had come for Tyaa's reckoning with Lankhmar.

'So I sent the birds forth to take the old tribute, bidding them punish when tribute was refused, or when the woman was notorious for vanity and pride. Swiftly they regained all their old cunning. Tyaa's altar was fittingly decked. And Lankhmar learned to fear, though not knowing they feared Tyaa. It shall not be so for long!' Here the voice became piercingly shrill.

'Soon I shall proclaim Tyaa openly. The doors of the temple will be opened to worshipper and tribute-bringer. The idols of the Great God will be cast down, and his temples broken. The rich and insolent women who despised Tyaa in me will be summoned here. And this altar will feel again the sweetness of sacrifice.' The voice rose to a screech. 'Even now it begins! Even now two interlopers will feel Tyaa's vengeance!'

Sound of a shuddering inhalation came from Stravas' throat, and he rocked futilely from side to side against his bonds. Fafhrd pried frantically at the loosening lashing of his right hand. A portion of the black birds rose at command from their perches – but then settled uncertainly back, for the trilling command was not completed.

The other falconer had returned and was advancing toward the altar, his right hand raised in solemn salute. There was no bird on his wrist now. In his left hand he carried a bloody shortsword.

The shape on the altar eagerly edged forward into the moonlight, so that Fafhrd saw it clearly for the first time. It was no giant bird or monstrous hybrid, but a woman muffled in black draperies with long, pendant sleeves. Her black hood fallen back revealed, white in the moonlight though stranded with gleaming black hair, a triangular face, whose glassily bright eyes and predatory aspect were suggestive of a bird, but also of an evil, oddly beautiful child. She moved in a crouching, short-stepped, fluttering way.

'Three in a night,' she cried. 'You have killed the third. It is well, falconer.'

Stravas could be heard saying in a gasping voice, 'I know you. I know you.'

Still the falconer advanced, until she said quietly, 'What is it? What do you want?' Then the falconer leaped at her with catlike swiftness and advanced the bloody sword so that it glittered redly against the black fabric covering her bosom.

And Fafhrd heard the Mouser say, 'Move not, Atya. Nor command your birds to any evil action. Or you will die in a wink, as your falconer and his black pet died.'

For five choking heartbeats there was dead silence. Then the woman on the altar began to breathe in a dry, strangled way, and utter short, broken cries that were almost croakings.

Some of the black birds rose from their perches and beat about uncertainly, dipping in and out of the shafts of moonlight, though keeping clear of the altar. The woman began to sway and rock from side to side. The sword followed her unalterably, like a pendulum.

Fafhrd noted the second falconer move up beside him, raising his shortsword for a throw. Putting all his strength into one mighty leverage of wrist and forearm, Fafhrd snapped the last of the lashings, ponderously heaved himself and the chair up and forward, caught the falconer's wrist as it started to whip the shortsword forward, and hurtled down with him to the floor. The falconer squealed in pain and a bone snapped. Fafhrd lay heavily atop him, staring at the leather-masked, gauntleted Mouser and the woman.

'Two falconers in a night,' said the Mouser, mimicking the woman. 'It is well, Fafhrd.' Then he continued pitilessly, 'The masquerade is over, Atya, Your vengeance on the highborn women of Lankhmar has come to an end. Ah, but fat Muulsh will be surprised at his little dove! To steal even your own jewels! Almost too cunning, Atya!'

A cry of bitter anguish and utter defeat came from the woman, in which her humiliation and weakness showed naked. But then she ceased to sway and a look of utter desperation tightened her decadent face.

'To the Mountains of Darkness!' she cried out wildly. 'To the Mountains of Darkness! Bear Tyaa's tribute to Tyaa's last stronghold!' And she followed this with a series of strange whistles and trillings and screams.

At this all the birds rose together, though still keeping clear of the altar. They milled wildly, giving vent to varied squawkings, which the woman seemed to answer.

'No tricks now, Atya!' said the Mouser. 'Death is close.'

Then one of the black fowls dipped to the floor, clutched an emerald-studded bracelet, rose again, and beat with it through a deep embrasure in that wall of the temple which overlooked the River Hlal. One after another, the other birds followed its example.

As if in some grotesque ritual procession, they sailed out into the night, bearing a fortune in their claws: necklaces, brooches, rings and pins of gold, silver, and electrum set with all colors of jewels, palely rich in the moonlight.

After the last three for whom no jewels were left vanished, Atya raised her black-draped arms toward the two outjutting sculptures of winged women, as if imploring a miracle, gave voice to a mad lonely wail, recklessly sprang from the altar, and ran after the birds.

The Mouser did not strike, but followed her, his sword dangerously close. Together they plunged into the embrasure. There was another cry, and after a little the Mouser returned alone and came over to Fafhrd. He cut Fafhrd's bonds, and pulled away the chair, helping him up. The injured falconer did not move, but lay whimpering softly.

'She sprang into the Hlal?' asked Fafhrd, his throat dry. The Mouser nodded.

Fafhrd dazedly rubbed his forehead. But his mind was clearing, as the effects of the poison waned.

'Even as the names were the same,' he mumbled softly. 'Atya and Tyaa!'

The Mouser went toward the altar and began to saw at the lashings of the cutpurse. 'Some of your men tried to pepper me tonight, Stravas,' he said lightly. 'I had no easy time eluding them and finding my way up the choked stairs.'

'I am sorry for that – now,' said Stravas.

'They were your men too, I suppose, who went jewel-stealing to Muulsh's house tonight?'

Stravas nodded, uncramping loosened limbs. 'But I hope we're allies now,' he answered, 'though there's no loot to share, except for some worthless glass and gew-gaws.' He laughed grimly. 'Was there no way to get rid of those black demons without losing all?'

'For a man plucked from the beak of death, you are very greedy, Stravas,' said the Mouser. 'But I suppose it's your professional training. No, I for one am glad the birds have fled. Most of all I feared they would get out of hand – as would surely have happened had I killed Atya. Only she could control them. Then we'd have died surely. Observe how Fafhrd's arm is swollen.'

'Perhaps the birds will bring the treasure back,' said Stravas hopefully.

'I do not think so,' answered the Mouser.

Two nights later, Muulsh, the money-lender, having learned something of these matters from a broken-armed falconer who had long been employed to care for his wife's songbirds, sprawled comfortably on the luxurious bed in his wife's room. One pudgy hand clasped a goblet of wine, the other that of a pretty maid who had been his wife's hairdresser.

'I never really loved her,' he said, pulling the demurely smiling wench toward him. 'It was only that she used to goad and frighten me.'

The maid gently disengaged her hand.

'I just want to hang the coverings on those cages,' she explained. 'Their eyes remind me of hers.' And she shivered delicately under her thin tunic.

When the last songbird was shrouded and silent, she came back and sat on his knee.

Gradually the fear left Lankhmar. But many wealthy women continued to wear silver cages over their features, considering it a most enchanting fashion. Gradually style altered the cages to soft masks of silver network.

And some time afterward the Mouser said to Fafhrd, 'There is a thing I have not told you. When Atya leaped into the Hlal, it was full moonlight. Yet somehow my eyes lost her as she fell, and I saw no splash whatever, although I peered closely. Then, as I lifted my head, I saw the end of that ragged procession of birds across the moon. Behind them came, I thought, a very much larger bird, flapping strongly.'

'And you think ...' asked Fafhrd.

'Why, I think Atya drowned in the Hlal,' said the Mouser.

IX: THE PRICE OF PAIN-EASE

The big barbarian Fafhrd, outcast of the World of Nehwon's Cold Waste and forever a foreigner in the land and city of Lankhmar, Nehwon's most notable area, and the small but deadly swordsman the Gray Mouser, a stateless person even in careless, unbureaucratic Nehwon, and man without a country (that he knew of), were fast friends and comrades from the moment they met in Lankhmar City near the intersection of Gold and Cash Streets. But they never shared a home. For one obvious thing, they were by nature, except for their companionship, loners; and such are almost certain to be homeless. For another, they were almost always adventuring, tramping, or exploring, or escaping from the deadly consequences of past misdeeds and misjudgments. For a third, their first and only true loves – Fafhrd's Vlana and the Mouser's Ivrian – were foully murdered (and bloodily though comfortlessly revenged) the first night the two young men met, and any home without a best-loved woman is a chilly place. For a fourth, they habitually stole all their possessions, even their swords and daggers, which they always named Graywand and Heartseeker and Scalpel and Cat's Claw, no matter how often they lost them and pilfered replacements – and homes are remarkably difficult to steal. Here, of course, one does not count tents, innlodgings, caves, palaces in which one happens to be employed or perhaps the guest of a princess or queen, or even shacks one rents for a while, as the Mouser and Fafhrd briefly and later did in an alley near the Plaza of Dark Delights.

Yet after their first trampings and gallopings of Nehwon, after their second, mostly womanless, adventures in and about Lankhmar – for the memories of Ivrian and Vlana haunted them for years – and after their ensorceled voyage across the Outer Sea and back, and after their encounters with the Seven Black Priests and with Atya and Tyaa, and their second return to Lankhmar, they did for a few brief moons share a house and home, although it was a rather small and, naturally, stolen one, and the two women in it ghosts only, and its location – because of the morbid mood they also shared – most dubious and dire.

Coming one night half drunk by way of Plague Court and Bones Alley from the tavern at Cash and Whore named the Golden Lamprey to an inn of most merry yet most evil recollection called the Silver Eel – on Dim Lane, this, halfway between Cheap and Carter – they spied behind it the still uncleared cinders and blackened, tumbled stones of the tenement where their first loves Ivrian and Vlana had, after many torments, been burned to white ashes, some atomies of whom they might even now be seeing by the murky moonlight.

Much later that night and much more drunk, they wandered north beyond the Street of the Gods to the section of the aristocrats by the Sea Wall and east of the Rainbow Palace of Lankhmar's Overlord Karstak Ovarta-mortes. In the estate of Duke Danius, the Mouser spied through the spiked wall and now by brighter moonlight – the air there being cleansed of night smog by the gentle north seawind – a snug, trim, well-polished, natural wooden garden house with curvingly horned ridgepole and beam-ends, to which abode he took a sudden extreme fancy and which he even persuaded Fafhrd to admire. It rested on six short cedar posts which in turn rested on flat rock. Nothing then would do but rush to Wall Street and the Marsh Gate, hire a brawny two-score of the inevitable night-long idlers there with a silver coin and big drink apiece and promise of a gold coin and bigger drink to come, lead them to Danius' dark abode, pick the iron gate-lock, lead them warily in, order them heave up the garden house and carry it out – providentially without any great creakings and with no guards or watchmen appearing. In fact, the Mouser and Fafhrd were able to finish another jug of wine during their supervising. Next tightly blindfold the two score carriers – this was the only difficult part of the operation, requiring all the Mouser's adroit, confident cajoling and Fafhrd's easy though somewhat ominous and demanding friendliness – and guide and goad the forty of the impromptu porters as they pantingly and sweatingly carried the house. They went south down empty Carter Street and west up Bones Alley (the garden house fortunately being rather narrow, three smallish rooms in a row) to the empty lot behind the Silver Eel, where after Fafhrd had hurled aside three stone blocks there was space to ease it down. Then it only remained to guide the still-blindfolded carriers back to the Marsh Gate, give them their gold and buy them their wine – a big jug apiece seemed wisest to blot out memory – then rush back in the pinkening dawn to buy from Braggi, the tavern-master, the worthless lot behind the Silver Eel, reluctantly chop off with Fafhrd's fighting axe the garden house's ridgepole and beam-horns, throw water and then disguising ashes onto the roof and walls (without thought of what evil omen this was, recalling Vlana and Ivrian), finally stagger inside and collapse into sleep on the naked floor before even looking around.

When they woke next evening, the place turned out to be quite nice inside, the two end-rooms each a thick-carpeted bedroom with highly erotic murals filling the walls. The Mouser puzzled as to whether Duke Danius shared his garden-concubines with a friend or else rushed back and forth between the two bedrooms all by himself. The central room was a most couth and sedate living room with several shelves of expensively bound stimulating books and a fine larder of rare jugged foods and wines. One of the bedrooms even had a copper bathtub – the Mouser appropriated that one at once – and both bedrooms had privies easily cleaned out below by a parttime and out-dwelling houseboy they hired that night from the Eel.

The theft was highly successful, they had no trouble from Lankhmar's brown-cuirassed and generally lazy guardsmen, no trouble from Duke Danius – if he hired house-spies, they botched their not-too-easy job. And for several days the Gray Mouser and Fafhrd were very happy in their new domicile, eating and drinking up Danius' fine provender, making the quick run to the Eel for extra wine, the Mouser taking two or three perfumed, soapy, oily, slow baths a day, Fafhrd going every two days to the nearest public steam-bath and putting in a lot of time on the books, sharpening his already considerable knowledge of High Lankhmarese, Ilthmarish, and Quarmallian.

By slow degrees, Fafhrd's bedroom became comfortably sloppy, the Mouser's quite fussily tidy and neat – it was simply their real natures expressing themselves.

After a few days Fafhrd discovered a second library, most cunningly concealed, of books dealing with nothing but death, books at complete variance with the other supremely erotic volumes. Fafhrd found them equally educational, while the Gray Mouser amused himself by picturing Duke Danius pausing to scan a few paragraphs about strangulation or Kleshite jungle-poisons while dashing back and forth between his two bedrooms and their two or more girls.

However, they didn't invite any girls to their charming

new home and perhaps for a very good reason, because after half a moon or so the ghost of slim Ivrian began to appear to the Mouser and the ghost of tall Vlana to Fafhrd, both spirits perhaps raised from their remaining mineral dust drifting around-about, and even plastered on the outer walls. The girl-ghosts never spoke, even in faintest whisper, they never touched, even so much as by the brush of a single hair; Fafhrd never spoke of Vlana to the Mouser, nor the Mouser to Fafhrd of Ivrian. The two girls were invariably invisible, inaudible, intangible, *yet they were there.*

Secretly from each other, each man consulted witches, witch doctors, astrologers, wizards, necromancers, fortune tellers, reputable physicians, priests even, seeking a cure for their ills (each desiring to see more of his dead girl or nothing at all), yet finding none.

Within three moons the Mouser and Fafhrd – very easy-amiable to each other, very tolerant on all matters, very quick to crack jokes, smiling far more than was their wont – were both rapidly going mad. The Mouser realized this one gray dawn when the instant he opened his eyes a pale, two-dimensional Ivrian at last appeared and gazed sadly at him one moment from the ceiling and then utterly vanished.

Big drops of sweat beaded his entire face and head from hairline down on all sides; his throat was acid, and he gagged and retched. Then with one fling of his right arm, he threw off all his bedclothes and raced naked out of his bedroom and across the living room into Fafhrd's.

The Northerner wasn't there.

He stared at the touseled, empty bed for a long time. Then he drank at one swallow half a bottle of fortified wine. Then he brewed himself a pot of burningly hot, triple-strength gahveh. As he gulped it down, he found himself violently shivering and shaking. He threw on a wool robe and belted it tightly around him, drew on his

410

wool boots, then still shivered and shook as he finished his still steaming gahveh.

All day long he paced the living room or sprawled in one of its big chairs, alternating fortified wine and hot gahveh, awaiting Fafhrd's return, still shaking from time to time and pulling his warm robe tighter around him.

But the Northerner never appeared.

When the windows of thin and ash-dusty horn yellowed and darkened in the late afternoon, the Mouser began to think in a more practical fashion of his plight. It occurred to him that the one sorcerer he had *not* consulted about his horrible Ivrian hang-up – just conceivably because that was the one sorcerer he believed might not be a faker and quack – was Sheelba of the Eyeless Face, who dwelt in a five-legged hut in the Great Salt Marsh immediately east of Lankhmar.

He whipped off his woolen stuff and speedily donned his gray tunic of coarsely woven silk, his ratskin boots, belted on his slim sword Scalpel and his dagger Cat's Claw (he'd early noted that Fafhrd's ordinary clothes and sword Graywand and dagger Heartseeker were gone), caught up his hooded cloak of the same material as his tunic, and fled from the dreadful little house in vast, sudden fear that Ivrian's sad ghost would appear to him again and then, without talking or touching, again vanish.

It was sunset. The houseboy from the Eel was cleaning out the privies. The Mouser asked, rather wildly and fiercely, 'Seen Fafhrd today?'

The lad started back. 'Yes,' he said. 'He rode off at dawn on a big white horse.'

'Fafhrd doesn't own a horse,' the Mouser said harshly and dangerously.

Again the lad started back. 'It was the biggest horse I've ever seen. It had a brown saddle and harness, studded with gold.'

The Mouser snarled and half drew Scalpel from her

mouseskin scabbard. Then, beyond the lad, he saw, twinkling and gleaming in the gloom, a huge, jet-black horse with black saddle and harness, studded with silver.

He raced past the lad, who threw himself sidewise into the dirt, vaulted up onto the saddle, grasped the reins, thrust his feet into the stirrups – which hung exactly at the right height for him – and booted the horse, which instantly took off down Dim Lane, galloped north on Carter and west on the Street of the Gods – the crowd scampering out of the way – and was through the open Marsh Gate before the guards could draw back their ragged-edged pikes for a thrust or advance them as a formal barrier.

The sunset was behind, the night was ahead, damp wind was on his cheeks, and the Mouser found all of these things good.

The black horse galloped down Causey Road for sixty or so bowshots, or eighteen score spear-casts, and then plunged off the road inland and south, so suddenly the Mouser was almost unsaddled. But he managed to keep his seat, dodging as best he could the weaponed branches of the thorn and seahawk trees. After not more than a hundred gasping breaths, the horse came to a halt, and there facing them was Sheelba's hut, and a little above the Mouser's head the low, dark doorway and a black-robed and black-hooded figure crouched in it.

The Mouser said loudly, 'What are you up to, you wizardly trickster? I know you must have sent this horse for me.'

Sheelba said not a word and moved not a whit, even though his crouching position looked most uncomfortable, at least for a being with legs rather than, say, tentacles.

After a bit the Mouser demanded still more loudly, 'Did you send for Fafhrd this morning? Send for him a huge white horse with a gold-studded brown harness?'

This time Sheelba started a little, though he settled

himself quickly again and still spoke no word, while of course the space that should have held his face remained blacker even than his draperies.

Dusk deepened. After a much longer bit, the Mouser said in a low, broken voice, 'O Sheelba, great magician, grant me a boon or else I shall go mad. Give me back my beloved Ivrian, give me her entire, or else rid me of her altogether, as if she had never been. Do either of those and I will pay any price you set.'

In a grating voice like the clank of small boulders moved by a sullen surf, Sheelba said from his doorway, 'Will you faithfully serve me as long as you live? Do my every lawful command? On my part, I promise not to call on you more than once a year, or at most twice, nor demand more than three moons out of thirteen of your time. You must swear to me by Fafhrd's bones and your own that, one, you will use any strategem, no matter how shameful and degrading, to get me the Mask of Death from the Shadowland, and that, two, you will slay any being who seeks to thwart you, whether it be your unknown mother or the Great God himself.'

After a still longer pause the Mouser said in a still smaller voice, 'I promise.'

Sheelba said, 'Very well. Keep the horse. Ride it east past Ilthmar, the City of Ghouls, the Sea of Monsters, and the Parched Mountains until you come to the Shadowland. There search out the Blue Flame and from the seat of the throne before it, fetch me the Mask of Death. Or snatch it off Death's face, if he's at home. By the way, in the Shadowland, you will find your Ivrian. In particular, beware a certain Duke Danius, whose garden house you recently purloined, not altogether by chance, and whose death library I imagine you have discovered and perused. This Danius person fears death more than any creature has ever in history, as recorded or recollected by man, demon, or god, and he is planning a foray into the

413

Shadowland with no less a purpose than to slay Death himself (or herself or itself, for there even my knowledge stops) and destroy all Death's possessions, including the Mask you promised to procure me. Now, do my errand. That is all.'

The numb, astounded, yet still unhappy and suspicious Mouser watched the dark doorway for as long as it took the moon to rise and silhouette herself behind the sharply angled branches of a dead seahawk tree, but Sheelba said not another word, nor made a move, while the Mouser could think of not a single sensible question to ask further. So at last he touched his heels against the flanks of the black horse and it instantly turned around, carefully single-footed to Causey Road, and there cantered east.

Meanwhile, at almost exactly same time, since it is a good day's ride from Lankhmar across the Great Salt Marsh and the Sinking Land to the mountains behind Ilthmar, city of evil reputation, Fafhrd was having the same identical conversation and making exactly the same deal with Ningauble of the Seven Eyes in his vast and mazy cave, except that Ningauble, as was his gossipy wont, talked a thousand words to Sheelba's one, yet in the end said nothing more than Sheelba.

So the two disreputable and mostly unprincipled heroes set out for the Shadowland, the Mouser prudently following the coast road north to Sarheenmar and there cutting inland, Fafhrd recklessly riding straight northwest across the Poisoned Desert. Yet both had good luck and crossed the Parched Mountains on the same day, the Mouser taking the Northern Pass, Fafhrd the Southern.

The heavy overcast, which began at the watershed of the Parched Mountains, thickened, though not a drop of rain or atom of mist fell. The air was cool and moist and, nourished perhaps by underground water of most distant source, thick green grass grew and an open forest of black cedars sprang up. Herds of black antelopes and black reindeer nibbled the endless grass to a lawn, yet there were no herdsmen or human folk at all. The sky grew darker yet, almost a perpetual night, odd low hills topped by congeries of black rock appeared, there were distant fires of many hues, though none blue, and each vanished if you approached it, and you found no ash or other sign of it at its site. So the Mouser and Fafhrd well knew they had entered the Shadowland, death-feared by the merciless Mingols to the north, by the bone-proud, invisible-fleshed ivory Ghouls to the west, to the east by the hairless folk and bald beasts of the shrunken yet diplomatically subtle and long-enduring Empire of Eevarensee, and to the south by the King of Kings himself, who had a standing rule that instant death be the lot of any person, even his own vizier or most-beloved son or favoritest queen, who so much as whispered the name 'Shadowland', let alone discussed the dark area in any wise.

Eventually the Mouser sighted a black pavilion and rode toward it and dismounted from his black horse and parted the silken drapes of the doorway and there behind an ebony table, listlessly sipping white wine from a crystal goblet, in her and his favoritest robe of violet silk, sat his beloved Ivrian, with an ermine wrap about her shoulders.

But her small, slender hands were death blue, the color of slate, and her face of like hue and vacant-eyed. Only her hair was as livingly glossy black as ever, though longer than the Mouser recalled, as were her fingernails.

She stared her eyes, which the Mouser now saw were faintly filmed by grainy white, and parted her black lips and said in monotone, 'It delights me beyond my powers of expression to see you, Mouser, ever-beloved, who now have risked even the horrors of the Shadowland for sake of me, yet you are alive and I am dead. Come never again to trouble me, my darlingest love. Enjoy. Enjoy.'

And even as the Mouser hurled himself forward toward her, smashing to one side the frail black table, her figure grew somewhat faint and she sank swiftly into the ground as if it were diaphanous, gentle, unfeared quicksand – though solid turf when the Mouser clawed at it.

Meantime, a few Lankhmar leagues to the south, Fafhrd was suffering exactly the same experience with his dearly-beloved Vlana, slate-faced and slate-handed – those dear, long, strong fingers – actress-clad in black tunic and red stockings with dark brown hair agleam, except that before she too sank into the ground, she ended, being a rather rougher woman than Ivrian, by intoning in a voice that was most strange for being a lifeless monotone rather than the spirited accents the words implied, 'And now exit fast, you beloved booby, sweetest man in live world or Shadowland. Do Ningauble's idiot job, which will almost certainly be your death, stupid boy, for you've most unwisely promised him. Then gallop like Hell southwest. If you do die by the way and join me in the Shadowland, I'll spit in your face, never speak you a single word, and never once share your black mossy bed. That's what death's like.'

As Fafhrd and the Mouser, though leagues apart, simultaneously tore like terrified mice from the two black pavilions, they each sighted to the east a steel-blue flame rising like the longest and gleamingest of stilettos, far higher than any other flame they'd seen in the Shadow-land, a most narrow, bright-blue flame deeply stabbing the black overcast. The Mouser saw it a bit to the south, Fafhrd a bit to the north. Each frantically dug heels in his horse and galloped on, their paths slowly converging. At that moment, their interviews with their beloveds huge in their memories, to encounter Death seemed the best thing in the world to them, the most to be desired, whether to kill life's awfulest creature, or by him be killed.

Yet as they galloped along, Fafhrd couldn't help thinking of how Vlana was ten years older than he, and had looked all of that and more in the Shadowland, while the Mouser's mind couldn't avoid touching the topic of Ivrian's basic silliness and snobbery.

Yet they both galloped on willfully, wildly, joyfully, toward the blue flame, which grew ever thicker and brighter, until they saw it came from the huge central chimney of an open-gated, open-doored, low, vast black castle on a low long hill.

They trotted into the palace side by side, the gate and doorway both being wide and neither man recognizing the presence of the other. The black granite wall before them was indented by a wide fireplace in which blue flame shone almost as blindingly as the naked sun and shot its fiercest flame up the chimney, to make the flame they had noted from afar. Before the fireplace stood an ebony chair, cushioned with black velvet, and on that most graceful of seats rested a shining black mask, full-faced, with wide-open eyeholes.

The eight iron-shod hooves of the white horse and the black one sounded a dead clank on the black flagstones.

Fafhrd and the Mouser dismounted and moved, respectively, to the north and south sides of the ebony chair, upholstered with black velvet, on which rested the spangled mask of Death. Perhaps fortunately, at that time Death himself was away, on business or vacation.

At that instant, both Fafhrd and the Mouser realized he was promise-bound by oath to Ningauble and Sheelba, to slay his comrade. The Mouser whisked out Scalpel. Quite as swiftly Fafhrd whipped out Graywand. They stood face to face, ready to kill each other.

At that instant a long, glittering scimitar came down between them, swift as light, and the black, glittering mask of death was cloven precisely in two, black forehead to black chin.

Then the swift sword of Duke Danius went licking right at Fafhrd. The Northerner barely parried the blow of the mad-eyed aristocrat. The gleaming blade swept back toward the Mouser, who also barely shoved aside the slice.

Both heroes likely would have been slain – for who in the long run has might to master the insane? – except that at that instant Death himself returned to his customary abode in his black castle in the Shadowland and with his black hands seized Duke Danius by the neck and strangled him dead within seventeen of Fafhrd's heartbeats and twenty-one of the Mouser's – and some hundreds of Danius'.

Neither of the two heroes dared look at Death. Before that most remarkable and horrid being was a third finished with Danius, his foolish foe, they snatched up a gleaming half of a black mask each, sprang each on his horse, and galloped side-by-side like twin lunatics of the frantickest sort, ridden even harder than they rode their powerful white and black horses by that cosmically champion jockey Fear, out of the Shadowland southwest by the straightest path possible.

Lankhmar and her environs, to which they swiftly returned, were no great good to them. Ningauble and Sheelba were both most angry at getting only half a mask apiece, even though it was the mask of the most potent being in all universes known and unknown. The two rather self-centered and somewhat irrational archimages, intent on and vastly enamored of their private war – though they were undoubtedly the cunningest and wisest sorcerers ever to exist in the world of Nehwon – were entirely adamant against the very sound four arguments Fafhrd and the Gray Mouser advanced in their self-defense: one, that they had stuck to the magician-set rules by first making certain to get the Mask of Death (or as much as they could of it) out of the Shadowland at whatever personal cost to themselves and diminishment of their self-respect. For, if they had fought each other, as

Rule Two required, they would most likely have simultaneously slain each other, and so not even a sliver of a mask get to Sheel or Ning, while who in his sane senses would take on Death as an opponent? – Danius being a most crushing, present argument here. Two, that half a magical mask is better than none. Three, that each magician having half the mask, both would be forced to quit their stupid war, cooperate in future, and so double their already considerable powers. And, four, that the two sorcerers had neither returned Vlana and Ivrian in their lovely, living flesh to Fafhrd and the Mouser, nor vanished them utterly from time, so that there was no memory of them anywhere, as promised, but only tortured the two heroes – and likely the two girls also – by a final horrid encounter. In pets most undignified for great wizards, Ningauble magicked all objects whatsoever out of the home Fafhrd and the Mouser had stolen, while Sheelba burned it to ashes indistinguishable from those of the earlier tenement in which Vlana and Ivrian had perished.

Which was probably all to the good, since the whole idea of the two heroes dwelling in a house behind the Silver Eel – right in the midst of the graveyard of their great beloveds – had undoubtedly been most morbid from the start.

Thereafter Sheelba and Ningauble, showing no gratitude whatever, or remorse for their childish revenges, insisted on exacting from the Mouser and Fafhrd the utmost service established by the bargain they had set with the two heroes.

But Fafhrd and the Gray Mouser were never once again haunted by those two admirable and grand girls Ivrian and Vlana, nor even thought of them except with heart-easing and painless gratitude. In fact, within a few days the Mouser began the hottest sort of love affair with a slightly underage and most winsome niece of Karstak Ovarta-mortes, while Fafhrd took on the identical twin daughters, most beauteous and wealthy and yet on the verge of turning to prostitution for the excitement it promised, of Duke Danius.

What Vlana and Ivrian thought of all this in their eternal dwelling in the Shadowland is entirely their business and that of Death, on whose horrid visage they now could look with no fear whatever.

X: BAZAAR OF THE BIZARRE

The strange stars of the World of Nehwon glinted thickly above the black-roofed city of Lankhmar, where swords clink almost as often as coins. For once there was no fog.

In the Plaza of Dark Delights, which lies seven blocks south of the Marsh Gate and extends from the Fountain of Dark Abundance to the Shrine of the Black Virgin, the shop-lights glinted upward no more brightly than the stars glinted down. For there the vendors of drugs and the peddlers of curiosa and the hawkers of assignations light their stalls and crouching places with foxfire, glowworms, and firepots with tiny single windows, and they conduct their business almost as silently as the stars conduct theirs.

There are plenty of raucous spots a-glare with torches in nocturnal Lankhmar, but by immemorial tradition soft whispers and a pleasant dimness are the rule in the Plaza of Dark Delights. Philosophers often go there solely to meditate, students to dream, and fanatic-eyed theologians to spin like spiders abstruse new theories of the Devil and of the other dark forces ruling the universe. And if any of these find a little illicit fun by the way, their theories and dreams and theologies and demonologies are undoubtedly the better for it.

Tonight, however, there was a glaring exception to the darkness rule. From a low doorway with a trefoil arch new-struck through an ancient wall, light spilled into the Plaza. Rising above the horizon of the pavement like some monstrous moon a-shine with the ray of a murderous sun, the new doorway dimmed almost to extinction the stars of the other merchants of mystery.

Eerie and unearthly objects for sale spilled out of the doorway a little way with the light, while beside the doorway crouched an avid-faced figure clad in garments never before seen on land or sea ... in the World of Nehwon. He wore a hat like a small red pail, baggy trousers, and outlandish red boots with upturned toes. His eyes were as predatory as a hawk's, but his smile as cynically and lasciviously cajoling as an ancient satyr's.

Now and again he sprang up and pranced about, sweeping and re-sweeping with a rough long broom the flagstones as if to clean path for the entry of some fantastic emperor, and he often paused in his dance to bow low and loutingly, but always with upglancing eyes, to the crowd gathering in the darkness across from the doorway and to swing his hand from them toward the interior of the new shop in a gesture of invitation at once servile and sinister.

No one of the crowd had yet plucked up courage to step forward into the glare and enter the shop, or even inspect the rarities set out so carelessly yet temptingly before it. But the number of fascinated peerers increased momently. There were mutterings of censure at the dazzling new method of merchandising – the infraction of the Plaza's custom of darkness – but on the whole the complaints were outweighed by the gasps and murmurings of wonder, admiration and curiosity kindling ever hotter.

The Gray Mouser slipped into the Plaza at the Fountain end as silently as if he had come to slit a throat or spy on the spies of the Overlord. His ratskin moccasins were soundless. His sword Scalpel in its mouseskin sheath did not swish ever so faintly against either his tunic or cloak, both of gray silk curiously coarse of weave. The glances he shot about him from under his gray silk hood half thrown

422

back were freighted with menace and a freezing sense of superiority.

Inwardly the Mouser was feeling very much like a schoolboy – a schoolboy in dread of rebuke and a crushing assignment of homework. For in the Mouser's pouch of ratskin was a note scrawled in dark brown squid-ink on silvery fish-skin by Sheelba of the Eyeless Face, inviting the Mouser to be at this spot at this time.

Sheelba was the Mouser's supernatural tutor and – when the whim struck Sheelba – guardian, and it never did to ignore his invitations, for Sheelba had eyes to track down the unsociable though he did not carry them between his cheeks and forehead.

But the tasks Sheelba would set the Mouser at times like these were apt to be peculiarly onerous and even noisome – such as procuring nine white cats with never a black hair among them, or stealing five copies of the same book of magic runes from five widely separated sorcerous libraries or obtaining specimens of the dung of four kings living or dead – so the Mouser had come early, to get the bad news as soon as possible, and he had come alone, for he certainly did not want his comrade Fafhrd to stand snickering by while Sheelba delivered his little wizardly homilies to a dutiful Mouser ... and perchance thought of extra assignments.

Sheelba's note, invisibly graven somewhere inside the Mouser's skull, read merely, *When the star Akul bedizens the Spire of Rhan, be you by the Fountain of Dark Abundance,* and the note was signed only with the little featureless oval which is Sheelba's sigil.

The Mouser glided now through the darkness to the Fountain, which was a squat black pillar from the rough rounded top of which a single black drop welled and dripped every twenty elephant's heartbeats.

The Mouser stood beside the Fountain and, extending a bent hand, measured the altitude of the green star Akul. It

423

had still to drop down the sky seven finger widths more before it would touch the needle-point of the slim star-silhouetted distant minaret of Rhan.

The Mouser crouched doubled-up by the black pillar and then vaulted lightly atop it to see if that would make any great difference in Akul's attitude. It did not.

He scanned the nearby darkness for motionless figures ... especially that of one robed and cowled like a monk – cowled so deeply that one might wonder how he saw to walk. There were no figures at all.

The Mouser's mood changed. If Sheelba chose not to come courteously beforehand, why he could be boorish too! He strode off to investigate the new bright archdoored shop, of whose infractious glow he had become inquisitively aware at least a block before he had entered the Plaza of Dark Delights.

Fafhrd the Northerner opened one wine-heavy eye and without moving his head scanned half the small firelit room in which he slept naked. He shut that eye, opened the other, and scanned the other half.

There was no sign of the Mouser anywhere. So far so good! If his luck held, he would be able to get through tonight's embarrassing business without being jeered at by the small gray rogue.

He drew from under his stubbly cheek a square of violet serpent-hide pocked with tiny pores so that when he held it between his eyes and the dancing fire it made stars. Studied for a time, these stars spelled out obscurely the message: *When Rhan-dagger stabs the darkness in Akul-heart, seek you the Source of the Black Drops*.

Drawn boldly across the prickholes in an orange-brown like dried blood – in fact spanning the violet square – was a seven-armed swastika, which is one of the sigils of Ningauble of the Seven Eyes.

Fafhrd had no difficulty in interpreting the Source of the

Black Drops as the Fountain of Dark Abundance. He had become wearily familiar with such cryptic poetic language during his boyhood as a scholar of the singing skalds.

Ningauble stood to Fafhrd very much as Sheelba stood to the Mouser except that the Seven-Eyed One was a somewhat more pretentious archimage, whose taste in the thaumaturgical tasks he set Fafhrd ran in larger directions, such as the slaying of dragons, the sinking of four-masted magic ships, and the kidnapping of ogre-guarded enchanted queens.

Also, Ningauble was given to quiet realistic boasting, especially about the grandeur of his vast cavern-home, whose stony serpent-twisting back corridors led, he often averred, to all spots in space and time – provided Ningauble instructed one beforehand exactly how to step those rocky crooked low-ceilinged passageways.

Fafhrd was driven by no great desire to learn Ningauble's formulas and enchantments, as the Mouser was driven to learn Sheelba's, but the Septinocular One had enough holds on the Northerner, based on the latter's weaknesses and past misdeeds, so that Fafhrd had always to listen patiently to Ningauble's wizardly admonishments and vaunting sorcerous chitchat – but *not*, if humanly or inhumanly possible, while the Gray Mouser was present to snigger and grin.

Meanwhile, Fafhrd standing before the fire, had been whipping, slapping, and belting various garments and weapons and ornaments onto his huge brawny body with its generous stretches of thick short curling red-gold hairs. When he opened the outer door and, also booted and helmeted now, glanced down the darkling alleyway preparatory to leaving and noted only the hunch-backed chestnut vendor a-squat by his brazier at the next corner, one would have sworn that when he did stride forth toward the Plaza of Dark Delights it would be with the clankings and thunderous tread of a siege-tower approaching a thick-walled city.

Instead the lynx-eared old chestnut vendor, who was also a spy of the Overlord, had to swallow down his heart when it came sliding crookedly up his throat as Fafhrd rushed past him tall as a pine tree, swift as the wind, and silent as a ghost.

The Mouser elbowed aside two gawkers with shrewd taps on the floating rib and strode across the dark flagstones toward the garishly bright shop with its doorway like an upended heart. It occurred to him they must have had masons working like fiends to have cut and plastered that archway so swiftly. He had been past here this afternoon and noted nothing but blank wall.

The outlandish porter with the red cylinder hat and twisty red shoe-toes came frisking out to the Mouser with his broom and then went curtsying back as he re-swept a path for this first customer with many an obsequious bow and smirk.

But the Mouser's visage was set in an expression of grim and all-skeptical disdain. He paused at the heaping of objects in front of the door and scanned it with disapproval. He drew Scalpel from its thin gray sheath and with the tip of the long blade flipped back the cover on the topmost of a pile of musty books. Without going any closer he briefly scanned the first page, shook his head, rapidly turned a half dozen more pages with Scalpel's tip, using the sword as if it were a teacher's wand to point out words here and there – because they were ill-chosen, to judge from his expression – and then abruptly closed the book with another sword-flip.

Next he used Scalpel's tip to lift a red cloth hanging from a table behind the books and peer under it suspiciously, to rap contemptuously a glass jar with a human head floating in it, to touch disparagingly several

426

other objects and to waggle reprovingly at a foot-chained owl which hooted at him solemnly from its high perch.

He sheathed Scalpel and turned toward the porter with a sour, lifted-eyebrow look which said – nay, shouted – plainly, 'Is *this* all you have to offer? Is this garbage your excuse for defiling the Dark Plaza with glare?'

Actually the Mouser was mightily interested by every least item which he had glimpsed. The book, incidentally, had been in a script which he not only did not understand, but did not even recognize.

Three things were very clear to the Mouser: first, that this stuff offered here for sale did not come from anywhere in the World of Nehwon, no, not even from Nehwon's farthest outback; second, that all this stuff was, in some way which he could not yet define, extremely dangerous; third, that all this stuff was monstrously fascinating and that he, the Mouser did not intend to stir from this place until he had personally scanned, studied, and if need be tested, every last intriguing item and scrap.

At the Mouser's sour grimace, the porter went into a convulsion of wheedling and fawning caperings, seemingly torn between a desire to kiss the Mouser's foot and to point out with flamboyant caressing gestures every object in his shop.

He ended by bowing so low that his chin brushed the pavement, sweeping an ape-long arm toward the interior of the shop, and gibbering in atrocious Lankhmarese, 'Every object to pleasure the flesh and senses and imagination of man. Wonders undreamed. Very cheap, very cheap! Yours for a penny! The Bazaar of the Bizarre. Please to inspect, oh king!'

The Mouser yawned a very long yawn with the back of his hand to his mouth, next he looked around him again with the patient, worldly smile of a duke who knows he must put up with many boredoms to encourage business in

427

his demesne, finally he shrugged faintly and entered the shop.

Behind him the porter went into a jigging delirium of glee and began to re-sweep the flagstones like a man maddened with delight.

Inside, the first thing the Mouser saw was a stack of slim books bound in gold-lined fine-grained red and violet leather.

The second was a rack of gleaming lenses and slim brass tubes calling to be peered through.

The third was a slim dark-haired girl smiling at him mysteriously from a gold-barred cage that swung from the ceiling.

Beyond that cage hung others with bars of silver and strange green, ruby, orange, ultramarine, and purple metals.

Fafhrd saw the Mouser vanish into the shop just as his left hand touched the rough chill pate of the Fountain of Dark Abundance and as Akul pointed precisely on Rhantop as if it were that needle-spire's green-lensed pinnacle-lantern.

He might have followed the Mouser, he might have done no such thing, he certainly would have pondered the briefly glimpsed event, but just then there came from behind him a long low 'Hssssst!'

Fafhrd turned like a giant dancer and his longsword Graywand came out of its sheath swiftly and rather more silently than a snake emerges from its hole.

Ten arm lengths behind him, in the mouth of an alleyway darker than the Dark Plaza would have been without its new commercial moon, Fafhrd dimly made out two robed and deeply cowled figures poised side by side.

One cowl held darkness absolute. Even the face of a Negro of Klesh might have been expected to shoot ghostly bronze gleams. But here there were none.

In the other cowl there nested seven very faint pale

greenish glows. They moved about restlessly, sometimes circling each other, swinging mazily. Sometimes one of the seven horizontally oval gleams would grow a little brighter, seemingly as it moved forward toward the mouth of the cowl – or a little darker, as it drew back.

Fafhrd sheathed Graywand and advanced toward the figures. Still facing him, they retreated slowly and silently down the alley.

Fafhrd followed as they receded. He felt a stirring of interest ... and of other feelings. To meet his own supernatural mentor alone might be only a bore and a mild nervous strain; but it would be hard for anyone entirely to repress a shiver of awe at encountering at one and the same time both Ningauble of the Seven Eyes and Sheelba of the Eyeless Face.

Moreover, that those two bitter wizardly rivals would have joined forces, that they should apparently be operating together in amity ... Something of great note must be afoot! There was no doubting that.

The Mouser meantime was experiencing the smuggest, most mind-teasing, most exotic enjoyments imaginable. The sleekly leather-bound gold-stamped books turned out to contain scripts stranger far than that in the book whose pages he had flipped outside – scripts that looked like skeletal beasts, cloud swirls, and twisty-branched bushes and trees – but for a wonder he could read them all without the least difficulty.

The books dealt in the fullest detail with such matters as the private life of devils, the secret histories of murderous cults, and – these were illustrated – the proper dueling techniques to employ against sword-armed demons and the erotic tricks of lamias, succubi, bacchantes, and hamadryads.

The lenses and brass tubes, some of the latter of which were as fantastically crooked as if they were periscopes for seeing over the walls and through the barred windows of other universes, showed at first only delightful jeweled patterns, but after a bit the Mouser was able to see through them into all sorts of interesting places: the treasure-rooms of dead kings, the bedchambers of living queens, council-crypts of rebel angels, and the closets in which the gods hid plans for worlds too frighteningly fantastic to risk creating.

As for the quaintly clad slim girls in their playfully widely-barred cages, well, they were pleasant pillows on which to rest eyes momentarily fatigued by book-scanning and tube-peering.

Ever and anon one of the girls would whistle softly at the Mouser and then point cajolingly or imploringly or with languorous hintings at a jeweled crank set in the wall whereby her cage, suspended on a gleaming chains running through gleaming pulleys, could be lowered to the floor.

At these invitations the Mouser would smile with a bland amorousness and nod and softly wave a hand from the finger-hinge as if to whisper, 'Later ... later. Be patient.'

After all, girls had a way of blotting out all lesser, but not thereby despicable, delights. Girls were for dessert.

Ningauble and Sheelba receded down the dark alleyway with Fafhrd following them until the latter lost patience and, somewhat conquering his unwilling awe, called out nervously, 'Well, are you going to keep on fleeing me backward until we all pitch into the Great Salt Marsh? What do you want of me? What's it all about?'

But the two cowled figures had already stopped, as he could perceive by the starlight and the glow of a few high windows, and now it seemed to Fafhrd that they had stopped a moment before he had called out. A typical sorcerers' trick for making one feel awkward! He gnawed his lip in the darkness. It was ever thus!

'Oh My Gentle Son ...' Ningauble began in his most sugary-priestly tones, the dim puffs of his seven eyes now hanging in his cowl as steadily and glowing as mildly as the Pleiades seen late on a summer night through a greenish mist rising from a lake freighted with blue vitriol and corrosive gas of salt.

'I asked what it's all about!' Fafhrd interrupted harshly. Already convicted of impatience, he might as well go the whole hog.

'Let me put it as a hypothetical case,' Ningauble replied imperturbably. 'Let us suppose, My Gentle Son, that there is a man in a universe and that a most evil force comes to this universe from another universe, or perhaps from a congeries of universes, and that this man is a brave man who wants to defend his universe and who counts his life as a trifle and that moreover he has to counsel him a very wise and prudent and public-spirited uncle who knows all about these matters which I have been hypothecating—'

'The Devourers menace Lankhmar!' Sheelba rapped out in a voice as harsh as a tree cracking and so suddenly that Fafhrd almost started – and for all we know, Ningauble too.

Fafhrd waited a moment to avoid giving false impressions and then switched his gaze to Sheelba. His eyes had been growing accustomed to the darkness and he saw much more now than he had seen at the alley's mouth, yet he still saw not one jot more than absolute blackness inside Sheelba's cowl.

'Who are the Devourers?' he asked.

It was Ningauble, however, who replied, 'The Devourers are the most accomplished merchants in all the many universes – so accomplished, indeed, that they sell only trash. There is a deep necessity in this, for the Devourers must occupy all their cunning in perfecting their methods of selling and so have not an instant to spare in considering the worth of what they sell. Indeed, they dare not concern

431

themselves with such matters for a moment, for fear of losing their golden touch – and yet such are their skills that their wares are utterly irresistible, indeed the finest wares in all the many universes – if you follow me?'

Fafhrd looked hopefully toward Sheelba, but since the latter did not this time interrupt with some pithy summation, he nodded to Ningauble.

Ningauble continued, his seven eyes beginning to weave a bit, judging from the movements of the seven green glows, 'As you might readily deduce, the Devourers possess all the mightiest magics garnered from the many universes, whilst their assault groups are led by the most aggressive wizards imaginable, supremely skilled in all methods of battling, whether it be with the wits, or the feelings, or with the beweaponed body.

'The method of the Devourers is to set up shop in a new world and first entice the bravest and the most adventuresome and the supplest-minded of its people – who have so much imagination that with just a touch of suggestion they themselves do most of the work of selling themselves.

'When these are safely ensnared, the Devourers proceed to deal with the remainder of the population: meaning simply that they sell and sell and sell! – sell trash and take good money and even finer things in exchange.'

Ningauble sighed windily and a shade piously. 'All this is very bad, My Gentle Son,' he continued, his eye-glows weaving hypnotically in his cowl, 'but natural enough in universes administered by such gods as we have – natural enough and perhaps endurable. However' – he paused – 'there is worse to come! The Devourers want not only the patronage of all beings in all universes, but – doubtless because they are afraid someone will some day raise the ever-unpleasant question of the true worth of things – they want all their customers reduced to a state of slavish and submissive suggestibility, so that they are fit for nothing whatever but to gawk at and buy the trash the Devourers offer for sale. This means of course that eventually the Devourers' customers will have nothing wherewith to pay the Devourers for their trash, but the Devourers do not seem to be concerned with this eventuality. Perhaps they feel that there is always a new universe to exploit. And perhaps there is!'

'Monstrous!' Fafhrd commented. 'But what do the Devourers gain from all these furious commercial sorties, all this mad merchandising? What do they really want?'

Ningauble replied, 'The Devourers want only to amass cash and to raise little ones like themselves to amass more cash and they want to compete with each other at cash-amassing. (Is that coincidentally a city, do you think, Fafhrd? Cashamash?) And the Devourers want to brood about their great service to the many universes – it is their claim that servile customers make the most obedient subjects for the gods – and to complain about how the work of amassing cash tortures their minds and upsets their digestions. Beyond this, each of the Devourers also secretly collects and hides away forever, to delight no eyes but his own, all the finest objects and thoughts created by true men and women (and true wizards and true demons) and bought by the Devourers at bankruptcy prices and paid for with trash or – this is their ultimate preference – with nothing at all.'

'Monstrous indeed!' Fafhrd repeated. 'Merchants are ever an evil mystery and these sound the worst. But what has all this to do with me?'

'Oh My Gentle Son,' Ningauble responded, the piety in his voice now tinged with a certain clement disappointment, 'you force me once again to resort to hypothecating. Let us return to the supposition of this brave man whose whole universe is direly menaced and who counts his life a trifle and to the related supposition of this brave man's wise uncle, whose advice the brave man invariably follows—'

'The Devourers have set up shop in the Plaza of Dark Delights!' Sheelba interjected so abruptly and in such iron-harsh syllables that this time Fafhrd actually did start. 'You must obliterate this outpost tonight!'

Fafhrd considered that for a bit, then said, in a tentative sort of voice, 'You will both accompany me, I presume, to aid me with your wizardly sendings and castings in what I can see must be a most perilous operation, to serve me as a sort of sorcerous artillery and archery corps while I play assault battalion—'

'Oh My Gentle Son …' Ningauble interrupted in tones of deepest disappointment, shaking his head so that his eye-glows jogged in his cowl.

'You must do it alone!' Sheelba rasped.

'Without any help at all?' Fafhrd demanded. 'No! Get someone else. Get this doltish brave man who always follows his scheming uncle's advice as slavishly as you tell me the Devourers' customers respond to their merchandising. Get *him!* But as for me – No, I say!'

'Then leave us, coward!' Sheelba decreed dourly, but Ningauble only sighed and said quite apologetically, 'It was intended that you have a comrade in this quest, a fellow soldier against noisome evil – to wit, the Gray Mouser. But unfortunately he came early to his appointment with my colleague here and was enticed into the shop of the Devourers and is doubtless now deep in their snares, if not already extinct. So you can see that we do take thought for your welfare and have no wish to overburden you with solo quests. However, My Gentle Son, if it still be your firm resolve …'

Fafhrd let out a sigh more profound than Ningauble's. 'Very well,' he said in gruff tones admitting defeat, 'I'll do it for you. Someone will have to pull that poor little gray fool out of the pretty-pretty fire – or the twinkly-twinkly water! – that tempted him. But how do I go about it?' He shook a big finger at Ningauble. 'And no more Gentle-Sonning!'

Ningauble paused. Then he said only, 'Use your own judgment.'

Sheelba said, 'Beware the Black Wall!'

Ningauble said to Fafhrd, 'Hold, I have a gift for you,' and held out to him a ragged ribbon a yard long, pinched between the cloth of the wizard's long sleeve so that it was impossible to see the manner of hand that pinched. Fafhrd took the tatter with a snort, crumpled it into a ball, and thrust it into his pouch.

'Have a greater care with it,' Ningauble warned. 'It is the Cloak of Invisibility, somewhat worn by many magic usings. Do not put it on until you near the Bazaar of the Devourers. It has two minor weaknesses: it will not make you altogether invisible to a master sorcerer if he senses your presence and takes certain steps. Also, see to it that you do not bleed during this exploit, for the cloak will not hide blood.'

'I've a gift too!' Sheelba said, drawing from out of his black cowl-hole – with sleeve-masked hand, as Ningauble had done – something that shimmered faintly in the dark like ...

Like a spiderweb.

Sheelba shook it, as if to dislodge a spider, or perhaps two.

'The Blindfold of True Seeing,' he said as he reached it toward Fafhrd. 'It shows all things as they really are! Do not lay it across your eyes until you enter the Bazaar. On no account, as you value your life or your sanity, wear it now!'

Fafhrd took it from him most gingerly, the flesh of his fingers crawling. He was inclined to obey the taciturn wizard's instructions. At this moment he truly did not much care to see the true visage of Sheelba of the Eyeless Face.

*

435

The Gray Mouser was reading the most interesting book of them all, a great compendium of secret knowledge written in a script of astrologic and geomantic signs, the meanings of which fairly leaped off the page into his mind.

To rest his eyes from that – or rather to keep from gobbling the book too fast – he peered through a nine-elbowed brass tube at a scene that could only be the blue heaven-pinnacle of the universe where angels flew shimmeringly like dragonflies and where a few choice heroes rested from their great mountain-climb and spied down critically on the antlike labors of the gods many levels below.

To rest his eye from *that*, he looked up between the scarlet (bloodmetal?) bars of the inmost cage at the most winsome, slim, fair, jet-eyed girl of them all. She knelt, sitting on her heels, with her upper body leaned back a little. She wore a red velvet tunic and had a mop of golden hair so thick and pliant that she could sweep it in a neat curtain over her upper face, down almost to her pouting lips. With the slim fingers of one hand she would slightly part these silky golden drapes to peer at the Mouser playfully, while with those of the other she rattled golden castanets in a most languorously slow rhythm, though with occasional swift staccato bursts.

The Mouser was considering whether it might not be as well to try a turn or two on the ruby-crusted golden crank next to his elbow, when he spied for the first time the glimmering wall at the back of the shop. What could its material be? he asked himself. Tiny diamonds countless as the sand set in smoky glass? Black opal? Black pearl? Black moonshine?

Whatever it was, it was wholly fascinating, for the Mouser quickly set down his book, using the nine-crooked spy-tube to mark his place – a most engrossing pair of pages on dueling where were revealed the Universal Parry and its five false variants and also the three true forms of the Secret Thrust – and with only a finger-wave to the ensorceling blonde in red velvet he walked quickly toward the back of the shop.

As he approached the Black Wall he thought for an instant that he glimpsed a silver wraith, or perhaps a silver skeleton, walking toward him out of it, but then he saw that it was only his own darkly handsome reflection, pleasantly flattered by the lustrous material. What had momentarily suggested silver ribs was the reflection of the silver lacings on his tunic.

He smirked at his image and reached out a finger to touch *its* lustrous finger when – Lo, a wonder! – his hand went into the wall with never a sensation at all save a faint tingling coolth promising comfort like the sheets of a fresh-made bed.

He looked at his hand inside the wall and – Lo, another wonder – it was all a beautiful silver faintly patterned with tiny scales. And though his own hand indubitably, as he could tell by clenching it, it was scarless now and a mite slimmer and longer fingered – altogether a more handsome hand than it had been a moment ago.

He wriggled his fingers and it was like watching small silver fish dart about – fingerlings!

What a droll conceit, he thought, to have a dark fishpond or rather swimming pool set on its side indoors, so that one could walk into the fracious erect fluid quietly and gracefully, instead of all the noisy, bouncingly athletic business of diving!

And how charming that the pool should be filled not with wet soppy cold water, but with a sort of moon-dark essence of sleep! An essence with beautifying cosmetic properties too – a sort of mudbath without the mud. The Mouser decided he must have a swim in this wonder pool at once, but just then his gaze lit on a long high black couch toward the other end of the dark liquid wall, and

437

beyond the couch a small high table set with viands and a crystal pitcher and goblet.

He walked along the wall to inspect these, his handsome reflection taking step for step with him.

He trailed his hand in the wall for a space and then withdrew it, the scales instantly vanishing and the familiar old scars returning.

The couch turned out to be a narrow high-sided black coffin lined with quilted black satin and piled at one end with little black satin pillows. It looked most invitingly comfortable and restful – not quite as inviting as the Black Wall, but very attractive just the same; there was even a rack of tiny black books nested in the black satin for the occupant's diversion and also a black candle, unlit.

The collation on the little ebony table beyond the coffin consisted entirely of black foods. By sight and then by nibbling and sipping the Mouser discovered their nature: thin slices of a very dark rye bread crusted with poppy seeds and dripped with black butter; slivers of charcoal-seared steak; similarly broiled tiny thin slices of calf's liver sprinkled with dark spices and liberally pricked with capers; the darkest grape jellies; truffles cut paper thin and mushrooms fried black; pickled chestnuts; and of course, ripe olives and black fish eggs – caviar. The black drink, which foamed when he poured it, turned out to be stout laced with the bubbly wine of Ilthmar.

He decided to refresh the inner Mouser – the Mouser who lived a sort of blind soft greedy undulating surface-life between his lips and his belly – before taking a dip in the Black Wall.

Fafhrd re-entered the Plaza of Dark Delights walking warily and with the long tatter that was the Cloak of Invisibility trailing from between left forefinger and thumb and with the glimmering cobweb that was the Blindfold of True Seeing pinched even more delicately by its edge

438

between the same digits of his right hand. He was not yet altogether certain that the trailing gossamer hexagon was completely free of spiders.

Across the Plaza he spotted the bright-mouthed shop – the shop he had been told was an outpost of the deadly Devourers – through a ragged gather of folk moving about restlessly and commenting and speculating to one another in harsh excited undertones.

The only feature of the shop Fafhrd could make out at all clearly at this distance was the red-capped red-footed baggy-trousered porter, not capering now but leaning on his long broom beside the trefoil-arched doorway.

With a looping swing of his left arm Fafhrd hung the Cloak of Invisibility around his neck. The ragged ribband hung to either side down his chest in its wolfskin jerkin only halfway to his wide belt which supported longsword and short-axe. It did not vanish his body to the slightest degree that he could see and he doubted it worked at all. Like many another thaumaturge, Ningauble never hesitated to give one useless charms, not for any treacherous reason, necessarily, but simply to improve one's morale. Fafhrd strode boldly toward the shop.

The Northerner was a tall, broad-shouldered, formidable-looking man – doubly formidable by his barbaric dress and weaponing in supercivilized Lankhmar – and so he took it for granted that the ordinary run of city folk stepped out of his way; indeed it had never occurred to him that they should not.

He got a shock. All the clerks, seedy bravos, scullery folk, students, slaves, second-rate merchants and second-class courtesans who would automatically have moved aside for him (though the last with a saucy swing of the hips) now came straight at him, so that he had to dodge and twist and stop and even sometimes dart back to avoid being toe-tramped and bumped. Indeed one fat pushy proud-stomached fellow almost carried away his cobweb, which he could see now by the light of the shop was free of spiders – or if there were any spiders still on it, they must be very small.

He had so much to do dodging Fafhrd-blind Lankhmarians that he could not spare one more glance for the shop until he was almost at the door. And then before he took his first close look, he found that he was tilting his head so that his left ear touched the shoulder below it and that he was laying Sheelba's spiderweb across his eyes.

The touch of it was simply like the touch of any cobweb when one runs face into it walking between close-set bushes at dawn. Everything shimmered a bit as if seen through a fine crystal grating. Then the least shimmering vanished, and with it the delicate clinging sensation, and Fafhrd's vision returned to normal – as far as he could tell.

It turned out that the doorway to the Devourers' shop was piled with garbage – garbage of a particularly offensive sort: old bones, dead fish, butcher's offal, moldering gravecloths folded in uneven squares like badly bound uncut books, broken glass and potsherds, splintered boxes, large stinking dead leaves orange-spotted with blight, bloody rags, tattered discarded loincloths, large worms nosing about, centipedes a-scuttle, cockroaches a-stagger, maggots a-crawl – and less agreeable things.

Atop all perched a vulture which had lost most of its feathers and seemed to have expired of some avian eczema. At least Fafhrd took it for dead, but then it opened one white-filmed eye.

The only conceivably salable object outside the shop – but it was a most notable exception – was the tall black iron statue, somewhat larger than life-size, of a lean swordsman of dire yet melancholy visage. Standing on its square pedestal beside the door, the statue leaned forward just a little on its long two-handed sword and regarded the Plaza dolefully.

The statue almost teased awake a recollection in

440

Fafhrd's mind – a recent recollection, he fancied – but then there was a blank in his thoughts and he instantly dropped the puzzle. On raids like this one, relentlessly swift action was paramount. He loosened his axe in its loop, noiselessly whipped out Graywand and, shrinking away from the piled and crawling garbage just a little, entered the Bazaar of the Bizarre.

The Mouser, pleasantly replete with tasty black food and heady black drink, drifted to the Black Wall and thrust in his right arm to the shoulder. He waved it about, luxuriating in the softly flowing coolth and balm – admiring its fine silver scales and more than human handsomeness. He did the same with his right leg, swinging it like a dancer exercising at the bar. Then he took a gently deep breath and drifted farther in.

Fafhrd on entering the Bazaar saw the same piles of gloriously bound books and racks of gleaming brass spy-tubes and crystal lenses as had the Mouser – a circumstance which seemed to overset Ningauble's theory that the Devourers sold only trash.

He also saw the eight beautiful cages of jewel-gleaming metals and the gleaming chains that hung them from the ceiling and went to the jeweled wall cranks.

Each cage held a gleaming, gloriously hued, black- or light-haired spider big as a rather small person and occasionally waving a long jointed claw-handed leg, or softly opening a little and then closing a pair of fanged down-swinging mandibles, while staring steadily at Fafhrd with eight watchful eyes set in two jewel-like rows of four.

Set a spider to catch a spider, Fafhrd thought, thinking of his cobweb, and then wondered what the thought meant.

He quickly switched to more practical questions then, but he had barely asked himself whether before proceeding further he should kill the very expensive-looking spiders, fit to be the coursing beasts of some jungle empress – another count against Ning's trash-theory! – when he heard a faint splashing from the back of the shop. It reminded him of the Mouser taking a bath – the Mouser loved baths, slow luxurious ones in hot soapy scented oil-dripped water, the small gray sybarite! – and so Fafhrd hurried off in that direction with many a swift upward overshoulder glance.

He was detouring the last cage, a scarlet-metaled one holding the handsomest spider yet, when he noted a book set down with a crooked spy-tube in it – exactly as the Mouser would keep his place in a book by closing it on a dagger.

Fafhrd paused to open the book. Its lustrous white pages were blank. He put his impalpably cobwebbed eye to the spy-tube. He glimpsed a scene that could only be the smoky red hell-nadir of the universe, where dark devils scuttled about like centipedes and where chained folk gazing yearningly upward and the damned writhed in the grip of black serpents whose eyes shone and whose fangs dripped and whose nostrils breathed fire.

As he dropped tube and book, he heard the faint sonorous quick dull report of bubbles being expelled from a fluid at its surface. Staring instantly toward the dim back of the shop, he saw at last the pearl-shimmering Black Wall and a silver skeleton eyed with great diamonds receding into it. However, this costly bone-man – once more Ning's trash-theory disproved! – still had one arm sticking partway out of the wall and this arm was not bone, whether silver, white, brownish or pink, but live-looking flesh covered with proper skin.

As the arm sank into the wall, Fafhrd sprang forward as fast as he ever had in his life and grabbed the hand just before it vanished. He knew then he had hold of his friend, for he would recognize anywhere the Mouser's grip, no matter how enfeebled. He tugged, but it was as if the

Mouser were mired in black quicksand. He laid Graywand down and grasped the Mouser by the wrist too and braced his feet against the rough black flags and gave a tremendous heave.

The silver skeleton came out of the wall with a black splash, metamorphosing as it did into a vacant-eyed Gray Mouser who without a look at his friend and rescuer went staggering off in a curve and pitched head over heels into the black coffin.

But before Fafhrd could hoist his comrade from this new gloomy predicament, there was a swift clash of footsteps and there came racing into the shop, somewhat to Fafhrd's surprise, the tall black iron statue. It had forgotten or simply stepped off its pedestal, but it had remembered its two-handed sword, which it brandished about most fiercely while shooting searching black glances like iron darts at every shadow and corner and nook.

The black gaze passed Fafhrd without pausing, but halted at Graywand lying on the floor. At the sight of that longsword the statue started visibly, snarled its iron lips, narrowed its black eyes. It shot glances more ironly stabbing than before, and it began to move about the shop in sudden zigzag rushes, sweeping its darkly flashing sword in low scythe-strokes.

At that moment the Mouser peeped moon-eyed over the edge of the coffin, lifted a limp hand and waved it at the statue, and in a soft sly foolish voice cried, 'Yoo-hoo!'

The statue paused in its searchings and scythings to glare at the Mouser in mixed contempt and puzzlement.

The Mouser rose to his feet in the black coffin, swaying drunkenly, and dug in his pouch.

'Ho, slave!' he cried to the statue with maudlin gaiety, 'your wares are passing passable. I'll take the girl in red velvet.' He pulled a coin from his pouch, goggled at it closely, then pitched it at the statue. 'That's one penny. And the nine-crooked spytube. That's another penny.' He

443

pitched it. 'And *Gron's Grand Compendium of Exotic Lore* – another penny for you! Yes, and here's one more for supper – very tasty, 'twas. Oh and I almost forgot – here's for tonight's lodging!' He pitched a fifth large copper coin at the demonic black statue and, smiling blissfully, flopped back out of sight. The black quilted satin could be heard to sigh as he sank in it.

Four-fifths of the way through the Mouser's penny-pitching Fafhrd decided it was useless to try to unriddle his comrade's nonsensical behavior and that it would be far more to the point to make use of this diversion to snatch up Graywand. He did so on the instant, but by that time the black statue was fully alert again, if it had ever been otherwise. Its gaze switched to Graywand the instant Fafhrd touched the longsword and it stamped its foot, which rang against the stone, and cried a harsh metallic 'Ha!'

Apparently the sword became invisible as Fafhrd grasped it, for the black statue did not follow him with its iron eyes as he shifted position across the room. Instead it swiftly laid down its own mighty blade and caught up a long narrow silver trumpet and set it to its lips.

Fafhrd thought it wise to attack before the statue summoned reinforcements. He rushed straight at the thing, swinging back Graywand for a great stroke at the neck – and steeling himself for an arm-numbing impact.

The statue blew and instead of the alarm blare Fafhrd had expected, there silently puffed out straight at him a great cloud of white powder that momentarily blotted out everything, as if it were the thickest of fogs from Hlal the River.

Fafhrd retreated, choking and coughing. The demon-blown fog cleared quickly, the white powder falling to the stony floor with unnatural swiftness, and he could see again to attack, but now the statue apparently could see him too, for it squinted straight at him and cried its metallic 'Ha!' again and whirled its sword around its iron head preparatory to the charge – rather as if winding itself up.

Fafhrd saw that his own hands and arms were thickly filmed with the white powder, which apparently clung to him everywhere except his eyes, doubtless protected by Sheelba's cobweb.

The iron statue came thrusting and slashing in. Fafhrd took the great sword on his, chopped back, and was parried in return. And now the combat assumed the noisy deadly aspects of a conventional longsword duel, except that Graywand was notched whenever it caught the chief force of a stroke, while the statue's somewhat longer weapon remained unmarked. Also, whenever Fafhrd got through the other's guard with a thrust – it was almost impossible to reach him with a slash – it turned out that the other had slipped his lean body or head aside with unbelievably swift and infallible anticipations.

It seemed to Fafhrd – at least at the time – the most fell, frustrating, and certainly the most wearisome combat in which he had ever engaged, so he suffered some feelings of hurt and irritation when the Mouser reeled up in his coffin again and leaned an elbow on the black-satin-quilted side and rested chin on fist and grinned hugely at the battlers and from time to time laughed wildly and shouted such enraging nonsense as, 'Use Secret Thrust Two-and-a-Half, Fafhrd – it's all in the book!' or 'Jump in the oven! – there'd be a master stroke of strategy!' or – this to the statue – 'Remember to sweep under his feet, you rogue!'

Backing away from one of Fafhrd's sudden attacks, the statue bumped the table holding the remains of the Mouser's repast – evidently its anticipatory abilities did not extend to its rear – and scraps of black food and white potsherds and jags of crystal scattered across the floor.

The Mouser leaned out of his coffin and waved a finger

445

waggishly. 'You'll have to sweep that up!' he cried and went off into a gale of laughter.

Backing away again, the statue bumped the black coffin. The Mouser only clapped the demonic figure comradely on the shoulder and called, 'Set to it again, clown! Brush him down! Dust him off!'

But the worst was perhaps when, during a brief pause while the combatants gasped and eyed each other dizzily, the Mouser waved coyly to the nearest giant spider and called his inane 'Yoo-hoo!' again, following it with, 'I'll see you, dear, after the circus.'

Fafhrd, parrying with weary desperation a fifteenth or a fiftieth cut at his head, thought bitterly, *This comes of trying to rescue small heartless madmen who would howl at their grandmothers hugged by bears. Sheelba's cobweb has shown me the Gray One in his true idiot nature.*

The Mouser had first been furious when the sword-skirling clashed him awake from his black satin dreams, but as soon as he saw what was going on he became enchanted at the wildly comic scene.

For, lacking Sheelba's cobweb, what the Mouser saw was only the zany red-capped porter prancing about in his tip-curled red shoes and aiming with his broom great strokes at Fafhrd, who looked exactly as if he had climbed a moment ago out of a barrel of meal. The only part of the Northerner not whitely dusted was a mask-like stretch across his eyes.

What made the whole thing fantastically droll was that miller-white Fafhrd was going through all the motions – and emotions! – of a genuine combat with excruciating precision, parrying the broom as if it were some great jolting scimitar or two-handed broadsword even. The broom would go sweeping up and Fafhrd would gawk at it, giving a marvelous interpretation of apprehensive goggling despite his strangely shadowed eyes. Then the broom would come sweeping down and Fafhrd would brace

446

himself and seem to catch it on his sword only with the most prodigious effort – and then pretend to be jolted back by it!

The Mouser had never suspected Fafhrd had such a perfected theatric talent, even if it were acting of a rather mechanical sort, lacking the broad sweeps of true dramatic genius, and he whooped with laughter.

Then the broom brushed Fafhrd's shoulder and blood sprang out.

Fafhrd, wounded at last and thereby knowing himself unlikely to outendure the black statue – although the latter's iron chest was working now like a bellows – decided on swifter measures. He loosened his hand-axe again in its loop and at the next pause in the fight, both battlers having outguessed each other by retreating simultaneously, whipped it up and hurled it at his adversary's face.

Instead of seeking to dodge or ward off the missile, the black statue lowered its sword and merely wove its head in a tiny circle.

The axe closely circled the lean black head, like a silver wood-tailed comet whipping around a black sun, and came back straight at Fafhrd like a boomerang – and rather more swiftly than Fafhrd had sent it.

But time slowed for Fafhrd then and he half ducked and caught it left-handed as it went whizzing past his cheek.

His thoughts too went for a moment fast as his actions. He thought of how his adversary, able to dodge every frontal attack, had not avoided the table or the coffin behind him. He thought of how the Mouser had not laughed now for a dozen clashes and he looked at him and saw him, though still dazed-seeming, strangely pale and sober-faced, appearing to stare with horror at the blood running down Fafhrd's arm.

So crying as heartily and merrily as he could, 'Amuse

yourself! Join in the fun, clown! – here's your slap-stick,' Fafhrd tossed the axe toward the Mouser.

Without waiting to see the result of that toss – perhaps not daring to – he summoned up his last reserves of speed and rushed at the black statue in a circling advance that drove it back toward the coffin.

Without shifting his stupid horrified gaze, the Mouser stuck out a hand at the last possible moment and caught the axe by the handle as it spun lazily down.

As the black statue retreated near the coffin and poised for what promised to be a stupendous counter-attack, the Mouser leaned out and, now grinning foolishly again, sharply rapped its black pate with the axe.

The iron head split like a coconut, but did not come apart. Fafhrd's hand-axe, wedged in it deeply, seemed to turn all at once to iron like the statue and its black haft was wrenched out of the Mouser's hand as the statue stiffened up straight and tall.

The Mouser stared at the split head woefully, like a child who hadn't known knives cut.

The statue brought its great sword flat against its chest, like a staff on which it might lean but did not, and it fell rigidly forward and hit the floor with a ponderous clank.

At that stony-metallic thundering, white wildfire ran across the Black Wall, lightening the whole shop like a distant levin-bolt, and iron-basalt thundering echoed from deep within it.

Fafhrd sheathed Graywand, dragged the Mouser out of the black coffin – the fight hadn't left him the strength to lift even his small friend – and shouted in his ear, 'Come on! Run!'

The Mouser ran for the Black Wall.

Fafhrd snagged his wrist as he went by and plunged toward the arched door, dragging the Mouser after him.

The thunder faded out and there came a low whistle, cajolingly sweet.

Wildfire raced again across the Black Wall behind them – much more brightly this time, as if a lightning storm were racing toward them.

The white glare striking ahead imprinted one vision indelibly on Fafhrd's brain: the giant spider in the inmost cage pressed against the bloodred bars to gaze down at them. It had pale legs and a velvet red body and a mask of sleek thick golden hair from which eight jet eyes peered, while its fanged jaws hanging down in the manner of the wide blades of a pair of golden scissors rattled together in a wild staccato rhythm like castanets.

That moment the cajoling whistle was repeated. It too seemed to be coming from the red and golden spider.

But strangest of all to Fafhrd was to hear the Mouser, dragged unwillingly along behind him, cry out in answer to the whistling, 'Yes, darling, I'm coming. Let me go, Fafhrd! Let me climb to her! Just one kiss! Sweetheart!'

'Stop it, Mouser,' Fafhrd growled, his flesh crawling in mid-plunge. 'It's a giant spider!'

'Wipe the cobwebs out of your eyes, Fafhrd,' the Mouser retorted pleadingly and most unwittingly to the point. 'It's a gorgeous girl! I'll never see her ticklesome like – and I've paid for her! *Sweetheart!*'

Then the booming thunder drowned his voice and any more whistling there might have been, and the wildfire came again, brighter than day, and another great thunderclap right on its heels, and the floor shuddered and the whole shop shook, and Fafhrd dragged the Mouser through the trefoil-arched doorway, and there was another great flash and clap.

The flash showed a semicircle of Lankhmarians peering ashen-faced overshoulder as they retreated across the Plaza of Dark Delights from the remarkable indoor thunderstorm that threatened to come out after them.

Fafhrd spun around. The archway had turned to blank wall.

The Bazaar of the Bizarre was gone from the World of Nehwon.

The Mouser, sitting on the dank flags where Fafhrd had dragged him, babbled wailfully, 'The secrets of time and space! The lore of the gods! The mysteries of Hell! Black nirvana! Red and gold Heaven! Five pennies gone forever!'

Fafhrd set his teeth. A mighty resolve, rising from his many recent angers and bewilderments, crystallized in him.

Thus far he had used Sheelba's cobweb – and Ningauble's tatter too – only to serve others. Now he would use them for himself! He would peer at the Mouser more closely and at every person he knew. He would study even his own reflection! But most of all, he would stare Sheelba and Ning to their wizardly cores!

There came from overhead a low 'Hssst!'

As he glanced up he felt something snatched from around his neck and, with the faintest tingling sensation, from off his eyes.

For a moment there was a shimmer traveling upward and through it he seemed to glimpse distortedly, as through thick glass, a black face with a cobwebby skin that entirely covered mouth and nostrils and eyes.

Then that dubious flash was gone and there were only two cowled heads peering down at him from over the wall top. There was chuckling laughter.

Then both cowled heads drew back out of sight and there was only the edge of the roof and the sky and the stars and the blank wall.